THE WEREWOLF SERIES

BEAST BORN

BOOK ONE

Her flesh soared through the air with a sickening wet splash. Blood rained down upon the man who had ripped open her throat with his bare hands, or rather, his claws. His hand was bulging and hairy compared to the rest of his body, looking grossly deformed. His fingernails were curved and sharp, drenched in blood that dripped slowly off the tips. The woman was choking, gagging, and unable to breathe. Her eyes bulged in shock and horror. She miserably flailed her arms in vain, knowing her fate was sealed. Crimson fluid gushed out of her mouth with rippling pressure, spewing down her beaten, bloody body.

She fell to her knees; her hands were clasping at the torn remains of her throat. She attempted to breathe in air like a desperate fish out of the water, but only gargles of pain and anguish filled the dead silence in the filth-ridden alleyway. The man looked down upon her and grinned with malicious glee. A burning stare was within his wild yellow eyes. He curled his lip in spite.

"Scum!" he growled before swatting his hand across her throat a second and final time. The last of her neck ripped away, causing her spine to be severed from her being like melted butter. With nothing keeping it up, her head thudded down beside her body. Blood spurted out of the gaping stump where her head used to be as her body began to spasm and slump to the floor, going ultimately still. Her head rolled next to the man's feet as he looked down at the lump and laughed. He then kicked it further down the alleyway.

Watching her body for a moment, the man then spat in the puddle of blood forming around his feet. It didn't matter what traces of him or what evidence he left behind. He knew when the body was found tomorrow; none but only his own kind could track him. No traces of what she was would be left behind either.

He waited for a second to make sure the process had already begun. Her previous flawless pale skin was starting to wrinkle. It grew old and frail within seconds. Her plump life filled body was shrinking and withering before his eyes. The police had come across many bodies like this over the years, and humanity could never explain it.

The man's hands then shrank and changed themselves, returning to being human-sized in appearance. The black bulging hairy claws deflated slowly, faded in color, and their hairs receded into his flesh. He was a very tall man, nearly seven feet in height, and his frame was broad with a dense muscular build. He was clean-shaven, with long raven black hair flowing down past his neck and shoulders. He wore a black trench coat with a matching black shirt, trousers, and thick heavy boots. His yellow-colored eyes narrowed when he heard the rustle of others coming closer. He knew he would have to be on the move quickly, and there was more blood still to spill tonight.

He knew they had nested here in this city for the last few weeks. He and his kind had come here to either scare them away or clear them up one at a time. This woman was his fifth kill since coming here. He figured there couldn't be much more because they never traveled in too large groups. They were creatures that stalked the night because they feared the sun with skin as pale as the moon itself and piercing red eyes. They feasted on the blood of humans because they believed humanity was cattle for their exclusive use. However, he had no plans on letting that happen tonight. He grinned as he tensed his legs before crouching down for a moment and then the man leaped high into the air as though shot out of a cannon. As he soared upwards, this speed was usually not humanly possible, and It remained barely visible to the human eye. His leg kicked against the side of the wall, then to the next one. He was pushing himself up and up before landing on the roof in a matter of seconds. He looked on into the night and gazed up at the moon, overcome with his senses. He threw his head back and howled out into the night. A deep echoing wolf's call flooded the night's air. He then tensed his muscles and left onward into the night.

CHAPTER ONE

Arthur Thorn was walking home from school. It was a sunny afternoon in the middle of summer though Arthur still sighed with exhaustion as he walked onward on a hot day down the path of the street. He was glum that he was nowhere near the weekend yet, so he just strolled on by with a sullen face. He was purposely keeping his head down and eyes on the pavement as always. He wore a plain back shirt with matching trousers and shoes, a whole ensemble. He preferred to wear the color black; he felt comfortable in it. Other kids in school made fun of him for wearing it, but he didn't care. At least he told himself he didn't.

Arthur was of average height for his age with pale skin, freckles, and bright ginger-colored hair. He felt that his hair color was the reason was bullied at school. Because no matter where he was, someone had a problem with him. People had often told him he had a bad temper, and his hair was the reason behind that. He didn't think so. He thought getting angry because someone is bullying or annoying you didn't mean you were an angry person, only normal. Though if something tried to hurt him physically, he couldn't do much about it with a temper or none. He was a thin person who didn't exercise, but he wasn't fat either. Arthur was just weak and regular as far as he was concerned. He didn't know how to fight either way. He heard of other kids doing karate after school, but his family couldn't afford any lessons, so he could only remain as a punching bag for others.

He walked on with his eyes casually looming as he walked past the other houses on the street. Some people were in their front gardens doing garden work like planting flowers or trimming hedges. Arthur just let his mind wander as he looked away from them, often going into his private little world of thought. School today wasn't too bad, not like other days. He had a few Math lessons in the morning, then English, and two Science lessons in a row. It was always dull but nothing too hard for him. He wasn't stupid and often achieved average marks. He managed to drone on through it all without anyone bothering him. He never acted out in class, so teachers didn't pay him any mind, and no one in his class bothered to talk to him, so other students didn't distract him either.

Break and lunchtimes were a different matter, though, because people didn't ignore him then. He had the usual names and jeers thrown his way as he walked through the playground and hallways. Mainly from kids in groups of their friends thinking they were so tough and trying to impress. Nothing he wasn't used to; he didn't go to his regular hangout spots where he was left alone or to try and look for any of his friends. He just spent the short time given to him walking around, sometimes looking longingly at the larger group of people. He sometimes stood at far distances and would watch them laugh, and play fight with each other with a touch of envy. Arthur hated them because of how they treated him, but part of him also wished to be accepted. It almost looked sometimes as though a group of friends at school was a small family. That's how it looked to him, though not that his own family was anything like them; they were smiling too much.

He sometimes spent his lunch and break time indoors. Arthur was sometimes sitting in an empty classroom that wasn't being used or in the school library, reading. To his displeasure, the popular kids often would come into the library to cause trouble. He did everything he could to avoid them. They were the ones that bullied him the most. They saw him as an easy target. Few of his friends could defend him, and he was quiet and timid when confronted. They teased, pushed him around, and only laughed if Arthur lost his temper and tried to make them leave him alone, they never did.

The last lesson of the day, though, Arthur was barely paying attention. He wasn't distracted, just unmotivated. Arthur didn't care about what the teacher was explaining and counted the seconds until the bell went. None of his friends offered to walk home with him. They didn't want the trouble anymore. Arthur told them he didn't mind, but he did. He was often upset that there was never anyone he could count on to be with him.

As Arthur continued walking, a smooth, cool breeze blew against his face. He stopped for a moment and closed his eyes. He was feeling the gentle wind fly by him, smiling fondly. The small, subtle whistle strolled past his eyes and wavered against his hair, making his ginger locks feel like bristling tree branches. He enjoyed these tiny amounts of peace he got after school finished.

Arthur looked on ahead of him after that. The pavement he walked on was cracked and broken, decaying and rotten. Arthur lived in his city's poorer areas, so many streets and neighborhoods were broken down and forgotten. He walked past many broken fences with tattered falling to pieces houses not far behind them. The houses themselves were falling apart just from the outside view. Smashed windows with discarded bricks and broken bikes left in their gardens. He could see huddles of kids and adults in hooded clothes standing around outside certain houses that Arthur knew never to go near. Sometimes Arthur heard about muggings and sometimes even stabbings only a few streets from his own. Arthur walked by a couple of deserted houses, either unsellable or abandoned, and they looked the worst he could see. There was no glass left in any window and the building was often squatted in by homeless and dangerous people. These were places where Arthur could smell the mold from them just by walking by. Though he thought, at this point, he felt like it was probably the house's mold that was holding it together. Arthur had also heard about some of the prettier and more expensive homes that were broken into and robbed now and then. The smell of abandoned rubbish left on the sidewalk for weeks on end was nauseating as he walked past them. It was a place riddled with filth that Arthur always had to carefully navigate around to avoid getting close to what smelled like a year-old banana peel stuck to his shoe.

The police hardly kept the peace. They were too busy dealing with the whines of the higher-class people in the select areas to bother with Arthur's community down here. In his neighborhood, justice was often found by locals themselves. Those who had friends looked out for each other, a notion Arthur felt he couldn't be more unfamiliar with.

Ahead, Arthur saw a familiar tunnel he had to walk through. On top of it were train tracks that led to the station. A few feet within the tunnel were a group of boys Arthur didn't want to go near. But he had already come this way, and the other way home would take too long. Arthur didn't want to get in trouble for being late from his parents. He sighed and put his head down again, hoping today they might be too tired and not bored enough just to leave him be. But Arthur hoped for that every day, and each time he was proven wrong.

Arthur approached the tunnel to the sounds of snickering and saw the vicious-looking grins of five boys leaning against each of the walls. The light quickly faded from his body as he entered underneath the tunnel and he was surrounded in little darkness. Luckily, there was at least enough light for him to see those around him. He said nothing and tried to continue forward, but the leader of this group of bullies stood out in front of him.

"Not so fast, ginger," the boy growled at Arthur.

This kid was one year older than Arthur. He was also large, broad, and muscled. He was undoubtedly more than his superior in fighting. The others laughed and chuckled as Arthur didn't lift his head.

"Just let me past Gary," Arthur mumbled sadly. The bully Gary shook his head and then he grabbed Arthur by his collar.

"Shut up, freak!" he snapped, pulling Arthur close.

Gary wore a grey hoodie. They all were wearing hoodies in different colors with dark-colored jeans. Arthur tried to push back and get the bully off him. His sulk was beginning to vanish as his temper flared quickly. Gary saw this and laughed, then he pushed Arthur back hard, causing him to fall to the ground. His head smacked against the concrete pavement as he landed. The sharp pain was racing through his skull. Arthur gritted his teeth against the pain as he slowly got up with the group around him jeering.

"Aww, did ginger hurt himself?" one of them jeered.

"Ha, wuss," said a second one hatefully.

"Dirt like you belongs on the ground," the last chuckled. Gary gazed at Arthur. He was grinning smugly, relishing his pain and soaking up the feeling of power. Gary's friends were cheering him on to do more. Arthur clenched his fists and shot up to his feet.

"Leave me alone!" Arthur barked, clenching his fists. The pain in his head was clouding his judgment, and now he was only furious in agony. Arthur was readying himself for a fight. It was one he would lose, but his temper took hold as his heartbeat began to race and fire flared through his veins. He despised this person so much that it burned inside him.

The group around him laughed as Gary moved in, grabbing Arthur by his shirt and throwing him hard against the tunnel wall. Arthur coughed as he hit the dirty rotten bricks and looked on straight into the face of Gary, who curled his lip and spat in Arthur's face.

"Shut your face scum," he snarled. He pulled his fist back and grinned. Arthur struggled and tried to get away, but he couldn't move. The other bullies had moved into place and held him there by his arms. All of Arthurs' confidence was now sapped from his body in this position. His anger was now replaced by fear in a millisecond. He was struggling now with little hope. Arthur's teeth gritted in terror, he felt like a caged animal in an abattoir. He hated this feeling. He was helpless, too weak, and too cowardly to help himself. Gary smirked as he saw the panic on Arthur's face.

"Loser!" he called at him before then he spat at him again.

"Take it like a man," Gary finished throwing his fist forward. His knuckles connected with Arthur's face sharply, but Gary didn't stop there. A few more punches were thrown at his left eye, followed by a few more at his cheek, and a lot more in his stomach, which harshly winded him. Arthur cried out in pain with each blow. The smacking sound of Gary's fist connecting with his fleshly face filled Arthur's ears as the sharp pulsing pain of Gary's strikes vibrated across his skull. Arthur was coughing, and his body was going sluggish and limp. These beatings were harsh, but at the very least, Arthur was glad that his body had grown used to them. The pain drained him of all his fight and will to struggle. His body was too busy reacting to the pain for even the thought of fighting back to rear its tiny head. All he wanted to do was slink into the ground for safety and wait for them to stop. The other bullies eventually let go of his arms, and Arthur fell to the floor like a sack of bricks, coughing and gasping for air with his head ringing from Gary's punches. The bullies began laughing and walking off, calling for Gary to follow. Gary stood there for a moment and looked down at Arthur. He was throwing insults down at Arthur one last time before going, but Arthur couldn't hear him correctly. With a final kick in Arthur's stomach, Gary moved on out of the tunnel to catch up with his friends.

Arthur lay there for a moment, getting his breath back. He was gasping as he held his stomach, which felt like a nail bomb had just detonated in his gut. He was already feeling his face swelling. The pain was throbbing, his left eye was at least able to open, but it would bruise badly as it always had.

Arthur went through this pain a lot, but he was used to it. He already had bruises everywhere. He wasn't bleeding this time, but the pain ached and throbbed immensely. He just had to keep going until it stopped on its own. Arthur had learned very quickly that there was no point telling an adult about what happened to him. Not his teachers at school because the bullies would lie and say he had insulted them and followed by claiming he threw the first punch. Plus, with the bullies' friends backing them up, the bullies always won over. It didn't matter if the teachers did believe him; they couldn't give him the justice he deserved. Growing up, he was told that if someone in school hurt him, go to the teacher. But Arthur quickly realized that all teachers ever did was tell them off, give them detention, or something else completely useless. Arthur would prefer just to hit them back, eye for an eye. But he never could.

After maybe what felt like five or ten minutes, Arthur struggled to his feet. He wanted to stay there a bit longer, but he didn't dare be late home. His stomach was hurting, and his face was throbbing, but he was glad he was at least able to walk. He picked up his school bag that he had dropped and continued forward past the tunnel.

Arthur continued walking home, glad that he was now only a few minutes from his house. He knew his mother would question the marks on his face. He would say he got into a fight. With how the area was, his mother knew it happened often. He wouldn't admit it was bullies, and he would then have to endure her chiding on how dangerous these areas are and how his fighting would leave him stabbed or worse one day. He hated lying to his mother, but he knew she would only worry more if she knew he was being bullied like this all the time. She certainly couldn't do anything to stop it, and if she went to Gary's parents, his horrors would only double. Keeping things this way meant she would only think he was just acting like a typical teenager. She would continue to rant until he made his usual apologies, and she would go on her way back into the kitchen to continue with dinner.

Arthur actually didn't mind his mother telling him off. He felt the complete opposite. It was nice to know she at least cared about him. His father, however, would just say the same thing each time.

"Did you win, boy?" in his gruff tone, and each time, Arthur would lie and say yes only to then receive a mild nod as his father sat down to drink. The only one in his family who knew he was being bullied was his younger sister Alice. She was scared for him every time he came home with any visible mark. She was only eight, but he had asked her to keep it silent and that telling on him would only cause him more grief. She didn't understand why but Alice did as he asked. She always did anything her brother said.

She listened to him because Arthur was her hero in her eyes. She adored her older brother and most of the time, she always hugged him to try to make him feel better. Alice was young and innocent but she somehow managed to see the suffering Arthur felt behind the fake smile he gave the rest of the family. Arthur, in turn, always tried to protect his sister from anything he could. When she cried, he wanted to make her laugh, and he would read her to sleep most nights and hold her when she had nightmares, rocking her until she felt safe enough to fall back asleep. There wasn't a thing Arthur wouldn't do for his little sister, even if he were helpless. He wasn't going to give up trying to be a good big brother because he felt like it was the only good thing he could do in his life.

Arthur knew he would probably spend some time with Alice after he got in. He usually did it before dinner was ready. She liked to play with her dolls, or if she wanted him to, he would help her with some of her schoolwork. Her Math sums he preferred doing because they were easy for him. His father wouldn't get home for a short while after Arthur, but he would be expecting food as quickly as possible as he finished his beer. Arthur sighed and shook his head as he came up to the house, staring at it for a moment.

It was very run down. It was a two-floor house with three bedrooms, white paint peeling along the outside and chipping left and right. The top left window was smashed, and the side walls were spray-painted with marks in the door from where heavy stones were thrown at it, even the odd knife. The fence was wooden and rotted, nearly falling apart. The small front garden was overgrown and never tidy. It was always in disarray, but it looked like almost every other house in the neighborhood, so he didn't care much. He walked from the gate and up to the door. It was unlocked, so Arthur wiped his feet on the outside mat, sighed one last time, and took a deep breath to try and act a little cheery, putting on his mask.

Arthur felt the inside of his house was a perfect complement to the outside. While his mother tried her best, the carpets were stained with juice and food, which often caused the place to always have a strange smell no matter how much it was hoovered or cleaned. The wallpaper along all the walls was the same dull beige color, and most of it was extremely old and peeling. His father never bothered to redecorate. The kitchen was clean, so his mother's food never made him sick. Arthur walked in and left his school bag next to the door knowing it would be there for him in the morning. He looked upwards at the ceiling and squinted at the plain light bulb hanging from bare wires. As the door closed behind him, the sound of footsteps from the kitchen approached him. His mother came out into the hallway with a smile on her face.

"Hi honey, did you have a good d-" she didn't finish her sentence and her smiling face instantly snapped into a scowl.

"What happened!? Look at your face!" she gasped, rushing over to inspect her injured child frantically.

"Have you been fighting again?!" she enquired mournfully. Arthur sighed and nodded, holding his head down. His mother was young-looking, in her early thirties with long blonde hair. She was wearing a white apron with a purple dress under it. She walked closer and knelt. She lightly held his head up with her hand. Her eyes scanned over his bruises and wounds, humming and tutting; her worry was evident on his face as she fussed over him.

"You silly boy. You get yourself into more and more trouble each day. It's your temper, I bet. You need to control yourself, baby. You can't smack every person who looks at you funny." Arthur sighed again; everyone always said it was his temper. Every time he tried to defend himself, his temper was what adults would decide was the problem. It was always the same assumption but from a different person.

"Sorry, mum, things just got out of hand, but it's not as though I was going up to people starting fights." She shook her head.

"I know, baby, but if someone says something mean to you, you just ignore it and keep on walking; reacting will accomplish nothing," she lectured in a scolding way.

"Accomplishes nothing?! Well, why should they get away with it, why should they hurt me without justice for me!" Arthur shouted in his head. But he was too tired to say it out loud and argue back, so he just nodded again.

"I know, sorry, mum," he replied in a defeated murmur. She kissed his bruised cheek and gave him a hug which caused Arthur to wince slightly in pain.

"At least your OK, sweetie. Clean yourself up, OK? Dinner won't be much longer. Your father...is coming home early today." A look of worry went across her face as she then quickly stood back up and straightened her apron with specific attention.

"I better keep an eye on it; I don't want it to burn," she finished hurriedly before walking away from Arthur and back into the kitchen. Arthur sighed again when she was back in the kitchen. He said nothing else and just walked up the stairs. He saw his sister's room at the top of the stairs directly to his left, which had pink stickers of fairies and cute animals on the white door with her name written in a bright red crayon. He decided he would spend time with his sister, but he needed a little time to himself first. He walked to the end of the upstairs hallway to his room. He came upon it, just turned the handle, and walked in.

Arthur's room was his sanctuary. It was a place of peace where he could escape from the entire world and all its problems. Here in this small space,

Arthur knew he could simply exist as he saw fit. He could be who he is and not how he is meant to be. Arthur felt that all creatures, be they humans or animals, need one place they can call ultimately their own. A place that they know they are safe within that is secure and understands them just as much as they know themselves. He felt that this space was his perfect solace from the world and all the bullies that seemed to inhabit it. It was his world that he created for no one else but him. Arthurs' parents disapproved of his decorating preferences and he only got around it because they believed it was merely a phase. It wasn't, and a vital part of him knew he wasn't just some typical rebellious teenager. He felt like this room reflected his soul, and it was his paradise.

Arthur stepped inside and he was immediately greeted by the dark space of his black-painted walls. He flicked the light switch on the wall, and his red-tinted light bulb lit up the room with its bloody rays. The bulb was turning everything in his sight an intense red color. He loved this place because it was precisely the way he liked it. Arthur walked through the mess on his floor. He was too old for toys now, but he had comic books and his pencils and sketch pads dotted around along with discarded clothes that needed washing. His feet were kicking aside the worn clothes as he made his way to his bed. He smiled at the different posters along the wall of his favorite bands. The CD he liked to listen to was already in the player, which he switched on and pressed the play button. Then within seconds, his favorite metal music was in the air. Though he didn't play it too loud because he didn't want to bother his sister with the sound, and the walls weren't that thick. Arthur then sat down on the black sheets on his bed and closed his eyes, letting wonderful sounds fill his ears.

Metal music has always been Arthur's primary favorite genre of music. He heard it at an early age, maybe nine or ten, and fell hard in love with it within minutes of his first song. Since then, he had been on a binge of endless dozens of bands he found. He had always spent his pocket money on new CDs of his best groups. The feeling of metal made him feel invincible in a fun way. Its power through the speakers filled him with energy, and as he listened, he would picture himself in extraordinary situations with the music in the background. He was daydreaming of fantasy-like battles where he alone would fight armies in the hundreds himself. The strum of an electric guitar to him felt like liquid fire rushing through his veins. That even the very opening melody of any song continuously pumped him up. The way the rest of the instruments meshed with the guitarists and the vocalists singing and roaring to Arthur was heaven.

As the music filled the air, the guitars sounded strong before the lyrics began flying. Arthur lay down flat on his bed as he listened. He put his hands behind his head and stared up at the ceiling. The song properly began now, and the vocalist began to sing out his lines, causing a smile to slide up both sides of Arthur's face. He took in a deep breath and let all his feelings go into the air, letting all his problems leave his body carelessly.

Arthur winced a little as his stomach was aching from his beating earlier. He could already feel the bruising begin. His face was banged up, but he hadn't seen the damage on his torso yet. There would be different patches of black and purple that would spread across him in their own time. Arthur thought ahead as his mind drifted to his music. He wondered if he would have to endure this sort of torment forever, even as an adult. Arthur didn't think so the more he thought. He hadn't ever heard of adults picking on each other for hair color and trying to hurt and devour the weakest person in the group just because they weren't strong. Arthur then remembered what he learned about wars in school. He recalled learning about old wars with people killing each other over religion. Some countries had civil wars with more political nonsense that he didn't personally care about much. Then he thought about the more recent conflicts that plague the world, in the eastern parts of the globe where people were fighting. Soldiers and citizens were living in a world he couldn't even imagine, where his pain was probably laughable to them.

As those thoughts floated across his mind casually, he pictured how he would be in such situations. He didn't see himself as a soldier when he was older or anything like that. He wasn't sure what he thought he would be. Arthur continued to stare at his ceiling and thought about himself for a few seconds as that thought became stuck in his mind. He thought about where he saw himself one day. Arthur then shook his head and sighed. He still had years of school left, so he figured he would worry about it when teachers and his parents told him he had to care, and even then, Arthur just thought he would probably pick the first job he could. Arthur, however, doubted it would be anything he loved to do. From what he saw, no adult he ever met worked a job they loved, so what chance did he have?

There were subjects in school he did enjoy, though, some more than others. English was what he seemed to like the most because creative writing was his favorite thing to do. He thought he had a good imagination and loved writing short stories in his spare time about powerful heroes. They were mighty and super strong but also kind to people weaker than them. They were heroes that would strike down those who bullied others and punish the wicked viciously, killing them without hesitation. His teachers didn't criticize his grammar and punctuation much, but they would often try to steer him onto their ideas of what he had to write about in class. He hated that. He thought it wasn't fair to try and control someone's expression. He thought that's how people become zombies as adults. They would go through their life with the same expression and attitude until they randomly kill a street full of people in their midlife crisis one day. Arthur thought they did that because they woke up one day and realize their entire head is full of other people's ideas and none of their own. His answer was simply to continue his writing in private, away from the teachers' eyes. Inside the drawer of his bedside table next to his bed were short stories and lists of story ideas he wanted to continue writing. He sometimes thought that maybe if he were lucky, he could end up an author one day. On that notion, a few small taps on his door broke his train of thought. They came from his little sister Alice who was there to see him. Arthur smiled and spoke up.

"Come in," he called back with a cheery tone; his mood rapidly improved from being allowed a few minutes to decompress from his day. Plus, he never liked to be moody towards Alice. The door opened a few inches, and his little sister entered the room.

His little sister Alice was the sweetest child he knew. Other girls her age were perfectly nice kids, but his little sister was born so innocent that it always warmed his heart and brought a small glimpse of light to his world when he was able to see her constantly smiling face. There were, of course, times she didn't smile. Times when she was hurt or terrified even. Arthur wasn't sure if it were just his simple big brother nature or something deeper inside him, but he always fought to his utmost instinct to protect her from any evils in this world as he could. He loved her unconditionally. Arthur always had the best relationship with his sister. She seemed to him to be the only person he could trust in his entire life, and he knew she would never turn on him, no matter what.

She stood at the door no more than a few feet tall, wearing light purple clothes. Her shirt had a cute fairy printed on the front. She wore soft pink slippers on her feet with her purple jeans above them. She had pale skin, solid green eyes, and strong blonde hair like their mother that hung down past her shoulders. It was always brushed and kept neat. She had a small nose and tiny ears, often making her eyes look bigger than they were. Her face was flawless, with no strange birthmarks or anything that kids at her school point out to make fun of her. Often quite the opposite as he heard his little sister Alice was extremely popular at her small child's school and had many friends. Even though sometimes she came home crying because some jealous girl had pulled her hair and called her some mean names. Arthur knew how she felt from that kind of teasing. Therefore, he always knew what to say and how to cheer her up.

Arthur was always happy to see Alice having friends who looked out for her. However, sometimes it made Arthur slightly jealous of his younger sister because she has friends who would stick up for her when his own wouldn't. He often envied the innocence of his sister from the side of the school life he endured. He figured older siblings would dislike their siblings because of it, but some deep part of him could never truly be angry with her for anything.

Alice walked into the room and winced a little as the metal music blasted into her ears. Arthur got up from his bed and turned the music down a little. Alice smiled at that and ran over to her brother, leaping into his arms. Arthur laughed as he caught her. Arthur then lifted her and hugged her tight. His bruises hurt from the contact, but he ignored them as best he could because if Alice knew he had been hurt, she would get upset. Alice squealed with joy as her older brother hugged her and set her down. She looked up at him, smiling like a lit beacon. Arthur smiled back at her with genuine joy to see her.

"How's it going, sis?" he asked, smiling widely, rubbing her head with his hand.

"Fine, I got home earlier and I've been bored waiting for you to come home," she answered cheerfully; her voice was light and squeaky. Arthur often joked with his sister, claiming that she was the spitting image of a cartoon character when she was excited. He chuckled and patted her head again.

"Well, I'm here now. Do you want to play with your dolls? Need help with some homework?" She shook her head at him.

"No, I finished all my sums earlier; I did all five of them by myself!" she said with beaming pride. Arthur whistled, acting impressed.

"Bloody hell, you'll be running the stock exchange if you carry on like this," Arthur answered proudly. Alice giggled, loving the praise as all little children did.

"I'm the smartest girl in my class," she added, her smile widening. Arthur chuckled and nodded.

"I bet you are and the cutest as well," he finished tapping her nose. She giggled again, but then her smile dropped quickly. She walked over and climbed onto his bed, leaning next to him. She was fidgeting with her fingers looking scared as she looked down at her feet.

"Mummy is nervous about making dinner..." she said in a quiet voice. Arthur sighed and wrapped his arm around her shoulder, hugging her close.

"Don't you worry about that, OK? Just stay quiet and out of the way, and everything will be fine." She nodded but said nothing, squeezing her arms around Arthur. She was often quiet in moments like these. Arthur reached over and opened the drawer in his bedside cabinet. He pulled out a red hardback book and smiled as he opened it.

"How about a few chapters before dinner?" he offered, holding one of her favorite books to be read to when they spent time together. She lifted his head and looked at Arthur. A small smile returned to her face as she nodded. She got comfortable leaning next to Arthur.

"Yes, please," she answered sweetly. Arthur hugged her closer, opened the book to the correct page, and started reading to her. Alice was silent and still as the words softly glided out of Arthur's mouth, going from page to page. The two hugged each other close, enjoying this small moment together before their father got home

CHAPTER TWO

Arthur's father was not a kind man. The people Arthur had to deal with at school, like Gary, who beat his face earlier, didn't scare him half as much as his father did. Johnathan Thorn worked in a factory, some miscellaneous work that was the best he could get with no decent qualifications. It was harsh manual labor which meant his father was bulky and muscular. But it was also tiresome and stressful, which meant his father often drank at a pub after work before he came home, and alcohol did not improve his mood. Arthur's father hadn't been treated well by his dad when he was young. Arthur's grandfather adopted the old-fashioned ruling of his house with an iron fist. Therefore, when Arthur's father entered the home, everyone behaved well, and those who weren't were punished.

It hadn't always been unpleasantness with his father. Arthur would remember times when he was smaller. His dad would make jokes occasionally, laughing with him and his mother in a usual family way. He had taken Arthur fishing and camping a few times, and Arthur remembered that he enjoyed those times when he was little. Then he grew older, and those memories seemed to evaporate into mist in his mind. Now, all that appeared to be present in his mind whenever he thought of his father was the drunken beast that wouldn't go away. He didn't enjoy it; Arthur felt very scared often. Not just by his father alone but also because he thought he had no one to turn to if he ever got in serious trouble. His mother loved him and worried about him the same as any mother does, but it wasn't the same. His mother was compassionate and sweet but didn't have the confidence for confrontation and allowed herself to be controlled and ordered around. Arthur loved his mother immensely, but he knew he could never rely on her to do anything other than what his father demanded from her. Arthur also worried that his father would just up and leave them alone one day, putting everything on Arthur's shoulders to care for his mother and sister. Arthur didn't know what he would do then. His father was a horrible man, but he was also the only thing stopping the family from starving in the cold. In return for food and shelter, all he expected from his family was complete obedience and absolute rule over the entire house. Not a fair exchange in Arthur's eyes, and he longed for the day his father would learn how horrible he makes his family feel.

With a thunderous slam of the door, Arthur's father stumbled past the frame and stepped into the house, reeking of alcohol. He had enough bile from his mouth to melt the wallpaper. Arthur and his sister flinched as their father slammed the door behind him. Arthur heard him call their mother.

"Where's dinner?! I'm home now, aren't I? Can't be that hard to bloody put together!" Arthur heard his voice snarl. Arthur did not hear his mother's response clearly as she wouldn't raise her voice at him for fear of triggering his rage. Arthur listened to the flustered patter of his mother's footsteps darting towards her now-present husband in the house, and she said something that seemed to reason him towards the living room where his chair was. Arthur then heard his father grab another beer from their fridge and go to the front room to sit in his big chair. Arthur sighed as he prepared himself mentally. As he got up from his bed, Alice gripped his hand tightly.

"Don't go," she pleaded with a croaky squeak. Alice was scared for her brother. Arthur looked back and gave her a reassuring smile.

"Everything will be fine, I promise," Arthur said and walked out of his room and down the stairs.

Arthur could smell the alcohol from his father as he reached the bottom of the stairs. His father stood at the height of nearly six foot five. He was a towering giant over everyone Arthur had met in his entire life. He was wearing his oversized grey overalls with short dark brown hair and a rough grimace of a face with minimal signs of any facial features that could be considered pleasant. His excessive drinking over the years landed him with a bloated beer belly that sprouted upward and nearly cast a shadow over him as he lay in his chair. But despite his large stomach, he presented an impressive broadness with imposing arm muscles. Arthur arched his head in the kitchen to quickly look at his mother. She was rushing around with a look of panic on her face that made Arthur's stomach churn. Arthur turned the other way and walked into the living room, where his drunken father sat with his beer.

His father saw Arthur walk in and nodded in his direction, taking a large gulp from the beer can in his hand. Then holding the can down, his father studied Arthur's face. Though despite what Arthur had expected, a slight smirk appeared on his face.

"Been fighting again, eh boy?" he slurred out in lazy words. Arthur looked away for a moment and nodded.

"Yes, sir," he answered in the manner he knew his father preferred. His father chuckled without looking at him.

"Heh!" he applauded with a stupid drunken grin slapped across his face.

"I remember when I was your age, boy... I got into fights every day, most of the time every hour." Arthur nodded awkwardly, knowing that if his father knew the truth, the truth that his son wasn't fighting people and beating them up, that he was the victim of constant bullying, his father would make his life even more miserable. But Arthur noted that this had put his father in a better mood; he had been drinking more than Arthur had expected. Arthur also knew, however, that his father's temper could be triggered easily, like an unstable volcano looking for any excuse to explode, so he tried to remain passive and agreeable.

"How was work, dad?" Arthur asked casually. His father's smile slowly melted as he sighed bitterly.

"Bloody pain, boy! Your father got written up again today. The sodding supervisor has it out for me; I know it! He doesn't nitpick anyone else there on their work, just me...two more write-ups, and I'll get a dock in my pay." Arthur nodded slowly.

"I'm sorry to hear that," Arthur replied blandly in his usual emotionless tone. His father looked up at his son, who was looking back at him. Arthur kept his expression neutral, giving away nothing to be used against him.

"Shut up! Do you even know what you're sorry about!? You have no idea of sodding work, do you!? You just go to bloody school and wouldn't know a decent day's work if your life depended on it! You little toe rag!" Arthur held his head down and spoke softly.

"Sorry, sir," Arthur finished. He then turned away from his father, who was now muttering angrily to himself as he continued to drink. Arthur, once out of his father's earshot, sighed with relief. His dad was a very unpredictable person. Arthur felt he handled that better than it could have gone down. A few minutes later, his mother shouted out that dinner was ready. Now was the time when all of them would be treading on very thin ice.

It was complete silence around the dinner table as they sat in their chairs.

Arthur and Alice were staring at their plates, saying nothing sitting across from each other. Their father sat at the far end, drinking another beer and belching now and again without covering his mouth. A small vein was building on their father's forehead. He was growing more impatient by the second. Arthur was secretly praying inside for his mother to be quicker with the food for all their sakes. Arthur looked up from his plate at Alice; her little face was bland and inexpressive. She didn't move an inch and looked like a tiny human doll was in her place. Arthur cast a quick eye at his father. He was still in his work clothes. His father then downed his last beer before angrily crushing the can in his fist, and throwing it behind him. His breathing was growing heavier, like a raging beast building up steam. Arthurs' silent prayer was then answered as his mother came out of the kitchen with plates in her hands. Arthur saw relief wash across Alice's face at the sight of them; his own was similar. Their mother placed all three plates in front of them and smiled as she went to get her own. Arthur looked down at the plate to see what was for dinner. Potato mash with sausages and vegetables on the side, their father's favorite. Their mother then sat down next to their father with her plate. Arthur noticed his father hadn't moved. He just stared at his plate wordlessly. Alice was tucking into her mash as their mother was getting herself comfortable. Worry raced across Arthur's face. He looked at his father's plate for any problems, but nothing seemed amiss. The mash wasn't too hard or too soft. It was exactly right. The vegetables were perfectly cooked too, but that didn't matter much as his father didn't enjoy eating vegetables.

"Oh no!" he cried in his head, seeing that the sausages looked burned. They were too brown, almost black. Arthur watched his father with hawkish concentration, not sure how he would react.

In honesty, he knew how his father would react. How badly though he couldn't predict. He readied himself to leap to his mother's aid at a moment's notice, not that it ever did any good.

"Do you think I'm an idiot" his father muttered darkly. Alice's fork froze by her mouth, their mother looking up in shock, eyes shaking.

"What's wrong, honey?...is something...wrong?" she asked weakly. The head of Arthurs's father snapped in her direction and eyed her cruelly as though gazing at an unwelcome guest in his home.

"I break my BACK working for this family, and you serve me burnt food like I'm some bloody mongrel!" he finished with a roar getting to his feet in a flash. Alice whined and began to get away from the table out of reach.

"Back in your seat NOW!" he roared at her. She shot back in her seat and froze solid. Arthur just eyed his father, waiting for him to move.

"Please, honey, I... I didn't mean to; I can make you something else if you want...anything at all. Please, just...calm down," Arthur's mother pleaded feebly.

"ARE YOU ORDERING ME AROUND IN MY HOUSE!" he screamed before raising his arm and throwing it aside with a quick, decisive swipe, slapping their mother across the face hard, sending her flying to the floor screeching in pain. His mother's face reddened as she cried, her hands held against the mark. Arthur leaped from his chair and darted in front of his mother, standing before his father, spreading his arms.

"Dad, please stop!" he cried out. His father snorted in disgust at his son.

"You're a worthless, miserable SOD!" he roared back, curling his hand into a fist.

"I'll teach you some respect, BOY!" his arm flew forward and connected with Arthur's face knocking him back into his mother. The room went dark and fuzzy around Arthur. He lost his senses and only saw colored shapes in front of him. His father stood over the pair, glowering, his arms tensed.

"Bloody ingrates!" he spat out. Turning away from the table, his father then walked away, grabbing his coat and slamming the door as he left the house. Arthur was still barely conscious. His mother was sobbing, and Alice was frozen in her seat.

Arthur regained his senses after a few moments. His head was ringing in pain. Half of his face felt completely numb. He was sure he would be in agony later, but that didn't matter to him right now. He stumbled to his feet and turned around, kneeling by his mother.

"Are you OK, mum?" he asked. His voice was croaky and near tears. His mother looked up at her son. She was still holding the side of her face; it was completely raw and stinging terribly to the touch. Tears, having flown down her eyes, dampened the apron she was wearing. She nodded slowly.

"Don't worry about me, Arthur. It was my fault... a wife should provide for her family...it's my fault... I should have known better..." she muttered feebly. Her head went down again, and she began sobbing uncontrollably again. Arthur lost it at those words. They pierced his heart with a sharpness that rivaled any knife in the world. He fell into tears as well and went to hug his mother for comfort. But to his surprise, his mother didn't accept his embrace. She didn't hold him softly into her arms and coo soft words to him so they could heal together from the ordeal as a mother does. Instead, she pushed him away sharply. Arthur fell backward and looked up at his mother with confused eyes, and she glared back at him.

"You made him leave!" she hissed hurtfully.

"I always told you to listen to your father no matter what, now look what you've done. How could you, Arthur!," she snapped, tears falling now from glaring eyes. Arthur stared back at her with his jaw dropped, unbelieving what he was hearing.

"I was only trying to keep that monster away from you, mum!" he said in defense, tears now flowing down his eyes.

"How dare you!" she snapped back angrily.

"That *monster* is your father and my husband! You will do as he says and never defy him again. Next time Arthur, stay out of it!" she finished. With one last glare, his mother returned to her tears. This time Arthur didn't try to reach out to her. He was still recovering from what he had just heard from his mother. Their father had been hurting them for years but never once had his mother blamed him, never. He had tried to jump in the way before. To hold his father back, he had always reacted badly, but she never took his father's side over his own. Arthur looked at his mother, the same woman fussing over his bruises no more than a few hours ago when he came home. Who was worried and concerned like every normal mother. Now she had thrown him aside when he tried to protect her. Arthur's heartbeat was growing faster. Tears weren't enough to handle all of this. Arthur got to his feet like a wobbling drunk, his eyes blared and his head still fuzzy. He looked towards Alice, who looked at him, her face still saying nothing. He walked over to her and held out his hand.

"Let's go upstairs, sis..." he said with a strained kindness, his composure hanging on by a single thread left. She shook her head at him.

"Daddy said not to move. I won't until he comes back, Arthur," she answered quietly; Arthur froze in place.

"Even she sided with him..." he thought to himself. Arthur retracted his arm and looked at her oddly, and turned away from both of them. The family he tried to protect from his abusive father had turned on him. He walked towards the door and pulled on his jacket, which was a medium-length leather coat. He opened the door and walked out, feeling like he was not sure why he should bother to return at all.

Arthur was storming down the streets with unbridled rage, his body feeling like a tsunami of conflicting pain. He felt anger, sadness, and betrayal. All mixed into a swirling spout inside of him. Arthur had tried to protect his family from the bully that was his father. The mother he loved, and the sister who adored him and whom he always had tried to protect. He didn't know why he bothered when everyone around him seemed to be against him. So, he wandered on, feeling scorned by everyone he met in his entire life. He didn't care even where he was walking. He was only glad it was as far away from his family as possible.

Arthur wasn't sure how far he had walked. He only looked up often to check the roads for oncoming cars. It had now been a good couple of hours since he left his house. It was dark out with only a few streetlamps every few roads keeping him in the light. He could tell he was at least still in his side of town from how terrible the streetlamps were around him; one in every five was working. The still run-down houses were around him. He sometimes felt like he was walking around the aftermath of a war zone. The streets were empty, the night air was cold, and the sky bore several large black clouds threatening rain.

Proudly beaming in the night sky was a full moon, large and shining strongly. It showered down its rays upon him as though the rock itself had an eye looking down at Arthur. He couldn't help himself. He stopped dead next to an alleyway staring dumbly at the moon, and its immense still shine in the air was near hypnotic. Arthur had always felt this when he gazed at a full moon. Every second he looked at it, he noticed more and more detail about the glowing rock. He noticed the small patches and patterns that lay upon its surface staring back at him. It was not just a clean sheet of rock. Without realizing it, a few minutes went by until Arthur regained himself. He looked around and chuckled at himself, thinking he was being a little silly for staring at the moon for so long. He began to move down the street when he heard a voice caress his ear from the alleyway to his right.

"My boy, over here," it whispered.

It was a woman's voice. The sound was young and melodic in its tone. Arthur squinted down into the dark alleyway, seeing a tall, slender figure in the darkness. Arthur wasn't a bloody idiot, especially with these streets. He certainly didn't plan on being mugged or murdered by some psycho. He stood his ground and kept his eyes firmly on the figure, ready to run the second they did something suspicious.

"Aww, there's no need to be afraid, my boy, come closer." The voice sounded weird this time to Arthur.

Arthur took a small step forward as the voice spoke more. It was still mysteriously alluring, almost like a lullaby, soothing and enticing. Arthur felt propelled to walk towards the mesmerizing voice and whoever owned it.

"That's it, sweet boy. Keep coming," it soothed at him. Arthur took another step as though his feet were not his own. He felt like he was being dragged forward by an unseen rope. Arthur had now come within a few feet of the figure. It held out an arm. It was a slender, thin arm with a golden silk glove stretching down to the elbow. The long, delicate fingers beckoned for him to move. Arthur came away from the light of the streetlamp and entered the shadows of the alleyway. He now was face to face with his strange caller. The sound of her sweet chuckling could be heard.

"Very good, my sweet boy," she cooed sweetly. Then, very quickly and sharply, she seized Arthur by his arm, pulling him forward in front of her. He was now an inch from her face. Arthur could barely see the woman. All his eyes revealed to him was a tall, slender figure with long hair, shrouded in shadows with thin but extraordinary long arms.

"Very good stupid boy, now you get a present, you get to provide nourishment to a god!" she hissed violently. Her mouth opened, revealing two long, razor-sharp fangs within her mouth. Arthur tried to resist and run away, but he couldn't break free. She hissed, then with a shriek, she threw her head forward and bit down with her jaw upon his bare neck.

In the space of that millisecond, Arthur thought he was dead. He thought this crazed monster woman would devour him like an animal and leave him dead in the alleyway to be found by the police or morning joggers tomorrow. He thought fate had decided to end his existence right here and now on this night in cold blood. Arthur then quickly realized that fate had agreed for him to not have his life end tonight. A fast and powerful figure leaped from the shadows from behind the woman in the blink of an eye. It then dashed forward the second the woman's head came within breaths of Arthurs' neck. A huge bulging, black hairy fist shot forward, connecting sharply with the woman's jaw. Through Arthur's ears, it was like the sound of a log breaking against a tree that echoed through the airways as the woman was hurled back harshly, smashing against the wall of the alleyway. Arthur collapsed onto the floor out of the woman's grasp. He felt like his heart was beating four times faster than it's ever been in his life. He looked up at the figure that had just saved his life. It was a man nearly seven feet in height. He was pale-skinned. thin but broadly built with seemingly large muscles. He wore a black vest with black trousers, long flowing black hair hanging from his head, and his face scarred to pieces. The man looked down at Arthur and cast an eye over him to check for any signs of injury.

"Lad, are you OK?" he grunted, his voice deep and scratchy. Arthur was stunned to speak for the moment, so he just nodded shakily at the man. Before another word was spoken, the woman snapped to her feet with inhuman speed and hissed like an insane cobra at the man.

"Filthy mutt, I'll teach you to mess with the divine," she spat out like a cursing elderly woman. She raised her hand and pointed her incredibly long sharp nails at him, her now beaten bloody face twisted with hate. The man gazed at her with a look of contempt. He raised his arms, adjusting his body and lowering his knees a little.

"Try it," he grunted. The woman shrieked again and lunged at him. The speed both people fought with was barely perceivable. Arthur could still see both exchanging blows, but it was as though their limbs had trailed behind them as they moved. It looked to him like continuous blurs as they fought in the cramped space of the alleyway. Arthur crawled back several feet to stay out of the way, as well as gain a better look at what exactly he was seeing. He couldn't figure out what unique humans these two seemed to be. He had watched boxing, and other fighting matches on his family's rubbish television before, but he had never witnessed such an impossibility before.

The tall man moved as though he weighed nothing as the woman screeched with each attack. She was swiping her claws at the man like a wounded animal backed into a corner. His strike towards her jaw had cut her face, and she was now bleeding heavily from her mouth. The man moved with exact precision. He predicted her attacks before she even made them, blocking or dodging when he needed to and striking back twice as hard. The woman hissed as she took another blow to her eye. She then growled and swore, slashing with her long nails, trying to gouge out his throat in a single slash. But the man was a better fighter than she was. He hadn't taken a single attack from her. She then jumped back, dodging a punch he threw at her, and she snarled.

"Bloody mongrel!" she spat out, her face bloody and bruised and her right eye beginning to swell. The man snorted and raised his arms again.

"You're not getting away," he stated simply. She hesitated and tucked both her arms inwards until her hands were next to her breasts. She then jolted both her hands forward for an attack to lance him with both hands at once. Arthur saw the man but didn't react in time. That he didn't notice the woman shooting with both of her hands. Arthur saw that the man only saw her left hand and now his mysterious savior was going to be killed by her right. Arthur was scared to death, but he refused to sit there and let his rescuer die. Arthur jumped to his feet, took in a deep breath, and lunged forward throwing a punch at her as the tall man had done for him. The tall man had caught her left hand as Arthur's fist embedded sharply into her ribcage. The man was taken by complete surprise, looking oddly at Arthur. Her right arm went weak, and Arthur could feel his strike stab deep into her body, shocking her immensely. The woman screamed in agony. The tall man immediately wrapped his hand over her mouth. He looked at Arthur and smiled, nodding his thanks. The woman moaned and tried to struggle against him, but the fight was over, and she had no strength left. The tall man gripped the other side of her head with his other hand and sharply twisted her head, snapping her neck. The woman shuddered for a moment then went still in his hands.

Arthur was stunned as the tall man released the woman. She tried to kill him and got killed in return. Earlier today, he had been solving fractions in Math class, and now he just witnessed a person murdered before him. It was something he had never seen in real life before. It seemed oddly different from the films. This was more real and extremely terrifying. He decided not to think about it for now. He would try to leave it at that.

"Thanks," the tall man grunted, catching Arthur's attention. He looked up and saw the tall man brushing himself off, trying to rub the woman's blood into his clothes. Arthur breathed and faced the man with his back straightened.

"No...problem," Arthur replied blankly. He was clearly in shock from the attack. The tall man chuckled, looking down at the woman.

"Not many of them left in this city, she was their leader, and they'll probably scatter after they find her dead." Arthur had no idea what he was talking about. Arthur looked back down at the woman and noticed something impossible. The woman's body was different. Her hair had gone a bright, solid grey. Then her skin wrinkled, her sharp nails disappeared, and her body looked crooked and deflated. Her bones under her skin were now obvious to see. Arthur took a step back and looked. The young flawless fanged woman had disappeared and been replaced with a haggard, weakened old-looking witch.

"What!? How?!" Arthur stuttered. The tall man shook his head.

"It happens when they die. It's so no evidence is left behind for their lot to be traced," he answered plainly, speaking as though Arthur was meant to know what he was even talking about.

"What do you mean 'their lot'?" Arthur asked back. The tall man looked Arthur over for a brief moment and he then shrugged.

"Doesn't matter to you, perhaps," he answered in return strangely, a tone that suggested more context than Arthur could attempt to assume. Arthur took another step back, uncertain and sensing danger. The tall man chuckled and held his hands up safely.

"Don't be scared, kid. I won't hurt you. I understand if you're shaken up." The tall man caught Arthur's face wound he got from his father.

"Did she hurt you anywhere else?" he asked kindly. Arthur looked away.

"That wasn't her...," he replied in a low tone, saying nothing else. The man raised an eyebrow but just nodded and didn't pry further. He held out a hand to Arthur with a friendly smile.

"My name is Cratos Mane. It's nice to meet you." Arthur looked back up and saw the scarred man smiling with what seemed like sincerity, and he smiled back. Arthur wasn't sure how to respond to genuine pleasantness. He took the man's extended hand and shook it. His grip was immensely strong, like two steel pincers snapping shut. However, Arthur refused to wince at its strength. He, in turn, was trying to squeeze as hard as he could back.

"I'm Arthur Thorn, thanks for saving me." Cratos nodded and released his grip, turning his back on Arthur.

"See you around, Arthur Thorn," he said finally with a friendly smile. Cratos crouched somewhat, then, without saying another word, he leaped into the air, kicking himself side to side between the walls until he was on the roof. As Arthur watched him, the man quickly vanished from his sight, gone to the world, leaving Arthur alone in the alley next to the crumbled, ashy remains of the creature that had nearly taken his life. Arthur shook his head in astonishment, still comprehending the last five minutes of his life. Arthur turned away and headed back into the streets, leaving the alleyway and heading home.

CHAPTER THREE

Arthur didn't get back home until nearly two in the morning. Any other person would be dropping at the scene with exhaustion, but Arthur didn't think he would be sleeping a wink tonight. No one was awake when Arthur got in the house. He could tell his father was home from the sound of his monstrous snoring echoing through the house. The encounter in the alleyway was replaying through his mind like a broken film on loop. From the moment he was lured into the alley to Cratos saving him, then murdering the woman and vanishing in the blink of an eye. It was mind-boggling. A thousand questions were buzzing through his head.

"How did they move so fast? Why did that woman have long, sharp teeth, and how did he jump like that? What did Cratos mean by 'their lot'? Who were these people?" were questions that repeated inside his mind. What was driving Arthur mad the most was that there was no way he would never have any of these questions answered because he figured he would never see that man again in his life. Arthur wandered through the house, saying nothing at first and ignoring how hungry he suddenly was, remembering how he didn't finish his dinner. Then he thought about what happened at dinner. His father was probably drunk enough tonight to forget about it, but he knew his mother would remember. Those thoughts were quickly wiped away by what happened tonight again, that he was nearly killed. The woman who, at first, had seemed normal, then revealed her long sharp nails and weirdly long teeth. She was like some weird creature, the sort he saw in films once though he couldn't remember the name of what the monsters were. He wasn't a horror movie buff anyway. He walked upstairs and entered his room very quietly, knowing not to wake anyone up. Instead, he didn't turn on the lights and went straight to his bed, not even bothering to get undressed. He thought about the man who saved his life, named Cratos Mane. Arthur couldn't stop thinking about how he would now be dead if it weren't for him. When Cratos shook his hand and didn't spit in his face like other kids often did. Arthur was just now glad that tonight was over and that hopefully, tomorrow wouldn't be any worse than tonight.

The following morning was filled with an uneasy silence. Arthur drifted downstairs saying nothing, remembering that woman's face as she opened her mouth and bared her fangs like a vicious snake at him. His mind then flashed to the look on her face as he cracked her ribcage with his fist. He sat at the table and began eating a small bowl of porridge his mother had made for him. It had a tiny bit of sugar on the surface for flavor, but he didn't even notice. Arthur was chewing and swallowing mechanically, not bothering to look up at anyone, mumbling thanks as his mother poured him some orange juice which he drained in nearly one gulp. Alice sat a few chairs away from him, eating her porridge as well. Arthur raised his head a little and looked at her. She made eye contact with him but immediately looked away. Arthur faced back down and finished his food, not meeting her gaze again. Once the bowl was empty, he washed it in the sink and put it away in the cupboard. He said thank you again and walked out of the room, grabbing his bag by the door; as he left, he noticed his mother didn't wish him a goodbye like she usually did.

On the way to school, Arthur met up with his friend Jack. Jack Mortum was someone Arthur had known since going to preschool together. Jack was sometimes distant, but they remained friends even as their personalities grew somewhat different over the years. No matter what, Arthur was always there for his friends because he knew how rare they were in the world.

Arthur met up with him by a fence post a few yards away from the school gate. They were never hassled there. They knew if you stick to the same place in school for too long, you become a target. Arthur was still thinking about last night. He wasn't sure if he should tell Jack or not. Odds are his friend might not even believe him, but he wasn't sure he could trust Jack to keep it to himself even if he did. Jack was his closest friend, but in his life experience, he was hesitant to trust many people, and Jack had let him down plenty of times. He would have to think more and decide while they were talking on the way. Arthur walked past a corner and saw him up ahead. Jack had short blonde hair, wearing dark blue trousers with a black shirt and a denim jacket. He was often a 'ladies' man at the school, given he already had seven ex-girlfriends under his belt. They were still barely teenagers, but Arthur was continuously impressed with that number. Jack was growing into a more popular guy, but he still tried to stay Arthur's friend. Jack saw Arthur walking up and waved a hello, smiling. Arthur smiled back and waved in return.

Jack smiled as he saw his friend approach, noticing the dark rings around Arthur's eyes.

"Hey mate, not sleep well?" he pointed out, chuckling. Arthur sighed nervously. He didn't feel like telling him what happened for the moment and simply shrugged.

"Being so close to the weekend is always the hardest, I guess," he laughed back with obviously fake, insincere humor.

"I know right, it's right before us yet just away from our fingertips, agonizing!" Jack replied with a chuckle. Sometimes, Jack's voice was a tad high-pitched, but he managed to catch himself if he thought he was speaking too excitedly. Arthur pretended to laugh again, but Jack wasn't returning the false humor, noticing the face bruise across Arthur's face. Jack knew they were given from a punch. Arthur saw Jack catching it; then he rubbed it, chuckling.

"Gary. He caught me on my way home again. Scumbag!" Arthur growled darkly. This time very sincerely. Jack narrowed his eyes but chose to say nothing. These morning lies were an uncomfortable formality these days. Arthur saw that Jack would know precisely where that face bruise came from. It's the reason Jack stopped coming around Arthur's for dinner anymore. Arthur understood that Jack couldn't stand watching his friend go through what he did at home. So, Jack simply nodded at his friend, and the two began to walk down the road in silence for a moment letting the air clear from that awkward exchange a moment ago. Once a few minutes had passed, jack spoke up.

"You get your homework done for the second period?" he asked plainly. Arthur winced. He completely forgot to do it after he got home. The shock of his attack made him forget. For a moment, Arthur pictured using that as an excuse for why he didn't do his homework. He would bet his teacher hadn't heard THAT excuse before. He thought about how he would say it.

"Sorry, sir, a monstrous woman attacked me with fangs trying to kill me only to be saved at the last minute by a thin, tall man with inhuman speed and strength who killed her right in front of me. Is it all right if I hand it in tomorrow?" Arthur couldn't help but laugh out loud at the insane idea of it, shocking Jack a little.

"What's so funny?" Jack asked, confused. Arthur recovered himself and waved a hand at his friend.

"Doesn't matter, you wouldn't get it," he finished with a chuckled and shook his head before answering his previous question.

"No, I didn't do the homework, forgot about it." Arthur then exhaled with detached apathy. Jack nodded and smirked at him back.

"Guess I can count on not seeing your ugly mug during the break, have fun doing it then." The two came close to the school gate as the bell rang loudly, signaling for the students to get to their first class. Arthur shrugged and sighed again.

"It doesn't matter, less hassle inside the school than outside, right?" His friend gave Arthur a sad look, this time sincere. Nodding and saying nothing, the two walked past the big black gate and went to their first lesson to start a typically dull, unpleasant school day.

Arthur hurried on as his first lesson of the day was English. He always sat in the back of the room in the far-right corner. That way, people couldn't throw things at him. No one paid much attention to him unless the teacher spoke to him, in which case, he would give a quick mumbled answer. The other students were enough of an even mix of boys and girls, each of them in their friendship groups. The girls huddled together talking about new hairstyles they planned to get done at the weekend, and a few were talking about some films they had seen the previous night. The boys of the class also spoke about their interests to each other. They would go on about different cars they saw on some TV show and the ever-popular topic he would hear from boys, football. The other students in the class were like him. Those that weren't paired off with their friends just sat quietly and did their work. They were the intelligent bunch themselves, meaning that they were too busy studying to bother talking. When he was sure he wasn't being watched, Arthur would occasionally draw pictures on the inside of his workbook, just waiting for the bell to ring. The only friends he could chat with were mainly in his Math and science lessons, so he had to wait until then. Jack was in Math, so he was looking forward to it a little.

The lesson started the same, no one would shut up until the teacher came in, and even when she shouted at everyone three times, they were still mumbling and whispering to each other. But that was the best she could hope for, and she quickly began the lesson. Arthur's English teacher was an old, thin, angry woman. She was constantly snapping and shouting at the tiniest thing. Impossible to please, any work done was never good enough and thrown back in everyone's faces for correction. There were a couple of people who threw a few ginger hair jokes his way in hushed whispers. His temper flared, and his nails dug deep into his palms, but Arthur stayed quiet, so they got bored and left him alone. Arthur didn't bother drawing today in his book. His mind was still fixated on that tall man who saved him. He wondered where Cratos came from. He was clearly in his area hunting down those creatures, but where would he go next? Arthur could tell by his voice that he didn't have much of an accent. His language was English, but his voice almost seemed indistinct. Arthur felt a strange unease thinking about if he would see Cratos again. Some small part of him said he would. That was the exact part that made him dash forward to punch that woman and help Cratos. It made him feel that something was now different, not sure what, but something was indeed different. Before Arthur knew it, the bell rang, and he headed to his next lesson, doing what he could to avoid every other student in the halls. He felt as though they could all just be marching off a cliff, and realization wouldn't kick in until they were inches from the ground. They probably wouldn't care when they noticed either way.

Mathematics was a bore. When he was younger, Arthur used to be good at it, often going through different sums and equations like lightning. But the older he got, he lost interest in advancing his skills, and he slowly went to the bottom of the class in progression, barely scraping by as he didn't bother to improve. Arthur and Jack sat at the back of the classroom. A couple of Arthur's other friends named Ryan and Daniel were towards the front of the classroom. They greeted Arthur as he walked by but nothing else. Jack and Arthur would often talk to each other during the class, which helped the time go by during these lessons. Their teacher was a middle-aged man named Mr. Wreckson, nicknamed the wrecking ball for when he lost his temper. He could roar at a classroom and be heard in every other room on the entire floor when he wanted to. But he had a soft spot for certain students, and Arthur was one of them. When Arthur struggled with sums he was genuinely trying to solve, Wreckson would help him. He often spoke to Arthur about the bruises he came into school with. He was one of the few people who cared about Arthur.

The class started the same as in English, with everyone talking and messing around. Jack was speaking to Arthur about a television show he watched last night. Arthur listened and replied as best he could, but his mind was constantly flashing back to last night. So, all he could reply with were blank answers. It was the same usual lesson, sums put on the board for the class to copy down and complete. As Arthur worked silently, he felt a nudge on his elbow. Arthur snapped out of his lull and turned his head. It was Jack getting his attention.

"You OK, man? You've been spacing out all day. Did you stay up all night or something?" he asked skeptically as he finished a couple more sums. Arthur smiled and shook his head.

"Nah, mate, I've just got...a lot on my mind," he answered pleasantly, giving him a reassuring nod back.

"Like what, man?" Jack asked back, only receiving a shake of the head and a shrug back from Arthur.

"Don't worry about it. It's nothing really, I'll be fine when we're at the break, and I can breathe." Jack chuckled and put a smug look on his face.

"Don't count on it. You didn't do your homework, remember." Arthur groaned when he heard that. It would mean he would have to do it during break and miss out completely. Arthur's face dropped, and he continued his work. Jack stopped trying to talk to him and worked as well. The end of the lesson came, and Wreckson addressed the class.

"Right, you all know the drill. Those that completed their homework, hand it in with your workbook and go to break, and those that didn't stay behind to finish it by my desk." Everyone stood up and began shuffling towards the door, dropping off their work as they went out.

"See you at lunch, man," Jack said briefly, then he went on his way.

"Cheers," Arthur said back, and the pair knocked fists together, and he left. Finally, Jack came to the front of the class and sat at the front table next to Wreckson's desk. Arthur sighed and put a blank homework sheet in front of him with unsolved sums. Mr. Wreckson tutted and shook his head. Arthur was the only one left in the entire class.

"That's a shame, Arthur. But rules are rules. Sit down and get them done. If you finish them quickly, then you may be able to have some break time." His voice was kind and understanding as Arthur picked up his pen and began working through the sums in silence.

Ten minutes went by, and Arthur was nearly finished. He pressed on quickly in hopes of still getting a good enough time to meet and chat with what few friends he had. Out of nowhere, Mr. Wreckson began speaking to him.

"You used to be a lot better at Math, you know, Arthur, what happened?" Arthur looked up from his work, and then he looked away, uncomfortable.

"Nothing happened, sir. It just got a lot harder, that's all," Arthur mumbled in response. His teacher nodded, then sighed.

"I understand how you feel, Arthur; I get why you don't have as much motivation as you did once." Arthur couldn't help but snort at that remark.

"It's nothing to worry about, sir. I just didn't sleep well last night," he muttered, giving his teacher the same smile he had given Jack before. Mr. Wreckson, however, recognized the lack of conviction from Arthur and simply sighed.

"You would be surprised what I worry about, Arthur." he leaned back in his chair and looked sadly at Arthur, who looked up from his work and at his teacher.

"My father used to work in a steel mill," he began saying, eyes down, looking into his lap. He was no longer looking at Arthur.

"He had strong, callused hands. It was good for his work. He was a strong man. He had huge hands for welding and sawing." He looked up, and his eyes narrowed on the mark on Arthur's face.

"Punching too, that was what my father was best at, Arthur." Arthur's stomach turned to ice as his teacher eyed him carefully. Arthur avoided his teacher's gaze and muttered.

"I got this from some bullies, sir," Arthur mumbled, looking in every direction around the classroom except his teacher. Mr. Wreckson nodded curtly.

"Oh, I know, I'm sure there are bruises from bullies, but that mark came from a very large bully, in particular, didn't it, Arthur," he challenged gently. Arthur didn't answer. He said nothing and went back to his work.

"I DO understand how you feel Arthur, I can help you," Mr. Wreckson continued, trying to reach Arthur. Arthur's temper began to flicker. He gritted his teeth and pressed his pen harder against the paper.

"I can handle it, sir..." he said as calmly as he could. He didn't want to get angry at Mr. Wreckson. Despite the slight irritation coming through Arthur's tone, his teacher kept his calm and nodded.

"I can help in more ways than you think. But I cannot help you at all unless you can tell me anything about who gave you that mark and how." Arthur then sharply put his pen aside and pushed his completed homework hard on his teacher's desk. He stood up from his chair and grabbed his bag. He walked to the door only to turn back with a scowl.

"Nothing is wrong, sir!" Arthur said in an exhausted sigh before running out of the door. His teacher sighed as he looked over Arthur's work and began marking it. His teacher's eyes were slightly watery, and his hands started shaking slightly. He remembered terrible memories himself, hoping Arthur would come to him one day so he could help his student.

Arthur stormed down the stairs and hallways of his school with a furious scowl on his face. He imagined in his head what he wanted to say.

"MIND YOUR OWN BUSINESS! YOU DON'T KNOW ME OR ANYTHING ELSE, YOU IDIOT!" Arthur roared inside his mind. He was playing that sentence back-to-back in his head. He knew his teacher cared, but something about the way his teacher mentioned his problems seemed to have touched a deep nerve. Arthur clenched his fists, his arms tensing fiercely.

"What makes HIM think I need help, that I need ANYONE'S HELP?! I CAN LOOK AFTER MYSELF; I DON'T NEED ANYONE!" Arthur threw the door open that led to the field where he knew at least Jack would be. He walked about the grounds at first, needing to clear his head. He only had five minutes to relax before his following few lessons, and he planned to enjoy that as best he could.

He quickly spotted jack and moved on forward. The gardening staff had recently cut the grass on the field, so most of the students ran around throwing clumps of cut grass at each other. Jack was sitting by himself, leaning against a tree in the shade. Arthur saw him and quickly sat down next to him.

"I thought you'd be out sooner," Jack commented. Arthur breathed out a frustrated sigh.

"Wreckson had a lot to say," he grunted back, still holding back his rage and trying not to let it show in front of Jack. Jack nodded thoughtfully, choosing his following words carefully.

"About your face, I take it?" he asked casually. Arthur sighed impatiently again but nodded at his friend.

"Yes…" he answered blandly, then Arthur fell silent. Jack then looked out at the field.

"It helps to have at least one teacher in this dump to care about you, eh?"

Arthur shook his head again.

"I don't care. They're my problems, not his. All I need are my friends," Arthur finished, smiling a bit. Jack chuckled.

"How corny. Any friend in particular?" he asked, laughing. Arthur hummed, pretending to think.

"Well, you seem to be the only mate I can't count on sometimes." Jack chuckled again, then he smiled back at Arthur.

"Cheer's man, you know I've got your back."

"I know, man," Arthur replied, the pair knocking fists again. The bell sounded again, and the pair got up and headed for their following lessons. Arthur knew he had Science now.

Arthur knew there was only one reason he looked forward to each of his science lessons during the week, and it was that he got to sit next to his crush. Her name was Ashley Leyson. She was slightly shorter than him, with long brown hair stretching far down her lower back in a ponytail. She had somewhat darker skin with brown eyes and a warm sweet smile. She had a nice slender look which Arthur liked. Arthur had wanted to be her boyfriend for the past few years now. He had been friends with her for as long as he could remember. He would speak to her in Science, be her partner in projects, and spend the odd lunch break hanging out with her. He made it no secret with his friends that she was the girl he fancied out of their year group. He was sure she liked him back. He caught her smiling at him when she thought he wasn't looking, and the two laughed and trusted each other. The problem was Arthur never plucked up the courage to ask her out. He was terrified by the notion she would say no, and if she did say that, then they would never speak to each other again. Even if she wasn't his girlfriend, he liked having a crush on a girl and being able to think that she might one day go out with him. It was often a nice thought he had.

The lesson went by as their teacher was explaining the difference between elements and compounds, boring stuff to Arthur. Still, because Ashley loved science and always paid attention, Arthur pretended he was interested in the subject as well. Arthur succeeded in this one school subject purely because he pretended to like it and worked hard to impress Ashley.

"Do you have a spare pen?" Ashley asked Arthur as her pen had run out of ink. Her voice was smooth and light, always pleasing to Arthur's ears.

"Sure," he said coolly with a smile. He picked out a pen from his pocket and handed it to her.

"Thanks," she replied sweetly. Arthur looked away as he blushed, not wanting her to see. She returned to her work as Arthur looked at her for a second. To him, she was the most beautiful girl in the school. He figured he would ask her out eventually, and if he were feeling brave, it would be in the next few weeks he planned. He finished his work before the rest of the class. Ashley always finished hers before anyone else, and the two were chatting as the lesson began to end.

"Where did you get that mark?" she asked, confused. Arthur just shrugged.

"Got into a fight on the way home yesterday. A lot of people don't like me, I guess," he answered jokingly, trying to make her smile. Ashley did smile, and she patted him on the shoulder.

"You're such a nice guy. Why do people pick on you?" she asked caringly, her smile not fading in the slightest. Arthur turned his head and returned her smile.

"You'd be handsome as well if you gave your face a chance to heal," she added with a giggle. Arthur didn't have time to hide it this time, his face blushed like crazy, and with his pale skin, it showed. Ashley laughed sweetly at Arthur's face as he tried to cover his blushing. The bell rang, and they had to go to their next lesson.

"I'll see you at lunch, OK?" Arthur asked, smiling. Strangely, Ashley shifted uncomfortably and shrugged.

"Maybe, I'm meeting with my other friends. We'll see." Arthur's smile fell, but he nodded his head and went to his next lesson.

He had English again, simply doing the same work as before. Thoughts of Cratos Mane quickly resurfaced again as well as the alleyway fight. He recalled the event so thoroughly as though it had happened just a few minutes ago. But there were still a dozen questions littering his mind he couldn't answer.

"Were they some sort of superhumans? They might be experiments gone wrong. Broken loose from a laboratory and are now running wild? Or even perhaps aliens dressed up as humans?" Arthur couldn't help chuckle at that last suggestion, not sure what was wrong with his brain to think of something that absurd. The lesson flew by at an amazing time. It was as though the bell was ringing in a matter of minutes, and then it was time for lunch. Arthur now had a full forty minutes to hang out with his mates, which was exactly what Arthur felt like he needed. Arthur wasted no time; he packed up his books, grabbed his bag, and headed out to the field where his other mates were.

Along with Jack, Arthur had two other friends. They were Ryan Evers and Daniel Blane. Ryan was a short kid who was a little bit overweight with short brown hair and glasses. He wore dark green clothes, mainly black trainers. He was a mathematic wizard and was in the top class in the subject. He loved nerdy video games and played card games as well. Sometimes Arthur joined him in them, it was genuine fun, and it often gave him ideas of new stuff to draw and even write about for the future. Daniel was very tall and thin with long blonde hair. He wore a white shirt with a blue denim vest and black trousers and shoes. He was a musician. He played bass guitar as his main but could play pretty much anything else. He was in a band with some other people in the school and just like Arthur he loved Metal music. It was that which cemented their friendship, the trading of bands and new songs they each came across. They were good friends at times, and Arthur was glad he knew them. Though often the second anyone with a mean look came Arthur's way, they tried to back out and leave Arthur alone to face the problem himself.

The pair of them were chatting freely at the far end of the field by the metal gates that ran along the school's perimeter. Arthur could hear their conversation as he approached. Ryan was bragging about perfect marks on his Math test, and Daniel was trying to describe how this new song he came across was his most recent inspiration. They both noticed Arthur walk up and gave him a wave.

"Hey, Arthur!" Ryan chirped, his voice low and smooth

"Hey there," Daniel muttered friendlily after; his voice was often squeakier. Arthur smiled and waved hello, but he noticed one person was absent.

"Where's Jack?" he asked quickly.

"Bloody hell, are you two joined at the hip or something," Ryan joked. Daniel laughed, and Arthur chuckled himself.

"No, he just said he would see me at lunch, and I haven't caught sight of him yet," Arthur replied for them both to simply shrug at Arthur.

"Probably off seducing girlfriend number eight thousand," Daniel muttered scornfully.

Arthur knew Daniel didn't like Jack. Mainly because Jack dated his ex-girlfriend whom he still had feelings for without caring what Daniel thought. Arthur chuckled, ignoring the hate in his friend's voice.

"Probably, oh well, I'm sure he'll find us when he's done," he replied cheerfully, keeping the chat going.

"I noticed you weren't around at Break, Arthur, held back?" Ryan asked to which Arthur nodded.

"Bloody Wreckson took nearly all my break because I didn't do my math homework. Why does he care anyway?" Arthur asked bitterly. Ryan rolled his eyes at Arthur.

"It's his job, you idiot. You and Jack are in the lowest set for Math anyway. It can't be that hard." Arthur bit his lip, struggling not to remark on how Ryan is rubbish at Science. The one subject he could lord over his friend.

"Doesn't matter. Did you get up too much last night, Arthur?" He shook his head. If he didn't tell Jack what happened, he wouldn't tell either of them.

"No, just listened to some music and relaxed. Bit of writing and some drawing. You know my usual night." Both Ryan and Daniel noticed the significant mark on his face, but they never asked him, not even mentioning Gary and his thugs to him. Daniel smiled at Arthurs' answer.

"Was it that new CD I gave you?" Daniel had lent Arthur a new band to listen to a few days ago, claiming they were the best metal band yet. Arthur hadn't gotten around to it yet but didn't want to keep his mate waiting.

"Yeah, I did. I couldn't stop after just one song, man. You were right about what you said…" he replied feebly. Daniel grinned and went on for a few minutes about the band's rise to their fame. Arthur listened politely until Ryan cut in.

"Guys, Gary's coming towards us." Arthur turned around to see Gary walking towards the three of them with his friends from yesterday. Arthur felt his friends stiffen and take a few steps backward already. Arthur sighed, thinking he couldn't even have ten minutes of peace.

Gary and his friends made a feeble circle around the three of them. Gary was facing Arthur directly in his face. Daniel and Ryan shifted uncomfortably as the rest of Gary's friends were jeering and spewing insults at them.

"What do you want, Gary," Arthur muttered, exhausted and sick of this routine.

"Can't this wait until after school," he finished with an edge in his tone. Gary's face twisted as he scowled, not used to this amount of attitude from Arthur.

"Care to say that again, freak!?" he spat out at him. Arthur tensed his arms and fists, getting angry.

"I am not a FREAK!" he roared at Gary, not even making the bully flinch as Gary smiled at Arthur, who was now breathing heavily as his temper continued to build. Arthur noticed he didn't feel the same dread when looking at Gary as before. Things seemed different now. After Arthur had helped Cratos last night and after that fanged woman stared him in the eye as she went to kill him, Gary no longer made his knees shake after he punched her in the ribs despite his fear. The bully took a step forward, so he was closer to Arthur, who this time didn't look away but instead stared right back at Gary into his eyes. Arthur didn't blink. He was holding his back up straight and standing firm. Gary addressed Ryan and Daniel.

"Unless you two losers want what he's getting, get lost!" he snarled. The two hesitated but then quickly grabbed their bags. They said nothing to Arthur and walked away. Neither Daniel nor Ryan looked back, keeping their heads held down. Arthur didn't break eye contact with Gary, but on the inside, he was upset, even though he expected it by now.

Now Arthur was standing face to face with Gary, and all his friends took a few steps closer to Arthur. Every time they did that, it was a betrayal to him, each time. The bully curled his lips at Arthur.

"Do you think you've grown a spine now? Eh? you ginger freak! Accidents like you should have been thrown in the bin at birth! A mistake, that's what you are!" His friends all laughed at that, but Arthur's temper flared again as it always did when someone had gone this far.

"Then isn't it funny how you're so pathetic that the only person you can pick on is a 'Freak' guess that makes you lower than a freak yourself!" Arthur spat out slowly and venomously. Gary's eyes widened as he then spat clean in Arthur's face.

"SCUM!" Gary shouted spitefully. Arthur saw what was about to come next, so he immediately threw his fist forward, punching Gary clean straight in the nose. The strike missed his bully completely as Gary grabbed Arthur's fist in the air. His friends immediately jumped Arthur from behind. One swung a fist around, clocking Arthur in the side of the head. He fell aside when another one kicked his legs out from under him, making him fall to the ground. Right then, all of Gary's friends were kicking and stomping on his body as he tried to get to his feet. Gary waded into the mess with a curled lip, his face a demonic glare.

"You're going to regret that freak!" Gary then set about grabbing Arthur by the scruff of his shirt and wailing down punches on his face as his friends cheered him on.

After his beating was over, Arthur could have gotten up sooner, but he knew Gary and his friends would keep looking back until they were out of sight to ensure he was still on the floor. Once they had gone inside, Arthur struggled to his feet, groaning from the bruises that would soon smother the rest of his body. He usually preferred for Gary to wait for his wounds to heal before making new bruises. None of his bones was broken because they only stomped on his stomach. His lips were bleeding, and his other eye would be swelled by nightfall, but he was all right. He tried to ignore the pulsing sting of each strike and hobble on through the field to look for Jack. His friends would be off hiding somewhere, trying to steer now clear of Gary and his henchmen.

Arthur didn't know where Jack was but with each step; he was walking more quickly. Many of the other kids had watched what Gary had done, so no one bothered to call him names as he walked by. His head was held high with his bleeding lip, blankly walking past each of them. He came to the end of the field and turned the corner. This path led to the back exit of the school, where the car park was for the teachers. Arthur knew Jack well, and if he were trying to charm some new girl, he would do it there out of sight where they could snog in peace from catcallers or any stone-throwers. He came to the car park. A few dozen cars were all lined up next to each other, and at the far end was the long wooden bike shed. Behind, there was where Jack would be. Arthur walked forward past each car. As he came closer to the bike shed, he could hear the sound of giggling from a boy and a girl. Arthur smiled; he always admired what a ladies' man his best friend was and would only take a small peek to see before leaving the two of them alone. Arthur leaned against the wood of the shed, the two were heard kissing loudly, and Arthur smirked and leaned his head around to see. The girl that was wrapped in his best friend's arms, kissing him back intensely and giggling as he held her close, was Ashley.

Arthur was breathless. The first thing that went through Arthur's mind was the harsh wrenching words Jack had said to him only a few hours ago. He knew the kind of guy his friend was like, but Jack had never done anything like this before, and Arthur thought he never would.

"You know I've always got your back," now echoed inside his head. Those words were scornfully accompanied by mocking hysterical laughter by Jack as Arthur continued to watch the pair exchange saliva a few feet away from where he stood. Arthur watched Jack's hand gently caress her face as his lips pressed harder against her own. The girl he had a crush on, who he had liked for years. He felt a wrenched, twisted, and sickly feeling. He felt as though his heart had come to a complete stop. It felt as though a long, wide thin piece of glass, deep inside every part of his body, just shattered into a billion pieces. Arthur felt weak, dizzy, heartbroken, betrayed, and truly angry.

Arthur wanted to go over there right where Jack was and grab him with both of his hands. Then he would rip him away from Ashley and punch him, then he would just keep punching him repeatedly until his skin ripped down to the bone of his knuckles. The two broke lips and Ashley giggled again.

"Are you sure this is OK? Doesn't Arthur, you know, like me?" she asked, nervous. Jack chuckled smugly, running his hand over her hair. Her eyes closed a second to enjoy the feeling as he held her chin up and kissed her again softly. Pulling away, he stared deep into her eyes.

"Don't worry about Arthur. You're a beautiful woman. Not like the other girls here; you're a woman. You know that, right?" His voice was so smooth with each word, deep and enticing. It was the same tone he used on every girl he charmed. He was filling their head with his nonsense. He always said the same thing. She nodded nervously, and jack continued.

"Arthur's a loser," he said bluntly, somehow making Arthur feel like his legs were cut off him from the knees, and he just fell a foot down.

"You deserve better than the kid that gets bullied by every kid in school. You deserve a real man. That's me, babe." She blushed again, and she returned to kissing him. For three whole seconds, the two best friend's eyes met each other's unblinking gaze. Jack's eye opened in Arthur's direction, but he didn't move. Arthur said nothing, and neither did Jack. Very slowly, Arthur moved out of Jack's view and headed towards the back school exit. He hopped over the fence and began walking away, away from it all.

CHAPTER FOUR

Arthur was walking the streets blindly, not even bothering to look both ways as he walked past the roads. Several cars were coming to a screeching halt, followed by the drivers yelling at him as he walked on. Arthur felt completely numb. There was rage inside of him, a dark rage coupled with tremendous heavy sorrow. He felt like there were enough of his pain to swallow up the entire world. He didn't know where he was going, and he didn't care. He just decided to keep walking the streets. He knew if a police officer saw him, they might take him back to school because it hadn't finished, but none had bothered him yet. He didn't know what he would do if one did. That building was the last place in the world he wanted to go back to. He thought of going home. His mother would be angry when he left, but he wondered if she would understand if he explained. She might call his teachers and tell them he was sick and that he went home. Arthur might get in trouble, but it would be nothing too serious. He wouldn't be the first student who cut school during the day, so he knew most wouldn't care. He didn't want to go home anyway. So, for now, he simply wandered the streets. He felt like he could just walk until he starved to death for all he cared. He just needed to keep moving for now.

Arthur walked past the adults through the street; to them, he just looked like another typical sullen angst-ridden teenager shuffling along. His eyes didn't focus on anything else except the pavement a few steps ahead of him. The mental flashes of Ashley and Jack riddled his mind, shadowing his every thought as he tried to think about anything else. However, no matter what he attempted to focus on, the image of the pair together in each other's embrace would slingshot back straight to the front of his mind, haunting him. He figured that Jack didn't do it to spite Arthur purposely. Ashley may have felt slightly guilty, but he knew she had never promised him anything and so owed him no real explanation. Jack, however, just did whatever he wanted, and often to him, it didn't matter who he hurt. To Jack, if he didn't hurt Arthur physically, he wasn't a bad guy. Arthur assumed Jack would just carry on and think he could talk Arthur round to his way of thinking the next day. Arthur knew Jack would just do whatever he wanted and then drop her like an old jacket within a couple of months. This betrayal from Jack didn't just hurt his respect and pride. It insulted who he was as a person with those simple words.

"You deserve better than the kid that gets bullied by every kid in school. You deserve a real man, that's me, babe." That summed up for Arthur anyway, exactly how Jack saw their supposed friendship. Arthur didn't hate Ashley. She knew Arthur liked her, and maybe she liked him back, but Arthur knew she was free to make her own decisions, and he would have to deal with that. She was going to meet Jack, and she didn't want to tell him to his face, and he understood that.

Arthur looked up from the ground to see he had walked further than he thought. He saw a clock tower and looked at the time. He saw that he had been traveling with his thoughts for over three hours now. The school was out, and Gary and his thugs were probably getting bored waiting to jump him on the way home. He was on the other side of the city from where his school was. He was in the old warehouse district. Most of them were closed now, empty and evacuated. Dozens with condemned signs on them but the ones running the city couldn't be bothered with tearing them down to build anything else, so the area was dead and nearly lifeless. Not much around apart from the odd clothing factory that was going out of business. He walked around looking at each one. They were rusted, battered, and looking as though they were only days from falling inwards on their weight. The smell in the air was rancid. The filth and dirty streets were mixed with the stench of fish and salt from the docks. It made the place reek. Arthur felt sick from the smell, but he stomached the stench and carried on despite it. For some reason, he stopped at a particular building. From the outside, it looked no different than any of the other ones with the same rotten decaying front outside. It was riddled with smashed windows and a door chained shut by broken, rusted chains that no longer even locked it. Arthur would always look back on this moment and figured he could never explain why he felt the need to walk in. His feet moved towards the door. He looked around just in case he wasn't alone for whatever reason, as he didn't want some adult yelling at him. But no one was around, and he was completely by himself. His hand touched the rusty cold handle of the old factory door, and he opened it slowly, the door creaking and screeching from the rust as it opened slowly. Arthur grimaced as he struggled to open it wide. It was very heavy to push. Arthur saw the inside and walked in, not sure what to expect, and nothing on this planet could ever have prepared him for it.

The inside was pretty much what Arthur had expected it to be. A large empty vacated lot of space in the middle of the entire ground floor. To the sides were rickety rusted metal stairs that led up to a cleared-out office. Dust sailed through the air in an aimless direction. The light shone in from the window and touched the wooden floors of the factory. All else was in shadows around Arthur. The smell of wood and sawdust was in the air; it was pungent. Arthur coughed a few times, but he quickly adjusted to it and began walking through the factory. As he walked, his steps echoed throughout the entire building in suspended taps. He came to the middle of the factory and looked around. He wasn't sure why he had entered this factory, and he thought perhaps he just wanted one place he could go and be alone. He walked to the side and began climbing the rusted stairs. The metal taps of each step echoed louder than the wooden floor had. The stairs shook as he walked up. Any other person would have been scared about the whole thing collapsing with random metal pipes impaling him in seconds, and Arthur was one of them. His breathing went a little quicker as he panicked, but he carried on, hoping the fear would pass. He came to the top of the stairs and took a deep breath. He felt better now, and he then walked into one of the empty offices. The room was empty, saved for an old wooden chair in front of a worn-out wooden desk. He stepped forward again and sat in the chair, leaning back and staring at the ceiling. He couldn't fathom what he was doing there. Jack and Ashley were still buzzing through his head. His gut was still riddled with what felt like thousands of hissing angry snakes. Arthur didn't know what to do about the situation. He felt like he had nowhere to go, and personally, there was nowhere he did want to go. Arthur couldn't think of a place in the entire world where he was safe from hurt. He continued to sit there and just stare silently. The peaceful nothing of this room was oddly comforting. Before Arthur could sink further into his sorrow, a colossal crash exploded from outside the office in the warehouse. The noise was so loud it shattered through Arthur's eardrums. He jumped out of his chair and raced to the door, looking through the glass and seeing someone he thought he would never see again.

Cratos Mane had once again appeared in Arthur's life. The tall, pale man now was lying in the middle of the floor with metal and wooden shrapnel surrounding him on the ground. The building's wall had been wrecked, creating a large, jagged hole only a few meters from his body. The sunlight from outside was shining in, which illuminated the room further. Arthur then saw three figures standing in the warehouse hole, blocking the light with their bodies. Arthur saw them walk into the warehouse through the hole and stand around Cratos, who was lying on the ground. One was a man, and the other two were women. They all had pale skin and all wore what looked to Arthur were expensive designer clothes. The man wore a dark purple, silk-looking long-sleeved shirt given how glossy it looked in the light with black trousers that seemed to have strange patterns sewed into material down the legs with smart shiny shoes on his feet. The woman wore a similar silk shirt, but it was colored dark green with her sleeves rolled up, and the other woman's shirt was red-colored with her sleeves down and white cloth gloves on her hands. Instead of black trousers, they both had a skirt to match the color of their shirts with what Arthur thought were high heels on their feet. Their hair was styled and shiny. Each of them flinched and winced as the light from the hole Cratos entered through touched their faces, quickly moving into the safety of the shade. They stood over Cratos, who was groaning and wincing. Arthur could barely see the tall man clearly, but his face was beaten, and there was a heavy pool of blood bleeding from his right leg. The three people who stood over Cratos mocked him. The man of the three raised his leg and stomped his shoe hard on Cratos's chest. The sharp strike caused Cratos to roar out in anger and pain. However, to Arthur's surprise, it wasn't the pained scream of a man. It was different. It was a loud, beastly roar, deep and grizzly. Arthur's blood went cold when he heard it. Arthur thought it was an impossibly inhuman noise to exist, let alone come out of a man's mouth. He didn't even think a demon could make such a noise if they existed. The man who kicked Cratos said something to him, but Arthur couldn't hear from behind the office glass. The man knelt and gripped Cratos by his clothes roughly. The other two women did the same, and all three of them screeched like banshee burning in flames. Then with another feat of inhuman strength, they heaved Cratos up with their strength and sent him hurling upward through the air aimed straight towards Arthur and the office. In less than a split second, Arthur jumped down and crouched under the window by the door as Cratos smashed through the office window with glass raining down alongside him.

Arthur froze as he looked down at the man who saved his life only last night. He was a bloody mess. Shards of glass were sticking out of his body, making him look like a tall pin cushion. Cratos was moaning on the ground slightly. His teeth were clenched angrily. He was only wearing a now ripped-to-pieces sleeveless black shirt with rugged black trousers and heavy knee-high boots. Arthur could see the veins on his torso rising to the surface of his skin intensely. They were a deep unnatural purple color. His body was looking hairier than before, thick black hairs beginning to cover his pale skin slowly.

Arthur leaned in closer to see. He was right. Cratos's hair then thickened into what was looking like an animal's fur coat. The hair was as black as night itself. Cratos was growing too. His body was shaking and convulsing. His muscles were throbbing, expanding like a balloon being blown up. His legs began growing thickly like his arms. Cratos's hands twisted grossly. His fingers extended, and his nails at their ends doubled in size. They were now thin and looked razor-sharp. Arthur's eyes widened with shock. He crawled several paces away from the monster before him until his back hit the wall. Cratos was looking like a wolfman Arthur had seen in horror films. His hands were large and sharp, twitching as the glass in his body was slowly making its way out of his body. The flesh they came from quickly sealed up, leaving no mark behind. Only the blood on the ground that had been spilled remained. His wounds were now completely healed in a few seconds. Arthur couldn't believe it. He had no idea what was going on. The man who had saved his last night now had a thick black coat of fur covering his skin with hands twice their size with knife blades at the end of them. His head turned to the side, and his eyes jumped open, his pupils vertical instead of a circle with a strange yellow ring surrounding it. The whites of the outside were riddled with red veins. He frowned, his gaze locking onto Arthur.

"What...the hell...are you doing here...kid!?" Cratos growled in strained fury, his right eye twitching. He was looking like he was trying to hold himself back. Arthur was speechless as he looked at Cratos.

"Wha...what...are you?" Arthur replied with a stutter. Cratos sighed, exhausted. The pair then heard the stairs banging soundly.

"Someone is coming...hide...and stay hidden." Arthur didn't need to be told twice. He hurried across the floor and hid under the wooden desk as the door swung open. The male figure walked into the office. He called out behind him to the other two.

"I'll finish him off. Keep an eye out for any of his flea-ridden *friends* that might be lurking around!," he shouted, his voice smooth and confident, like a CEO of a huge corporation. He then turned his attention to Cratos.

"Poor little doggie," he called mockingly, casually brushing dust off his sleeves. Behind him entered one of the women. Arthur focused his eyes to see bright, powerful, red-colored eyes on the man. It reminded him of the woman's eyes the other night.

"Seems to be clear, but Jessica will shout if that changes," she said to the man as he walked in. The man didn't take his eyes off Cratos and just nodded. She looked at Cratos with a massive grin on her face. She again had moon pale skin and red eyes with long, red-dyed colored hair.

"You're going to pay for Morticia's death, you mutt," she hissed. Arthur frowned at the name drop. Arthur assumed Morticia must have been the woman that attacked him the other night. The man waved a finger at the woman who spoke.

"Hush now, my sweet, This wretch and his pack have taken more than just her." The man knelt over Cratos's transformed body. He looked over Cratos's changed appearance.

"What a disgusting creature you are, just another filthy animal, all of you," he noted. His lip curled in scorn. Cratos's chuckled wolfishly, like a sneaky predator.

"If I'm an animal...what does that make you... eh?" Cratos wheezed out with his deep, growling voice. The man snorted and punched Cratos sharply across the face, using the incredible sharp speed Arthur had witnessed last night. His speed was so fast that it was nearly a blur to the human eye.

"We are creatures of divinity. We are the chosen nightwalkers of greatness. You, a dog, could never understand such nobility. Like worms, you simply eat dirt. I am like a god." Arthur began to get increasingly nervous; the situation was growing worse. His hands spread around the area off the floor around him. His left-hand fingertips touched something metal. He looked to the side to see his hand over a discarded metal pipe. Without thinking, his hand gripped it tightly, and he held it close to him. He was not sure what he was planning to do with it but just having it made him feel a tiny bit safer. Cratos leaned his head up to those around him. The surface of his face faded away within seconds. Black fur spread over his entire skull, leaving not an inch of his skin left. His ears pricked up in size, and his mouth morphed outward, teeth growing large and sharp. The man sensed danger, but it was too late for him to react. Cratos's hand shot forward, impaling the man's stomach down to the middle of his fingers. Blood began to quickly spread across his silk clothing, drenching him in seconds in his sticky fluid. The man's body shook as he looked down with shock at his fatal impalement. Cratos then pulled him forward, so he was close.

"Gods don't bleed, you parasite!" Cratos snarled deeply in his eardrum and threw the body off to the side. The man fell across the room like a rag doll, dead before he hit the ground. His blood was emptying on the office floor like a ripped open water balloon from his stomach.

The woman in the room screamed for help as she pulled a large hunting knife from her waist, and then sharply attacked Cratos. Arthur saw that Cratos wouldn't dodge the attack. Without hesitating, Arthur jumped from the desk. He gripped the pipe high above his head with both hands. The woman heard Arthur emerge and turned her head only for her face to be immediately met with the sharp skull-cracking smash of the lead pipe burying itself firmly within the flesh of her face. The woman dropped her knife and stumbled backward a few steps. At that moment, Cratos rose to his feet behind her. His tall, lean black hairy body towered over her, casting a shadow darker than his fur. She wearily turned around to face him, only to be met with another attack. But rather than with a lead pipe, Cratos's gripped her arms sharply with his claws and swung his head forward. His mouth extended a few inches forward, revealing a savage row of immensely thick and sharp teeth that proceeded to clamp tightly over what was left of her face. She attempted to scream but was quickly muffled and drowned out by his jaw tightening sharply over her soft face. She tried a sharp screech in suppressed cries as her body jerked and shook from the meaty crunch Cratos took over her skull. Cratos ripped his head away viciously like a wild beast tearing flesh away from its prey. With a heartless shove, he threw her body to the floor, discarded. Blood was flowing from the giant vacant bite on the side of her head. If you looked deep into the crater Cratos bit into, you could see down past her skull that a large chunk of her brain was missing from her head. Cratos chewed what was in his mouth a moment and spat it out, disgusted.

"I'm sorry you had to see that kid," he said warmly, looking at Arthur, who was still holding the now bloodied pipe in his hands.

"Thanks again, kid. You shouldn't be here, but I guess I'm glad you were, or I'd be a goner." Arthur was utterly horrified. The sight and smell of the blood were enough to make him nearly throw up. He would have fallen to the floor crying hysterically if he weren't frozen with terror right now. He had witnessed two people demonically murdered before his eyes. Every instinct in his head right now was screaming like the inside of his brain was on fire. He attempted to say something, but his voice refused to let the sound out. Cratos held up a hand.

"Give me a moment, and I'll explain all of this to you. I owe you that much." Arthur nodded shakily and remained still as the third woman appeared in the doorway. She had heard the commotion but arrived too late. She saw the two dead bodies of her former allies and the now morphed body of the tall black-furred wolfman with blood-stained teeth and hunger in his eyes. Cratos turned his focus on their new visitor, hungry drool forming around his lips.

The woman took a step back, which was as far as she managed before Cratos leaped through the air and roughly grabbed her by the shoulders. The two then launched out of the office and onto the warehouse floor far down below, breaking the hardwood floor harshly as they landed. Arthur rushed out of the office after them and watched from the top of the stairs. Cratos had smashed the woman hard on the wooden floor, going through it with a large snapped splintered indent in the ground where her body was. Cratos rose and stood above her, snarling hatefully. Her eyes were wide with a panicked shock like a fish ripped out of the water. Her body was twitching but unable to move correctly.

The crash to the ground caused her limbs to be out of place and appeared bent at misplaced angles. A pool of blood pumped out around her body from the places wood had penetrated her flesh. Cratos cast an eye over the woman's twisted body to survey if she could attack him again. He saw she could not. He lifted his left leg high and snarled. The woman was sobbing slightly, begging for her life, he assumed. Cratos said nothing. He slammed his foot down on her body viciously. The sound of several cracks and snaps sailed through the warehouse air as her body went completely still. Arthur barely comprehended everything he had witnessed in the last five minutes of his life, but he continued to watch. As Cratos withdrew his foot, the woman he stomped on began to change like the woman in the alleyway did. With life fading from her body just like with the woman before, her body began to deflate and turn into lifeless skin, old bone, and dust.

Arthur turned his head to look back into the office to see the same had happened to the other two people.

"What the hell are these things!?" he thought to himself.

"Hey, kid! It's safe. You can come down," he heard Cratos say. He turned his head to see Cratos's body begin to shirk before his eyes slowly. His frame deflated as the black fur covering his body seemed to recede into his flesh. Within a few seconds, he had returned to the visual body of an average human. Arthur began to go down the steps towards where Cratos was standing, studying the man carefully. His body returned to its former pale complexion. His trousers legs were ripped and torn, but his waist remained intact, covering above his thighs. His vest was gone, revealing his bared torso. He now resembled the man he met the other night when he saved Arthur from the woman. Arthur observed the man's torso in detail. It was littered with hundreds of scars, some small others long and stretched around his back. Arthur's jaw dropped as he saw his wounds. Cratos chuckled at his reaction.

"You stop bothering to count the scars after a while," he laughed. Arthur looked up and saw his eyes had also returned to normal. Arthur took a step back himself. The adrenalin of the situation was now passing, and caution began to take over his senses. Cratos held his hands up with his palms facing Arthur and smiled warmly.

"Hey, kid, don't worry, I won't hurt you, I promise." Arthur was wary, but he guessed if the man meant to hurt him, he would have done so easily in that beast form he could turn into. Cratos sat down on the floor cross-legged and exhaled loudly.

"This will be tricky to explain. You'll want to sit down," he chuckled. Arthur did so and allowed the tall, amazing stranger to explain what the past two days were about.

"I am part of a particular and ancient old group of people who work in the shadows of every society in the world," Cratos began firmly. Arthur heard this, and his eyelids dropped slightly. The first part of Cratos's effort to explain only raised more questions. But he didn't interrupt.

"We work tirelessly to protect mankind from monsters who seek to enslave them," he coughed, rubbing his head as though he was trying to figure out what he was saying himself.

"Well, enslave them any more than they already have done, I guess," he added awkwardly.

"Who are these creatures?" Arthur asked impatiently, feeling Cratos wouldn't get to the point any time soon. Cratos thought for a moment and leaned in.

"They are creatures of incredibly amazing powers and abilities. Since the dawn of their existence, they have used their powers and ability to live for endless centuries to manipulate and control humanity. They use them as their cattle and subjects. They feed off humans to continue their existence, and because of that, their current generation sees themselves as living beings of divine nature." He snorted in spite as he finished that last word.

"Fools," Cratos snarled scornfully. Arthur was more curious, specific phrases caught his attention. "Live for endless centuries. They feed off humans." It was impossible, but to Arthur, which had sounded uncomfortably familiar. It sounded like things he has seen in horror films too. He remembered the woman that night and the three people Cratos had just killed. They all had fangs for teeth. The realization was slowly hitting, but he needed Cratos to say the name, that one word.

"Who are they!" he snapped impatiently. Cratos saw Arthur was catching on and he chuckled.

"Willful, that will do you good in the days to come," he laughed.

"You probably know of them but only in mythology. Films and media that have made you believe they are nothing but fantasy and fiction, used as a ruse to conceal their identity." Arthurs' fists were beginning to shake.

"A name. Please," he said through clenched teeth. Cratos leaned in closer until they were both face to face.

"They feed off the blood of humans, have long dangerous fangs with red eyes, pale white skin, and they seemingly live forever." He whispered the last word, which changed Arthur's concept of reality from then on.

"They are Vampires!" he hissed. With the utterance of that tiny word, everything that Arthur Thorn considered reality faded into mist, and everything he thought to be impossible just became possible.

Arthur knew it before he heard Cratos say it, but he felt it was still impossible. Here in the modern world, Vampires were silly fun mythical creatures used for books and films. Arthur had seen a few movies with Vampires. They were ugly, crooked-backed monsters with long fingernails and fangs. They all were meant to look wrinkled and a hundred years old. However, the four apparent Vampires he had just met in the last few days were all young-looking, wearing expensive clothes, and aesthetically attractive. They still had fangs and pale skin but little else to give them away. Cratos saw Arthur contemplating and chuckled again.

"It's a lot to take in, but trust me, kid, that's only the tip of the ice burg in this explanation." Arthur looked up and remembered how he started this story, with how Cratos belonged to a group fighting these Vampires. The lines inside his brain were connecting, dozens every second he just realized what Cratos now was. If Vampires existed, then the hairy wolf-headed, fur-wearing beast must be the other creature of myth. Arthur stuck out a finger in shock.

"You're a Werewolf!" he shouted in shock. Cratos firmly nodded.

"Yes, the Werewolf clan has existed since time was recorded, fighting against the Vampires as best we could as we watched them control and enslave humanity," he answered calmly. Arthur frowned.

"Why are you telling me all of this? What if I went to the papers or the news?" Arthur inquired, to which Cratos could not help but raise a bemused eyebrow.

"Yes, by all means, go tell anyone about the Vampires and Werewolves you met today and about the ancient war. If you don't end up in a white padded cell like most who have tried have done, then you'll be ostracized by everyone you know for the rest of your life. So, what do you think, going to tell anyone?" he finished smugly. Arthur rolled his eyes but shook his head.

"No, I guess not," he muttered, and Cratos nodded.

"If humans would believe this secret, then I wouldn't stop you from saying anything. You only get the explanation because you have seen everything firsthand. Vampires being at risk of discovery would have them cover up any legitimate cases, to begin with," he continued, which confused Arthur again.

"What do you mean? Nobody believes in Vampires; I still barely do." Cratos nodded slowly.

"Exactly, that's how cunning they are. Vampires have been unable to control humans outwardly. There aren't enough of them to win a war with humanity, especially since they don't like to fight for themselves," he then quickly held up a hand.

"I will explain another time about that," Cratos said hurriedly and then continued.

"They rule over humanity through politics and economics. They are high politicians, royalty, and corporate giants. At the top of all of them are Vampires that guide and rule over humanity, controlling and deciding what is real and what is fake. They control what the media tells humans and therefore can completely hide their existence." Arthur looked away and thought for a second. Vampires stood as the heads of all sources of power in the world. They are controlling humanity in the shadows without them knowing. They are leaders of countries, Royalty, and heads of larger corporations. Arthur then looked up at Cratos and narrowed his eyes.

"Explain what exactly Werewolves can do to stop the Vampires if they rule the entire world. How haven't they managed to kill you all then?" Cratos raised his eyebrow at Arthur

"Not very subtle, are you?" Cratos noted back dryly.

"Werewolves CAN fight back. There are more of us in numbers, and we are stronger than them physically. Something else I will explain another time. We use the monopoly they created against them. They are twice as scared of being discovered as we are. Especially in the more advanced society today with weaponry the way it is. It gives us a better chance to fight them in more discreet locations." He waved a hand around the room.

"Take this warehouse, for example. Vampires see themselves above humans, and Werewolves stand between them and the Vampires as a wall to protect people. We work to kill all Vampires and free humanity so they can control their destiny. While we vastly outnumber them along with being much stronger physically, they still have advantages that we do not."

"Which are?" Arthur asked, dubious still but too curious to stop asking questions at this point.

"Well, for example, Vampire cash flow is pretty much endless. They can buy anything air touches. Unfortunately, they often hire mercenaries or use military forces at their disposal to fight us when they don't want to. In media, they label us terrorists in more civilized countries and assemble many humans with large guns to mow us down." His face turned solemn then as his eyes looked away.

"I have been in such situations many times. It is not something fun to experience." He looked back up and smiled at Arthur again, eyes fixating on his hair for a few seconds.

"But it's not all bad. We are a massive family. We live lives of fantastic adventure. Even if they are short, they are amazing, and we are always on the lookout for recruits." Arthur began to feel a different vibe from the tall man now. Cratos stuck out his hand towards Arthur.

"Tell me, kid, how do you feel becoming a Werewolf and joining our cause to save the world?"

Arthur didn't know precisely how to react. As someone his age, when considering such a request, it was hard to judge correctly. Until now, the only choices he had were what music he would listen to while doing his homework or if he would play with his sister when coming home or do some drawing. Now, he was being asked how he wanted the rest of his life to play out at this exact moment. He guessed it was like when adults joined their countries' military. They had the choice of having to leave their home, their family, and friends. Having to leave the people who love you and look after you, especially those who would miss you and who you would miss yourself. Arthur did have such a choice himself. He had struggling times with his family and friends, but he did care about them deep down. He knew he would struggle not to be with them anymore, and he knew his mother and sister would especially miss him. Arthur knew they would be heartbroken if he left them. He wondered if authorities would bother to look for him. Many kids in his area ran away from home, and while the police had their usual inquiries and searching, they were seldom found and gave up after a few months. Not for any reason, they just lacked much funding, and the area was so rundown that it wasn't a national concern. He loved his sister a lot, and he didn't want to leave her to the cruel whims of his father, but often enough, he never hurt her. Arthur knew there were plenty of reasons to turn Cratos down, but after today he felt there was nothing left for him in this town that would give him much of a future. Even the girl he had feelings for had vanished into smoke. Arthur felt like he wanted a clean start. He knew it was selfish of him to leave all the people who cared about him behind. He knew he would regret it, but some part of him was telling him to do it. Telling him that staying where he was would lead him nowhere. Worse, he might end up growing up like his father, and the thought of that made him want to throw up. He was not sure what the right or wrong decision was, but there was a solid, silent voice he heard deep within himself. One that he had always ignored was now screaming at him to agree, leave and not look back. Arthur smiled firmly, deciding to go with his instinct. He stood to his feet. He looked at Cratos Mane sternly and nodded firmly.

"I accept," Arthur stated firmly.

"Make me a Werewolf," he finished without a hint of hesitation. Cratos smiled and stood up, nodding at Arthur's decision with a gaze of respect.

"You will make a good Werewolf. We only accept those who have proven themselves. But after your help last night as well as today, you have shown courage and strength in the face of fear." Arthur frowned and then spoke for a moment.

"Are the parameters to enter that easy?" he asked unthinkingly to Cratos, who chuckled and shook his head.

"It's more than just your actions. Werewolves can sense potential in a person. Your actions caught my attention. Sometimes we are proven wrong about a candidate for the clan, but we honestly need all the numbers we can get, so this happens often. I honestly believe at this moment that you will make an excellent member of the pack. Now please hold out your left arm." Arthur frowned, confused.

"Why?" he asked. Cratos stuck out his left arm and showed up the underside of his. There were more scars but smaller and in a circular row along his flesh, teeth shaped around the limb.

"A lot of mythology about Vampires and Werewolves is merely exaggerated, but one thing has always remained a fact for both of our species. We can only become one or the other by surviving a bite." Arthur's eyes narrowed.

"Surviving?" he asked skeptically. Cratos shrugged.

"You saw what I become, and it is not instantaneous either. Each Werewolf's ability and lifestyle change will appear to you after a lot of time and training. This puts a lot of strain on your body, but that will be explained further another time. For now, though, the venom that changes you must defeat your natural defense systems, and it can sometimes be dangerous. Are you still sure you want this?" Arthur thought for a second, but his answer was still the same. He nodded his head and looked Cratos in the eyes.

"Do it!" he stated. Cratos walked closer to Arthur and gripped his thin arm with his hands. He noticed Arthur tense nervously, and he raised an eyebrow.

"This will hurt but try to remain calm." Arthur nodded and breathed carefully. Cratos opened his mouth, and for a moment, his teeth looked like ordinary human teeth. Then, out of nowhere, they began to change in size, The front ones grew longer and sharper, and the back molars thickened in depth and length. Arthur was impressed.

"This is an ability of us towards the end of the change. You'll be taught about it in your training. Here it comes," he warned. In a Flash, Cratos Mane threw his head down and clamped his mouth around Arthur's arm. He dug all his teeth into the flesh of Arthur's arm. Arthur screamed and roared in pain, but he remained as still as he could. His body was shaking, and tears were flowing from his eyes, but he remained standing despite the shrieking pain coursing through him now, like liquid fire surging through his veins. He was determined to look back on this day and feel proud he kept his nerve. In a second, he felt woozy. He was suddenly tired and sleepy, unable to control himself. He felt Cratos's mouth detach from his arm, and Arthur fell to the floor, and the world of ordinary humans vanished from his sight forever.

CHAPTER FIVE

Arthur awoke with a throbbing headache. He was groaning as the darkness around his eyes cleared, and the roof of the factory was now in his sight. His breathing seemed very loud even though he felt he was breathing softly. He looked up at the ceiling and saw a remarkably high window with several dozen squares of metal frame in its design. He wasn't sure how he saw it so easily. He even heard the cars passing on the streets outside.

"That will pass in a few seconds," he heard Cratos say in a whisper. Arthur winced as his eardrums ached at how loudly he heard it.

"What the hell!" Arthur snapped, only to wince again at his own words.

"Easy," Cratos soothed, still whispering.

"You survived the process, but your body is still adjusting to the first stage of effects. It'll take a few moments." Arthur lay still and thought for a moment.

"The first stage? How many are there? So, I can hear and see better, but what else?" Arthur thought, the surge of his change overwhelming him. Arthur sat up and looked around the warehouse. The Vampire woman's body was still in the floor's wood, and it was now dark outside. He knew his family would be wondering where he was. The factory was much darker at night. As Arthur looked around, he felt a tiny chill from the sheer amount of still darkness. But despite the darkness, Arthur's vision was near perfect. Even in the darkest corner on the far side of the room, Arthur could see every discarded tool and piece of metal that lay bare. He smiled, finding this ability more remarkable by the second.

He rose to his feet when he noticed something. He felt strangely heavier. He looked down at his body and saw nothing was amiss at first glance. He was still wearing the same clothes and everything else, but he felt different.

"Role up your sleeve," Cratos voiced softly with a smug grin. Arthur did so, rolling up his sleeve so he could see his entire right arm. It hadn't increased in size, but the muscle definition was blatantly apparent. It was the sort of look that he had only seen on television. They were thick dark prominent lines from the top of his shoulder down along the arm.

"They will increase in size as well in time, especially for Crimson class. Your strength is key." Arthur looked up at him.

"Crimson class?" he whispered, feeling his hearing adjusting with every passing minute. Cratos waved it away.

"I'll explain later," he replied dismissively.

"You'll notice it all over your body. You are now a lot stronger and faster. So be aware that if you decide to hurt someone or even play fight with them, it can become dangerous to normal humans now." He dropped his whisper at the last word to empathize with it. Arthur looked at him seriously and rolled down his sleeve, his hearing starting to feel fine now.

"Yeah, ok, I'll remember," Arthur replied, nodding.

"Good, you don't want to end up muzzled," Cratos warned ominously. Arthur frowned again in confusion, but Cratos simply waved his hand again.

"You don't want to know. Now you head on home," he muttered. Arthur's frown deepened.

"What are you talking about; I can't go home now, can I?" Cratos laughed.

"It's a tradition. You'll thank me in the years to come. It will be your last day as the human Arthur Thorn. Meet me back here tomorrow night at midnight. Then your new life begins. You have one day to say goodbye to all those you care about. Use it wisely because it may be a long time before you are free to come back, OK?." Arthur nodded wordlessly. He walked away from Cratos, picked up his school bag, left the warehouse, and then began walking home, only now Arthur was a Werewolf.

The world looked completely different through Arthurs's new eyes. Not only was the night easily seen. He felt like how a sunny day looks when you put on sunglasses. You could still see everything; it's just the world in slight shade. Every time a car passed him on the streets he was walking past, it made him wince a little from the sight and sounds. Especially when he heard a car horn, but he felt as though he was nearly hearing everything around him. He could listen to all the sounds of every little animal scurrying in the bushes and bins around him in detail. He could even hear the soft-sounding conversations from people with their windows down. As he walked, he didn't feel himself growing tired at all, and he was walking fast. It was the excitement from everything he experienced around him, building momentum as his pace quickened. He barely felt his heartbeat increase as he moved. Arthur tensed his arms for fun, enjoying the feeling of his newly developed muscles moving when he did it.

Arthur was unable to hide a grin of joy. He had only been a Werewolf for a small while, and he was already twenty times happier than he had been in years. He decided to start running. Sprinting through the night streets of his city was exhilarating. Arthur zoomed from street to lane and across the roads, feeling like an Olympic athlete running the hundred-meter dash. He felt his heart beating rapidly now, but he had been sprinting at full speed for nearly ten minutes straight, and he only just started to feel tired. He was only a few minutes from home now. Before, it would have been an hour and a half's journey, but now it had only taken him twenty minutes since leaving the factory. Arthur then slowed down his running to a light jog, then regular running again. He felt a little sweat running down his back as his breathing gradually began to relax. Realization hit him now a little harder than it did when he was first told back in the factory. Arthur realized this would be the final time he would go this way through these streets for a long time. He would go through his front door for the last time, the last time he would see his family. As Arthur approached his front door, a slight feeling of loss surfaced in his stomach. He felt a little scared. He knew it was too late to go back now and went through the door anyway.

His house was completely silent as he walked through the door, darkness surrounding the entire space. Even out from the streets, Arthur still had his strange, improved vision. He could see the stairs in front of him perfectly. He easily saw the furniture in the living room and everything else in his home. Arthur smelled the air as he closed the door behind him. He caught the scent of what his family had for dinner earlier, chicken and vegetables. The smell was unmistakable. To his new nose, it was as though a fresh plate of food was before him at that very moment. He smirked as he put his bag on the ground. Arthur then looked over his house, his head feeling like it was swelling as his new abilities continued to build within him. He walked up the stairs quietly, making next to no sound. As he reached the top of the stairs, the sound of his father's immense slumber filled the air as though the brute was snoring through a megaphone. Arthur rolled his eyes, lightly opened the door to his sister's room, and walked in.

His sister's room was a regular little girl's room. Pink wallpaper with flower and fairy stickers slapped across the whole space. She had dolls and other smaller toys covering the floor with girly books on a set of shelves. Her bed covers were a mix of pink and purple, the same pattern as her curtains. Arthur walked across his sister's room quietly. His improved hearing was causing him to listen to every little feint breath she exhaled softly, like a snoozing kitten. He stood over her bed as she lay on her side, her eyes closed. She was utterly still. She looked so cute to him. She was like a cat among tigers that could do no more harm than a mild summer breeze flying through the trees. He knew leaving her behind would put a hole in his heart. A small lump festered in his throat as tears threatened to burst forth. They nearly won before Arthur inhaled deeply and blinked them back. He couldn't change his mind now. He sat on the edge of her bed next to her as she slept. She moved slightly onto her back. Arthur remained still, not wishing to wake her. When she stopped moving again, he smiled at her widely. This little girl used to look up to him as her hero. Arthur made a personal pact right there on her bed. He vowed that whatever happened in his future, he would come back to her. If only to make sure she was OK. He moved his arm forward, lightly brushing her forehead with his hand. Sighing with pained regret, he leaned forward and kissed her softly on her cheek, whispering gently.

"Goodbye, princess." Her face creased a little at his words, but she did not wake up. Arthur took one last look as he pulled away. Arthur then got to his feet and left his sisters room before he ended up crying. Knowing if he did, then he probably wouldn't be able to stop.

He wasn't tired. Despite what time it was, he didn't want to sleep, not yet anyway. He left his school bag downstairs but knew he would probably need to pack light to travel with Cratos. He rooted through his draws and pulled out an old pair of black combat trousers he never wore. They were practical but not too stylish. He grabbed another rucksack from under his bed. This was larger than his school bag and could store a lot more inside it. It was grey with a black skull on its face. He opened the top and filled most of the space inside with essentials. He filled it with pants, socks, other trousers, and shirts he wanted to bring. He wanted to make sure he had a reasonable number of changes of clothes. He thought of what else he might need. He opened his bedside table and saw his notepad and a few pens. He was never good at drawing, but he enjoyed it as a hobby and decided to pack them as well. He stopped and looked around his room. Once again, he felt a pang of sadness and melancholy. This small piece of space had been his sanctuary for years, and he was now leaving it forever. Just like with his sister a moment ago, he felt regret for leaving his possessions and his room behind. He smiled thoughtfully and embraced the moment, and then he sat on his bed and fastened his backpack up after putting in the last few bits of items. He looked at his clothes. He only had a few hours until he was meant to be up and ready for his last day as a human. He would have his last meal with his family and then tend to a few unresolved personal matters before meeting with Cratos. He felt his heart suddenly panic, beating faster the more he thought about it. For a long time now, his life had been the same thing repeatedly. It wasn't much fun, but he always knew what was coming the next day. Now he knew that if he went with Cratos, he couldn't predict anything that would happen to him. His life as a Werewolf was full of uncertainty. He knew he knew nothing about the world and would have to rely on Cratos for a lot. But he also knew, despite his distaste at the idea of being so helplessly vulnerable, that he could do nothing about it. He took a few deep breaths and tried to push those thoughts from his mind. He shook his head and chuckled as he lay back on his bed and closed his eyes, getting in a final nap in his bed, putting this room and all the memories he had with it behind him with one last sleep

Arthur awoke a few hours later, he rose and rubbed his eyes. Weirdly he didn't feel tired at all despite only sleeping a few handfuls of hours. He was confused at first, but he just shrugged it off. He figured it was another perk of being a Werewolf. Jumping off his bed, he stretched and looked at himself in the mirror. He felt a strange surge of confidence when he looked at himself. He smiled and continued to fix his hair the way he liked it, smiling. He grabbed his backpack and headed downstairs. It was the end of the week now, so he knew everyone at school would be eager to hurry through the day and get out, making him less of a target for people picking on him. He sat at the table and began to wolf down his breakfast as fast as he could. He was so fixated on eating his food that he forgot to say good morning or even look his mother and sister in the eye. They were now staring at him bewildered as though he had walked into the room with two heads. He stopped and slowly looked up at their faces and chuckled.

"Hello…" Arthur awkwardly muffled through a mouthful of cereal. His mother raised an eyebrow at her son. Something seemed different about him, but she couldn't tell exactly what. His sister narrowed her eyes at him, frowning with suspicion. His mother shrugged and returned to drying the dishes by the sink. His sister, however, quickly gulped down her food and spoke.

"Where were you last night?" she asked. Arthur was surprised that the question had waited until now.

"Mom said you were around a friend's house probably, were you?" she asked again. Arthur sighed; odds are, his father didn't even bother to ask where he was. Arthur decided to just go with it, which saved him from having to make a terrible excuse anyway.

"Guess I was then," he muttered uncomfortably. His mother said nothing and continued doing kitchen work, but his sister's gaze didn't lower. She knew there was something he wasn't saying. Arthur caught her looking at him and chuckled. He reached across the table and ruffled her hair.

"Cheer up," he chuckled playfully, trying to change the subject.

"End of the week, right?" he finished with a big smile. His sister's suspicion vanished, and she giggled. He laughed back at her and then finished the last of his breakfast. He got up from the table and started to go for his bag. He hesitated and looked back at his mother. He waited for a second then walked towards her.

"Mum?" he asked. She put down her plate at the sink and turned to face him. Arthur didn't know what to say, so he went forward and gave her an enormous hug, holding the embrace for a few moments.

"I love you, mum..." he said with honest adoration. His mother was bewildered; his son was never this emotional. But she simply smiled and hugged him back.

"And I love you, even more, honey," she cooed. Arthur smiled truly and released from her.

"Bye, guys," he then said quietly as he went for the door. They both said bye to him and returned to their morning, both unaware it would be the last time they saw him for a long time.

CHAPTER SIX

Arthur wasn't sure why he felt the need to give his mother such a dramatic last hug. He knew in his heart that the events from the other night at dinner were still hurting him. She had cast the blame on him for what his father had done. But despite that, he had the same feeling when he entered his sister's room last night. He felt the same pang of regret when he was about to leave the kitchen. No matter what, Arthur still loved his mother and always would. He smiled as he walked to school, taking his time and enjoying the day. He only had a few things to clear up then he would meet up with Cratos. The day was a fierce blast of sunlight, with not a single cloud in the sky to block the intense brightness. Arthur couldn't help but wince for several seconds before slowly opening his eyelids second by second as he slowly adjusted to the harsh light. He didn't realize that his new, improved sight would have a drawback. He then guessed that Werewolves are considered creatures of the night as well for a reason. The sun can be too bright for their enhanced eyes. Arthur now wished he had packed his sunglasses. But it was too late now. He guessed he could pick some up later.

As he had assumed, Jack wasn't by the gate to meet him. Arthur thought that he would probably try and avoid him all day. Jack was one of the last pieces of business he wanted to attend to before leaving. He already knew what he would say to his former best friend who betrayed him, and there was nowhere Jack could hide from him. He didn't want to speak to Ashley, though. Fortunately, Arthur didn't have a science lesson today, so he thought he wouldn't run into her if he were lucky. He didn't hate her. Arthur wished he did, but he couldn't bring himself to do so. He wasn't even sure he hated Jack that much. He walked slowly to the gate to the sound of the bell ringing; he smirked. For everyone else, this was the last day of school for the week; for Arthur, it was the last day of school for the rest of his life.

His first lesson blew by. English was usually a bore for him, but Arthur only cared about getting to his next class, Mathematics. He decided to do the work given to him without a word. Arthur noticed he felt strangely great. Even though he had gotten next to no sleep at all, he felt like a fully charged battery. He was feeling so pent up with energy to the point that he was struggling to remain in his seat. He couldn't explain it well, but he felt the need to run a hundred miles and then climb a mountain with his bare hands. It was distracting, but Arthur kept his head down and got on with his work, trying to vent the focus and power by getting as much done as he could. Now and then, he would look up from his workbook because he would occasionally notice something in the corner of his eye. Everyone else was working in their way, talking to their friends while writing or while not working at all.

Arthur noticed quite a few of the girls in the class were stealing glances at him. He barely knew half of their names, but he locked eye contact with a couple of them as they smiled at him. A few even blushed before quickly going back to their work. Arthur had no idea how to react at first, so he just casually nodded back at them and returned to his workbook though he was secretly beaming on the inside. Girls had never been interested in him, and now he was a Werewolf. They kept looking at him like he was the class's prize. He wasn't sure how, though. There was no way they could tell he had changed. They couldn't see his newly acquired defined muscles, and his body's size itself was still the same as any other day. So, Arthur couldn't fathom what exactly they were seeing in him. But Arthur was far from letting it bother him, so now he was smiling to himself throughout the rest of the class. He decided that whatever their reason was, Arthur felt he could soak it in for now. The bell went, and he handed in his workbook to his English teacher for the last time and headed for his next lesson. The sounds of some of the girls whispering far behind him, not knowing Arthur could now listen to everything they were saying with his new hearing. His smile was widening at what he heard from their gossip about him.

He was in Math class next, but Jack wasn't there. He knew his friend would be reluctant to see him, but Arthur just thought he would sit at a different desk, not cut class altogether. Mr. Wreckson didn't say anything to Arthur as he came in. He didn't even look in his direction the entire lesson. After how persistent he had been about Arthur's marks the other day, Arthur thought the teacher would have brought them up again to him, but he said nothing. Therefore, Arthur just did his work without anyone else bothering him until the bell rang for the break. Regardless of whether his teacher spoke to him, he had some things to say to him, though. After every student was out of the classroom, Arthur stood by his teacher's desk. Mr. Wreckson looked up from his work and raised a curious eyebrow.

"What's up, Arthur?" he asked pleasantly. Arthur sighed; he looked at his teacher's casual, smiling face and looked down at his feet.

"I just wanted to say sorry if I didn't answer like I should have yesterday, and I also wanted to say thank you," he replied with a genuine, appreciative tone, trying his best not to sound too awkward. His teacher went to answer back, but Arthur continued.

"No one ever really cared to ask about me the way you did yesterday, sir, and when I got hurt, it before was usually just blanked over. I knew you were only trying to help yesterday. So, you know. Yeah, thank you, sir. It meant a lot, and I will never forget it." Arthur's teacher stood up and chuckled, patting Arthur on the shoulder.

"My pleasure Arthur, we all go through tough times. It's the way of the world. Don't ask for an easy life Arthur, just the strength to endure a hard one." Arthur looked up at his teacher and smiled back at him, then nodded. His teacher's face dropped a little, and confusion entered his facial features.

"Arthur? Are you using bruise cream or something?" he asked. Arthur frowned at him, confused now. His mind clicked when he looked at himself in the mirror last night, not realizing he didn't have a single mark on him anymore. He winced; he was so caught up in how he now looked that he forgot about how his wounds had healed entirely, which he guessed was due to his new Werewolf blood. Arthur acted with a fake embarrassed chuckle.

"Yes, sir, why? Is it noticeable that I'm using it?" Arthur replied feebly, but his teacher simply shook his head.

"Not at all boy, it looks fine. If you ever need to talk, you can always come to me, Arthur," his teacher finished with a meaningful nod. Arthur smiled again and turned for the door.

"Thanks, I'll remember that. Goodbye, sir," Arthur said finally with a genuine look of gratitude in his eyes towards one of the few people from his old life who had genuinely tried to help him.

"Enjoy your weekend Arthur," his teacher replied. Arthur didn't answer as he left to head outside to find Jack. However, as he left, he felt a guilty weight had been lifted from his chest by apologizing to his teacher. He felt going forward, he would never forget Mr. Wreckson and how he had tried to help him.

Break time was even better than class. The sunny day made it perfect for nearly everyone to be running around having fun with each other. Arthur got a lot more looks from girls as he walked past them on his search to find Jack. Not that he was complaining from all the attention. He made a note to ask Cratos about that when he got the chance.

His confidence was flying through the roof right now. He had started from the bottom, and he felt like he had just been catapulted to the top. The noise around him became a lot more apparent as well. All the noise and every side scream by excited kids playing games were nearly deafening to him as he walked past them all. Arthur couldn't help but wince now and then as though a sharp pin had been jabbed into his eardrums. He couldn't see Ryan or Daniel around either. He wasn't angry at them for yesterday. It wasn't the first time they had done that, and he honestly would have preferred that they not get hurt. He wanted to say goodbye to them. They were always good mates to him, but he didn't know what he would say. He decided if he ran into them, he would say something, but he now had a different goal. Jack was his priority right now. He turned a corner, and amongst a group of giggling girls was Ashley, who spotted him immediately. All his previous bravado and confidence immediately vanished from his body, and he instantly turned around to go the other way. After no more than five steps, a girl's hand grabbed his shoulder. He sighed, turning around for a conversation he would give his newly acquired wolf powers not to have.

Ashley's face was a mix of discomfort and awkwardness. She didn't look Arthur in the eye right away and was struggling to speak. Arthur decided to talk first then.

"Look, Ashley, you don't need to worry about yesterday. It's fine," Arthur said casually. Ashley frowned, finally looking at him properly.

"Are you sure Arthur? I understand if you are angry at Jack and me. I should have told you that we had been talking and seeing each other. I know you like me, but I still said nothing," she muttered quietly. Arthur shrugged. He wasn't going to refute what he felt was correct.

"So, you two are a couple now?" he asked skeptically. She nodded then a smile returned to her face.

"We had been meeting in secret to avoid teasing, but we are open about it now. Yesterday cemented it. That's why I just hoped it doesn't tear you and Jack apart; I wouldn't want to be the cause of that." Arthur raised an eyebrow at that statement but didn't reply for the moment. Ashley squinted at

Arthur. She seemed to be genuinely upset and worried about him, which he couldn't help but appreciate. His feelings were still hurt, but she was right, he did like her, and he was at least glad to hear she was happy.

"Have you changed something, Arthur? Your hair or...something?" she asked strangely, her voice different. Arthur frowned and then realized whatever was making the other girls look at him was now affecting Ashley. He shrugged and pretended not to know what was going on.

"Nope. Nothing different at all. Why? Am I different in a bad way?" he asked slyly, clearly fishing for compliments. She smiled slightly.

"You may not believe me, especially after yesterday, but there was a part of me that did *like* you. But no, not different in a bad way. I don't understand what it is, but you're..." she didn't finish. Arthur smirked, his confidence surfacing once again. He moved slightly closer to her and extended his arms, hugging her tight to him. She gasped, but she didn't pull away. Instead, she hugged back. Arthur could feel her heart racing against his chest. He whispered gently into her ear.

"You are beautiful, Ashley. Out of the entire school, I have wanted to ask you out for a long time. But that doesn't matter now. Please don't feel bad. You have done nothing wrong. I hope Jack will make you incredibly happy, and nothing has changed between us. OK?" She was overcome for a moment before muttering her reply.

"OK, Arthur," she replied shyly. Arthur sensed she was feeling timid around him, which probably was an unusual experience for her. Arthur released her from the hug and smiled warmly. She looked at him and blushed slightly.

"Do you know where Jack is? I just want to say a few things, and everything will be fine. There's nothing to worry about, OK?" She smiled wildly at Arthur and nodded.

"Yeah, I was just with him a minute ago; he is by the tree down near the grass bank, I think." Arthur smiled at Ashley for a few moments, letting silence fill the air. Her face began to go red as she smiled and looked away.

"Goodbye, Ashley," he murmured and turned his back on her, heading for Jack. He was pleased with himself as he walked away. Arthur felt Ashley continuing to watch him as he walked away. He figured she would return to talking to her friends, completely bewildered by how easy that conversation went.

Jack was sitting lazily against the tree body, smiling like a fool in love as he looked out at the field of kids playing their games. Arthur approached Jack, but his friend didn't even bother to look back at him. Saying nothing himself, Arthur sat down beside him. The pair of them simply sat next to each other for a few moments. Jack took a final bite of his apple and threw it aside, not watching as it rolled down the bank. The tree branches above shaded them from the sun on the bank they sat on as the sounds of those playing were faint in the background. There was the smell of cut grass looming in the air gently. Jack smiled normally and then said the first word.

"Are you here to fight me?" he asked casually. Arthur chuckled, neither one of them moving their heads to face each other. They just continued to look out into the field.

"Wouldn't that be an interesting fight? I wonder who would win?" Arthur replied just as casually as though they were talking about the weather itself. Jack hummed slightly.

"I don't know, Arthur; I think I would have the edge on you," Jack mused.

"Tough talk from a guy who has never been in a fight his entire life," Arthur replied with a chuckle.

"Tough talk from the guy who has never won a fight his entire life," Arthur chuckled again with a few seconds of silence following.

"So, who's better, the guy who doesn't win or the guy who doesn't even bother?" Arthur suggested. Jack thought for a moment and answered.

"I would say you. At least you have experience in fighting; I guess." Arthur nodded.

"True, odds are you have a jaw of glass," Arthur said cuttingly.

"With the rest of my body to add as well," Jack responded, which made them both laugh. The laughter faded into silence again as the pair sighed.

"Do we have a problem, though?" Jack asked. His voice was more serious now, with the tiniest hint of worry embedded in his tone. Arthur shook his head.

"No. I spoke to Ashley before I came to see you. I know you two are a proper thing now. There's no point in me going mental now, is there?" Jack shook his head and chuckled.

"You really do amaze me, Arthur, you truly do," he said with what Arthur thought sounded like genuine respect, which he found odd for the self-obsessed Jack to say.

"Jack?" Arthur continued seriously. Jack frowned; Arthur saw he was now feeling uncomfortable.

"What?" he said nervously, sensing a change in the mood.

"Do you love her?" Arthur asked finally, and his friends' answer would decide his following action. As it turned out, Jack didn't waste any time thinking. He instantly smiled thoughtfully and then nodded.

"I truly do." Arthur nodded and let a small moment pass between them. Arthur then turned his body and immediately shot his arm out and roughly grabbed Jack by the scruff of his collar. Jack yelped out in shock as Arthur sharply pulled him close, face to face. Jack gazed into Arthur's eyes, now afire with a look of white-hot murder.

"Then I am only going to say this once," Arthur growled viciously. Jack's breath grew quicker with fear as he saw the dreadful gaze bellowing from his friends' pupils.

"Don't ever HURT her, Jack. Don't just dump her in a week like you always do. She might just be another girlfriend for you, but until yesterday, she was so much more to me. If you ever break her heart the way you have done to so many others, I swear I will find you, and I will break you into forty different pieces!" His last few words were spoken with a harsh growl in his voice. Jack was shaking. Without saying a word, Jack nodded in compliance. He was utterly speechless, stuttering only a few lines.

"O... K... Arthur, I promise." In literally a blink of an eye, Arthur released his friend and smiled warmly, as he did before.

"That's great to hear, Jack. You have a good one. I'll see you again one day, count on that." To Jack's surprise Arthur then just stood up and left him sitting there.

His next lesson after lunch was Gym class. Once a week, every Friday, he usually dreaded the subject. That was before, back when Arthur had the muscle strength of a jellyfish. Now he was different, and now he was stronger. He was also faster, so now he felt like it was his turn to shine.

He entered the changing rooms hearing the air filled with the laughter and joking of his Gym classmates fooling around while they dressed in their PE clothes. Arthur smirked as he walked past them all. Even the most athletic of his entire class with a fair bit of muscle bulk and other physical definition didn't even compare to what Arthur now had himself under his clothes. He came to a space at the back of the room and thought for a second.

"If they suddenly see that my muscles are now more insanely defined since last week, they'll think I've been taking steroids or something. I need to hide it for the moment," Arthur thought. He noticed the bathroom a few feet away. Arthur knew he would look like a five-year-old if he hid away to change, but no one would be mocking him by the end of the lesson, so he decided to go with it. He took his gym kit bag into the bathrooms and changed into his PE gear. He wore a long-sleeved shirt with black shorts and white trainers. The teacher came out of their office and yelled for everyone to get out onto the field. Arthur smirked as he went out of the bathroom and gently jogged after his class.

The boys and girls didn't do the same sports in his school. Both genders had classes that different sports teachers taught. That didn't bother Arthur, though, as before, he was too self-conscious about performing physical sports in front of all the girls in his year group, especially Ashley. He wondered what Ashley might be thinking as he jogged along the stone path towards the field. He wondered if she was still feeling shy about noticing the new him or if she had put it out of her mind. Arthur noticed Jack was in the group up ahead, but he was several people away from Arthur. Jack would see Arthur behind him and give him awkward glances now and then. He was still a little shaken up from his encounter with Arthur at the break. The class did the same every week. They lined up next to each other to await instruction from the teacher. The teachers were the last to come down to meet the class. He looked over the class and shouted for them all to do five laps of the entire field as a warmup. Several people groaned, but Arthur couldn't help but continue smirking. As one group, they all started running around. Arthur decided to test out his new skills in this lesson.

Three laps into the warmup, half of everyone was lagging and breathing heavily with exhaustion. The people who did best in the class were a bit red in the face but kept pace ahead of everyone. Arthur was barely breaking a sweat, and he was still fast-paced, jogging right in front of everyone. Arthur heard the confused mumbles and whispered to each other that he could easily hear.

"How's that ginger kid keeping up? Isn't he always at the back?" they would mutter, which Arthur could now understand clearly with his new wolf hearing.

"I don't know. It's weird," the other kids would continue. Arthur's ego continued to rise as he held back a mocking laugh. He was tempted to do a full-pace sprint the last few laps just to spite those doubting him, but he knew that would be too suspicious. For now, he was only testing his power, not seeing their maximum. As the warmup ended, the entire class was exhausted. Most of the class needed to drink out of their water bottles from just the warm-up. Arthur, however, felt his pulse only increase a little, and he was still barely sweating. Arthur caught sight of Jack looking at him the same way two-thirds of the rest of the class was. He was looking at him like he had just sprouted wings. The teacher shouted that the class would do Athletic sports today, similar to the events done in the Olympics. Arthur knew that wasn't uncommon. They sometimes did these lessons every few months rather than just football or Rugby every week. They would do the shot put, long jump, the one-hundred-meter dash, and others. Arthur said a silent thank you to whatever force was kind enough to give him this excellent opportunity to show off how powerful he had become in front of everyone who had already thought of him as nothing. First up was the shot-put sport. Arthur put himself at the back of the class. Not so he didn't go first as all the stronger kids did, but so he could throw it the furthest and then beat everyone else's score at the same time.

One by one, after the teacher shouted go, everyone launched the heavy ball as hard as they could. The strongest kids were boasting to each other about how far their ball went. The weakest and average simply stayed silent as they walked away from their throw. Arthur's turn with his row was next. He held the ball in his hand, feeling the weight up and down. To him now, it nearly felt as light as a tennis ball. He placed the ball by his neck and waited for the shout. Then when it came, he launched it as hard as he could. While the others in his row fell average and near to the further ones, Arthur's ball soared through the air like a shot bullet. Its distance was nearly double the length of the current furthest of the entire class. Arthur heard the surprised gasps of his classmates around then turned around to scowls and confused frowns. No one said anything to Arthur directly, not even the teacher of the class bothered as he then shouted for everyone to move on to the next event. As they moved on, the other kids would then speak about him to their friends in disbelief. Arthur winced at himself. Arthur realized he got so wrapped up in showing off that he forgot to hold back some of his strength, so he didn't stand out too much. He figured that if he didn't smarten up for the next few sports, he would end up having his blood tested for some drug in the nurse's office.

The long jump went very quickly. This time Arthur remembered to be more careful. He placed in the top numbers of the class this time, but he didn't launch himself past the end of the entire sandpit like he probably knew he could. Despite his minor control this time around, there were still suspicious mutters. As they all moved on to the hundred meters, Jack walked up next to Arthur.

"Hey man, what the hell is going on with you?" he muttered hesitantly, still reluctant to speak to Arthur at all. Arthur shrugged in response.

"What do you mean?" Arthur asked innocently, as though nothing was amiss for him. Jack scowled.

"Don't think I'm an idiot. None of us are. How the hell are you doing all this in PE? You're one of the worst in the class. Are you on something?" Arthur couldn't help but chuckle and think of his answer for a second.

"Why yes, I am. It's called Werewolf blood! You should try it. It is an impressive performance enhancer." Arthur, of course, didn't reply with that and lied instead.

"I have been training hard this past week, and this is just the fruits of hard labor," Jack hummed. He wasn't convinced, but he didn't say anything else and rejoined the others in the class. Arthur walked onward, smirking smugly.

Arthur debated how much energy he should use here as the class lined up for the hundred-meter dash. He still wasn't sure about his limits, so he didn't quite know how to restrain himself fully. This was a dash race which meant you were supposed to run at full speed. However, Arthur knew if he did run at full speed, he would finish before his teacher had even finished saying go. He wasn't sure if he would have the time to slow himself a little in this race. It was the last one of his lessons, and he wanted to place himself at the top again. Everyone had their go quickly. The teacher noted everyone's performance on his clipboard. Once again, Arthur was at the back of the class while everyone tried to outrun each other in the blink of a handful of seconds. A few had beaten their old times and were celebrating with each other. Large high fives and praises from their friends could be heard by everyone else in the class. Most of the highly athletic kids in his class teased Arthur a lot about his physique, and now Arthur felt it was time for some delicious payback. He lined up himself and crouched a little. The teacher yelled for them to go, and Arthur dashed off. He looked to his sides and noticed he already had a very suspicious lead. He quickly slowed his pace a little, and three others came near him. Arthur allowed two people to overtake him as they finished giving him third place but also beating plenty of other classmates' finish times. He heard the angry whispers of jealous students as they all lined up again. Some of them were muttering that Arthur had somehow cheated. The teacher gave them all a quick rundown. He said he was impressed with people's performances today and encouraged them to keep improving and beat their scores again the next time they did this. He then dismissed them to get changed and go to their next lesson quickly. Arthur was beaming with pride. He walked back with his head held extremely high. Arthur had put all those who had mocked him in the past in their rightful place. The class all walked up back to the changing rooms, the teacher ahead of them and gone right into the changing rooms already. A familiar but for once, a welcome voice shouted up at Arthur as he walked.

"Hey freak, don't you move!" Arthur turned around to face his last piece of business of the day, smiling.

Gary was walking up towards Arthur while quite a lot of the class made a large gap around him and watched, most hoping to see Arthur get slapped around for beating them in sports. Jack also stayed, but he noticed something was different. He had seen Gary pick on Arthur before, but Arthur acted too confident and calm about it. He noticed an almost smirking expression on Arthur's face. Arthur didn't even want Gary to leave him alone; he instead eagerly waited for the bully to march toward him. Jack stayed because, strangely, he expected something different to happen than what the others in the class were thinking.

Gary came face to face with Arthur, frowning as the punch marks he gave him yesterday had vanished. He was nearly beginning to question that before Arthur spoke up first.

"What do you want Gary, got bored chasing the red dot of a laser pointer?" he said mockingly. The class around him 'oohed' at the remark as Gary puffed his face up angrily.

"Shut up, freak, you ginger loser! And go back to your home in crapville!" he spat back. The rest of the class started giggling at the childish insults. Arthur was done playing. He hated being called a freak. He took an intimidating step forward and gave Gary the same death glare he gave Jack not long ago.

"Get the hell out of my face, you disgusting piece of trash, before I reshape yours!" Arthur growled deeply. Gary roared at that; he wouldn't stand for the likes of Arthur Thorn threatening him. As always, Gary pulled back his arm to punch Arthur. The whole class went silent, which was perfect for

Arthur, who was concentrating hard now. He sharpened his sight on Gary and observed his movements. Arthur was tensing his arms, ready to strike in a flash. Gary threw his arm forward with his fist hurtling towards Arthur's face as it had always done for as long as Arthur can remember. With all the speed his new abilities would grant him, Arthur shot his arm up and caught Gary's arm by the wrist, stopping it dead. Everyone in the class gasped in shock. Gary looked bewildered for a moment, then threw his other fist forward as a panic reaction. This time, not letting go of Gary's wrist, Arthur snapped his body to the side, only then letting go of his wrist at the same time causing Gary to lose his balance and fall to the floor. Everyone laughed as Gary hit the ground hard, Arthur looking down at him as he got to his feet quickly.

"Have a nice trip, Gary?" Arthur chuckled condescendingly. Gary's face was twisted with intense, fiery hatred. He screeched as he leaped for Arthur one last time like a tackling troll.

"You FREAK!" He bellowed. Arthur's temper flared. He jolted forward and gripped Gary tight by the neck, stopping the bully in his tracks. Gary choked and tried to pry away Arthur's hand, but it wouldn't budge even a millimeter. Arthur stared dead into Gary's eyes without blinking. With a snort of derision, he let go of Gary's throat and gripped his shirt instead, pulling him forward. Gary's knees buckled as Arthur held him up close. Arthur raised his other hand high and spat darkly in Gary's direction.

"Let's see how you like it," Arthur said quietly, swinging his hand down. His hand connected with Gary's cheek, slapping him in the face. Hard. As Arthur hit him, he let go of Gary's collar. The power of his slap sent Gary back to the ground. Gary then began to cry out in pain and shock like a wailing newborn. Arthur turned his back on Gary and looked at his classmates who were now staring at him, not with any cheer. They only looked on at Arthur with fear.

"What!?" he challenged out to them. Arthur looked around and saw every head look down at his gaze. He sighed, frustrated with all of them. Arthur did not have the patience for spineless onlookers.

"Move!" he ordered. A path was instantly made for him. As Arthur walked away to change, he heard the whispers from others behind him and the sound of Gary crying on the floor. He didn't stop and just carried on.

There was nearly complete silence in the changing rooms, Arthur changed in the toilet again, but he could hear almost every word said about him. The whole class was struck with awe. Arthur Thorn had just taken down one of the school's worst bullies with barely any effort. No one challenged him about it or even went to the teacher to tell on him yet. Now quite a few were even scared of him. Arthur smelled the strange scent of their fear through the room. It was a thin plant-like smell that scarcely touched his senses. But with his new nose, nothing escaped him now. Arthur had finished changing, and the bell went for everyone to go to their next class. Arthur had expected everyone to gossip about what he did to every student within a mile radius. But right now, he didn't care what they did. Arthur was feeling ecstatic about finally giving Gary what he deserved. It was sweet justice no teacher or parent could ever give him. Arthur felt that after all these years of having to take that monster's abuse, he finally had the strength to deliver what he always wanted. It was what he always dreamed about. He hadn't been a Werewolf a full day yet, and he already felt like it was the greatest blessing possible. Arthur walked out of the bathroom for complete silence to follow. All eyes were on him as he walked. Some were scared, others confused. He walked past Jack, who was squinting at him suspiciously. Arthur didn't bother to look his way. He was far too engrossed in the moment. As Arthur left the room, chatter started again once the door closed behind him. Arthur couldn't help but chuckle as he walked on to his next lesson before lunch, where he once again planned to leave early, but this time for good.

The next lesson flew by Just as it did earlier in the day. Arthur heard a few whispers of people talking about what he did to Gary. Girls were giggling, and everyone else was doing their usual work. Arthur was thinking over his day so far as he pretended to do his work in class. Since entering the school, people had been noticing as he went by them. They would look at him for a moment like Arthur was something they hadn't seen before. He remembered his encounter with Ashley and how he made her feel shy with whatever the Werewolf part of him was doing. Arthur confronted Jack using newly acquired confidence from this morning, and a rare spark of beastly intimidation surfaced as he spoke. He bested all the toughest and fastest of his class in sports, followed by immediately knocking down his lifelong bully. Arthur now wished he had been a Werewolf since birth. He felt that if he always had these abilities, he would never have had any problems with people like before. He felt like a whole new Arthur than the one who stepped out of his home this morning. Arthur felt he was growing into someone different before his very eyes. However, Arthur couldn't help but notice his head was swelling a little as these thoughts continued. Arthur wasn't an idiot, and he could tell he was getting a little full of himself. But he had to admit that he liked the feeling for once. Arthur was enjoying the sense of not feeling like a loser, like a victim. He wanted to feel like someone who could defend himself. Arthur couldn't help but be slightly worried that perhaps he would become like Gary if he only ever did what he felt like. As that thought entered his mind, he automatically assumed he couldn't. Gary had never gone through what he had, but Arthur also recalled threatening Jack earlier more casually than he would have done before he had his new strength. He knew he wouldn't have hurt him, but he also noticed how quickly he was ok with doing that suddenly. Arthur had hoped that a lifetime of being at the bottom would give him the humility to handle these powers sensibly and justly, but he was now second-guessing his self-control.

Arthur knew whatever instruction Cratos had in store for him would allow him to continue to become stronger, smarter, and more powerful. Arthur couldn't wait. He decided he would leave the second the lunch bell went. Arthur had a feeling he couldn't afford to remain in school for much longer. Teachers would soon learn what he did to Gary and try to speak to him. He held his hand up and looked at his palm; this was the hand he had slapped Gary with. Arthur wondered why he decided to slap Gary and not punch him. Arthur pondered if he was being careful of his strength, as Cratos had warned. He doubted that though. Arthur knew he had lost his temper. He slapped him because he wanted to humiliate the bully, even worse, as Gary had humiliated Arthur every day.

Then a tiny wave hit Arthur that he wasn't expecting, guilt. For some reason, the delicious taste of revenge had turned sour, and his surge of bravado began to dwindle within him. Arthur felt very wrong with this thought. He felt like something venomous inside him came alive. That flame of the thought flickered stronger inside him. He now began to question the resolve he gave himself before.

"But then doesn't that justify everything he's done to you by acting no different than him, back to him," his mind sneakily said, making his arms tense in anger. Arthur didn't even believe such nonsense. He wondered why Gary should go unpunished for his crimes; it's only right he should feel the pain he gives to others.

"But who are you to judge him?" his mind countered internally. Arthur's face grimaced as he answered, knowing this was a losing battle.

"His victim…" he thought shallowly, despite knowing that was no excuse. He wasn't an idiot and knew what his head would say.

"Yes, and as his victim, you were better than him, and he always knew that. Part of why he hated you so much was because you never truly went to his level. Well, today you have." The voice fell silent as Arthur said nothing else. The bell went, and Arthur quickly hurried out of the classroom and through the school back gates. Arthur Thorn was now leaving his school behind him forever. What had started as his best day ever had rotted and turned into his most shameful.

CHAPTER SEVEN

Arthur still had a lot of the day to go through before he had to meet Cratos back at the warehouse to start his new life. He wasn't sure what to do or where to go. Once again, he had cut school, so Arthur knew he couldn't stand out like he did yesterday. If he did, a police officer would catch him and bring him back to school. He checked his pockets as he walked through the streets. He had little money to do much. He thought he might get away with relaxing in some coffee shop for a while, but that would be boring. He was still feeling guilty for acting the way he did today, especially now that he was out of school. He was away from his fellow students' looks and giggles, and he was starting to see his behavior more different than he had at the time. The pain that Gary had caused him for so long weighed heavily on Arthur. He felt he couldn't leave without settling the score. However, now Arthur understood what that voice in his head was telling him and why he now felt terrible. Arthur shrugged his shoulders and sighed. He wasn't going to find Gary and apologize. Nor was he going to see Jack and take back what he had said to them. Arthur decided he would continue to shoulder his guilt as his punishment and carry on walking the streets aimlessly for as long as he needed to.

Arthur continued to walk with his uneasy feeling from how he acted. He knew nothing about the Werewolves as people. Arthur didn't know how their biology worked and what their society's rules were. Still, he assumed they wouldn't take kindly to an arrogant teenager amongst their ranks using his strength against normal humans as a tyrant. It quickly became evening as Arthur wandered further and longer. Once again, no adults bothered to try and stop him even though he had left school early. The dusk promptly began to go into the night. It was Friday, so Arthur knew his father would be out drinking with his friends late. Not that it was a problem. For Arthur, it was like giving his family the night off from being within his reach. Arthur's mother probably assumed he was at a friend's house again. He then let his mind play and wondered how long it would take her to realize he was missing. His sister would probably be the first to know. Part of him hoped they wouldn't miss him that much. It would be easier on his conscience if they were glad to be rid of him, he thought. He still remembered every inch of that night when the first Vampire attacked him and how his family turned on him in the blink of an eye when he tried to defend them. He struggled to hold a grudge and probably already forgave them in his heart, so the wish of his disappearance being easy to deal with was quickly flattened. However, no matter how he felt, he knew there was no going back now. The blood of the wolf was now within his veins, and he had to commit fully to his new life. This was the path he was on, and they would just have to go on without him, no matter how much it would wretch his soul.

More time passed as he walked. Arthur passed a pub on a mildly familiar street. The night was black, with only the street lights keeping the area around illuminated. He heard music and laughter from inside the pub. It was a sizeable, green-painted building with 'The frisky whiskey' above the front door as its name. Arthur's father let him taste beer once; it had been a year or so ago. Even from one sip, he didn't like the taste of it that much. It had a bitter, unpleasant tang to it on his tongue. Plus, he recalled seeing the kind of idiotic oaf it turned his father into, and that was something he wasn't interested in becoming, ever. But seeing how many other adults drank it, he figured he would probably change his mind as he got older. When drunk, of course, his father had told him stories about how Arthurs' grandfather forced him to drink his first pint when he was ten, then smacking him if he couldn't handle it. Arthur believed him. His grandfather was no different from his dad in that they were both bullies. The door to the pub suddenly swung open by two men dressed entirely in black. They threw a man out from the place and onto the ground, saying he was barred from coming in ever again. The man got to his feet and swore several times at the men and spat at the building. He then began to mumble underneath his breath a variety of different swear words. Arthur could see his breath nearly producing fog with the stench of alcohol. The man turned his head and spotted Arthur. He frowned.

"What the bloody ell are yo doin ere boy!" Arthur's father said with a drunken slur, his words incoherent and almost impossible to understand. Arthur only knew what his father was saying because he was used to it. Arthur looked up at his swaying drunken father with a raised eyebrow.

"Hey, dad," Arthur replied plainly, acting as cool as a cucumber.

"You all right there?" he smoothly added. His father sniffed and waved an arm sluggishly back at the pub.

"Bloody curs...can't handle teir booze," he answered angrily, then he refocused his attention back on Arthur.

"Why are you ere?" he asked again, scowling firmly at him. Arthur shrugged and looked around the night air.

"I'm out for a walk dad, been a rather rough day." His dad's scowl vanished, quickly replaced with a sinister smirk striding up the side of his face.

"Ha! Got yer ass kicked at school eh boy!" his father laughed, swaying in the air from side to side in his merriment.

"Pafetic," he hiccupped. Arthur shook his head solidly.

"The opposite actually, today I finally beat down the boy who's been bullying me for years in front of everyone, humiliating him completely." Arthur's father belched unpleasantly and frowned again.

"Bullied? Only the weak get bullied, boy. Why was itting im back bad?" Arthur's father was asking these questions like a confused infant. Arthur shook his head but maintained eye contact.

"Because I stooped to his level, dad. Because I became what I hated and enjoyed it while it happened, making me a bully myself. That dad, is truly pathetic." His father growled and spat on the floor again.

"Bloody kids teday, all turned into pansy hippy wusses. None of you are REAL men," his father slurred, standing up strong, puffing his chest out with the last word. Arthur shook his head again. This time he kept his calm. After how Arthur felt earlier, he wouldn't do what he did with Gary ever again. He decided he would handle his last demon as who he is, not who he hated.

"What would you know, father? You're a drunken bully yourself. You're no man. You're barely human," he hissed out his final word hatefully. Arthur's father took a step back, blinking several times. He was shocked beyond measure.

"Wer...wer....what?" he stuttered like a dumbfounded neanderthal.

"Sorry, was I too subtle?" Arthur asked. His father then realized what he had just heard, and his face twisted demoniacally. His features were darkening in the light into a near-delirious, nasty mess of wrath.

"You miserable sod! You bloody, damn, bloody..." his father didn't even finish. Arthur simply rolled his eyes as foam was nearly flowing from his father's mouth in blind fury.

"Calm down, dad," Arthur said gently. Two weeks ago, he would have screamed those words with panic and fear. Now he finally spoke with calm and steady poise. Arthur stood up tall and strong, looking his father straight in the eyes. His father HATED being told to calm down. The drunken ogre pulled his arm back, clenched his fists, and with a snarl, hurled it forward at Arthur's face.

Arthur's father would look back on the night his son disappeared and remember what had happened. Even though he was drunk out of his mind, he refused to allow the alcohol he consumed that night to erase even a second of what happened. No matter how he ever tried to figure it out, he never managed to answer how his son managed it. Surprise whipped across Arthur's father's face as he stood still in place as though he had just transformed into a statue. His eyes were quivering, refusing to believe what he was seeing. Without even blinking, his son shot out his hand and caught his father's fist in the air, inches away from his face stopping it dead. Despite his father's strength, his son grabbed his punch without his forehead even creasing. Arthur's face remained unchanged as he looked at his father with a severe eye. Not hateful, just serious.

"No more, dad. You will never hurt me again." Arthur leaned in closer to his father, who took an uncertain step backward. With instinct, Arthur's father used his other arm and swung it around to strike the side of Arthur's temple. Without breaking eye contact, Arthur threw his other arm up in the air blocking against the blow with his forearm. He saw the attack in some action film, and he was glad he managed to pull it off. Arthur let go of his father's fist and let his arm down. Both his father's arms slumped down by his sides like they had lost all feeling.

"I'm not going to let you bully me anymore either, dad. One more thing," he added. Arthur took a menacing step forward, as he had with Jack before. A dark, hallowing face materialized in front of his father's shaken-up one. His dad didn't move this time, and Arthur looked at him. Arthur wanted to throw a punch so dearly. Like Gary, he wished to hurt him. But Arthur, this time, caught himself before he could make that mistake. He looked at his drunken father with clear eyes. The person was a sorry, sad, and damaged man. He felt bad enough stooping to Gary's level earlier. Arthur then looked deep into his father's eyes and realized he didn't want to be the kind of person who hurts his own family, even if he hurts someone who does that themselves. Arthur sighed and instead leaned forward, so the two were nose to nose.

"It will be a long time before I will return, dad, but return I will. And when I do, If I find out that you EVER hurt mum or Alice again, I swear this. I leave for now, but if you ever hurt them again. I will come back, and I will kill you." His father's eyes widened, and his pupils shrank. He fell backward onto the ground and looked up at his son, who looked down on him, standing firm. Arthur then walked past his father, saying nothing else, proud of himself for remaining true to whom he is. In his life, he knew he would always look back and question if it was the right thing to do. If he should have punished his father the way he hurt Gary or if he was right for simply leaving him unmarked, something his father had never done.

It was midnight when Arthur arrived back at the warehouse to meet Cratos. He was a few minutes over the mark, but he doubted Cratos minded. Arthur then wondered what the Werewolf was doing himself all this time. He mentioned before that he was in the area with others, so Arthur wondered if he would meet other Werewolves too. He entered the place that changed his life. He walked in the middle of the wooden floor. The indent from where Cratos had crashed into the floor with the Vampire was still there, with the night seeming darker than before. Arthur's vision was still incredible within the darkness, and he loved it. He saw so much detail that would just come out as muddled shadows to his previous human eyes. He wasn't feeling anxious at all, and he was confident and ready for his destiny to begin. He thought about his father and the look on his face when Arthur first caught that punch. Then the moment when he blocked the second and finally stood up to him face to face. This time he was not wracked with guilt or shame like when he hit Gary. He hadn't stooped to his father's level and refused to give in to his selfish vile wishes this time. He was genuinely proud of himself.

"Been a busy boy," came a voice echoing around the room, Cratos's voice. Arthur turned around and looked around the room, going around in a circle. As he made a complete circle, he came face to chest with Cratos Mane, who was glowering down at him like a predator ready to strike. Arthur gasped as he took a shocked step back, looking up at the tall, pale, dark-haired man who was looking down on him with a raised eyebrow.

"How did you do that; I didn't even hear you?" Arthur said shakily.

"I'm Shadow class. It's our specialty," he answered, his tone icy. Arthur let the matter drop and smiled welcomely.

"Hey!" Arthur greeted cheerfully, but Cratos's expression remained unchanged.

"You acted very irresponsibly today. I have to say I am extremely disappointed. The boy I watched today was not the one who helped me not long ago. I had not expected hubris to warp your mind so quickly." Arthur's smile dropped as he then looked away, sad.

"How much did you see?" Arthur asked, downcast. Cratos breathed out heavily, exhausted.

"Everything since you went to school. You talking to that girl, I assume you were sweet on her. Your conversation with what I also assumed was a friend of yours, who you threatened, despite its noble intention from what I heard you say to him." Arthur's head rose with that word, confused.

"Noble?" he muttered back. Cratos waved his hand.

"That doesn't matter. What angered me was when you had your physical education lesson. Showing off your strength to others, your vanity as you beat them, purposely. I saw you realized you were drawing suspicion and acted more subtly, but you still tried your hardest to show them up. And then when that kid harassed you." His frown burrowed deeper in his head with an angry demeanor.

"What the hell were you thinking?! The Werewolves do not recruit those who use their powers to bully the weak," he growled. Arthur nodded at everything Cratos said, all the faults with his actions his conscience had already pointed out to him.

"I know. I'm sorry. That boy had bullied me so much for so long. He humiliated me every day, always hurting me. I wanted revenge," Cratos snorted with contempt.

"That's the worthless whines of a spiteful child. After helping me before, I was under the impression you were smarter than that!" Arthur's head dropped; he fell to his knees in despair. He hated himself once again. Cratos was right. At this moment, Arthur felt like Cratos had given these powers to the wrong kid.

Cratos knelt and put a hand on Arthur's shoulder. Arthur lifted his head to see a more understanding face, warm and caring.

"I understand Arthur. Weak people try and hurt those weaker than them, so they feel stronger. Like you did when you hurt him back, didn't you?" Arthur nodded thoughtfully; he remembered how powerful he felt when he hurt Gary.

"Those are the feelings of the sad and the hurt. When those people hurt others, it lasts seconds but leaves years of regret on the soul. When I saw you do that, I thought you were one of those people. It began to look like you were too damaged to be able to grow stronger and wiser, and I was close to changing my mind about you coming with me." Fear erupted into Arthur's stomach hearing that from Cratos. He had no idea how he would handle what he had become without a guiding mentor. As Arthur began to protest, Cratos shushed him.

"But then I saw you with your father. When you mentioned how someone else gave you that face mark, I realized who it was. I thought you were going to hurt your father like you did that kid. But you held back. You kept your calm and acted like the perfect levelheaded man that I would be proud to mentor." Arthur's face lit up, then a small tear went down his cheek. Cratos smiled at him.

"I saw the guilt on your face as you left your school, so we'll chalk this day up as experience. You must be careful, Arthur. If you're not careful, your human side will take your powers and corrupt you. They will turn you into a monster far worse than any Werewolf form can become. You would become no different than a Vampire." Arthur dried his eyes and nodded at Cratos.

"I understand. But what do you do? How do you stop yourself? What is the difference between revenge and justice?" he asked. Cratos looked at him thoughtfully.

"Justice is simply correcting what is wrong. It is the unemotional balance that is completely devoid of corruption. It is simply what is right. Revenge is making YOU feel better no matter what. Regardless of whom you hurt and, in the end, the one who is hurt the most, is you," Arthur nodded.

"I understand," he muttered back, taking in what he heard.

"Remember Arthur. When you hurt others, you must live with what you have done from then on." Arthur remained silent and simply nodded, taking Cratos's words to heart.

"I understand. I will become a worthy Werewolf, I promise." Cratos smiled warmly at Arthur.

"I know you will. You have the potential to become a fine Werewolf, just a little training here and there." Cratos nodded out towards the door of the warehouse.

"Let's go, Arthur Thorn. Your new life starts now." Arthur nodded and stood up straight, walking behind Cratos Mane as they walked out into the night. Arthur had no idea where they were going, but he didn't care. He felt he was no longer a human. From now on, he was a Werewolf.

CHAPTER EIGHT

The wild cat stalked through the forest with fierce growls. It wasn't used to being the prey and had been hunted as one for the last hour. It knew there were two of them, a large figure and a smaller one chasing it down. One was nearly completely silent as he stalked it, and the other smaller one was louder but still slightly refined in its approach. The wild cat was growing tired from the chase. It had been running for too long and now stood in an opening with several trees surrounding it. It raised itself on its hind legs and puffed up its shoulders, growling dominantly. It was trying to scare off what was chasing it. The night had come, and the forest was nearly entirely black in vision. The wild cat had hunted inside its home its entire life, but now it was struggling to catch sight of its predators. The forest itself wasn't quiet, though. The sounds of other creatures were vibrant in the night. Birds were squawking, and the rustling of smaller animals within their burrows and bushes rattled continuously. The noises distracted the wild cat as it constantly moved its body around, trying to peer on all sides. Its eyes were sharp, its heart pounding. There was a stronger rustle from the bushes to its right. The cat could tell the rustle was too big to be a smaller animal. Its head snapped to the right, and it roared. Its piercing shriek was trying to warn the predator off. There was another loud rustle, but the figure didn't emerge from the bushes. The wild cat sensed it had intimidated its prey and began to walk backward, eyes trained on the spot. As it stepped back, its tail lightly brushed against something hard. Its ears immediately snapped upright. It turned its head around only to see a tall, dark figure leaping upon its body mercilessly. The wild cat was taken by surprise, and it tried to twist its body around to escape the attacker, but he knew what he was doing. Within a few seconds, the figure wrapped its arms around the wild cat's neck and twisted his arms and his body sharply to the side, snapping its neck. The wild cat moaned softly, then went still, dead. Once the person was confident of their death, the feral cat went still and its killer stood up on his feet.

"It's dead," he called out to the bush the cat was distracted by. With another rustle from the bush, out emerged a very tall, black-dressed thin-looking figure. He couldn't be recognized with ordinary eyes, but with the enhanced vision from his Werewolf eyes, Arthur Thorn could see the wild grin slapped across his mentor's face.

"Well done, boy," he purred, clapping gently a few times.

"Done perfectly, we'll eat well tonight," he continued, pleased. Arthur looked down at the dead wild cat blandly and nodded.

"Yes, we will. Let's get it ready then," he muttered tonelessly before hauling the deceased creature on his shoulders as the pair then went on their way.

A few hours later, Arthur was sitting by the campfire. There were branches, twigs, and flammable roots thrown into the flame for kindling, along with a large log in the center that kept the flame burning. The orange flame was strong and steadily burned away brightly on the boy's face. He had to prod the large fat log in the middle of the fire with a stick now and then to keep the blaze going. He watched the sparks of embers dance away from the glow of the log as he jabbed at it. It spewed heat that roasted his face, knowing that the fire was now ready for the pieces of the wild cat Cratos had gutted and cut up to be cooked and eaten promptly. Arthur was starving. They had been hunting that cat for hours, and his rumbling stomach was a constant distraction. He had to crawl silently through bushes on top of brown, snapping leaves and twigs without making a sound. If Cratos weren't constantly with him, Arthur would have considered performing such amazing feats impossible to accomplish. If any other person claimed to move without making even the slightest sound, Arthur would have called them insane. But Cratos Mane was not insane, Arthur at least hoped. He sat cross-legged, looking deep into the fire. It was a frosty night, and the heat of the fire was captivating, as though it was staring back at Arthur as he gazed at it. His face and chest were actively roasted while his back was freezing up solid. This was another night like the many he had experienced since joining his mentor.

It had been three weeks since Arthur had joined Cratos Mane, and the two had been traveling the wilderness most of the way. Given that Arthur's disappearance would be wildly reported, Cratos had the two cover as much ground as possible so they wouldn't attract attention. Arthur felt any search for him wouldn't go past his hometown, and by the time they were three cities away, he knew no one would know his face. Arthur had asked why the pair weren't going through different cities and towns, to begin with.

"Tradition," Cratos grunted in reply. Arthur was told that this happens with what was considered 'new cubs' for the Werewolves. They had to learn to hunt and survive in the wilderness while adapting to being a new Werewolf. Cratos said they needed to be far from the distraction of civilization where they could hone their new abilities properly. This was because his Werewolf abilities were required to be properly trained before cubs could be around society again. He needed control over his strength and other powers, putting them to practical use every day so they could appreciate their talents and not take their abilities for granted. Arthur didn't like his new living arrangement. He would instead take a bed over the hard, muddy floor any day. However, he quickly understood why this was necessary, especially after how he had acted when he first became a Werewolf. He had disappointed his teacher at that moment, and now he was eager to prove himself to Cratos. So, Arthurs had lived like an animal for all these weeks without a single complaint. Even at night, when he was shivering from the cold, he still slept. The days he felt the stings of wounds he had received from animals they had hunted, he just gritted his teeth and carried on. Luckily, he healed remarkably quickly. From animal encounters, part of his new powers was that he could have his legs slashed open with claws and bite marks across his hands and arms, and within a few days, he would be fully healed with no scars. After seeing this, he noticed the scars on Cratos's face, asking why they hadn't healed.

"Wounds from Vampires never heal. Remember that. Those fanged monsters have ruined many a handsome Werewolf face," Cratos replied bitterly, his tone suggesting he was speaking more from experience than opinion.

There were still dozens of things that Cratos hadn't told or taught Arthur yet, and there were still many nights of cold hunting to go before he could be trusted to rejoin civilization again. He had often also wondered where about in the country they were. Before they had joined the animal kingdom, they had taken many trains and even a short private plane ride. The pilot that flew them was a fellow Werewolf friend who gave them a lift under the radar. Through Cratos's contact, the man had entered the city and provided the pair of them with enough supplies, like money and other identities, for them to go far enough. Cratos said Werewolves were ready to help each other just about anywhere in the world. Arthur had first thought it was because Cratos was concerned about police trying to track him down, but he soon realized that his teacher had a particular area in mind for his students' training. Arthur recalled Cratos had mentioned he had been hunting the Vampires that attacked him in the alley that night with other Werewolves. He asked if he would get in trouble for leaving his small Vampire hunting pack to train Arthur, but Cratos shook his head.

"No, it happens often. We are never short of recruits, and we never know when one will jump into our laps as you did. Any member of the pack is free to go off and train a new cub whenever they wish. Unless they are Beta's, they need permission from Cyrus." Cratos then dropped a name that Arthur didn't know, as well as these Beta's. Arthur had asked where they were precisely in the country, but Cratos refused to tell him. Arthur knew he wouldn't be told if he pressed the question, so he just nodded and moved on as always.

"Doesn't matter. Everywhere is pretty much the same. Worry about what's around you, not what it's called," Cratos would curtly mumble whenever Arthur was curious about their location. Arthur realized Cratos was keeping information on a need-to-know basis. So for now, Arthur was instructed to only worry about his training here in the forests and jungles.

As the cat cooked on the fire, the smell of its roasting flesh was making Arthur's mouth water. His stomach was growling in a way that would have made the cat they were about to eat shudder. Cratos looked over the meat with a studious eye and nodded.

"It's about cooked," he declared plainly. Arthur smiled and reached his arm in to take a piece of meat from the fire. As Arthur and Cratos traveled and ate from a campfire, Arthur noticed that his hands were incredibly more resistant to heat. Not impervious, but his skin seemed to have thickened not to burn as quickly as ordinary human flesh. Arthur was already picturing his first juicy bite only to have his hand slapped away by Cratos as he reached out. Arthur jumped in surprise and frowned at his mentor as he rubbed his slapped hand, frowning.

"What's wrong?" he asked. His stomach was rumbling in anger at the tease. Cratos held up a finger and smirked a very evil grin, as he always did when he produced a test out of thin air to Arthur.

"This is a new lesson. Self-control. You must look at this tender, juicy meat and remain still while I eat without letting your instinct take over and diving for the meat like an animal" Arthur's jaw dropped. He had spent hours hunting this cat, killing it, and then building a fire to cook the creature, and now he was being denied the fruits of his labor. He clenched his fists angrily.

"And why do YOU get to eat?" Arthur growled through clenched teeth, holding back the need to shout. Cratos's raised an amused eyebrow and snorted. He took a slab of meat off the fire in his bare hands and sank his teeth into it. He pulled away from the slab a sizeable thick chunk of meat. Cratos chewed for a few seconds and then swallowed loudly, exhaling in pleasure. The meaty scent drifted straight into Arthur's face as he sat there shaking in a near-blind fury.

"Because you have already displayed to me you cannot control yourself in the heat of emotion. Just as you assaulted your schoolyard bully in anger, you must now stave off your appetite in hunger. Now sit there and focus on how loudly I chew," he finished with a big grin. Arthur's mentor mentioned his mistakes at school often. Arthur had heard quite a few lectures on his temper in the few weeks they were together. Whenever Arthur questioned his mentor about a lesson or a correction of his attitude or opinion, out came that argument against him, always shutting him up. So there Arthur sat, his hunger making his very skin crawl as he saw his mentor take bite after bite of the wild cat's meat.

His eyes were barely blinking as the only thought going through his head was the unbelievable urge to leap forward and eat every piece of cooked meat on the fire. But despite it all, Arthur wanted to pass this test. So even though he had to fight his more basic primal urge, he sat there, fuming. His rage was building and building, nearly half tempted to strike out at Cratos himself. After his mentor had finished half of the meat in his hands, he belched loudly and smiled.

"Congratulations boy, you have done very well. You may eat now." Arthur shot his arm out only to hear one more thing.

"But you must still eat in a controlled manner. If I see you tearing that meat apart like a starved animal, I will throw it away, and you can go forage for some mushrooms. Understand?" Cratos warned. Arthur saw the firm expression on his mentor's face and nodded. He took a breath, steadied himself, and began taking sensible bites of every inch of every piece of his meat. The second it touched the tip of his tongue, it was the most extraordinary sensation ever. It tasted as though it was the first time he had ever eaten cooked meat before. Its tender, flavorful flesh was the greatest at this moment. Arthur relished every fat, juicy, salty bite of it.

The following day Arthur was awoken from truly little sleep by Cratos's morning shout.

"Get up! Vampires may sleep through the day, but we don't!" his teacher would yell cheerfully. Arthur groaned as he sat up. He didn't know how Cratos did this same routine every morning with a smile on his face. They had spent nearly all the night hunting that damn cat, and now he must rise at first light. He only got a handful of hours of sleep. Luckily for Arthur, he noticed that Werewolves recovered from fatigue and tiredness quickly. Otherwise, he would have dropped dead from exhaustion weeks ago. However, he also noticed that Werewolf recovery still took some time. As Arthur rose from the ground, his eyes were still half shut as he sluggishly sat up yawning. He felt like his belly was still full of the wild cat. Then out of nowhere, a wild burst of icy water slapped him in the face, covering him. Arthur jumped to his feet in shock and roared out in surprise. He looked around as he saw Cratos a few feet away from him with a bucket, now empty and grinning wildly.

"Now that's the kind of energy you need in the morning!" he laughed. Arthur lost his temper and ran angrily at Cratos, intending to batter his mentor to death with his bucket. Cratos had many supplies like buckets and pans from a small bag of essentials he traveled with, and all were collapsible or foldable for space. Cratos laughed as he jumped out of the way of the charging Arthur. Cratos would have looked like a matador against a bull in a fit of rage to anyone else watching. After a few minutes, Arthur gave up and swore under his breath darkly as he walked towards the nearest river to wash for the morning. Cratos began laughing to himself as he started his morning exercises. Arthur was expected to do his own once he returned.

Every morning Cratos had set him on a strict physical training regime since the day they started traveling. Because of his newly gained physique, Arthur was told he would have to do twice as much physical effort as anyone else to become stronger. He would need to push his body past even his Werewolf limits. It was always tiring, but Arthur couldn't hide a small spark of pride as he did the workouts. He was still a little bit big-headed about his strength and ability to achieve the tasks he was set. However, he made sure to hide his pride behind an intense stone mask of humility, especially in front of Cratos. He couldn't allow himself to seem overly confident, or Cratos would punish him. Cratos never physically hurt Arthur, but he was punished the way people in the military in films he had watched were punished. He would be given pushups and run up and down steep hills several times. After he saw Cratos would not become bored creating new, more tiring punishments, he quickly learned to mind his ego. He walked towards the stream shivering from the bucket of water, angry at Cratos but promptly getting over it. He had to admit it had at least woken him up.

Arthur was washing his hair casually from the stream. It had grown exceedingly long in the few weeks he had been with Cratos. His mentor had told him it was part of the change. Before he would go through his first transformation, nearly his entire body would grow hair. Cratos said he was free to shave as he wished. Arthur hadn't developed any facial hair yet, much to his dismay. Arthur had looked forward to having a goatee beard, but for now, only his ginger hair had grown down nearly past his shoulders. He hadn't brought a hairbrush with him, so it was very unkempt and wild-looking. He liked it; he felt like an old-age barbarian with it. It took a while to wash in the stream and the rest of him, but Cratos didn't mind him taking his time. He noticed his mentor was quite the 'clean freak' and constantly stressed about washing after they did any exercise or anything physical that made Arthur sweat. It was irritating a lot of the time; he could be worse than his mother was. Arthur paused his washing as that thought entered his mind. He thought a lot about his family now and then. Hoping they didn't miss him too much. He still remembered his mother throwing him aside that night, but he also knew she loved him deep down, as he loved her back along with Alice. He had scared his father before he left, and so he hoped he wasn't hurting the two of them anymore, but he wouldn't be able to know for certain for an awfully long time. Cratos sensed that Arthur missed his family and even his friends. Despite preferring to be a hermit, he never knew how much he would miss just being around people. Cratos was pleasant company for Arthur a lot of the time. When he wasn't teasing or teaching, he would try and make Arthur laugh, and tell him stories about places he had been and what he had seen around the world. Arthur always listened with interest. The pair laughed like old friends now and then on some nights together. But Arthur missed being around people his age, others who might understand how it feels to be like him. Cratos, despite not looking old, often had the mindset of an older man sometimes. He was very formal and didn't allow much silliness. Arthur had finished washing and pulled his clothes out of the stream, rinsed them out, and carried them on his shoulder back to Cratos.

The other clothes he had packed with him for his journey hadn't been touched much yet. Cratos was adamant about him washing and re-wearing the same clothes constantly. He didn't trust Arthur to keep track of keeping all his clothes clean, so for now, he was limited to only one set. But he was able to dry them by campfires often, so he wasn't wearing wet clothes. The other items he had packed were barely used as well. He had his notepad and the few pencils he had brought with him. He had sketched a few times, nothing complicated, and he only did this in the few hours he was awarded peace from training. Even Cratos understood the need for downtime. Whenever Arthur got out his sketchbook, Cratos would move to sit by himself a few meters away. He would cross his legs, firmly place for hands on the ground with his palms flat, and remain like that without moving apart from his breathing. He never explained himself for it, and Arthur felt the need not to ask. He assumed it was some sort of meditation, but it wasn't part of his training, so he was glad he didn't have to do it. He had no idea what Cratos was thinking about while he sat there, but Arthur figured it must be boring as hell remaining like that for so long. But despite that, Arthur enjoyed the minor piece of time he was allowed to himself. While he didn't tell Cratos, he was struggling to live like this. It was increasingly hard for him. He had never known a life of working hard for your food every night and training your body during the day. He wasn't prepared for how much his new muscles ached every time he woke up. The heat of the sun made his sweat river down his back, and at night, he felt his own eyes nearly freeze solid. However, he thought about his old life in comparison. It was a lot comfier than this one now. He had beds and furniture to relax on. But in that world, he was nothing. There it felt like he was on the bottom of everyone's shoe. Here, Cratos treated him with respect, he was a fair teacher, but he also treated Arthur like an equal friend. That feeling of finally seeing someone who genuinely cared for him, eye to eye, was worth all the days in the forest and more.

Arthur returned to their camp, the black ash smell of the campfire from the previous night in the air. The remaining bones and other unwanted pieces from the wild cat they ate last night were discarded in some bush, but the smell was still lightly roaming through the air. Up Arthur's nostrils, they still smelt like it was right under his nose, decomposing into a festering rot. Cratos was doing press-ups as Arthur came back into the clearing. The man never bothered to keep count anymore, and he just continued until he decided he was done, it seemed. Arthur, however, was still on set numbers. The amount was increasing every few days. Cratos had him start small, and more were added as he went. Arthur didn't need to be told or even addressed as he entered the camp. He set down his other clothes and began his stretches. First, Arthur had to stretch their arms for twelve seconds with each one. He started with the left arm, then the right. Then over his back, left, then right. Arthur finished with a stretch behind his back and then his front. His left leg was held behind him, then the right. The stretches had become the most annoying part of the workout for him. One day he decided to skip the stretch both before and after his exercises. Cratos said nothing at the time because he knew he didn't need to. The next morning Arthur was in absolute agony. His limbs, every inch of his body were in pain with every movement.

"Now you know," Cratos said formally; he didn't even look in Arthur's direction as he said it.

"From now on, you stretch," he finished, and since then, Arthur always stretched as though his life depended on it. But it had always been such a bore that wouldn't change. As he finished his stretches, he already felt ready for the first sets of pushups. He straightened his legs and held them together, heel to heel. He outstretched his arms and tipped himself forward, falling to the ground.

His palms were the first thing to touch the ground, his arms tensed instantly, and his face was millimeters from the dirt. He held himself there for a few seconds, his arm muscles flexing. Exhaling, he began to press himself up and down. The first twenty were easy for him. Now he barely felt his arms as he did it. With his newfound strength, a task like this almost felt mechanical to him as he did them. After the following twenty, his arms were finally beginning to feel the tension in the exercise, but Arthur held firm and continued without slowing his pace. His current number he had to attend today was sixty for a complete set. Once he hit sixty, he exhaled. He knelt for a few seconds to collect himself, then he spread his arms out wide from his body and did forty more. After finishing pushups, he moved to do sit-ups, followed swiftly by his squats, followed by a plank exercise where he held himself facing the ground raised straight by just his elbows and toes from the ground. Out of every activity, that was the most murderous on his stomach, especially since he had to do it right after his sit-ups.

After he had finished, he stood back up to recover himself. He was starting to sweat a little and he was breathing hard. Cratos was only mid-way through his sit-ups, going through numbers faster than a calculator with his speed. Arthur gave himself enough space and lowered his body. In a flash, he dashed forward several meters. When he was far away enough, he stopped in place and shot back to where he started, repeating the sequence ten times. After doing that exercise five times, Arthur was finished. He was breathing hard now. Arthur then took a long drink of fresh cold water they had collected from the river. As he gathered himself and was hydrated, Arthur waited for Cratos to finish his run, which he had done not long after Arthur had finished. Cratos smiled as he walked up to Arthur and patted him on the back, breathing hard himself and taking a drink of water.

"The morning warm-up is always the hardest," he chuckled. Arthur exhaled loudly and laughed with him.

"You know, for most people, that would be the exercise itself for the day." Cratos shook his head at Arthur, smirking cruelly.

"Not for Werewolves, I'm afraid. It's now time for today's tests." Cratos chuckled and gestured out for them to move.

His daily Werewolf training consisted of many tests, and they had started going through them immediately. Like last night with the piece of meat, many of the tests were designed to prepare his mental and personal strengths. His physique was easily tested and trained, pushed past his limits, and continued past that point which was easy to train up. A body could be molded, but Cratos said Arthur also needs to sculpt and refine his mind and willpower. Some tests required him to think on his feet. One of the first things Cratos had taught him was a simple phrase.

"What makes a man is not how he acts, but how he reacts," and since then, Arthur had been subjected to many tests that told Cratos exactly how he reacted to multiple situations. To see what his apparent instinct was in different scenarios.

One test required Arthur to withstand a range of insults while balancing on one foot on a log in still water. Cratos was testing his nerves, seeing what words or insults struck his core and pushed him over the edge to try and make him lose his balance and fall. Arthur struggled to pass the test at the time. He was gritting his teeth, furious. Cratos had said horrible things to him, and with his one trigger word, he snapped. His eyes exploded open. Arthur firmly placed his other foot on the log, then he leaped onto land where Cratos was standing and without hesitating, Arthur swung a punch straight at Cratos's face. However, his cunning mentor was already acting. Cratos grabbed Arthur's arm, and with the slightest push of his other hand, Arthur fell back into the water. Arthur thrashed around as he swam to the surface and then to dry ground, watching his mentor approach him by the edge. Arthur held out his arm, his face a twisted snarl of a beast.

"Go ahead!" he shouted at Cratos, waiting for the upcoming lecture.

"Say I failed! Say I lost my temper! Go on! Say it!" Arthur snarled in a fit of rage. Cratos said nothing. He simply nodded his head and gestured him back into the forest.

"Next test," Cratos simply muttered as he then walked away from Arthur as he stood up out from the water. Arthur was awe-struck that his mentor said nothing else.

Another test required Arthur to be placed into a snake pit without moving. Arthur wasn't even sure how Cratos managed to acquire as many snakes as he had, but he learned not to question the how with his teacher. Arthur had to sit crossed-legged and keep his eyes wide open without moving an inch. Cratos explicitly warned Arthur to remain completely still. Cratos said if he didn't move, the snakes would recognize the Werewolf blood in his veins and leave him alone. However, if he moved before they accepted his scent, they would see him as a threat and attack. Arthur always thought he liked snakes, but now, he hated them passionately in a few seconds.

In their droves, the slim creatures slithered around his body like he was their damn playground. Arthur felt goosebumps surfacing every time their long smooth bodies glided around his flesh. They ran across his legs, up along his back, across his neck, and they even slithered in his hair. He was told his Werewolf blood would attract them to him at first, but they would get bored and move on in their own time; he simply had to wait. His nerves were screaming for him to run, to throw the biters off his body, and escape to safety. The sound of their constant hissing was the only sound ringing through his ears like an orchestra of their endless noise rippling around his being like a torrent. His limbs were crying in agony to be scratched from the itching, from wanting to twitch even. He did his best to deny his compulsions. The most challenging thing he was struggling with was controlling his breathing. The more panicked he became, the more his chest grew with every quick breath, expanding larger and smaller every second. But Arthur remembered he was ordered to keep calm for this test, and he knew Cratos would be watching him. He watched the snakes move; he saw them crawl over his body. He studied them as they moved across him, his eyes darting from side to side, and they weren't attacking him. After a few minutes, they stopped hissing. They became much more docile and began to leave his body alone, just like Cratos said they would. Their tongues occasionally passed out between their mouths but nothing else. He slowed down his breathing upon feeling safe, more controlled, and steadier. Within the next minute, the snakes began to slither off his body and onward elsewhere in the pit away from Arthur, now uninterested in him, it seemed. Without saying a word, Arthur crawled out of the hole and looked at Cratos, not with anger but with understanding. He nodded at his mentor, and with an approving smile, Cratos nodded back. Nothing else was said as they both went hunting that night.

Over time, Arthur understood the meaning of each test and fail or succeed; he noticed he was still taking away with him the lesson they provided. It wasn't about winning or losing but building himself as a person. Cratos was trying to bring Arthur up and see how he reacted to the world, and how much of himself he was in control of. The tests were complex, some of them were life-threatening, but Cratos didn't tell him that the snakes in that pit were fatally venomous until later that night. As Cratos explained how even one bite from one of the snakes would have ended his life in mere minutes, Arthur's jaw dropped. Arthur was surprised and angry for a few seconds but understood why Cratos didn't tell him. He thought he would overreact and fail his test before he had a chance even to try and pass through it. Cratos had many tests ahead of them planned for his student, but one was the most important lesson he would need to learn for his entire life.

"Self. Control," Cratos had told him one night.

"The entire Werewolf race Arthur. All of us, every single one. We must always be in control of our emotions and our state of mind. We go through so much hardship and training. We study to achieve greater understandings and venture on near-suicidal quests of self-discovery so that we may control the raging beast that lies within us all. You know of this beast well Arthur," he said. Cratos looked hard into his pupil's eyes.

"You felt that beast when you were about to strike your bully when you saw how scared he was and remembered how much he had hurt you. You heard the voice whispering in your ear, making you hit him." Arthur said nothing but nodded. Cratos nodded himself, poking the fire with a stick one night while telling his student much more.

"Many of us make mistakes in life, Arthur; no man's heart is without weakness, boy. You will know both great joys." His expression darkened as the embers flickered towards his face, his dark gaze illuminated.

"And great suffering. This world has too much suffering for one man's heart to bear. A human man, when given terrible pain, can die. He can grow sad, depressed, suicidal even. Most in my experience of this world grow angry." He looked straight into Arthur's eyes now, not blinking.

"Anger is what you must be afraid of, boy. Not the anger of other men, not even the god's wrath itself. The anger you must fear the most is your own. Because if you give in to the whispering voice of the beast and allow rage to consume your mind, you will lose your soul to horrific oblivion. Its urging voice will make you commit sins even the darkest depths of any nightmares could not conjure up." Arthur saw Cratos's face fall, breaking his eye contact and returning to the fire's glow once more. Nothing else was said that night, but Arthur always remembered the pain radiating from his mentor's eyes and wondered what painful dark skeletons lay in his past. Arthur hoped that perhaps, Cratos Mane would tell him one night.

Since that night with Cratos, Arthur learned everything he could from each test he was given. He endeavored to train as hard as possible, harden his Werewolf powers, and become a creature of unbreakable resolve. But Arthur also made sure not to lose his soul while fortifying his mind in these trials. Arthur did not want to lose who he was as a human as he became Arthur the Werewolf. He felt he had to make sure he kept passions alive within himself. That was why he made it a crucial decision to continue drawing. Sometimes he drew the forest around him, the different colored flowers and trees. He drew animals that had gone past him, memorizing what they looked like as he let his pencils work. He didn't have an endless supply of pencils as he continued to sharpen the tips. He hoped Cratos would let him get more if he ran out at some point. Other times he just drew whatever came to mind. He tried to draw a Werewolf once, like the ones he had seen in films growing up. He remembered what Cratos had looked like as he turned into one. Cratos had muscular arms with black fur. He was thickly muscled, but his arms were not the bulging giants he had initially thought they all were. He sketched what he first felt the Werewolves were, giant monstrous creatures with arms the size of tree bodies. He drew one howling at the moon from the top of a vast crooked hill hanging off the side of a cliff. Arthur drew the size of the moon to be immense. He tried to draw it as though the wolf's body was nearly a shadow in its glow. Arthur had stopped when he noticed Cratos was looking at his drawing from behind him. His mentor studied the sketched image for a few seconds and smirked.

"It's good work, very authentic," Cratos chuckled, walking away to let Arthur continue.

"If only the moon were that big, the Vampires would never set foot outside their homes again," Cratos continued as he moved on. Arthur frowned, watching him go for a moment. Not sure why he only questioned the size of the moon and not the Werewolf when the creature Cratos had turned into wasn't nearly as large.

Today Arthur had followed Cratos for a new test that his teacher was acting exceptionally mysterious about, more than he had done for any of the other ones. He would tell Arthur nothing about it and simply instructed Arthur to follow him. After a few hours of walking, the pair came upon a small bay where the ocean met with the land. They both then waited on this bay as Arthur saw a ship emerge as a dot from a distance and come closer to the pair of them. Arthur enjoyed the scent of salt in the air as he was near the ocean. The waves were splashing and coursing all around him, which was profoundly and oddly pleasing for his Werewolf ears to listen to. The ship was white-colored, but it looked ancient and weathered. Arthur couldn't help but wince as the ship's smell of the rotten sea entrenched itself within his nostrils. The boat had approached the bay, stopping dead at the edge of the land. It then turned to the side in the water in front of the two. Arthur and Cratos looked upwards and saw a small rope ladder thrown down the side for them both to climb. Cratos gestured at Arthur for him to climb up first, and he did so without question. Cratos followed quickly behind Arthur as they made their way up the ladder and onto this strange ship. Cratos had Arthur swing their bodies over the railing as they reached the top and stood upon the boat's floor. Arthur felt unbalanced for a moment as the waves rocked the ship. Arthur had never been on a ship before and the ground moving despite his feet being solid on flooring was a strange experience. Then, almost instantly, with no warning or even a hint of physical alteration, everything seemed suddenly normal to him. His balance had almost immediately synchronized perfectly with the boat, and he no longer felt any sense of disorientation. Arthur blinked a few times, bewildered. It felt as though an invisible hand had grabbed the boat in the water and held it in place for him.

Arthur chuckled as Cratos came aboard right behind him. Cratos turned to face his contact, and he nodded firmly at him. The man who stood at the ship's helm nodded back. He moved his arms and hands along the helm, steering the ship out from the bay, making it turn, and all three headed out into the vast water ahead of them. Cratos walked away from Arthur and approached his contact. The pair then began to exchange words as the ship bounced up and down on the waves. Arthur didn't attempt to eavesdrop as he knew Cratos would know if he was spying. Instead, he walked towards the back of the boat, his hand sliding along the somewhat rusty railing as he did so. He watched and looked out at the ground they had departed from and wondered where he was going next and what possible test could his teacher have in store for him that required him to leave the land itself.

While Cratos relaxed on the ship and took a short nap on top of an uncomfortable-looking pile of fishnets, Arthur couldn't help but move towards the ship's captain as he steered the ship. The waves were bumping the boat, but he kept his balance better than he thought he would have even out at sea. Stepping next to the man, Arthur looked him over. He seemed to be wearing leather boots with grey trousers and a long black overcoat that was tightly fastened and buttoned-up, covering nearly the rest of him. He had a trim blond beard with a bald head that gleamed slightly against the sunlight. His eyes were dark, focused with a bright blazing yellow color that seemed to look onward for a thousand miles. Arthur felt a potent, overwhelming aura from this man. It felt very similar to how he observed Cratos when they first met. If the man had noticed Arthur come up next to him, he made no sign of it. Arthur was nervous, but after weeks in the woods with Cratos, he was desperate to speak to another person.

"So, do you…sail often?" he asked sheepishly, as he then instantly tightened his lips, grossly embarrassed at the stupid question he just asked. A few seconds passed with silence, only the sound of the waves around them splashing in the air. Arthur was about to retreat and sit next to Cratos in humiliated shame before the man suddenly answered.

"Been sailing for over ten years now," he grunted, his voice deep and gruff. Again, silence filled the air as Arthur attempted to respond.

"Is it mainly, people like… 'us' that you ferry?" he asked nervously. The man smirked slightly, but he didn't take his eyes off the waves.

"'US?' you say. Whoever do you mean by that?" he asked Arthur, chuckling. Arthur didn't know how to answer. He knew he was also a Werewolf, so Arthur wasn't sure why he was asking. Arthur looked around, which he then felt idiotic for as they were at sea, and spoke lowly.

"Werewolves. Do you ferry us Werewolves around often?" he finally spat out and proceeded to observe the man for his response carefully. However, the ship's captain simply went from a smirk to a full chuckle, his previous intense aura beginning to weaken as he seemed more approachable now.

"You cubs love that word. It's like a secret code name for you all. For me, it's as common as a spoon," he laughed, rolling his eyes. Before Arthur could answer, the man continued.

"Yes, I only offer my services to our race. There's me, pilots, and certain cargo drivers. We get our people to wherever they need to go worldwide as fast as we can. It is a giant travel network. Pretty convenient, eh?" he mused. His smile began to drop as he returned to focusing on the waves, steering his ship's helm gently as he maneuvered through the tides. Arthur thought about the idea of different Werewolf contacts all over the world helping everyone else.

"How much longer until we get there?" Arthur finally asked. He didn't want to bother the man who looked like he needed to concentrate. He smirked again and nodded ahead of them.

"Not much further, lad. Grab a seat until we get there. I have a feeling it'll be your last good rest for a while," he replied before laughing darkly and letting the conversation between them fall entirely dead. Arthur nodded thanks to the man and went back to sit next to the napping Cratos. The Werewolf captain's words seemed oddly ominous to Arthur as he looked onward out to sea, fearing what possible test could be next for him.

After they arrived, they had to walk miles with Cratos saying nothing to Arthur, only for him to follow. They left the boat, and Cratos thanked the captain as they went forward, and the captain went back to sea. As they traveled deeper into the searing hot lands, the thought of what it was Arthur was meant to be learning today surged in his mind. The heat was powerful. Its intense rays were raining down through the gaps in the trees with ferocious intent to cook and boil all living things it achieved to touch. Despite the pair being shielded from most of the sun's rays, Arthur was incredibly bitter that given one of the many wonderful curses of having ginger hair, his skin was noticeably pale and burned exceptionally quickly. He always hated the other kids who enjoyed the sun at breaks and lunches during the summers. They would bathe in the sunshine while he was forced to cower in the shade. Even when he did walk out into the sun, his face would burn up quickly, stinging and peeling for weeks. But this heat was something worse, Arthur was becoming further dehydrated every five steps, but Cratos would only permit them to take a drink out of their bottles a few times as they walked. His lips were as dry as hot desert rock. Arthur felt his entire body soaking and stinking with sweat. He could barely breathe; each gasp of air he took in rattled its way through his body and slithered back out of him painfully. Cratos was no different. The tall man was boiling and walking sluggishly the same way Arthur was, primarily thanks to the black clothing Arthur mused. Whatever this next test was, Arthur assumed it must have been essential for Cratos to put himself through this suffering.

After several more miles, Cratos suddenly stopped dead. It was past midday, but Arthur wasn't hungry. More than anything else in the world, he was thirsty. Without saying anything, Cratos took his water bottle and began drinking heavily. Arthur then did the same, taking a few welcome gulps. The feeling of the cold clear liquid sailing down his throat was a relief he had always taken for granted. It felt like a smooth washing wave of joy filling his body. With only two gulps, he pulled the water away from his lips and began to put it away in his pocket. Cratos shook his head and grunted while he drank.

"Finish it all," he declared. Arthur frowned, confused. He guessed they must be near a stream they could refill their drinks. Smiling, he put his bottle back in his mouth and drank it greedily, savoring every bit of it. As the bottle drained, Arthur exhaled with relief, smiled up at Cratos, who had finished his, and smiled back.

"Time for your lesson," Cratos smiled, though not with his usual pleasant grin and instead with a dark evil smile aimed straight towards his pupil. Arthur's smile vanished as Cratos's grew larger across his face. He only smiled like that when he was about to set an unbelievably lousy test. Little did Arthur know that this test would be the first building block that would be the making of him.

Cratos waved his hands all around the area where they stood. It was a random plain of jungle no different than the miles they had already walked through already. Trees, bushes, and vines simply surrounded them, and many creatures surrounded them, including some very infuriating insects.

"A tiger rules this part of the jungle!" he declared loudly. Arthur's eyes widened with shock as he looked around himself at the trees and bushes surrounding him.

"A...a... a tiger!" Arthur exclaimed with only a laugh from Cratos in response.

"That's right Arthur! A giant orange, white with black stripes, tiger! A tiger that is extremely territorial and seeks to destroy ANY trespassers that set foot on its land. And I have had us walk straight in the middle of it." Arthur felt his heartbeat race like a small newborn rodent that was twenty thousand feet in the air.

"This is your test, Arthur. It has good things and bad things. One of the good things is it has no time limit," he announced, still smiling like a gleeful demon.

"One of the bad things is, YOU do," he continued circling Arthur in steps like he was revealing a grand plan.

"I had you drink the last of your water, and only I know where the next stream is to have a drink is. With how hot this jungle gets during the day, you will become dehydrated quickly. Your test is simple enough, Arthur. Using the skills and lessons you have learned so far, you will hunt down and kill this tiger. I will be watching you always, but you will never see me. Once the tiger is dead, I will give you plenty of drink and food. If you fail, however," he then wiggled a finger in front of Arthur's face.

"Then it's YOUR flesh that will be feasted upon. Understand?" Arthur looked at his mentor with an open jaw. Several weeks into his training, he was already being asked to confront and kill one of nature's deadliest predators. With a truly angry sigh, Arthur simply nodded.

"I understand," he replied begrudgingly. Cratos clapped his hands and grinned.

"Excellent. The clocks ticking Arthur, and the night will be cold, but you grow more hungry, thirstier, and worst of all, weaker every hour that passes. Remember Arthur, use the skills you have learned so far, and you will succeed. It is time to test yourself and prove you can take your place as part of the world's greatest predators. Good luck, Arthur Thorn!" With that last word, Cratos Mane saluted Arthur and dashed off into the jungle. He was gone in seconds, leaving Arthur in the deadliest part of the jungle. His mission was clear; he had to hunt a tiger with a tiger now hunting him at the same time.

CHAPTER NINE

Arthur remembered everything Cratos taught him about hunting. Cratos had explained to him while they hunted their food all the careful nuances there were for hunting. The largest meal they had taken down was a mother lynx cat which was still nothing compared to a Tiger. Arthur remembered seeing something else when they took the creature down. It had a sheer ferocity that made Arthur panic as he quickly dispatched the animal of its life. There was particular urgency within nature, a force that compelled every animal to give one hundred percent of its willpower to stay alive. Arthur knew that the tiger would be no different, and every inch of that cat bearing down upon him would be the challenge of his life.

Arthur tapped into his trained knowledge, the critical elements of hunting. One was to know your prey. Arthur would have to cover the ground in the jungle. He would need to locate places where it slept, where it ate, the signs of its patrol route, and know what creatures it preferred to eat over others. Only by understanding its wants can he predict its actions, and then he would plan a strategy. A second key to hunting was silence.

"One who can move without making a sound will always catch their prey off guard. You cannot hear what isn't there," he was told from Cratos when they first began hunting together. Arthur remembered when Cratos was hunting and the sound of his mentor's feet when he was running alongside Arthur. How nonexistent the sound was. When Arthur's foot hit the ground, you would hear the break of a twig, the crumble of a leaf, or even the thud of his foot hitting the solid earth. Cratos moved as though he was running on thin air, his steps not even heard by Arthur's ears with his Werewolf senses. The more they hunted together, though, the lighter Arthur's feet became.

As he ran, he was able to control the strength of his legs and how much pressure he would put through his legs when he stepped down on the ground. He gradually learned to be using not his whole foot but the ball of his feet only. However, as good as Arthur became, he was never as silent as his teacher. He still needed time to master that. The third key to hunting was patience. Arthur had learned that the other night when Cratos restricted him from eating the juicy cooked meat from the wild cat. But Arthur also knew you could not always hunt your prey. Sometimes, you had to let it come to you. You had to wait and see what would happen; be patient and gather your thoughts as things happened. Like playing chess when he was in school, Arthur remembered seeing other people stare at their board for minutes on end without making a move. He knew he needed to be calm and collected, allowing whatever he was hunting to make a mistake before he did. His mind had to be clear and focused because sometimes you needed to wait. Only his prey could tell him how long he would have to linger.

Arthur was already feeling his thirst reappear, and it returned with a cruel vengeance. It had only been a few hours since Cratos had left him, but Arthur knew he was probably still watching him and would not intervene if he was in trouble. However, Arthur knew that if Cratos's pupil acted like a helpless child, then he wasn't worth saving. It was late afternoon, and the heat of the jungle was beginning to lift into a merciless cold night. His mouth dried quickly, and his appetite now grew. Around this time, he and Cratos started hunting for food. The hunger in his stomach was always a nuisance, but now it was a warning. He had until he died of either starvation or dehydration to kill the tiger before Cratos would save him, and he was already not faring well with each need. The heat was making Arthur as sleepy as he was thirsty. After all the miles of walking, he wanted nothing better than to just curl up by a tree and rest. But he didn't have such luxury. He was in a race against his stomach, and sleep would take up many precious hours he needed to use hunting down his prey. He focused his mind and fought off his fatigue, ignoring his rumbling belly and drying throat. Arthur focused on his task before he died, and if he did, all his training would be for nothing.

As he progressed in investigating the tiger as he roamed through the jungle, Arthur noticed the tiger's tracks early and began following them. Arthur was taking note of any critical areas the tiger had passed. He could tell by how dense the tracks were in the mud and how long the tiger had remained in an area. Arthur had noticed the tiger had stayed in one spot for an exceptionally long time. Arthur couldn't tell if it had been resting there, but the area showed signs that it had been there for some time. There were no scents of it relieving itself or signs of consumption either. He committed the same sight to his memory and moved on. He had already memorized two areas. One was by a large distinct tree. It had its bark sticking out like spikes, and Arthur noticed minor fractures of the tiger's hair by its base.

Arthur gathered that the tiger must use this spot as a possible scratching post and would return here. He collected a few of the tiger's hairs, seeing by the color and texture whether they were freshly plucked or old and had naturally molted. Arthur could tell they were fresh. The smell of the tiger was also becoming more vibrant in the air as he tracked the beast. The scent of its kills and the blood was on its breath. The flesh stuck between its long sharp fangs and the stench of fear that its former prey had left upon its fur. The second was by a bush where the tiger had disposed of its waste. From what he knew about specific animals, they could sometimes be private about where they emptied their stomachs, meaning it was a high possibility that the tiger only did that in certain areas. It was a weaker area for him to take notice of, but he hadn't come across many, so he kept it to mind. Arthur proceeded with an artful calm and quiet in his movements with his advanced senses, knowing silence was a greater asset than distance. If Arthur wanted to be just like Cratos, it was better to be silent and far away than noisy and close. Arthur knew the creature would stop for the night where it claimed its den was, and he would find it eventually. Arthur then considered striking the beast dead in its sleep, but he wasn't sure if Cratos would approve. His teacher set no rules about how he was to go about killing his prey, but he knew his mentor wanted to see his student use the lessons he was taught and that he might consider Arthur cowardly for striking while the tiger slept. He would need to think about it further, see how desperate he became further down the line. He guessed from how fresh the tracks on the ground were that he wasn't far behind the tiger. He also noticed faded paw prints by the fresh ones meaning this tiger was methodical. The new tracks next to the old ones told Arthur that it probably always followed the same route within its territory. These marks meant the tiger was in control of this area without much disturbance. The tiger didn't have to deal with any challenges for its land and, hence, had become either lazy or overconfident. Arthur thought either would prove its undoing if he acted correctly.

Arthur felt oddly proud as he stalked the beast. His footsteps were becoming lighter, and his mind was focused on the creature's movements. From its paw prints in the dirt and the way, Arthur had used what Cratos taught him to come to conclusions about the animal. Cratos had told him that only he knew where the nearest water source was, but he assumed if he followed the beast enough, the creature must need to stop to drink itself. Arthur knew he just needed to become the ghost of this jungle, to be there but unseen and unheard. He thought about how he would attack it if he came across the animal. Tigers are not stupid, and therefore wouldn't fall for a simple trap.

If Arthur plans to use its route against the creature, then tampering with its areas would cause alarm and ruin everything. No pitfalls or traps could be made without the beast sensing something was up. He was a Werewolf and thus strong, but a full-grown hunting tiger was mighty as well. Plus, Arthur lacked the teeth and fangs of a tiger; at least for now, he did anyway. Speed was essential, he needed to dodge the cat's strikes, or his stomach would be ripped apart in seconds. He considered crafting a knife out of sharp rocks to use to stab it. It would work, but it would take time to sharpen correctly. He would get to know the beast more first before he knew what weapon he needed for victory.

More tracking continued, it had become nighttime now, and darkness loomed everywhere. All around Arthur was darkness accompanied by the large bulging shadows of trees and bushes everywhere he looked. Even with his improved vision, he was struggling to maneuver around this environment. He was focused on maintaining absolute silence which was an incredible struggle. Even with the jungle turning into an icy fortress of barren cold, he still sweated in the subtle effort exerted not to make any sound. Arthur also knew there were snakes around him, and despite his tests before where Cratos had assured him that they wouldn't bother or strike him unless he gave them a reason to, he remained cautious of attack from anything.

"They don't like the smell of Werewolves. They will avoid you eventually. Just stay away from nests," Cratos had instructed him before, but given he didn't know if he was about to step on a nest, Arthur was careful regardless. The jungle insects and the constant crunching leaves beneath his feet were his most significant sources of rage at this moment. The insects were trying to use him as their home and food source, and the leaves and rustling bushes gave away his position every five feet. He remembered when he first arrived in the forests and jungles. The threat of tiny venomous creatures attacking him and ending his life was an intense fear at first. But now he knew his Werewolf body repelled other animals; it was a significant relief and allowed him to focus more on the tasks at hand. So, Arthur knew not to be afraid of anything snapping at his ankles or falling onto his neck, killing him instantly. Arthur wondered what animals liked the Werewolf scent and which ones didn't. He assumed cats didn't like Werewolves, thinking it was because Arthur was now part canine, but Arthur would remember to ask Cratos more thoroughly what animals would be on his side if he survived. The squawking and noises of the jungle lessened at night than they did before. He felt as though he was within the bowels of some giant creature, running through the depths of endless shadows as he walked. Seeing the tiger's tracks now was impossible. He could barely see his own feet as he walked, so instead, Arthur focused on his sense of smell. He closed his eyes and focused firmly on his other senses, concentrating as hard as he could. For several moments, Arthur stood utterly still. He closed his eyes and slowly breathed a few times. Arthur let the noises around him drown out, so only the shadows of the night smothered his body, allowing his very being to be one with the night of the jungle itself. Then sharply, exceedingly sharply, he sniffed inward heavily, gathering the scents of all that was around him. His new wolf nose caught the scents of dozens of different creatures, flowers, and even the cold night itself. The tiger's scent was also among them. Arthur focused his nose as he continued to sniff, narrowing down on the scent of the tiger, trying to push all the other smells aside and out of his mind. Then he had it. His mind locked onto that smell as though the beast was in front of him. Keeping the scent within the depths of his nose, he snapped his eyes open and began moving in its direction. Arthur was now going wherever the tiger was; he now had a direct line towards it, an invisible rope connecting his nose to its body which he would not allow to be severed easily. Arthur made his way forward with a true hunter's glare in his eyes. Soon the two predators would decide who the true ruler of this jungle is.

Arthur felt this tiger had already proven its arrogance by its lack of inspecting its land for intruders. He hadn't even heard the beast roar yet. A petty part of Arthur felt insulted that the tiger knew he was there but considered him to be tiny prey and not worth its time. Arthur very much looked forward to proving the smug cat wrong. After further tracking through his senses, he finally came upon the creature's den. It had made its home by the mouth of a cave-like entrance at the bottom of a large stony hill formation. Arthur didn't know how deep the cave was, but for now, he felt that did not matter as he saw the creature itself. The tiger was huge. Its body was immensely long, nearly twice the length of Arthur himself with what looked like exceptionally long legs which he knew would be perfect for leaping upon its prey. It had traditional orange and white fur with black stripes along the top of its body. It lay there sleeping soundly, the smell of its previous prey still fresh on its mouth from when it breathed out. Arthur stood there gazing at the creature; he was no more than several meters away from it. He wondered how he should engage it. Arthur thought over what he had learned so far. He had two locked locations in his memory from his searching. One tree is used to groom itself and one section of bushes for its leavings. Arthur followed multiple tracks in the ground, learning that it followed the same route each day except when chasing prey, of course. Now he knew where it slept; his only missing location for the beast was its water source. He wanted to attack, but leaping upon a tiger with his bare hands and no other plan would get him killed very quickly, even if he were as silent as he could be. Even with his Werewolf strength, one fast lucky slice with a tiger's claw would be his death. Arthur knew he needed more strategy before attacking. Like with the meat on the fire, he needed to be patient at this moment especially and not leap out like a frantic animal. So, for now, he continued staring at the monster and thought long and hard about his plan of attack. One wrong move and Arthur knew his life as a Werewolf would come to a quick and bloody end.

Arthur lay within the depths of large bushes, watching the creature sleep. He had no idea how much time had passed, but the darkness of nighttime was in full effect. Arthur didn't want to sleep. He felt that would make him vulnerable. Plus, there was nowhere safe for him to lower his guard. Arthur felt like the entire area was a danger zone until that tiger was dead. But regardless of his sensible paranoia, his body, however, tolerated none of his excuses. Sleep was knocking harshly at his conscious door, and he felt his eyelids grow heavier by the second. Arthur then thought of a tree he had walked past earlier. He remembered it was far out of the tiger's patrol route. To be safe, Arthur figured he would need to find some way to strap himself to a high branch to sleep. He then began to doze as he thought; his sight was going fuzzy. As he stared, the sleeping tiger was nearly doubling in his view, returning to normal and then doubling again. Arthur quickly realized that if he didn't find somewhere safe to rest soon, he would wake up to smell the wild fur of the beast wrapping its fangs across his face before it crunched him into his death. Arthur shook his head and retreated away from the sleeping tiger, memorizing where its den was. Arthur quietly walked at least a mile away from the tiger's home, finding one immensely tall tree with many branches. He needed to rest, or he would be fighting a tiger half-asleep, resulting in his certain death.

It was child's play to climb the tree branches. Arthur smiled confidently as he leaped from branch to branch, making his way up the tree using the extent of his Werewolf legs. He quickly rose upwards and finally landed on a larger trunk high up. Arthur then looked down at the ground and saw he was higher up than he thought. At first, Arthur felt a surge of panic spike up across the surface of his skin, his heart rate jumping and his brain screaming at the rest of his entire system to completely freeze up and turn his body to stone so that he wouldn't fall. However, Arthur, after all his training with Cratos, didn't panic. He remained still and calm. He observed his skin and steadied his body, and then he began to control his breathing. After a few heavy deep breaths, his breathing returned to normal, and his heart was regular. He looked back down at the ground and felt no fear. He looked back up and got to his feet. He was standing on a branch that was certainly wide enough for his body. His feet stood firmly on the trunk as though it was nearly a flat surface. The branches that stretched out from the end spread into enough foliage to hide a mammoth within its thickets. The trunk Arthur stood upon was wide enough for him to walk on casually, but he knew he would fall to his death if he rolled around in his sleep. Arthur spotted long vines wrapped across the tree, stretching far up and down its entire body, almost looking like veins on the surface of the body. Arthur looked at them curiously; they seemed like thousands of green snakes working together to slowly constrict a giant monster to death. He grabbed two of them and began to pull. The vines stretched like elastic and then sharply snapped away from the body of the tree. Arthur's muscles strained, and he continued to pull; they had stopped pulling off the tree and remained still in the air. Arthur's veins were pushing hard up against the skin of his forearm. After a few more seconds of pulling and straining, he felt his arm muscles begin to ache, and Arthur began to lose his strength. Arthur was starving and dehydrated, so these tree vines were beating him.

A cool breeze then passed by Arthur's face with a gentle, sweet caress. The night air went utterly still in his head. Arthur's pupils shrank into tiny dots; then, his body began shaking with surging energy. He clenched his teeth with enough force to bite through a diamond. His biceps bulged fiercely. Its mass was slowly expanding to nearly twice its original size. His grip tightened, and his shaking arms began to rip harder at the vines. Arthur's throat began to emit a low, deep growl like an old car engine struggling to run. The vines weakened within his grip from the tree's base, its layers snapping by its fibers one strand at a time. Arthur pulled harder, taking a step back in his state. He could no longer see out of his eyes; there was only the intensity of this moment in his mind. Arthur let loose a single, immense, bestial roar that echoed through the jungle's trees down to the bottom of their roots. With that monstrous heave, the vines snapped free, and Arthur flew backward on the branch. He lay there breathing heavily; his deep breaths exploded out in the air away from him. Arthur then turned onto his side and tried to get to his feet, his head was dizzy from the moment and adrenalin was still ablaze in his blood. He was gasping as he snapped back onto the middle footing, his body heaving up and down. He shook his head and gazed down at his arms. His veins were looking as though they were about to burst through his arm and attack him. His hands were viciously clenching the long strips of the vine in each palm, unable to release. Arthur began inspecting his body franticly. He was trying to figure out what had come over him. He couldn't explain why he suddenly went berserk like that. He was suddenly overcome with an intense sense of power and mind-erasing instinct. Arthur felt as though he wanted to not only rip off the vine but uproot the entire tree itself with one giant heave. What else Arthur had noticed was that he had no way of controlling it as the surge took over. It felt as though something just possessed him before he had time even to blink. Arthur felt more powerful than he had ever been in his life despite all his training, but he still felt shaken from that one instant. He was unable to stop whatever that mad rush of power was that took control of his body. Arthur simply sighed; he was far too tired, dehydrated, and starving to worry about this now. He had the vines he needed, and Arthur knew he had to rest. He was feeling woozier than before, and he knew if he didn't sleep soon, he would collapse. He lifted himself and began to swing the vines around himself. He tightened the vines around his waist with a firm knot and swung both ends around the tree branch he was lying on several times, then knotted the loose ends to his body again tightly. He lay back on the tree branch and firmly made sure he was stuck to the tree with the vines like he was the tree bark itself. He was overcome with whatever it was that sparked such an unexpected rush to obtain the vines. Unable to think of an answer to satisfy him, he quickly drifted into sleep. Arthur promptly fell into a deep sleep within moments. The clouds in the sky returned to cover the jungle, removing the moon's light from Arthur's face for the rest of the night.

Arthur was awoken early the following morning from the sound of a pounding roar bellowing through every inch of the jungle. The echo bellowed up to the heights of every tree and down to the deep catacombs of every cave. Arthur attempted to jump up in shock, only to be slung back down, letting out a high-pitched yelp as he hit his head against the tree trunk. He groaned with pain as he arched his neck over to look down as best as he could. The vines had worked perfectly and kept him firm against the tree branch while he slept. He wriggled his body with the tiniest bit of slack he had within vines to look over the edge. The tiger wasn't directly below him, luckily. His thirst was more present as his mind focused. His tongue was dry and thick in his mouth. His throat was parched, and it felt like sandpaper as he attempted to swallow even a tiny amount of saliva. He then noticed how hot he was. The sun was beginning to cook the jungle, ready for the day with intense heat. Arthur thought the temperature was blazing everything the light touched, which as he lay on the tree trunk, was himself included. In the distance, he could see the very lines of heat in the air. Arthur cut his fingernails against the vines holding him, snapping them loose with mere scratches and setting him free. He stood upon the branch and looked down at the ground; he needed to figure out where that roar came from. Arthur couldn't allow the tables to be turned on him. If the tiger was now hunting him, he had to meet its challenge straight back. He threw himself on the body of the tree and began to slide down to the bottom. Arthur knew that today, he would have his final confrontation with his prey.

The tiger was moving in an unstoppable rush, striding through the jungle like a madly possessed entity. All its previous patterns had now vanished. It was searching hard, and the thick scent of Arthur plagued its nose. The creature was snarling, growling, roaring randomly in a near-crazed state. Its warpath was unchallenged by anything as the behemoth roamed its territory. The ground thundered beneath its feet, claws visible and ripe for slicing. Arthur's stench never weakened, and the tiger was more than ready to rip its intruders to pieces the second it got the chance. Arthur wanted to deal with the tiger chasing him straight away, but his thirst was wearing him down hard and fast.

Arthur knew his need for water would only worsen as the day went on and the sun became more potent in the sky. He climbed down from the tree and quickly reached the ground in near seconds. He tried to run, but Arthur stopped his pace only after a few meters. He was out of breath, and his mouth felt like it was as rough as the bark on the tree. Arthur knew he needed something more than his bare hands in his condition. He looked around and saw there were several rocks by his feet. With no other options, he quickly knelt and spent the next few moments hastily sharpening several slate stones into the shapes of blades. He knew he had only a few seconds to do this because the tiger would soon be upon him, but Arthur knew if he faced the beast unarmed, he would be at an even worse disadvantage. Cratos had shown him how to create makeshift weapons in challenging situations, so he quickly carved them for practical use. He was making them sharp enough to cut with handles to grip without letting them break apart at the same time. He knew he needed them to have thick handles to grasp, and for the other end, to have thin and sharp points to lance the tiger. He used one larger stone with an edge to sharpen all the rest. As he quickly came to a satisfying finish, he heard another roar from the tiger that sounded a lot closer to him than he wanted. He knew he had to begin moving now. His thirst felt nearly like strangulation at this point, but he was out of options. Arthur moved although he was starving and dangerously dehydrated. Currently, it was either do or die. He now ran as best as his body would allow through the jungle with only four makeshift daggers. He held them to his body through holds made in the waist of his trousers to slot in. They wouldn't do well hitting against something for too long. Arthur figured that one would break after maybe five hits max, and he would need to switch it out with another. He knew he wouldn't last long slashing with them. Arthur planned to use them to pierce straight into the tiger's body and, hopefully, its organs. Arthur had also kept hold of an exceedingly long piece of tree vine he had ripped from the tree's hull. He grabbed as much as he could quickly before wrapping it around his body from his right shoulder across his torso like a sash. It was a tiny bit of armor, but Arthur knew he had to have some form of protection against the unstoppable visceral slashes from the tiger so his organs wouldn't instantly spill out. He was now running through the jungle himself to keep the beast chasing him until he found the best place to engage it.

Arthur knew predators enjoyed the chase more than striking the prey itself sometimes. He knew about the rush of adrenalin as it grew closer and closer with every passing second and how they would smell the scent of the fear flying back, hitting the predator in the face and enticing its appetite even more with the seductive promise of easy prey. Arthur wanted the tiger to become drunk, enthralled by his intent to kill. It was a roll of the dice and a dangerous one, but Arthur had run out of time and needed every minute he could milk to think of a more legitimate fighting strategy. But it seemed luck was against him today, given his bodily needs was weighing down on him like thick chains. He came out of a large thicket of bushes only to come to a grinding halt. He ran forward a few paces and ran his hand over the tall rocky stone wall surrounding his area. His eyes were bewildered; he looked left and then right. The wall was nearly three times his height without even a dent in the work. It must have been old given how shaky it looked, and it ran far in both directions. He had hit a dead end. A fierce roar bellowed from behind him as the tiger leaped from the thickets of the bushes and came into full imposing view of Arthur. Arthur turned around and thudded his back against the stone wall, looking straight at the tiger, which was now licking its lips as it locked eyes with Arthur.

Over nine thousand thoughts were rushing through Arthur's mind. He came up with a different solution every millisecond, but each was just as stupid and suicidal as the last. He went through his options carefully in his mind as the tiger walked side to side, carefully looking at Arthur and sizing up its meal. Arthur thought the tiger was waiting for its prey to make the first move. He thought of his options. Run? The only direction he would go would be left or right, and either one he chose would give him no more than three seconds before the tiger leaped on his back, and it would be over. Climb? He hadn't tested out the full strength of his Werewolf nails yet, nor did he know how old the wall would be. It could have been here for decades or only a handful of years, so the odds weren't great on success there. There was much erosion in the stone, but he wasn't sure he wanted to roll the dice. Even if his nails worked, the second he turned his back on that tiger, it would leap, and if even one of its claws touched him, he was dead. Fight? That seemed to be the only option left. Arthur breathed in heavily. He still had his carved stone knives across his waist, and despite his thirst and hunger, he would try to use his muscles to the best of their ability. Not allowing the tiger to leave his line of sight, Arthur flexed his arms and legs, tensing his muscles. He crouched down slightly, lifting his heels. Arthur then slightly bent his knees and held his arms behind his back, both hands gripping the handles of two of his stone knives and very slowly bringing them out in front of him. The tiger ceased its walk and straightened up its shoulders as he did that, making itself appear larger. The beast growled deeply from the back of its throat as it stared at Arthur, as though warning Arthur to stay still and die without a fuss. Arthur narrowed his gaze with a trained sense of determination. He didn't plan to die anywhere without giving out a few mortal blows himself, and this tiger was no exception. He held his knives in front of his body, and the tiger let out one giant roar. Arthur felt his eardrums sting as its bellow went through his entire body like a ghost. Arthur acted on something deep and foreboding from within himself. A new instinct he had from being a Werewolf. His eyes focused angrily, and Arthur stuck his head forward and summoned a roar of his own. He screamed a howling storm towards the tiger and leaped forward with both his stone daggers raised. The tiger met his jump and lept itself in retaliation. The pair soared through the air at each other. This battle would decide who the true predator of this jungle was, the wolf or the tiger.

CHAPTER TEN

The two clashed mid-air as the tigers' claws met firmly over the sharp edges of Arthurs' stone blades he was holding in front of him. There was a scraping noise that raced through Arthur's ears as the pair hit the ground sharply. Arthur landed on his feet, the tiger on its hind legs with the top part of its body held up from Arthur's knives causing Arthur to feel the full force of its heavy body. The tiger roared and threw its head forward to bite off Arthur's whole face. If Arthur had reacted a millisecond later, he would have died. He immediately let go of his knives and ducked down. The tiger's body lunged forward as he did. It then jerked its torso so it could follow Arthur and pressed on with all the power in his legs. Arthur clenched his fist, and without hesitating, he twisted his body and uppercut punched the tiger harshly, striking the beast from the bottom of its jaw. The tiger took the strike and snarled in pain as it was knocked a few spaces back. Arthur jumped back several feet to gain some distance in case the tiger lunged. He immediately replaced his dropped knives with his last pair from his waist slots. Once they were gone, that would be it. The tiger shook its head a few times from the strike and whined softly, followed by rage, which quickly overtook its pain. The tiger roared once again; its eyes became a narrowed pincer upon Arthurs' being. Arthur was breathing heavily with exhaustion. When they met, and he felt the weight of the tiger's body against him, it took nearly all his strength to land that blow, and it only threw the tiger's balance off a bit. Luckily, adrenalin quickly overtook his fatigue, and he rapidly began to shake with anticipation. Arthur scowled at the tiger with pure hatred. His spike in adrenaline had pushed him past simple reactions and had made him fully embrace the intent to kill. Arthur had all new energy bursting through his veins. The tiger pounced forward at Arthur, ready to finish him off.

Reacting on his instinct alone with his reflexes at their current height, Arthur dodged the tiger's pounce with a simple twist of his body, not even moving his feet. He then jerked to the side at a close, right-angle shape. The tiger's claws flexed into the ground beneath its feet acting eager and agitated, ready to dig into Arthur's flesh. The tiger's eyes were fixated on Arthur's chest, licking its lips. With a mountainous heave, the tiger jumped at him with both its claws slashing wildly. Arthur then leaped himself, but as the two came close again, like the first time they had clashed, Arthur sharply and suddenly twisted his body to the side in mid-air. Then as the beast passed his body in the air as the two crossed, down came Arthur's right arm, plunging the dagger in that hand straight into the side of the tiger's body. The tiger shrieked with surprise and pain. Yelping sharply, it slammed harshly onto the ground below. Still recognizing Arthur as an immediate threat, the tiger regained its stance after only a few moments, refacing Arthur again as it rose shakily back onto its legs. Arthur eyed his target carefully, looking over its wound. Blood was seeping strongly from the edge around the knife, flowing down and onto the ground by its feet. The tiger's body was shaking, and it trained a demonic glare upon Arthur coupled with rapidly growing desperation. Arthur saw the tiger's body prepare for another attack, and he once again lowered his body and readied himself for the tiger to attack, remembering a wounded animal could be even more deadly than a healthy one.

The tiger was seriously wounded, and supposedly, Arthur now had the advantage. He thought that maybe if he dragged the fight out, perhaps the creature would bleed to death. But even with the tiger's strength slowly fading from its wound, Arthur was struggling to maintain his previous vigor at this moment. No scratch was on him so far, but the strain from fighting the beast had just dehydrated him further. Adrenalin was now the only thing left powering his body. He wasn't sure whether he now had the time to try and outlast the tiger. He was worried his body might give out without warning and that he might drop unconscious. Each breath he took sounded like an old gust of wind blowing through a haunted house, dragging against his lungs as though fishhooks were pulling them up through his mouth. He was in trouble, and he knew he needed to attack before he couldn't raise his limbs anymore. The stone knife was impaled deep, and the tiger limped as it walked slightly. Every few seconds, it winced with clear anguish. Arthur kept count of each time it winced; it was precisely like clockwork. Arthur stepped in towards the tiger slowly, a small toe at a time. The tiger growled as he did, its claws reappearing from its paws in a warning gesture. He was a few feet from the beast, nearly within swiping distance from its claws. He needed to take a gamble here, so he decided to roll the dice. The tiger roared, then mid-way through its shout, it winced again. That was Arthur's chance. It whined in pain as he leaped forward, shooting his final stone knife forward like a charged lance, aimed straight at the tiger's forehead. This attack was one suicidal plunge toward a quick death.

Fate, however, had a rather irritating way of suddenly hating Arthur Thorn. The tigers' wincing didn't make a lick of difference with the creatures' defensive reflexes. Without even its eyes open, the tiger swatted aside Arthur's knife like it was a bothersome fly. Then with its other paw, the tiger swept its limb across and sliced clean down Arthur's chest with four long, razor-sharp claws. At that moment, it was as though time had completely gone still for him. Arthur's eyes shook with disbelief. The whole world went black and white as blood sprayed from the bloody trenches that were now embedded in his chest. The sliced flesh of his chest muscle was torn like soft butter. His blood flowed freely on the ground, puddles quickly turning into pools by his feet. Arthur stumbled backward a few steps with unbelieved trauma, as though his brain had not yet realized what happened to him and his body was too busy bleeding out to inform his senses.

Arthurs' eyes wandered to the tiger that had moved a space backward to resume wincing from its wound. It now felt comfortable to deal with its pain as Arthur was now out of a threatening range. Arthur wasn't even sure the beast knew what it had just done correctly, that perhaps it had just slashed out at random and struck gold. Suddenly Arthurs' breathing problem had turned into mist before his eyes. Even though the wounds hadn't even begun to hurt yet, he was still in shock. Arthur's head slowly looked down at his wounds. They were long and deep. The tiger's eyes opened and gazed upon the deeply injured prey before it. The smell of blood was thick in its nostrils, causing its pupils to expand. Veins strengthened within the whites of the tigers' eyes as the sweet scent of blood caressed their senses. Arthur's body was shaking more, twitching, and he was beginning to struggle to keep himself composed with his injury. His eyes began to fade completely white; his teeth slowly began to grow longer. A few of his teeth were sharpening in his mouth. The nails of his fingers were growing longer, growing pointed. The tiger sensed something different with Arthur and acted quickly. With another roar, it leaped forward for the final kill, its jaw wide open to sink its teeth straight into Arthur and finish him off.

This change felt similar to last night when Arthur struggled with the vines, but it wasn't as strong within him. There was no immense surge of strength. His arms remained the same size, and he was still completely conscious of himself. It was something deeper that had broken free of its chains deep within him. It was a primal instinct that refused to die. As the tiger came within arm's length, Arthur shot out both his arms, slashing aside both tigers' paws to its sides. With speed unseen by the tiger as its arms fell down and still in the air from its lunge. Arthur then threw his hands straight at the tiger's jaw, gripping the top and lower with his bare hands. The two hit the ground struggling, the tigers' fangs jammed deep in the palms of Arthur's hands, going through the top of his hand clean. Blood exploded from his hands, but his arms held firm. The tiger tried to thrash and twist its head free, but Arthur drove his nails within the face of the tiger. Arthur began screaming manically like a flaming monster. The whites of his own eyes were straining with thick red veins as Arthur remained solid. The tiger felt the unnatural strength upon its skull and began screeching down Arthur's face, panicking fiercely for its life. The tiger brought its arms back up and gripped Arthur's back. Its long claws sank into his flesh deep and hooked in solid as though they were butcher's meat hooks buried deep into the bottom of his back muscles. Arthur only roared louder, his strength increasing. He began to stand taller, raising himself as though his body moved without strain, forcing the tiger onto its hind legs. The tiger started to drag its claws down through his back; if its claws cut down enough, just like the strike Arthur received across his chest, then he was dead. Arthur threw his head to the sky and roared once again in an uninterrupted bellow. It was a shout that ordinary people would think could summon thunder from the skies. It was the howl of a Werewolf. Arthur snapped both his hands aside left and then right, snapping the tiger's jaw apart and its neck in one final powerful blast of his strength. The tiger shuddered in his arms and went still almost immediately, dead. A few moments passed, maybe even minutes. Arthur's eyes returned to normal. As though by magic, his strength evaporated from his body, and he fell to the floor with the dead tiger still in his arms. Suddenly he felt drowsy, and his eyelids went heavy. He couldn't fight it off. He still felt blood rushing out of his chest and down his back, especially with the tiger's claws falling out of them, allowing every hole to bleed freely. Arthur fell asleep with his kill now growing cold in his arms. Arthur had won, and now he began to grow unconscious even though he knew falling asleep meant bleeding to death in the jungle. To Arthur, it seemed his title of king of the jungle, will be short-lived.

Arthur awoke to the sound of soft clapping. His head was a throbbing mess, and every muscle in his body ached, screaming at him in blind fury. He tried to move, but an explosive burning sting from his back and chest sent him dead still as a corpse on the small bedding he had been placed within. He winced for a few seconds until the pain went, and then he opened his eyes and arched his head up to see a long grey blanket covering him. It was nighttime now, and he was close to a campfire to be kept warm. He looked over the area around him. It wasn't the jungle area he fought the tiger in. He had been taken to some different place. The noise of the wilds was close to him. He seemed to be resting at the mouth of a small cave, the forestry outside. He felt it didn't matter where he exactly was anyway, he couldn't move a muscle, and his head was pounding.

"The champion awakes!" said the voice of Cratos Mane after the clapping stopped. Arthur turned his head to see his mentor cross-legged a few feet away from Arthur, watching over him with a proud smile.

"How are you feeling, champ?" he asked pleasantly. Arthur coughed violently and swore up into the sky from the pain.

"That good, eh?" his mentor chuckled.

"I was worried there for a second. I thought that tiger had you; new Werewolf cubs cannot usually tap into the Wolf form part of themselves until their first stage starts. Without it, you would have died," his teacher noted casually. Arthur frowned for a second, confused. Then he remembered. After the tiger slashed the front of his body open, Arthur lost his temperance and broke the tiger's jaw and neck. His mind also drifted to when he went wild in the tree's vines, which he knew felt different.

"But the vines?" Arthur muttered in a muddle strained croak out loud. Cratos coughed uncomfortably.

"That was different and will be explained very soon. For now, rest. You have been unconscious for nearly a full day." Arthur was breathing fine now. He also couldn't feel his former thirst or even hunger. Arthur guessed that Cratos must have fed him and given him water while he rested. He remembered his wounds and how fatal they truly were. He wondered how he didn't bleed to death.

"How am I alive?" he asked Cratos with genuine awe.

"I said before that Werewolves heal quickly. As long as you didn't have any organs ripped out of you, flesh wounds especially heal in no time. At an even faster rate especially given what time of the month it is." Arthur rolled his eyes, thinking that was some sort of gender joke, but he saw his mentor's eyes were deadly serious.

"What do you mean?" Arthur asked him. Cratos nodded up to the sky, his expression now deadly serious, as though gazing upon an incoming enemy itself.

"When the clouds clear, either tonight or tomorrow night, you'll know then. For now, rest, your wounds are still healing, and you should be fine for tomorrow. Then you can complete your next test." Arthur wanted to ask what he meant but knew from experience he wouldn't tell him, so he instead closed his eyes and continued to rest for the night, thankful to at least be alive.

When Arthur awoke again, his headache was gone, and he could sit up from his blanket without wincing from the pain this time. He looked down at his chest and saw thick lines that resembled scars from the tiger attacks. At first, Arthur grinned; he liked the look of the scars on his body and looked forward to telling the tale behind them to other Werewolves. But that excitement was quickly squashed when he remembered that Cratos said only scars from Vampires remained. His face went glum, and he then stood up and stretched, enjoying the morning sun hitting his face. He felt as proud as a peacock from his victory. He had tracked the tiger well and fought it on its terms out in the open. He didn't need to make any traps or use dirty tricks. He felt proud of himself for how he fought.

"Careful," Arthur heard Cratos purr from behind him.

"If you don't keep an eye on your head swelling, I'll deflate it for you," Cratos warned intently. Arthur lessened the wide grin on his face and chuckled.

"Same to you, mate," he answered back, only for his mentor to then laugh.

"You're gaining a sense of humor. Good. Don't lose it," his teacher cheered. Arthur turned around and smiled at his mentor, then spread his arms like a displaying showman.

"So, then, my illustrious mentor, how did your number one pupil do on his test?" Cratos raised an amused eyebrow which quickly turned into a stern look.

"I'll let you have that one but don't push it," he started, then his face turned warm and genuinely proud.

"You did great Arthur! You exceeded my expectations by miles. You trailed the tiger and fought it amazingly. Many new cubs have failed this test, and I am proud you did it!" Arthur beamed back at his mentor, caught himself, and forced himself into a modest smile, bowing his head slightly.

"Thank you, my teacher," he answered back, putting on an overly formal voice.

"That's better," Cratos returned, humor in his voice. Arthur saw his clothes by the blanket and padding, unsure of where Cratos acquired them and saw how torn to shreds they were.

"Your backpack with your spare clothes is here. Quickly change. We have a place to go too." Cratos threw the pack by Arthur's feet, and he began to put fresh clothes on.

"Where are we going?" he asked calmly, dressing in clothes near precisely like his previous lost ones.

"To the tigers' cave," Cratos answered simply.

"Why?" Arthur asked, and Cratos replied without looking back as he tied the laces of his boots.

"We are going for you to learn a lesson about both accountability as well as responsibility," he answered ominously. Arthur frowned at the cryptic response. He stood up tall and walked after his mentor, unsure of what could be in that tiger's cave for him to see.

It turned out that Cratos hadn't taken Arthur that far away from the jungle area he had fought the tiger in. Arthur had healed well, but his legs protested the movement strongly as he attempted to walk. Arthur grunted at the pain as they went forward. Cratos promised it was only a few miles walk. Arthur was still feeling the bravado of his victory going through his head; he felt the courage to finally try and pry some information on the Werewolves out of his mentor, feeling he had finally earned some answers.

"Cratos?" Arthur began, eyeing his teacher carefully as he attempted to pick his mentor's brain.

"Hmmm?" his mentor responded casually, unaware of Arthur's curious intent.

"Explain more about this wolf thing I tapped into when I defeated the tiger. I need to know." Cratos was silent for a few seconds before hesitantly answering.

"Things like these are hard to explain fully, at least at first. I do not enjoy hiding things from you, Arthur. If I explained one thing, I would have to explain several more and then several more for each of those several things. Therefore, until you come to experience these things one step at a time, it can just be a confusing spider web of tips and hints." Arthur sighed, annoyed and exhausted. He understood what his mentor was saying but still didn't enjoy it. Even though he had just taken down a tiger, he felt he was still being treated like a child.

"But," Cratos added, sensing his students' disappointment and not wishing to rob his student of his post-victory pride.

"There is one thing I can say. There is a reason the training process has been this many weeks so far, as well as why you had that specific test just now," Cratos finished.

"Go on," Arthur replied. Cratos had now severely piqued his curiosity.

"It didn't appear full yesterday, but I know it will tonight. This night of the month is when the moon will be at its strongest and full." Cratos went silent for a few moments to let that sink in with Arthur as they continued walking. Arthur knew a little of Werewolf mythology and how the people only changed into the beast at a full moon. But he had thought, given he saw Cratos change at will, that it didn't matter.

"What will happen when the moon comes out," he asked, suddenly nervous. Cratos sighed; his facial features twisted left and right from Arthur's view. It looked as though he was struggling to find one straight answer in a sea of answers.

"You will enter the first stage of your Werewolf transformation, and the tiger was only a test to see if you are ready for it. For you will face something a lot more deadly than the tiger." Cratos's words began to dig deep into the depths of Arthur's stomach, scaring him a tiny bit.

"What's that?" Arthur asked hesitantly. Cratos stopped walking, turned around sharply, and stared deep into his pupil's eyes.

"You will meet with the beast that lies dormant inside you, and you will have to fight against it. Our kind isn't given automatic control of ourselves when we turn into our wolf forms; it has to be won."

"What happens if I lose?" Arthur asked, and Cratos sighed, a pained exhale.

"The beast will take control of your conscious. It will completely inherit your mind and reign control of your entire body. It will then go on a rampage of death, and you will have to either be put down or spend the rest of your life as a raging, uncontrollable beast in chains." The pair was nearly upon the tigers' cave as that notion swam around inside Arthurs' head. Arthur had thought the tiger was the battle that would make him a true Werewolf; it seemed that the big cat was just the appetizer. Tonight, he would have to battle another savage beast, only this time; the stakes were a lot higher.

They then came upon the cave entrance where Arthur had tracked the tiger the previous night. It was no different than the last time he was here, although the last time he saw it, bushes had covered him, and now he and his mentor stood at the mouth of the cave entrance. Arthur broke the silence after a few seconds.

"So then, what are we doing here? I can't see much accountability here. Just rocks and a cave." Arthur couldn't see inside the cave, which meant it must have run far and deep inside. The light of the day shined around most of it, but the further in he looked, darkness swept around, and his vision was silenced. Cratos sighed.

"Don't overreact at first, but you must understand," he said. Arthur was going to ask what that meant, but before he could, Cratos whistled sharply. The whistle echoed down the cave. At first, nothing happened, the noise of the whistle vanished, and silence once again took the area around the pair. Arthur rolled his eyes; whatever Cratos was here for wasn't here. Arthur began to ask Cratos if they could leave when he was suddenly cut off again by a sound, but this time it wasn't from his mentor. Within the shadows of the cave, three small figures emerged from the darkness. They were mewing and whining softly. The three figures came to the cave's mouth to meet the pair, and the light touched them. Arthur's breath caught in his throat, his eyes widened, and his heart skipped several beats as he gazed upon three tiny, orange-colored tigers with black stripes and white patches staring up at him with curious eyes. Arthur stared back at them, and tears formed in his eyes. The tiger he had killed had been a mother to these three tiger cubs before him, who he had just made into orphans.

The three small tiger cubs whined and growled softly at the strangers, not sure how to react to them. Arthur remained still as he stared at the now motherless creatures, all alone in the world now because of him. He wanted to cry, to fall to his knees and sob at their presence begging forgiveness, but he was still too overcome to breathe normally. Cratos nodded somberly.

"This is what being a Werewolf can result in, Arthur. Look carefully at them," he said mournfully. However, Arthur didn't need to be told; his eyes were switching from one to the other. All three looked up to him as though expecting something. He wasn't even sure if they knew that their mother was dead. The three cubs purred slightly and walked up to Arthur, sniffing around his legs and such. He wondered why at first, but then he realized;

they probably smelt their mother's scent on his body still. That nearly pushed Arthur over the edge, the three cubs nuzzling against him like happy cats.

"Every action in this world, Arthur, has an equal reaction. To Werewolves, this belief is an absolute," Cratos said, beginning to speak as Arthur slipped slowly into total despair.

"That is why Werewolves train to their limits and beyond. It is why we learn to control our anger and emotions. Because apart from Vampires, we are the most capable creatures on the planet and those with capability have responsibility. For every action, there is accountability for its consequence." Arthur fell to his knees, and he looked deep into the small cub's faces, reaching out and gently touching their fur. Each one of them welcomed the touch.

"Every time you kill, it affects more lives than just the one you ended. Every action creates either a solution or problems for others. This consequence is something you must always be aware of, Arthur. In the human world, you can be a hero or a tyrant, and the latter is the easiest for you to succumb to. The lesson, Arthur, is to know that there will always be consequences for more lives than just yourself." Arthur turned his head away from the cubs and looked down, ashamed. He felt like a monster, a horrible piece of living trash. Now without a mother to take care of them, the little tigers would starve and die, alone in the darkness of their cave, whining for the comfort and love of a mother they will never see again because of him.

Cratos bent down and gripped Arthur's shoulder gently; his pupil looked up at the black-haired man with his eyes full of tears, ready to burst forth. Cratos pulled Arthur into his arms and held him against his chest, buried in his clothing. Arthur's body shook for a moment before he finally let go and cried. Tears streamed from Arthur's eyes as he wailed and moaned into Cratos like a newborn child. Not only did salty water sail from his eyes, but also a mountain of grief was thrust upon Arthurs' entire being within seconds of looking at the orphaned cubs. Cratos held Arthur tight against him, hugging his grieving friend and patting his back as the boy cried his heart out. Cratos was shushing gently, saying soft words of comfort.

"It's OK. It's OK, Arthur. Let it out. You must grieve," Cratos voiced gently. Arthur remembered how he felt when he slapped Gary and how horrible he felt afterward. He had been genuinely guilty about bullying the boy back. Arthur realized that his actions did not just affect Gary. If he had used too much strength and killed him, his parents would probably have cried their eyes out. Even Gary's friends, scum as they were, would also be saddened and grieve at his death, and they all would go on through their life then without him. Arthur understood that his actions affected more people than he thought. Arthur breathed in heavily and knew he would remember that the responsibility of using his Werewolf powers made him accountable for any pain he caused, intentional or accidental. Arthur stopped crying and lifted his head from Cratos's chest. Cratos stared at Arthur's face and saw the lesson had dug deep into his student's very bones. He smiled proudly at Arthur.

"Now the lesson is learned, I will share some information with you. You have earned it." Cratos then gestured his arm towards something. Somehow a slither of hope flourished within the guilt running through his body like a potent poison. He looked intensely at his mentor, who nodded at the cubs. Arthur heard the rustle of footsteps come from behind the pair of them. Arthur leaped to his feet and saw a man emerge into the light.

"Arthur, meet Genric. He is the Lone Ranger of this area." Cratos declared formally. The man stepped up towards Arthur and held out his hand towards Arthur smiling.

"Greeting's cub! Excellent job on passing your test. By the look on your tears, I would say you've learned our top lesson. I heard most of it getting ready to come out!" His voice was light and friendly. He almost sounded like the person who greets you at the doors of a supermarket. He then gestured to the bushes he had emerged from with his thumb.

"I had to wait for Cratos's cue. Now then, time for some good news!" Arthur looked this friendly man over. His entire outfit was fashioned from large leaves and vines. They covered his torso and ran across his waist down to his knees, seemingly knotted together by the vines though Arthur didn't know how the leaves were merged. He had long black hair like Cratos with muscled but filthy arms. The only parts of his body from the neck down not covered by jungle greenery were nearly completely covered in mud. He held an extensive and welcoming grin buried beneath a thick bushy beard matching his hair color despite his shabby appearance. Its length nearly ran past his chest cover. Arthur thought he looked like a wild man who had never lived in civilization in his entire life. But despite that, Arthur finally noticed something more distinct on his face, his eyes. They gleamed with the Werewolves' signature yellow color, which was looking upon Arthur warmly. Not wanting to seem rude, especially in front of Cratos, Arthur took the man's hand and shook it.

"Oh yeah. Hi there. I'm Arthur Thorn," he greeted back, trying to regain his original voice from his previous weak, weepy tone. The man named Genric beamed as he then enthusiastically shook it. Arthur couldn't help but wince as the muddy claw vice locked on his hand in the shake. Genric withdrew his hand and chuckled.

"Sorry about that! I forget cubs aren't strong yet. I'm only used to dealing with regular Werewolves." Arthur looked to the side and decided to ignore that intentional jab, and he instead pressed on what the man had said before.

"So, what is the good news? I doubt it will help," Arthur asked with his face again dropping. The unexpected excitement of meeting Genric had sunk back into him as the weight of the tiger had retaken the helm within Arthur. Genric saw Arthur's face drop, and he reached out to pat Arthur on his shoulder.

"It wasn't your fault the tiger died, Arthur," Genric said calmly. Arthur's head shot up like lightning, and he gazed into Genric's eyes to see if he was weirdly messing with him. However, all Arthur saw looking back at him was a warm, understanding face that nodded to confirm what he said to Arthur, who was now more confused than ever.

"But...but I killed the tiger. I tapped into some of my wolf strength and ended its life completely!" he exclaimed frantically, not sure if Genric was being literal or metaphorical with what he said. Genric's face changed then; it twisted into confusion too. Genric's head faced Cratos.

"He tapped into his Werewolf strength before his stages?" he asked Cratos, who nodded uneasily back, shrugging his shoulders.

"I'm guessing the full moon last night is the reason why but I'm not sure how he tapped into it exactly either," Cratos answered uneasily. Genric thought for a moment. He then shook his head and refaced Arthur.

"It doesn't matter right now. I guess it can happen. Arthur," he said, his tone turning severe to recapture Arthur's attention as he had slipped back into melancholy. Arthur observed Genric with no idea what this dirty Werewolf was about to say. Seeing Arthur return to the moment, Genric's smile also resurfaced as he continued.

"I'll keep this simple. Mainly because I have mushrooms for lunch, and I will not be lucid for a good few hours after that."

"Genric!" Cratos snapped. Genric looked over at Cratos, who gave him a stern look, his eyes communicating to Genric saying,

"The BOY doesn't need to hear that!" Genric gulped and nodded at Cratos continuing to speak to Arthur.

"The mother tiger was sick, Arthur. She was extremely sick in the head. If you hadn't come here to kill her, then she would have died in a short time, after going on a pain-induced rampage and most likely killing her cubs in the process." Arthur was silent for a few seconds, letting Genric's words sink. His eyes went to the cubs, which were still close by mewing at the three of them. He thought hard, letting the wires connect in his head. He killed a tiger with sick cubs that would die anyway, and if the tiger hadn't been killed, it would have died, killing her children. Arthur pulled himself out of his train of thought with a few follow-up questions.

"What was the tiger sick with?" he asked curiously. He felt he needed to know the details precisely for his guilt to let him sleep. Genric tapped the side of his head with his left hand a few times.

"Brain disease. As Cratos said, I am a Lone Ranger, and it is my job to protect ecosystems and the creatures that live within them. There are also plenty of recon and other Shadow class-related missions. But anyway, I have been treating the world's animals for many years, and I diagnosed the poor kitty not too long ago. Please don't ask how; it's a messy story. But I knew how much longer the poor thing had left, and if Cratos hadn't gotten in touch with me for your test, I would have had to put down the poor thing myself. But then you came along for me. When stars align, eh?" he finished with an excited chuckle. Arthur thought hard; it made sense to him.

"But the tiger didn't seem to be acting like it was sick or anything." Arthur couldn't help but counter, his curiosity running the controls in his brain right now. Genric smirked.

"I do love it when people think illness is always noticeable. You'd be surprised how many humans walk around with something wrong with them, minutes away from death without knowing it," he remarked smugly. Arthur began to feel embarrassed about the challenging question, but Genric continued speaking. This man seemed to have strange energy to him. Arthur figured that perhaps he didn't talk to other people that often.

"I was first alerted by the creature's *subtle* difference in its behavior. You would need to know what to notice to see it but trust me, the poor thing was sick. Its mind became increasingly agitated as time passed. It was becoming more aggressive; it spent less time with its cubs and more time patrolling its territory. It was on the verge of no longer being able to provide for the cubs. That is why the tiger became so fixated on you when you began waltzing around its home. You were the poor tiger's final obsession, Arthur." Silence hung in the air for a few seconds as Arthur understood. He didn't rechallenge Genric and nodded in acceptance.

"However!" Cratos butted in as he saw Arthur's shoulder begin to relax.

"That doesn't take anything away from the lesson after Genric explained all of that to you, Arthur. You were lucky this mother tiger was already dying for you to learn this, Arthur."

"Not sure 'lucky' is the right word there, but ok," Genric muttered, uncomfortably looking at the orphan tiger cubs. Arthur looked at his teacher and nodded at him.

"I understand Cratos. Thank you, I will not forget this," Arthur then looked at Genric and nodded at him.

"And you too, Genric. Thank you for helping me." Genric continued smiling at Arthur as he then reached out and ruffled Arthur's hair with his grimy, muddy hand, leaving filth behind as he spoke.

"No problem, cub! You seem to be a decent kid. You handled this test better than most cubs do." He then pulled his hand away and continued smiling as Arthur smiled back, genuine relief running through his mind. The mewing of the tiger cubs then became apparent in his ears again. Arthur looked down at the fragile cubs, then at Cratos and Genric.

"What will happen to the cubs? Without a mother, how will they survive," he asked worriedly. Genric waved a hand at Arthur as though he had just asked why water is wet.

"That's where I come in, cub. I sadly lack the stripes, but I will keep an eye on the little ones, bring them food and keep anything with sharp teeth away from them until they've grown enough to start hunting. Then once they're big enough to look after themselves, I'll just observe them no differently than I did their mother." Arthur grinned as he heard that. While he still felt grief at taking the tiger cubs' mother away from them, Arthur was glad to hear they would still be given a chance to live themselves. Arthur nodded at Genric, then faced Cratos.

"So, what happens now?" he asked firmly, feeling a new sense of being in himself now. He knew he had taken this lesson to heart, and he could already feel it making him stronger inside. He had returned to holding his head up high. Cratos sighed and smiled uneasily.

"Now, Arthur. It is time for your hardest test yet. It is time for your first Stage," he answered. Genric whistled sharply and looked at Arthur.

"Good luck, kid. It's been great meeting you. I hope I get to again," he finished with a cheerful grin, his tone jolly sounding as though he had just complimented Arthur on a new outfit. Genric walked away from Arthur and walked towards Cratos; the pair shook hands and nodded at each other. Genric gave a final wave at Arthur before walking back into the jungle, vanishing from sight after a few moments. Arthur watched as Genric left. He was another Werewolf he had met apart from Cratos and the boat captain. The man seemed friendly, but there had been a strange aura to him that made Arthur feel uneasy. He looked at Cratos and looked him dead in the eye.

"Cratos, I'm ready," Cratos then nodded at Arthur, and the pair walked away from the cave with the tiger cubs mewing after them as they left. Arthur felt his pang of guilt in his stomach as he heard the lasting of their mewing, but he tried to focus instead on whatever this new test was. After fighting a tiger head-on, Arthur now thought he was ready for whatever was next for him to overcome.

CHAPTER ELEVEN

"Is this really necessary?" Arthur commented dryly, his hands clenched around the metal bars of his large cage.

"Maybe not," Cratos responded with a familiar smug smirk running up the side of his face.

"But it's easier to throw things at you this way," he mused jokingly. Arthur rolled his eyes and let go of the bars, sighing. Cratos had taken Arthur to a secluded place that the Werewolves had built worldwide for this very reason. Cratos had told him all new cubs were trained several rigorous days and nights to prepare for their first full moon with Werewolf blood. Arthur had been told he was fortunate with his time. He had become a Werewolf right after the last full moon, which gave him more weeks than some did to prepare.

"There are some with only twenty hours to prepare for their first stage," Cratos had told him to help ease Arthur's anxiety as his test was coming close.

"What happens to them?" he asked back, only receiving a shrug from Cratos.

"It depends. Some people have more mental strength than others. Although I have seen men take the challenge of the first stage only after mere hours of being bitten and come out successful. It depends on the inner strength of a person. It's your soul's strength that determines whether you are truly worthy of the powers you hold." Arthur now wondered how many other times he would be tested to see if he is 'worthy' of being a Werewolf.

The cage Arthur was locked in was locked up tightly. Cratos had explained that this was in case new cubs failed to seize control of their body from the beast. He also mentioned how two other Werewolves usually oversaw this night to assist in olden times. They would pin the cub down to the ground with their mentor until the result was finalized.

"The cage method was introduced for two reasons," Cratos explained, continuing to help keep Arthur's mind from worrying too much.

"One reason is that it is always tricky to find an extra couple of Werewolves on short notice, and two, the process wasn't without fault. Sometimes the cub would fail, break free and roam around killing. The cages were built in secluded places all around the world. They are in every country, city, town, or even small village where the Werewolf population is strong. They are meant to be easy access for recruits to come too from wherever their teacher was training them." Cratos had marched Arthur to one that lay within a secret cave that was located halfway down a waterfall behind the falling water itself. Every Werewolf knew where most of the cages were located. Cratos himself coincidentally knew the location of nearly every single one he claimed boastfully. He guided Arthur past the thrashing waters of the waterfall and within the cave, pushing him into the cage and locking the door behind him. Only then did he explain everything about it. It was a few hours now until the full moon would be shining down upon the land. The cave was Werewolf constructed. Where the cage was placed, a large tunnel was hollowed out upwards through the ceiling straight to the outside. This ceiling hole was so moonlight would shine firmly down upon him. Arthur was beyond nervous. Leading up to now, he had a lot of training from Cratos. But despite his nerves, he still felt that he was ready for this challenge after defeating the tiger.

"Any advice?" Arthur asked as the pair sat crossed-legged within the cave, the sound of the crashing waterfall rife in the air around them. Cratos rubbed his chin for a few moments and hummed.

"Hard to say; each encounter is different. The Werewolf blood takes over your entire body, and as a result, your brain is also extremely affected. The beast you face tonight will be created with elements of your psyche. It lies within the depths of your subconscious, whispering in your ear in weak moments, trying to make you give in. The only instruction anyone can offer is just to fight back with everything you have." Arthur thought about that. Arthur was told that this beast lived within his subconscious. Therefore, Arthur figured it had access to not only his memory and his thoughts, but it also knew all his desires and even desires he may not know himself. He anticipated the idea that the beast may try and use his mind against him somehow.

"But it's a savage beast, right?" he thought. It took over your body and killed people; there was no way the thing itself would hold conscious thoughts. Arthur told Cratos his thoughts, and his mentor nodded.

"You are correct. The beast will know everything about you. The reason the creature turns savage when they take over the body is that it goes insane. The subconscious merges with the conscious making the mind whole. No creature is capable of such presence, so it goes mad and then goes on a rampage." Arthur sighed; the more Cratos told him, the more his opponent seemed impossibly invincible to defeat.

"Do not lose hope, Arthur," Cratos said warmly.

"The beast has been here since you woke up in that warehouse; it is YOUR mind and YOUR body, not the beasts. Remember that. YOU are the Werewolf. That thing is just an unpleasant result, the bad with the good. There are thousands of Werewolves in the world, Arthur, and they all had the mental strength to defeat their Beast. So can you. I believe in you," Cratos explained, smiling at Arthur, who then beamed at his mentor's faith in him. Arthur, however, then frowned as a curious thought popped into his head.

"Why tonight, why does the moon hold power over us? Also, Why aren't you going through this as well right now?" Cratos smiled grimly at Arthur as he responded.

"That is a much more complicated situation," he started uneasily.

"Did you ever learn about the planets in school?" Cratos asked to which Arthur nodded. He knew about the planets revolving around the sun by some gravitational pull; he always paid attention to science to look good to Ashley.

"Good, that saves time. Well, as the planet rotates around the sun, so does the moon around the earth. The moon holds many benefits to our planet, and it holds its magnetic force within the earth's gravitational pull, which means-," Cratos stopped when he saw Arthur's eyes droop slightly. His mentor saw that Arthur was expecting a less technical explanation. Cratos coughed and started again.

"Seems this is what I get for taking you OUT of education," he muttered, causing Arthur to frown.

"Anyway," he continued quickly.

"Long story short, our blood changes our bodies in ways that the light of the moon triggers a chain reaction of cells in our bodies, causing the primal instincts within our subconscious to come alive and into our present mind. Do you understand?" While Arthur still felt it was a wordy explanation, he did understand somewhat. He nodded his head, gesturing for Cratos to continue.

"It is weird hearing this all sound somehow logical," Arthur chuckled. Cratos rolled his eyes.

"Either way, it's the way our blood changes our bodies for our conscious that allows us to fight the beast back, and thus we can turn into our Werewolf forms at our leisure. But such a stage is extremely far away from you. Now, you need to work on stopping the beast from eating your soul, metaphorically speaking, that is." Now Arthur rolled his eyes.

"Gee, thanks," Arthur replied sarcastically; his mentor had gone from reassuring Arthur of his strength to mentioning how he could have his entire soul devoured. Arthur smirked then he nodded firmly.

"Well, fair enough. How long now?" Cratos looked up at the sky through the hole and narrowed his eyes at it.

"A few hours, I believe. The second the full moon hits your skin, it'll start. Be ready, Arthur, you're in for the fight of your life." Arthur was breathing carefully, not allowing nerves to overtake him like in the pit of the snakes.

"But again, why don't you have to go through this? I thought all of us did this our entire life, you said," he started again, trying to distract himself further.

"Yes, but after you finish your stages and your body makes its first start to the stages, the Werewolf also changes its, let's say, routine and strikes its challenge on a different day. No longer bound to strike during the full moon, it even sometimes picks a time at random to catch us off guard. It's only those going through the stages that have to suffer it exactly every full moon." Arthur still squinted at his mentor.

"But it's been a month since I joined you; I haven't seen you need to go through this," he challenged skeptically.

"That's because I had my encounter with my inner beast while you were hunting the tiger, so I dealt with it then." Arthur nodded, satisfied with the answer, and he then sat back in wait for the beast to strike.

Cratos had left Arthur by himself. He told Arthur he was going hunting and would return shortly. The time had approached, and darkness swept through the cave completely. Arthur was focusing his thoughts on the sound of the waterfall. Now and then, Arthur looked up through the hole above him. The sky was nearly black, with clouds smothering his vision. Any moment a gap could appear and trigger his test with the moon's light. He struggled to control his heart rate; his nerves twitched continuously, coupled with a spiked pit of fear burrowed in his stomach. He was ashamed to admit it, but he was scared. The bravado of fighting the tiger had vanished from his mind, and he was terrified of the beast winning. The last few weeks had been hard training. The morning exercises, the tests that strained his mental and physical sanity, and being thrown into the deep end to see if he could hunt down a tiger. But despite it all, all the testing and teasing, collapsing on the floor every night tired out of his mind, he felt truly alive. In retrospect, his old life seemed like a black hole, sucking all the positive emotion and creativity; it was abusive mentally and physically. He hated it to the core of his person. Day two with Cratos Mane as a trainee Werewolf and Arthur fell in love with his new life, rising from the ashes of his former life. He would ultimately be exhausted from one night of training and then reborn to experience a new life the following day. That was how he felt after every test. Within the space of a few weeks, Cratos Mane had drilled moral lessons into Arthur that he thought he couldn't have learned as a human with a dozen lifetimes. Not with what the world is today. Since joining the Werewolves, Arthur had gained things he thought he would never again feel. He now had gained his self-respect and a feeling of honor and dignity. Arthur didn't want to give those things up. He didn't want to lose his life after only a few weeks of living for the first time.

A bit of time had passed, and Arthur was breathing calmly now. He knew the time was only minutes away. Arthur prepared himself. He closed his eyes and focused his mind, readying himself for any form of trickery the beast would try and sway him with. As well as any sort of physical effort he had to put in. Cratos had told him stories of past cubs who threw themselves around the cage-like madmen. They would slam themselves on the metal bars, often breaking bones or suffering deep fractures. He was breathing calmly, keeping his mind clear. He wished Cratos was here for moral support, but he still hadn't returned. He figured whatever he was hunting was very elusive, and Arthur secretly scorned the quick creature for it. His mind drifted slightly as the waterfall sound still carried through the air. It had been a few weeks since he left home; he wondered if there had been much of a search for him. Every time he thought of home, that was usually his first thought. How hard had people tried to find him? Arthur then wondered how quickly they gave up when there was no sign of him. He acted highly suspicious on his last day there when he was showing off his new powers. If Arthur had seen someone behave like that all day and then suddenly disappear from the face of the earth, he would have assumed the government or aliens had stolen and experimented on them.

Arthur suddenly felt his entire body tense as though a bolt of lightning had just struck his brain. It felt like fire was coursing through every vein in his being. Its seething intensity was like a hoard of thousands of burning spiders riddling up and down his insides. Arthur could barely move. With all the effort he could manage, Arthur arched his neck and looked upwards, his eyes staring dead center at the white illuminating light in the skies that was the moon, at its fullest and most potent. Arthur couldn't control it. His body began to shake, feelings began to disappear from his body, and Arthurs' mind went numb. He felt his muscles starting to bulge vigorously. His pupils were beginning to shrink and disappear. A deep dark growl formed in the back of his throat like a horrible monster was emerging from his mouth. The last thing Arthur saw was the moon and its thick beam of light in his vision as the world around him faded into shadows. The first stage of his transformation was upon him, and it was his time to answer the Werewolf howl within himself.

Arthur suddenly found himself existing within an absolute black abyss. Nothingness surrounded his being within a complete dark void. He was standing on his feet. The cage he was locked in, the cave, and the light of the moon had all vanished from the world he previously perceived, and now he stood in an endless universe of shadows. He gazed down at himself and saw he was no longer even wearing clothes; he was only visible in his human form. He looked around, seeing only blackness and hearing not a single whistle of even wind, only silence. He wiggled his toes where he stood. He wasn't even sure what he was standing on; for all Arthur knew, he was floating in mid-air somehow despite feeling solid ground on his soles. He stamped his foot where he stood; the ground he was on was hard. It wasn't rock or dirt, just some form of solid matter. There was no warmth, no cold; he felt nothing. No breeze passed him, nor could he feel his breath as it slowly died out of his mouth. He held up his hands and looked at them. He wasn't in the darkness of the night because he saw his own body entirely as though he was somehow now luminous. He called out loudly into the black space. He heard his voice plain and clear, and it echoed out far, vanishing into a faint whisper within seconds of speaking. His voice carried briefly out into what seemed like an endless void of nothing.

"Where the hell am I?" he muttered, angry and increasingly more agitated. Arthur was unsure of where he was and was becoming much more defensive at being caught off guard. As though answering his question, a loud thunderous roar exploded out of the shadows ahead of him from seemingly nowhere. Arthur had to cover his ears from the intensity of the screech. It sounded like a chaos god itself tore its way into existence and began raining down a monsoon of wrath. Arthur looked up and around, still nothing in sight. But given the roar, Arthur knew full well what creature had made it. He crouched down slightly in defense and raised his arms in front of his face. Arthur was clenching his hands into fists, eyes snapping around himself, ready for anything. He began moving in small circles, covering every direction he could around his being in case anything snuck upon him. Arthur was prepared for the beast, wherever the moon had taken him. Whether or not this was some sort of secret magical plain where cubs were tested or whatever his mind had somehow conjured up in some kind of lucid dream experience. Even if it was one or the other, he was ready for a fight. Arthur spread his arms out, welcoming anything that looked upon him, and roared at the top of his lungs,

"Where are you!" he bellowed. Instantly in response came a whisper straight into the depths of Arthur's ear.

"Here!" the Beast replied

Arthur whirred his body around, only for every functional muscle in his body to become instantly voided of feeling and fall limp within seconds, as a vast hairy shadow smothered claw vice gripped his throat. It lifted him off the ground choking him slowly. Arthur's hands lay limp by his sides as his legs dangled in the air. His mouth was only making choking noises as he looked forward at the monster that controlled the hand strangling him. The creature before him could only be described as Goliath in size and stature. Cratos in his wolf form was thin, muscularly defined, and agile, but this beast before him was a shadow-infused demigod of a hulk with tree trunk-sized muscles and an enormous wolf head with piercing bright yellow eyes, staring straight at Arthur. Its torso was the width of nearly Arthur's total height. Its muscles were thickly defined, like an inch-deep carved piece of wood with the size of what Arthur could assume from his position as probably more than nine feet high.

The beast had no scent, and its form nearly blended within the darkness around it, though it was present before Arthur's sharpened eyes, looking like an ethereal behemoth of a Werewolf. The Werewolf leaned its giant head in and opened its mouth, revealing a long row of dozens of sharp fangs, glistening somehow within the beast's thick saliva. Arthur gurgled feebly within its grip, and the Werewolf roared once again. Arthur, this time, was unable to shield his ears from the loud storm blowing his hair back as it passed his face. Arthur gazed deep into the creature's horrible yellow eyes and scowled, gritting his teeth in anger. He knew he had to fight back. Slowly, very slowly, he raised his arms, wrapping his fingers around the beast's single grip, trying to pry them away from his throat. The beast snarled at his attempt and twisted its body vertically, before slamming Arthur's body into the ground with its feet in a flash. Arthurs' body felt as though it had shattered like broken glass from the beast's tremendous strength. His being, rippling from the shockwave of force waving through his body, sent Arthur coughing and roaring at the pain.

"You are a feeble worthless worm!" The beast said in a deep animal ridden tone of pure contempt. The giant beast let go of Arthur's neck and stood upright, towering over Arthur like a king cobra over an injured ant. It gazed at Arthur for a moment and snarled.

"Pathetic coward," it grunted. Arthur coughed and took in a painful lungful of air, twitching in pain from the beast's slam on the ground. Arthur felt whatever solid surface they were on was strong and very sturdy. Arthur looked up at the beast and spat what tasted like blood towards the ebony titan. It fell short and hit the beast on its foot. The Werewolf looked at his foot, then back at Arthur.

"Was that your best, you worm?" it challenged, loath radiating from its tone. Arthur coughed again and spoke shakily, but his eyes were trained straight on his foe.

"Come closer...and I'll show you," Arthur snarled through painful words. The beast's eyes widened, and it roared out in a fit of rage. Arthur, this time held his face still, no flinching or even blinking. The beast finished and looked back at Arthur, who smirked and spoke again, his voice sturdier this time.

"The weakest dogs...bark the loudest...you stupid mutt," Arthur grunted through strained breaths, finishing with a mocking wink. The beast howled in fury and then brought its left arm back like an archer pulling back on the string of his bow. It held in place for a solid second before then hurling its clenched clawed fist downward towards Arthur like a falling meteorite. Arthur was completely still as it fell, then within the single second of the fist connecting with him, Arthur rolled out of the way and jumped to his feet, all in the flash of a single moment. His body felt like it was throbbing in pain, but he pushed that aside for the moment. The giant fist hammered into the ground as its head snapped up, looking at Arthur, who was now on his feet next to him.

"You think you scare me!" Arthur snapped angrily into the dark hairy features on its face.

"I've been scared by worse bullies than you," he spat with contempt. The beast chuckled darkly, pulling its claw off the ground, slowly raising itself, and then gently approaching Arthur.

"I know every last one of your fears, boy," the Beast said, coming toe to toe with him with a vicious gleeful life within the depths of its horrible eyes.

"I know everything you have ever feared. Every terror you have ever felt. From a monster in your closet to your dread of mortality itself!" The beast bent down, so the pair was face to face.

"You're in my world now boy, you think you're tough, but I know deep down what it takes to cripple you completely." Arthur stared dead into the beasts' eyes without blinking and firmly said.

"This is my body. My mind. Nothing is yours here. This is my world; you're just an unwelcome guest, and I want you gone from my mind." The beast threw its head back and roared with laughter, ceasing only to shake its head.

"You are a foolish boy. If it weren't for ME, that tiger would have ripped you to shreds! When you needed the vines on that tree, especially when you wanted to punish that bully from your school. Without me, you would just go back to being the weak victim you truly are at heart, boy!." Arthur crouched slightly and scowled.

"My strength is my own, not yours. And if you won't go, I will make you leave!" Arthur snarled confidently. The beast's eyes then widened, and the beast grinned with malicious joy.

"And how will you do that, freak!" it spat. Arthur's rage flared, and he leaped into the air.

"Like this!" he roared, taking the battle to the beast with his fists. The beast saw Arthur fly towards it. It simply snorted, curved its claw inward, and swatted its arm outwards sharply, knocking Arthur out of the air as though he was just a bad smell. Arthur cried out at the beast's attack but refused to give up. As he went for the ground, he twisted his body correctly, landing on his feet. Arthur looked up and growled through gritted teeth. The beast snarled and charged forward at him like a lumbering bull. Arthur saw the beast approaching him in a charge and side-rolled left, dodging him. The beast continued to growl and spit in anger as it turned its body in response, building itself a frenzy of rage. The beast spun around and locked its gaze on Arthur with thirsty eyes. Thinking quickly, Arthur brought his foot forward and met the beast's stare. At the same time, both charged at one another. Arthur dashed forward towards the beast, arms held out and his hands tense, ready to strike.

The beast galloped forward on both its legs and once again swatted its arm out when it came within arm's length of Arthur. This time Arthur had been expecting the swat. Instead of rolling again, Arthur ducked down, dodging the attack by the thinness of a hair, and crouched down as low as he could. As the beast looked down to react, Arthur shot himself upward with a powerful jump, shooting his arm upwards with a firmly clenched fist at the end and punched the beast square in the face. His fist connected sharply with the beast's chin, causing the Werewolf to stumble backward slightly. Arthur seized his chance. He landed back on his feet and crouched low again, but this time with all the strength he could muster, he twisted his body sharply to the left with his leg stuck out and swept its leg. Arthur's shin crashed through the beast's legs while it was off-balance, and the beast fell to the ground like a sack of bricks. The beast cried out in surprise as its back hit the floor, and Arthur leaped straight on its body and sat clamped on its torso, looking dead into its face with pure hatred.

"Don't call me a freak," Arthur spat out like venom and then began wailing his fists down on the Werewolf, slamming the edge of his knuckles deep in its face.

One after the other, The beast's head was hitting the floor below it in recoil as Arthur pulled his arms back, bringing forward hit after hit. As Arthur struck every blow, he roared hellishly. Arthur was becoming intoxicated with the adrenalin of the moment. He felt like he could win; Arthur felt in control now that he was in charge of this world. He was the one who owned his body and his mind. This beast was an intruder in his head. To Arthur, this beast obeyed his rules. Punch after punch, the thudding noises of Arthur's fists pelting against the creature's savagely rough face grew louder in Arthurs' ears, like punching against a thick wad of hairy tree bark. He felt once again that feeling of pure power he felt when he had hurt Gary. The power when he told off Jack and when he took down the tiger. He was the victim to NOONE anymore; he felt a rush of –

"Arthur, stop now, boy!" came a firm shout from the beast. Arthur froze in place; he had one arm back and another stopping still on its face after another punch. Arthur slowly looked down at the dark Werewolf that had commanded him to stop with a look of horror and disbelief. Arthur ceased his attack, and now he felt as though he was a hollow, brittle piece of clay. As Arthur gazed at the head of the wolf, it now possessed the face of a man that had terrified Arthur his whole life since he was a small boy. Added to that, it had just roared at him as the man always used to do before he went berserk. Arthur stared down with a look that was now pure terror as, despite still maintaining the whole body of the terrifying Werewolf, it now bore the somehow morphed head of his father. Arthurs' father was now staring up at him with a wicked look smothering every drunken wrinkle of his horrible malice-filled face. Arthur remained utterly still, looking straight into the exact face of his bully of a father; the wolf's arms shot out forward and wrapped both its claws around Arthur's throat. Sitting up as it did and began squeezing his neck, the tables had now turned.

The beast quickly realized that, while its body easily defeated Arthur with his strength, its dark wolf-like head didn't scare the boy. Arthur had seen Cratos as a Werewolf and didn't feel dread or terror. The beast had rooted around inside Arthur's head for the moment while Arthur had been hailing him with punches. That mental invasion allowed it to locate the prime source of what it took to truly make Arthur Thorn shiver, his bully of a father. Arthur stood up to his father the night he had left his town, but that was when he had become a Werewolf. After that day, he felt strong, but Arthur wanted to prove himself not to hurt his father but merely scare him back. Arthur would always reflect on that night with pride. But those few minutes couldn't wash away all the years the man had tormented Arthur and his family. The Werewolf knew that the most, and now it bared his father's head and voice, seizing back control over their battle. It was like a chess game, and Arthur just felt he was put in check, and he was terrified that now he was one move away from checkmate.

Arthur felt like a lifeless stone statue within what he now considered his father's grip. Every single horrible memory of every time his father had hurt Arthur flashed through his brain at super speeds as his breath was silenced completely.

"Worthless little ingrate," his father snarled into Arthur's face. His arms vigorously tensed as his strength increased.

"What a waste of my seed you always were. I hated you the second I set my eyes on your very being." Arthur's spirit was ripping itself apart at the words. In front of him was a mouthpiece for every self-blame he had put upon himself in secret on nights he cried himself to sleep after beatings.

"I wouldn't have been surprised if you weren't my son at all. You're such a weak, feeble runt. You are no son of mine; you have no father, mistakes like you have only the dirt." Tears ran down Arthur's cheeks as he choked within his father's grip, each word cutting deeper and deeper inside himself as he just wanted to disappear into nothing. He wished he could tell himself that it wasn't real, that his father wasn't 'really' saying these things, and it's just the Werewolf exploiting what he always felt himself. But there was that growing nugget of knowledge that told him that despite the fact his father had never said those words, he probably would have if it crossed his mind.

"Why do you think your idiot of a mother threw you aside that night? She thinks the same as I do; you were always unwanted! Not a child but an irritation that wouldn't go away, I would have welcomed fleas in my home before you any day!" Arthur began to feel the life drain from his eyes. Despite the darkness that already presented itself around him, the wolf father before him began to fade from his vision in pieces. Arthur was giving up; his father was right.

"You're not even a real person, you're a complete nobody, and in a few minutes, you'll be banished in this darkness forever until your body is dead. It's what you deserve, you freak. You –"

"Arthur, no! Don't listen!" came the loud crying sound of Alices' voice, his little sister interrupting their dad. Arthur's eyes blurred back into full vision, and he even saw the beast looking around confused.

"Don't listen to him, big bro; it's all lies! We loved you. Me and mummy always loved you. Don't listen to Dad; you know the truth. You always had power inside you. Find the strength, fight back!" his sister finished with a screeching cry.

"Silence!" bellowed the beast in response, the voice of his father fading a tad in frustration. It was all in vain, though. Arthur threw his arms up with renewed vigor and latched his fingers around his father's hands. As though there was no resistance, he began prying them apart as though they were child's fingers. His father's eyes flashed in shock.

"No, you don't, you little worm!" he snarled, trying to fight back. Arthur threw his father's arms aside, and he dropped to the floor, now free from its grip. Arthur was amazed at how easily he managed to free himself. The sound of his sister gave Arthur the will to fight back that he desperately needed. Arthur understood now that this was HIS mind, and he could only be beaten if he allowed it.

Arthur looked up at the still towering beast standing before him with the enraged head of his father, and he still felt scared; he still felt the same fear he always felt growing up. However, the sound of his sister's voice made him remember why he stayed in that house so long. He remembered why he didn't give in and why he never gave up in the misery of his father's tyranny. The second Alice was born, his mother had placed her within those soft pink blankets in Arthur's arms and said to him.

"That's your little sister Arthur. You're her big brother, and you have to look after her," she cooed sweetly. Arthur had gazed down at her tiny face with her wide eyes that had only been opened for a few minutes, and they stared directly back at him. The two shared a look for a moment, and then Alice, as a baby, giggled. The newborn baby giggled further, staring up at Arthur, and she reached out her little arm towards him, which was met by a couple of Arthur's fingers for her little fingers to wrap around. As Arthur investigated her innocent face, he knew he would look after her, that now Arthur had something in his heart that he would always fight for.

The beast roared at Arthur; its voice was more like the Werewolf tone than his father's now. The beast was enraged that its attempt to manipulate Arthur had failed. Arthur didn't even flinch as he attacked. Without blinking, Arthur crouched down, held in his left arm, clenched his fist tight, and shot it out like a speeding bullet, striking the beast sharply in the stomach like a charged lance. The beast fell backward, howling through the air and hitting the ground hard.

"That's enough now!" Arthur thundered, standing firm, glaring at the beast as it struggled to its feet.

"Shut up, worm. Do you think you're strong now? You're not! You're still weak, and I will ALWAYS haunt your nightmares!" With his father's head, the beast stood up straight on its legs and spread its arms.

"I am the voice of your inner conscious boy! You know this; you cannot hide from your fears!" Hit then outstretched a finger and pointed at Arthur, grinning.

"You will never stop shivering at my call," he said with hollow malice. Arthur's scowl deepened as he pointed a finger of his own at the beast.

"No more!" Arthur said again, the shadows around the pair beginning to shake as though the ground was experiencing a mild tremor. The beast frowned with uncertainty but then maintained its presence.

"You do not control me, judge me, or have ANY idea about who I am!" Arthur continued to shout; the ground beneath them shook further as Arthur spoke. The tremor had escalated into a near earthquake. The Werewolf began to stumble as it roared in defiance, its voice for words suddenly gone.

"I am nobody's mistake. I am my own person, and most importantly, you stupid bulging bully! I am NOT afraid of you anymore!" That last word sent the world around them into chaos. The beast roared again as the ground below its body rippled and broke around it like a frozen lake cracking into pieces. Arthur noticed that several holes in the land had appeared, starting to circle the monster. Its head was shaking in the earthquake of the world around them, and Arthur saw within a few seconds that his father's face disappeared and the wolf head of the beast had returned, angry and roaring in cosmic fury.

Suddenly as the shaking of the ground began to subside, a strange thing happened. Sprouting from one of the holes around the Beast looked like an endlessly long silver snake. A thick metal chain flew into the air and shot over the Werewolf's body and into a hole on the other side. As the chain buried into the other side of the Werewolf, it went taught on the beast's dark flesh. The beast roared with shock, but before it could pull at it, another chain had shot into the air across from the first one, shooting high and plunging into the hole on the other side of it, slamming hard on the beast's body like the first one.

"No!" the beast finally said after a flurry of endless roars; more chains erupted from the ground in a hysterical outburst, racing into the air and falling into their opposing hole over the beast's body. Within seconds, the chains wrapped around the Werewolf that lay within the darkness of his mind. Before Arthur's eyes, the beast was now trapped and unable to move. The chains rattled and clinked at the beast's attempts to break them, but the chains held firm, not even stretching against its struggle. Arthur let his hand fall by his side, and he looked at the beast and spoke.

"Listen to me," Arthur called out. The Werewolf ceased its struggle and looked at Arthur, bitter in its defeat.

"You have lost here. Every time you surface and throw my self-doubts, my fears, and every worry that I burrow in my mind at me, I will be right here to meet you each time. I will always be ready to hear your whispering voice trying to corrupt me, and I will never let you win. I hope you're comfortable in those chains, you monster! Because I will sooner die before I release you from them!"

The Beast was silent for a few seconds. It remained still within its wraps and looked down at the floor for a few moments. Arthur did not take his eyes away from it. After a brief time of straight silence, the beast chuckled and then began laughing. Its head shot up violently, and its piercing yellow eyes stared deep at Arthur's again.

"You will see soon enough. You will discover you will need me in the days to come." The chains began to pull at the beast's body; instead of the ground cracking beneath the monster, it instead turned into what looked like quicksand before Arthur's eyes. The giant Werewolf began sinking into the dark floor before it, still chained.

"At your most desperate moment, you will release me, and I will save our lives. You hold more secrets within yourself than even your mentor knows." Arthur said nothing and watched this hideous monster disappear from his sight, hopefully for a very long time. It carried on speaking as it sunk into the black earth, Its body being swallowed up like the best itself was simply morphing into the ground than sinking into it. As its shoulders disappeared, leaving only its head remained, the Werewolf grinned viciously and finally said.

"I'll be in touch." Then it sank away from Arthur, leaving him alone in the darkness. Arthur sighed for a few moments, then looked around, hoping there wouldn't be any more surprises. Before he could say anything, a great wave of sleepiness fell upon him, and he fell to the floor as though he had just been hit by paralysis. He was then on the ground soundly asleep and victorious in his first trial stage as a Werewolf.

CHAPTER TWELVE

"You did it!" Cratos cried with joy in proud laughter. The first thing Arthur heard as his mind came back to reality was the boasting cries of joy and happiness ringing in his ears.

"You cut it damn close there, Arthur! I was readying my hand to cut your damn throat open! But you did it, boy! Well done!" Cratos was laughing and holding up Arthur's hand in victory. His mind was still dazed after waking from his Werewolf slumber. In return for his mentor's rapid show of affection, all he could muster was a weak smile and a nod in appreciation. Cratos noticed the daze still on Arthur's face and laughed, leading him to a freshly made fire to eat some of the deer he had killed and cooked while Arthur was fighting.

Arthur sat by the fire and ate in silence. He was eating mechanically, filling his stomach up until it was full. His appetite was ravenous. Cratos had told him that was common after a fight with the Beast inside. The mental anguish drains a person of all their energy, and the stomach is left empty when they awake. Arthur was pretty much given the whole deer to eat himself with plenty of fresh chilly water to wash it down with. After half an hour of silence, when Arthur felt he had eaten his fill and his mind was entirely his own again, he looked around the cave the pair were in. The waterfall was still thrashing at the mouth of the cave. The moon had vanished from the sky as it was now early morning. The first peaks of the sun's light were faintly shining through the hole at the top of the cave; he was glad he had won.

While eating, Arthur had thought long and hard about his encounter. He pondered about meeting the dark Werewolf within his mind in that shadow-ridden plain of existence. He thought about fighting the Beast, winning for a moment before his father appeared. Hearing all those words the world had told him with his father's voice and his own deep and darkest thoughts that he had always dreaded hearing. His stomach went cold as he remembered that part and his face was solemn. He then remembered what had saved him, what gave him the strength to stand back on his feet and remember that all those bad thoughts were simply all that was. He knew they were only thoughts and nothing else that could hurt. He remembered his little sister. Just hearing her voice reminded him that she was the very reason Arthur had taken up the will to fight against his father. Not for himself but for her. That was what gave him to strength to fight for himself now, and he would never forget that. Arthur nearly felt older as he woke up like he had aged a few years. He felt like his mind had grown sharper by his experience. He thought that he now understood the actual reason to believe in himself. He didn't fight just for his sister; he left home and her, and now he needed to depend on his inner strength. But it's remembering where that strength came from that allows him to keep growing for himself so he could be ready against anyone who would make him doubt himself the way the Beast had.

"It's an ugly thing, isn't it," Cratos had said; the cheer vanished from his voice and his face was just as melancholy as Arthur's now. Without saying anything, his train of thought now broken, Arthur looked at his mentor and nodded.

"It was so dark, so evil," Arthur croaked. His mentor looked at him for a moment and nodded back.

"We each see something different," Cratos had told him, rapidly grabbing his attention.

"I don't know what you saw or what was said or done to you. But every one of us is confronted by the very worst of our demons. That is a prime test of our strength; we must be willing to be subjected to the very worst horrors even our mind can throw at us and remain standing. I have seen many a good Werewolf driven mad finally by what their beast had thrown at them. The longer you live, the more it has to say and show. I won't lie to you, Arthur. It doesn't get easier," Cratos finished with his eyes dropping on the fire. Arthur knew his mentor remembered something painful as he sat there, but he still hadn't shared it yet. Arthur thought for a moment and then nodded.

"Good," Arthur answered firmly. Cratos looked up, frowning in confusion.

"What do you mean?" he asked, puzzled.

"I saw a couple of things when I fought the Beast that I never wanted to see again. And I heard things said to me that I was always terrified of hearing outside my own mind," Arthur explained, Cratos nodding as he did.

"But thinking back, now that I have seen those things and heard them. They no longer hold the same fear over me that they once did. The faces still scare me, and the words still hurt but nowhere near as much as before I heard them. I feel stronger from getting through them, and each time I am presented with the same pain that I know inside myself, the stronger I will become because it will hurt me less and less. I don't want it to become easier, Cratos." Arthur looked his mentor in the eyes and smiled.

"I just always want to keep growing stronger from it," Arthur finished. Cratos smiled and closed his eyes for a moment, nodding his head.

"Spoken like a true Werewolf Arthur Thorn," he replied with genuine admiration in his tone. He opened his eyes, and Arthur returned a serious but friendly smile.

"Thank you, Cratos, for helping me become stronger." Cratos's eyes began to fill with water slightly, and he looked away from Arthur and stood up.

"Well, we can't sit around all day getting emotionally mushy. It's time to move on from this blasted land, finally," Cratos said hurriedly as he wiped his eyes dry. Arthur looked on at his mentor and chuckled, catching on to his words.

"Where are we going now? You're not going to take me to Greenland for a lesson on igloo building, are you?." Cratos laughed and wagged a finger at Arthur.

"Oh, definitely not, so don't worry. You have passed your first stage Arthur, and now things are going to start happening to you at a high-speed rate and for proper preparation in that field, we need the absolute best in the business to teach you. Pack your things, Arthur; we are heading to the home of all Werewolves in the world."

As Cratos had expected, within the few hours, the pair had begun traveling back to civilization, and Arthur had dozens upon dozens of questions for his mentor, which he pretty much didn't answer. There was always just the same response.

"You'll see for yourself." This answer was quickly becoming rapidly annoying for Arthur's ears, but he kept his temper as low as he could. The pair had left the jungle and forests and was nearly upon the world of humans again. After a month in the wild, hunting wild cats and tigers, Arthur wondered how he would look at the real world again. After his experiences and lessons learned, he was in no way the same boy that had walked into these lands. Arthur doubted he was now a man; he knew of plenty of experiences he had yet to go through before he had earned that title. But Arthur felt he had grown more mature, so now he had a better understanding of things that had left him confused before. He knew from his studies at school that history was full of many great philosophers who dedicated their entire lives to studying what life means. Great questions like the meaning of our existence had plagued humankind and its minds for centuries, with no real solid answer. Some guesses, theories, and even prophecies, but nothing was ever finite. Arthur had learned more in the months inside those forests learning remarkable things he would never have in school. He learned much about the world and what lies within it, being with Cratos so far.

But most importantly, Arthur knew he had learned much about himself. Day by day, he came to understand himself more. By going through these inner trials, Arthur felt he was developing a solid foundation of self-confidence within himself that he had thought never could exist. It took the call of his little sister to remind him of that foundation, and he would never forget it. But now, he wondered what sort of people he would find at the home of the Werewolves. He would be surrounded by people who had gone through the same tests he had and hundreds more. They would be people who had the strength, both mental and physical, of near-impossible standards. Arthur only hoped he would meet up to their standards.

The pair had stopped for a moment to rest and drink more water in their travels. The scorching heat of the jungle took its last stab at roasting both of them before they were out of its range, sweating them down to the bone. As they sat on a path, drinking greedily from their water, Arthur had begun his next series of questions for Cratos. During their travels, Arthur decided to narrow his questions to fewer specific ones, hoping to find an answer that way.

"Where exactly IS home?" Arthur asked, grabbing his mentor's attention.

"I mean, where in the world? Does it have a name?" he continued quizzically. Cratos pursed his lips and thought for a moment.

"Hard to say, it has many names, no definite one for our people. But Werewolves from different countries and lands, call it something different. Given your country of origin, I guess you would refer to it as 'Wolf kingdom'." Arthur rolled his eyes, unsure if Cratos was making a royalty joke, but he nodded, allowing Cratos to continue.

"As for where exactly. Given its location facility requirements, it was built within Europe. There are different strongholds and more minor places of refuge in nearly every country, but the main base for us is in Europe." Arthur nodded, pondering on this new information, his first tiny look into the infrastructure of the Werewolf world.

"Built-in Europe, you say, where exactly was it built?" Cratos then tapped the ground with his foot and smiled.

"Underground," He answered pleasantly. Arthur frowned with confusion.

"The home of all Werewolves is underground? How is that possible?" Cratos chuckled with his familiar smug tone.

"It's quite simple. With the Vampires controlling the human world, we needed to exist outside of their radar. We know the Vampires know where we are, but they leave us alone unless they want to dig up every country in Europe. As for the how?" He raised his hand to Arthur, and his fingernails slowly transformed into claws, extending out before his eyes.

"Patience!" Cratos growled with wicked glee. Arthur's eyes widened for a split second, and Cratos burst out laughing, causing him to frown.

"What?" Arthur snarled, not enjoying being the butt end of Cratos's humor. Cratos continued chuckling until he finally returned his nails to normal and wiped away tears of laughter.

"You are too gullible, Arthur. We didn't use our nails; we used regular excavation tools. We have tunnels stretching from miles to miles across the entire kingdom with different carved-out structured caverns built for our other needs."

"Other needs?" Arthur echoed back to his teacher, his temper beginning to rise at his teacher's endless Vagueness.

"You'll see for yourself," he blandly answered, causing Arthur to throw his empty water bottle at his mentor. Cratos ducked out of the way and laughed. Arthur calmed himself down and thought about it for a moment. The Werewolf Kingdom was located below all of Europe by an endless series of dug tunnels and burrowed caverns. Even if they were able to do this, Arthur didn't understand something.

"What about earthquakes and tremors? How do you stop the whole place from collapsing?" Arthur inquired, feeling this was a rare chance to sneak some answers from Cratos about the Werewolf world. Cratos rubbed the back of his head uncomfortably; he was trying to figure out the best way to detail this response.

"Many Werewolves have interests and professions of their own outside of their work for the race. We have had many architects, stonemasons, construction people, and highly creative engineers. They see what was constructed previously in the past, and they adapted with innovative technology to reinforce what we have created as strongly as they can, and for the most part, it works. As science and new advancements develop in the world, we are always a step ahead, and we use the best of what we must to strengthen our home, its defenses, and especially its structure. But every now and then, a tunnel collapse. Barely any Werewolves die as a result though, they simply run as fast as possible to another tunnel entrance and escape it. But the caverns, especially in the throne room, are perfected to the ultimate in safety. So don't worry, you'll be fine when we're there. I have been going for years, and I have never had an accident." Arthur once again caught a keyword from Cratos, 'throne room.' It sounded like an expansion of the kingdom name he was given before, but he assumed it must be where all the leaders of the Werewolves met or something. As expected by his infuriating mentor, the answers he received only made his curiosity worse. The pair got up from their rest and continued forward, nearing the end of the jungle and soon back into civilization.

After a prolonged expedition of travel, Arthur found himself walking through the streets of the real world once again. After a month in forests and jungles, Arthur had now returned to society's most immense jungle of them all. As they left the clearings of the grassy lands behind them for good, it was only a short walk before they reached their following form of transport, which eventually led to them walking the streets of a strange city. Cratos seemed to know where they were going all the time; Arthur wouldn't be surprised if his mentor turned around and told him he had mapped out every place in the world in his mind. The pair were now walking past people unnoticed. Arthur wasn't sure how. Their clothes must have stunk of sweat, they washed them in the rivers every few days, but the pair had been living in forests and jungles for nearly an entire month. He didn't understand how people weren't looking at them like they had just crawled out of the ground like moles. As though sensing his confusion, Cratos spoke up quietly next to Arthur.

"People like us can blend into crowds very easily. In the sense of how pheromones attract creatures with their smell, we also give out a scent to others than repel in a way. They walk past us without looking unless we draw attention. Although I have this effect at a stronger rate than you do, remain close to me, and we won't draw attention from anyone. This ability is a vital way we can move around the world without our enemies locating us." Arthur listened carefully, knowing Cratos was choosing his words carefully. Arthur guessed that words like 'Vampire' and 'Werewolf' would set alarms off and for all Arthur knew, they had already walked past a few Vampires. Only now did Arthur realize how genuinely vulnerable he was. In the jungle where there were only him and the animals, he felt in control but now, he was a sitting duck.

Arthur recalled when Cratos explained how the Vampires were the world's leaders in terms of control. He explained how they secretly rule with politics, influence, and corporations. Arthur couldn't help but feel increasingly anxious about what was around him or, most importantly, who was around him and who noticed him. The Vampire forces could be everywhere, and they were looking for him and would happily kill him without hesitating if found.

Within only one month, Arthur had forgotten entirely how loud humans could be. The forests and jungles themselves were never quiet, with the squawking of birds and the mating calls of wild animals now and then. But as Arthur walked through the streets with Cratos, it seemed like every person around him was chattering to save their lives. It seemed like millions of words a minute needed to be said, or their heads would explode. He winced now and then when a poorly made car backfired, screeched in the road, or honked its horn. There would be people shouting at each other and calling their friends from several feet away at the top of their lungs. Not only was it hurting his ears, but it was infuriating him immensely. Arthur wanted nothing more than to throw his arms apart and roar into the sky.

"WILL YOU ALL SHUT THE HELL UP?!" But he felt that might draw attention to him and Cratos, so he held his tongue and continued to keep an eye out at the city life around him, trying his best to ignore the endless chirping of these birds.

Arthur had no idea what country the pair of them were within. Arthur once again had taken a lot of different forms of transportation once leaving the jungle. From boats to a few secret plane journeys in their time, they would be anywhere for all Arthur knew. He had studied an atlas in geography at school but not thoroughly enough to memorize anything significant he could use when traveling. Plus, there were places in the world with several jungles and forests, so that didn't narrow it down much for him as Arthur thought about it. The chattering of the locals, while annoying, was in a language he didn't understand. With the people of the city themselves, Arthur struggled to find any racial majority to help him place where he might be though it wouldn't prove anything finite even if he had. But where he was, it seemed strangely diverse. But given he only knew one language and there was truly little cultural diversity at his school. He still couldn't narrow it down as to what language it was. He asked Cratos again, but he simply grunted in response.

"It doesn't matter. We won't be here long." Arthur exhaled angrily; there were times his mentor treated him like an equal friend and others when he was treated like an ignorant child, and it was insulting to feel like a dog on a lead. Wherever they were, the city they were in wasn't exactly the cleanest either Arthur noticed as they walked through the streets. It had its signs of poverty. Some roads were in disrepair, vehicles were old and shabby, and houses and shops looked barely clean. Homeless people littered the empty alleyways they walked past. Some regular citizens walked around, but Arthur couldn't help but notice there was more wrong where he was than right. It was a sweltering day with next to no clouds in the sky, so the heat was battering down on everyone. Arthur couldn't help but feel sorry for the poorer people he walked past. He saw even children sitting against the walls, huddled up and begging for change. If Arthur had any money on him, he would have given some. As Arthur observed every space he was walking around, Cratos suddenly stopped walking dead in the street.

"What is it?" Arthur asked. He saw a severe look on his mentor's face as his eyes narrowed and sharpened around him, his head twisting and turning. He then turned to face Arthur and nodded at the building that stood before him. The brick was white with a single shabby brown door and no windows. There was a sign above the door saying, 'The doghouse'. Arthur had walked past a few places like this, seeing drunken men and women stumbling out of the open doors. They must have been pubs and taverns, he assumed.

"A bit early for a drink, isn't it?" Arthur remarked humorously. Cratos's face didn't change, and he looked around with intense concentration. Arthur noticed his measuring eyes scoping the place around him. Arthur didn't know what Cratos was trying to detect that Arthur couldn't, but he didn't interrupt and let his mentor focus. After a few seconds, his gaze dropped to Arthur.

"This is one of the many safe spots for our kind. It is a meeting place for Werewolves within this city. We must make sure we haven't been followed.

If 'they' find any places like this, then we are usually raided by police no more than an hour later." Arthur caught on immediately and began searching the crowds walking past them. Nothing seemed suspicious from his glance. It looked like no people were hanging around the area for too long. It looked as though people were just walking by, wholly blank-faced to their existence as it had been since they entered the city. Arthur knew he would miss things Cratos would be able to see, so even though he saw nothing suspicious, it was Cratos's evaluation he trusted. Arthur stepped up beside Cratos, and his mentor tapped on the door softly three times. At the near top of the door, a small rectangle opened with a mouth appearing inside.

"Password?" the man challenged in an intense voice. Cratos cleared his throat and then answered clearly.

"Moonlight," he answered. The man said nothing, and the rectangle opening snapped closed. For a few seconds, nothing happened, and Arthur thought Cratos had said the wrong phrase. Then, a series of clicks were heard, the sound of chains rattling and hinges moving.

"They take security seriously," Arthur muttered in a faint voice. Cratos smirked at that. The door opened a few centimeters, and Cratos slipped through the opening without saying anything. Arthur took one last look on the street, seeing nothing amiss, and finally stepped through the door as well. The wooden door then snapped shut behind him, re-clicking as it was locked up. Across the road, though in the darkness of an alleyway that even Cratos hadn't seen, was a tall man dressed in all black with a pale face, red eyes, and a grinning smug look. After a few seconds, he pulled out a phone, pressed a button, and spoke quietly into the mouthpiece.

"It's me, another hideout has been located, and the interest target has been identified, track my signal and be here as soon as you can. And bring quite a cavalry." The man then put the phone back in his pocket and continued to stare at the brown door grinning devilishly.

The inside wasn't exactly as Arthur had expected. Growing up in his hometown, Arthur had seen the inside of many bars and pubs, although this one seemed to have an exciting theme. There wasn't anything in the bar itself that stood out, but rather it was more the crowd within that made it stand out to Arthur. The room was filled with oversized carved wooden chairs and tables littering the room. The walls around them were built with heavy grey bricks cemented together. What hung from the walls was a different range of weapons. Spears and swords were crossing each other in display around every wall surface. There were also different paintings of people Arthur didn't recognize which hung across the place randomly. The floor was hard solid wood painted black. To the far left of the site was a massive fireplace with a roaring orange fire within it. Lying at the back of the room in the middle was the bar. The front of the bar was a deep mahogany brown color with a massive array of shelves behind the bartender, displaying differently decorated bottles of various alcohol nearly everywhere in sight. A sizeable black speaker in each top corner of the room was bolted by thick metal bars to the walls. The room was filled with people, drinking and talking, some laughing and others with menacing expressions on their faces.

They were all heavily built people, physically speaking. They were all looking like age-old warriors, even the women. All of them bore huge defined muscles, with scars littering their faces and exposed flesh. Some had ordinary clothes on, but many were wearing what looked like thick leather armor over the top of dark clothing with shin and forearm guard protection. Most had long hair, passing their shoulders and going down their backs. Many women had theirs tied up in different fashions, and Arthur even spotted some men with strange, braided hair designs. Like outside the bar, the inside of the place was very racially diverse; he spotted about every race he knew, all within groups of each other speaking freely. A lot of the people were also heavily tattooed. Arthur saw a vast array of distinctive designs, animals, and colors covering their bodies, even on their faces. Arthur was amazed; it all looked terrific from his eyes. He had always wanted a tattoo. Arthur then noticed that the Werewolves must be very accepting people. He had learned in History and English classes how discriminating a lot of the world was. Cratos had never mentioned how tolerant and accepting the Werewolf society seemed to be, and he liked it.

Arthur took a few steps into the place only to be greeted with the sweet sound of metal music blasting through the air. He didn't recognize the band or song, but he knew the excellent strumming of the guitars and the other instruments meshing into the powerful blast of sound that riddled the air around him in a chaotic wave of power. The lead singer was singing in a different language, but that didn't bother Arthur one bit, it was the music itself he was listening to and the voice singing over the sound was still unique. Arthur couldn't help but start nodding his head to the beats and smile. He didn't realize how much he had missed his precious music while he had been away from humanity. Cratos chuckled as he saw Arthur taking in the sound.

"I take it you're a fan of Metal?" Cratos asked ironically. Arthur looked back at his mentor and nodded.

"I've loved it ever since I heard it when I was little," he replied with a euphoric vibe in his tone. Cratos laughed, then nodded and winked.

"Wait until we get to the Wolf Kingdom. I think you'll be pleasantly surprised then if it's Metal you like."

Arthur wanted to press more on what he meant when a man approached the pair. He walked with a confident stride in his stature, dark skin covered in multiple black tattoos of different symbols running up his arms and even onto his bald head in patterns Arthur didn't recognize. As this man got closer, Arthur noticed his immense height, taller than even Cratos a bit, dawning thin but thickly defined muscles, also very much like Cratos. He wore tightly strapped deep brown leather armor with a sleeveless black vest beneath it, thick heavy black trousers with steel-toe-capped boots. The man presented Arthur with a fearsome blazing stare; his yellow-colored eyes around his pupils that Arthur felt could burn a hole through his face. The man's lip curled hatefully as his chest puffed up as though he was about to leap and murder Arthur right on the spot. Arthur himself froze, not sure how to react. He wasn't sure if he had angered the man somehow without noticing. He doubted he would be able to fight the man if he decided to attack him. Arthur instead waited for him to speak.

"Who are you?! Speak!" he snapped at Arthur. His voice was deep in tone and surprisingly commanding. Arthur wondered if maybe he was the man who asked for the password at the door. Arthur, this time scowled, he didn't like being snapped at like that, and he glared back at the man.   A surprising bolt of confidence sparked within himself, and so Arthur narrowed his eyes at the man.

"Make me," he hissed back. The man leaned in close, and his eyes looked as though they were carved from the very rage of a demon.

"Come now, Delfer, don't frighten the boy," Cratos said, calm and friendly. The man held his face for a few more seconds, then pulled back and laughed, smiling and his stare suddenly became pleasant and welcoming. Arthur relaxed and breathed out, glad it was just a joke.

"I just wanted to see if your new cub had a backbone; I have to say I'm quite impressed," the man chuckled, then facing Cratos, his smile widening.

"It's been a while, old friend," he greeted, holding out his hand. Cratos took it and shook back, the pair wrenching their hands together in a death grip for an extended time, not breaking eye contact with each other.

"Glad to see you haven't gone soft," Delfer noted, gritting his teeth.

"Same to you, old man," Cratos answered back with a wide smirk on his face, veins straining around his forehead. The pair released their grip, and Delfer nodded to an empty table.

"Shall we catch up then, old friend?" Cratos nodded, and the three went to sit down in the Doghouse pub.

"Arthur Thorn, allow me to introduce you to Delfer Septus, one of the laziest of our kind you will ever meet," Cratos had said in a playful tone as he drank his pint of beer deeply. The man named Delfer laughed back.

"This coming from the man who spent the majority of his training with our teacher Marthal, bedding every woman that batted their eyelids at him!" Cratos choked on his beer and coughed discreetly, blushing slightly and then nodding towards Arthur.

"HE doesn't need to hear such things, Delfer, please be careful of what you say." Arthur rolled his eyes, he wasn't an innocent child, and Arthur knew full well what they were talking about in front of him. Looking at Cratos Mane, Arthur would never have pegged him as a ladies' man. When Arthur pictured ordinary people who enjoyed getting all dressed up and going out to nightclubs and dancing, he imagined Cratos going to a graveyard to meditate or something. But despite Cratos's words, Arthur still laughed and winked at his mentor.

"Stories I will get you to share one day," Arthur warned at him, causing Delfer to laugh.

"The boy has a sense of humor. That's a good thing to have in our world, boy, don't forget it." Arthur smiled at Delfer and nodded. He was drinking a glass of orange juice because Cratos refused to allow him to drink alcohol yet. Delfer asked Cratos why Arthur couldn't drink any alcohol.

"He only just passed the first stage," he answered, and Delfer just nodded and left it at that. Arthur didn't know that his fight with the Werewolf inside himself had anything to do with a simple pint of beer, but he didn't want to disrespect Cratos in front of others by arguing. He felt that might make him look like a child, and he wanted to make a good impression in front of Delfer.

"So then, what brings you around here? I haven't seen you in this city for about five years now, right?" Cratos nodded firmly.

"Around that time, I recall; however, we see each other during the Eclipse celebration each time, so it hasn't been that long." Delfer nodded back, and Arthur just continued to drink. He made a mental note to mention this Eclipse thing later to his teacher, and hopefully, after Cratos has had more pints, and will be willing to say a lot more when drunk. Delfer turned his attention to Arthur and looked him over with a studious eye.

"Crimson class eh, strange for you to take one of them on Cratos," He noted. There was that phrase again, 'Crimson class', Arthur noticed, still wishing to know what it meant exactly. Cratos had mentioned it before, referring to himself as 'Shadow class', and he was dying to know what I meant.

"Yes, ordinarily, I would have given him to a teacher who would have trained him in that way earlier, but I thought mixing in some Shadow class ideology and lessons would do him a lot of good. Stop him from becoming an arrogant muscle head like most of them," Cratos concluded with a slight edge in his tone on the last few words. Delfer chuckled and rolled his eyes.

"I dare you to say that to Blane to his face," He replied dryly, finishing the last of his pint, which had been his fifth one since Arthur had met him. He didn't know how many the man already had.

"Blane is the minority of the Crimsons. Levelheaded, smart, and discreet, the kind of Crimson I want Arthur here to be." Arthur smiled oddly at that, glad his mentor had such a high opinion of him.

"Well, if he learns well enough, I'm sure Cyrus will be pleased to add more elites to the Beta's," Delfer noted, still looking Arthur over and judging him.

"How long ago did he pass the first stage?" he asked passively.

"Literally the other night, it was a close call, though, but he will be fine from now on. I am sure of it." Arthur was starting to get a little annoyed that the pair was speaking as though he wasn't there. Delfer could have easily asked him that question; Arthur felt he wasn't a show and tell. Arthur also made a mental note to remember these names the pair was dropping. This Blake and Cyrus seemed to be essential Werewolves in the Werewolf society by how Cratos spoke of them. Delfer mentioning these 'Betas' as well struck his curiosity. Arthur speculated they must be the clan's strongest fighters who were just below the leader.

The two continued to speak of different people, places, and times they had spent together that Arthur didn't even bother to try and listen and make sense of. He drowned the pair out and refocused on the music playing. It was playing loud, but he noticed that he heard nothing when he and Cratos were standing outside the pub. Arthur gathered that the building must be greatly soundproofed. The other people in the building took no notice of the three of them. Not even Arthur, despite he was the only person of his age in the building. New cubs must be nothing new to their sight either. There were plenty of Werewolves that resembled that of Cratos and Delfer in his view. A lot were very tall and slender yet immensely defined in their muscles. Ranging from medium-sized to arms nearly the size of tree trunks, it was amazing. In the world Arthur used to live in, if you wanted a physique like that, you had to train like a bodybuilder every day of your life for years. He remembered when he first woke up from the bite that Cratos had given him. His body had automatically changed and had given him a fighter-grade physique. But his arms still hadn't expanded in size yet. Cratos had told him they would eventually, but he also said that Werewolves still train extremely hard regardless of their biology, giving them a superhuman edge. Arthur looked at the Werewolf people and their giant arms with envy. He knew he was young and still apparently had many changes and trials to go through before he would be considered a full-fledged Werewolf. Still, Arthur couldn't help but feel inferior to all these people. He then wondered what it would be like in the Wolf Kingdom; he would probably feel like a cat among tigers.

Arthur also noticed that even the women around the room easily rivaled most of the men he saw, and they carried their own fair share of scars, too, as he observed the space further. They appeared every inch of a fearsome fighter as the men did. This distinction was another significant difference from his previous life. The girls in his school had the mindset of only being skinny rather than fit, god forbidding if they developed big muscles. They all desired soft mushy thin arms and bodies just like the models in magazines they had read.

Contrary to that, the women here were rippling with strength and power just like everyone else, but as Arthur looked at them, he still noticed some were quite attractive women. Their strength was oddly appealing to Arthur in a strange way he couldn't quite explain. He felt suddenly sprung with a sense of first glance respect that he considered strangely desirable. The women with the larger muscles were red-headed like him, which was a fun coincidence, just like the men were also, oddly. The people with the darker hair looked more like Cratos and Delfer did, but the gingers of the room seemed to-

"Taking in the view, lad?" said the voice of Delfer, breaking his concentration. Arthur looked back at Delfer quickly and nodded, blushing slightly. Delfer laughed.

"Don't be embarrassed, boy. You'll find it won't be as much of a struggle to charm them as it would have been as a human," he said with a wink. Arthur frowned in confusion.

"What do you mean?" he asked. Cratos took notice of his confusion and frowned.

"Do you remember that day in school you had when you first joined us?" Cratos asked casually.

"How did that trial go anyway?" Delfer asked, cutting in.

"The usual, bad. Overconfident, arrogant, fat-headed. Like always with new cubs. He managed to redeem himself though." Delfer nodded and allowed Cratos to continue.

"Remember how I explained on the street that we let out certain pheromones that repel people from noticing us?" Arthur nodded dumbly.

"Do you remember that day at school any attention other girls were giving you?" Arthur thought for a second; he then remembered that Cratos was right. The girls at school that day were looking at him and whispering flattering things about him to each other all day. Arthur felt as though suddenly every girl in the school fancied him.

"Yeah," he answered back quickly.

"They had never even looked in my direction before, but on that day, they couldn't tear their eyes off of me," Arthur said with a chuckle. Delfer began chuckling as well.

"That's how we are to humans, especially to the opposite sex. Werewolf scent is three times as strong and appealing to humans. Ever heard the phrase, Animal magnetism?" Delfer explained. Arthur shook his head. It sounded familiar, but he didn't know it. Delfer rolled his eyes as Cratos drank his drink, enjoying its flavor and savoring not having to be the answer machine for once.

"It's simple really. The pheromones you put out, especially given your age specifically, work on human women as though it is some sort of airborne drug, causing them to become infatuated with you within mere seconds half of the time." Arthur sat back for a moment to take in all that information. Given how the girls at school responded to him, he had anticipated an answer like this, but he hadn't expected it to be as great as he thought. To hear he was irresistible to human women, as though he was upgraded to charm that even surpassed Jack.

"It works both ways as well, though," Cratos cut in, noticing the sight of his student's head inflating.

"Female Werewolves also possess the ability to charm male humans in the exact same way." He then held a finger at Arthur with a raised eyebrow.

"But it is no different than the rest of our powers and abilities, Arthur. It is not a plaything for you to abuse and start breaking human women's hearts. It is wrong to take advantage of anyone, Arthur." Delfer also nodded as he downed his drink.

"I have to agree, be careful with this charm, boy. It can cause a lot of pain to people," Delfer finished smacking his finished drink back onto the table. Arthur nodded thoughtfully. He knew that lesson all too well. Arthur had seen many girls from school crying hysterically in tears. The sadness was caused by his friend Jack after he casually dumped them for no reason. Arthur didn't need to see orphan tiger cubs this time to learn this lesson. It was a lesson he had already witnessed first-hand. Delfer clapped his hands and smiled.

"Enough grim talk already! Let's grab a couple more drinks. I am itching to hear how our new pup here came to be walking with you, Cratos. The last I heard, you were hunting down some Vampire nobles. Let's grab a few more drinks." Cratos smiled at his friend.

"We would be happy too, Delfer, but we are on our way to Europe. Now that Arthur has passed his first stage, he needs to start training with the other cubs, as you know." Delfer nodded and sighed with exhaustion. Arthur felt like this wasn't the first time Cratos had skirted drinking with Delfer.

"I see. So, you'll need some essentials, some money, and the like?" Delfer mumbled, disheartened. Cratos nodded, smiling as though he had simply asked Delfer to pass him the napkins.

"That's why we came here; I had a feeling we would run into you," he answered cheerfully. Delfer shook his head, smiling.

"I hope one day you just stop by to say hello," Delfer grumbled, but Cratos simply smiled back.

"The Eclipse festival should be in a few months. We'll exchange pleasantries then, OK?" Delfer nodded and got up from his chair.

"I have what you need in the back room. I'll only be a few minutes." Cratos bowed his head in thanks as Delfer walked away from the pair to the back of the pub as he then went through a brown door, closing it sharply behind him. Arthur finished the rest of his drink and listened to the music. Several different songs had come on since they were here. Still no bands Arthur recognized as they changed different Metal genres a few times, but each was just as good as the last. Cratos noticed Arthur taking in his surroundings and coughed.

"So, what do you think of our people?" Cratos asked Arthur casually, his drink turning him more merry than usual. Arthur smiled back, beaming.

"So far, so good, Delfer seems friendly, and everyone else here looks very impressive!" Cratos rolled his eyes.

"Don't let appearances fool you, Arthur," Cratos warned. He then tapped his chest with his left hand.

"It is in here where a man should be judged. I do not doubt any one of our brothers and sisters here at all. I am just saying be careful who you instantly trust. OK?" Arthur nodded.

"Fair enough. By the way, I meant to ask. I noticed some of the people here with darker hair looked more like you and Delfer, and I wondered if-" Arthur's question was cut off As the brown wooden entrance to the bar exploded open off of its hinges into everyone. Everyone in the building jumped to their feet as dozens of figures in black Armor entered the room and held guns up.

"Vampire raid!" roared one of the Werewolves in the bar. The first shots were fired, and then the room was turned into a raging bloodbath of carnage and chaos. The people who burst into the room held up guns and other weapons only to be instantly met with a round of dozens of blaring Werewolf roars.

CHAPTER THIRTEEN

Through Arthur's eyes, a million things happened in an instant. Arthur had seen Cratos fight the Vampire women who attacked him at a speed that made his eyes feel blurred. Now Arthur was seeing the same thing again but multiplied by dozens. In the attack, some of the Werewolves remained in their human forms, grabbing the various swords and axes that hung from the wall. They were all roaring with monstrous howls and dashing forward towards their gun-wielding assailants. Their legs were nearly invisible to the eye as they ran. Their arms shot forward to reach their targets before they would be filled with bullets, fighting for their lives. Their claws ripped, their long-fanged teeth biting, and their prey spilled lots of blood. One of the men in the black armor that blew the door open shouted an order. Following that, all the other soldiers fired their weapons at the swarm of Werewolves. The bullets began filling the air and plummeting deeply into the Werewolves' bodies. On impact, the metal pierced their skin open but somehow did not stop their charge forward. Blood exploded from the beasts' bodies like ruby fireworks from every direction. But despite the hail of bullets ripping their bodies to pieces, they didn't cease their assault; the front line came within claw reach, and then the carnage started.

Arthur noticed something interesting when the Werewolves attacked. There were plenty of black fur-colored Werewolves just like Cratos, tall, slender, and fast. But there were also others among them in the fray. Some of the people who turned into enormous bulky Werewolves had immense bodies the size of those he had heard about in fantasy. Werewolves who had been giants in the room in their human form had just tripled themselves in size and stature. But what stood out the most was that their fur wasn't black like the slimmer wolves. Instead, the fur Arthur saw on the giant Werewolves' hairy bodies was a dark red. It looked as though their entire body had just been dyed vermillion, and their fur was a powerfully dark shade of blood. A few others, only a handful were a dark yellow color themselves, but they were not as big as the red Werewolves, but they were not as thin as the black-furred Werewolves. They had the size to them, but they were bigger than the black-furred slim Werewolves. Arthur guessed their physique was in the middle when comparing. The rest of the Werewolves attacking had normal, brown-colored fur, just like in all the movies, the same as every Werewolf stereotype.

The red-coated Werewolves were the first to dive forward at the attackers, taking most of the bullet's fire. Blood was drenching their ruby-colored fur as they roared in both agony and wrath. They drove their claws upon the heads of those carrying the guns on the front line, instantly ripping them from their shoulders with a twitch of their arms. More Werewolves ran and attacked from the sides and corners around those that had charged the front. Their nails pointed straight and held together in a row like hand blades. With speed unseen by the gunmen's eyes, they sliced and slashed those that came within their range, hacking up bodies like wet paper against a chainsaw. The people that had charged in were fully clad head to toe in heavy black combat armor, looking like the perfect likeness to black ops soldiers. Even with the eyes of a Werewolf, Arthur could only recognize mere after-images of the violence before him. The other Werewolves, the golden ones, and brown ones, simply joined the fray of attacking. They slashed and roared their way into the bloodbath with their other reddened family members. Sadly, within seconds, many Werewolves hit the ground, going still in seconds, their bodies rippled and riddled with gunfire. While the Werewolves tore through the armored soldiers like they were made of cardboard, it seemed for every one they killed; four more took their place with fresh ammo ready to spend. The room was deafening; Arthur hadn't heard gunfire in real life before, only ever in films on television. The actual sound of guns firing on a screen and guns firing only a few feet away from his ears was a massive difference in volume, and with Werewolf hearing to add on, that made it even worse. The noise of a hail of bullets going through the air a second at a time made Arthur reel in agony. The Werewolves roaring as they fought and died did not make the noise any easier to bear.

Cratos acted away from Arthurs' sight as his student gazed at the battle with a dropped jaw, still not reacting from the carnage that had unfolded in his lap. By the time Arthur turned his head to look at Cratos, his mentor had already transformed himself back into his tall, black-furred Werewolf form. His eyes were burning with rage as he snarled. He looked at Arthur and nodded towards the back door towards the pub's back room, away from the chaos. He wanted Arthur to head towards the room Delfer had gone into to grab the supplies Cratos had asked for before they were attacked. Arthur however, didn't want to run. For some reason, some strange part of him wanted to join in the fight as well. He turned his head back to the battle and saw the littered bodies of Werewolves that had been cut to pieces with gunfire, and his blood boiled. Witnessing his own kind slaughtered like cows before his eyes. His shoulders began to shake angrily as his arms tensed. He took an angered step towards the massacre, suddenly at that moment. All noise from the room began disappearing into whispers in his ear as a red haze of rage swarmed over his senses. He began eyeing the soldiers he planned to rip in half down the middle of their bodies with his bare hands. He took another step when a hand gently gripped his shoulder, careful not to puncture a hole in his flesh with its claws. Arthur turned his snarling face around to see the wolf face of Cratos leering intensely at him. It looked nothing like his mentor in his human form. Arthur hadn't seen Cratos in his complete wolf form since the warehouse. Now he was just another one of the dozens of other black-furred Werewolves in the room. Then Arthur looked into his mentor's present piercing yellow eyes, yet still seeing the same care of his teacher that had looked after him this entire time.

Cratos shook his head slowly but firmly. Arthur had pretty much guessed that Cratos meant if the Werewolves that hadn't already died fell, then he probably wouldn't last long either. Arthur took another look at the battle before him. More soldiers from outside were beginning to move into the space. Cratos began to snarl with impatience; he nodded again towards the back door. Arthur realized that if he didn't listen this time, he wouldn't get another. Swallowing his pride, Arthur turned his back on his wolf brethren as they died in the gunfire and ran as fast as he could to the back door. Cratos covered Arthur from sight with his own body as Cratos joined the fray. As Arthur got to the back door, he pushed the wood, but it wouldn't budge. Arthur clenched his fist and slammed it on the door several times.

"I'm not a Vampire! I'm a Werewolf! OPEN!" he shouted in desperation. The door flew open, then a hand reached out and sharply grabbed Arthur by his collar and yanked him inside, the door snapping shut behind him. The next face he saw was the severe and stern frown of Delfer.

"Arthur, we have to act fast! There's an escape tunnel through here. We have to go down it NOW!" Arthur looked behind Delfer and saw that other Werewolves in the room were already bolting the door behind him shut. They were in their human form but worked fast without hesitation. They were bolting the door along the edges with giant metal nails with some sort of gun.

"Wait!" Arthur cried in shock.

"Cratos didn't get in!" he called out. Delfer shook his head at Arthur; his expression was pained.

"I know, but he would have wanted it this way. What matters is keeping you safe. I know what Cratos wants, Arthur. Now hurry!" The room was now what Arthur had expected. The back rooms of a bar were usually filled with boxes and crates of beer for when the stuff in the front runs out. This room was a sealed off-white blank room with a large square metal door in the middle of the floor. Delfer dashed forward and opened the door. There were five other Werewolves with Arthur and Delfer. They all went through the floor hatch first after dropping their guns without saying anything to the pair.

"Arthur, hurry now!" Delfer called angrily. Arthur scowled at Delfer and shook his head miserably.

"I'm not leaving Cratos behind!" he pleaded stubbornly. Delfer sighed, angrily exhausted.

"We REALLY do not have time for this, Arthur. Cratos will be fine! He has come through tighter situations than this. We have dealt with this before, boy. We have to deal with it all the time. But IF he does die, don't you think he would at least have wanted you to get away rather than rushing out there to help him only to be immediately gunned down!" Arthur didn't have an answer for that, he stayed silent, and his eyes began to water slightly. Delfer held his hand out and nodded at Arthur. The door behind them began to bang loudly. Someone was trying to knock it down. Arthur closed his eyes and ran forward, taking Delfer's hand and climbing down through the escape tunnel, leaving Cratos behind in the chaos of the attack to live or die.

The next twenty minutes were nothing but full-powered sprinting. Even Arthur's added Werewolf strength had his limits, and racing none stop was taking its toll on him. Were it not for his training in the jungle, he would have collapsed ten minutes ago. Delfer and the other five men kept a consistent pace without even sweating, and Arthur didn't want to look weak in front of them, so he kept on running without complaining. The tunnel was a straight line going away from the bar. It was nothing but the brown earth with long thick wood bars stretching across the ceiling and walls, reinforcing it for cave-ins. Arthur felt his chest and stomach aching with pain, his breathing was loud and apparent, but he remained as silent as possible. Delfer was next to Arthur as they ran; he ran an eye over Arthur and saw he was struggling.

"Heroe! How much further?" Delfer asked, for Arthur's sake. The man at the front thought for a moment.

"Not far, we're nearly there, but the Vampires will be already in the tunnel or about to be. We'll need to set the charges off soon, so we need to move faster." Delfer looked at Arthur again and spoke to him quietly.

"Keep going; don't focus on your breathing. Divert your mind to something else." Arthur nodded, but despite Delfer's advice working, it only added to his guilt as his mind could only drift to thoughts of Cratos and how he left him behind. Cratos Mane had been Arthur's only true friend his entire life, and Arthur felt like a miserable coward for leaving him behind. The first bunch of Werewolves he had met at a time, and within moments they were all slaughtered right before his eyes, cut down like dogs in the dirt. It then reminded Arthur of the Vampires themselves and how this was their entire fault; it made him sick.

"Will they all die?" Arthur asked in a huff, his breath still strained. He had been expecting a solemn yes in response followed by a voice filled with regret. But instead, he saw Delfer think about it a moment before he answered.

"Not necessarily," he mused honestly.

"As I said before, we deal with this all the time. The Vampires flush out our minor meeting points like this. The outcome isn't always the same. Sometimes most of us escape. But the Vampires, this time, managed to get some sort of Special Forces with automatic firing weapons. This means they have been watching this spot for a long time. Cratos entering must have sealed the deal." Arthur frowned.

"Why? How do they know who Cratos is?" Delfer heard that question and couldn't help but chuckle. The Werewolves ahead of Arthur exchanged looks with each other and continued running.

"Guess he never told you. Unbelievable. Always so bloody secretive," Delfer commented, smirking. Arthur was going to demand more answers when one man at the front threw his arm forward, pointing ahead.

"There's the exit, quick, everyone. Up the ladder, and I'll throw the switch!" The group got to the end with a final heaving sprint. There was a metal ladder against an earthen wall before them; a metal circle hatch at the top with light was seeping through the edges. Saying nothing, every man went up the ladder. The one in front pushed the cover off the top and scrambled into the open. Delfer went ahead of Arthur as he looked at the last Werewolf.

"What are you going to do?" Arthur asked. The Werewolf nodded back down the tunnel, then at a switch attached to the wall next to him. There was a long black wire that led from the metal switched along through the tunnel.

"Blow the tunnel apart; the scum won't be following us now!" he said with dark hatred in his voice. Arthur saw the strange pleasure in his eyes and then quickly climbed up the ladder, escaping the tunnel and leaving the advancing Vampires behind him, with no way back now for Cratos.

Arthur arrived inside a small grey cemented room. He climbed out from the ladder, standing up straight. He observed his surroundings for a moment. There were no windows, just grey walls, one of which had diverse types of guns inside a small crate next to it and only a metal door for an exit. The door itself was loaded with several metal bolts running from the top of the frame down to the bottom. The last man climbed out and closed the utility hole cover behind him. The other men were immediately grabbing the guns stacked by the wall and bolting the hatch cover shut. Within seconds the ground began to shake immensely. Arthur felt the room rumbling and vibrations rattling through the floor beneath his feet. Arthur could hear the tunnel collapsing from afar; the noise was echoing through his ear. Arthur winced as the other Werewolves laughed after the shaking died down.

"I hope a lot of them were chasing us," one said, chuckling. Arthur shook his head, wondering if the floor below him was about to give away. The tremor faded, and the men sighed with relief. Delfer nodded at them.

"You guys go ahead and follow usual procedures. We only have a limited time frame to get confirmation of any survivors. Go!" The men nodded and left the room, closing it behind them. Arthur was confused; he looked towards Delfer.

"Procedures? What do you mean, Delfer?" Arthur watched Delfer step on the metal man cover a few times, testing it was bolted down firmly with his foot. Satisfied, he turned around and sternly looked at Arthur.

"Usually when a Werewolf spot is raided, the Vampires like to take as many hostages as they can to 'extract' information out of each of them," Delfer answered sternly, his previous playful personality Arthur had met before was now completely replaced. Arthur's face went a little pale; the thought of Cratos being tortured wasn't nice and presented unsettling imagery in his mind. Delfer coughed into his fist uncomfortably.

"Usually, in situations like that, a Werewolf would bite off their tongue to bleed to death or take their life in whatever way presented itself so they cannot betray their brethren." Arthur's eyes widened, figuring Cratos was already dead. Arthur slowly lowered his head, looking at the floor and feeling like he was about to burst into tears. A hand touched his shoulder, and he looked up to see an understanding face of Delfer looking at him.

"But this is different, Arthur. Sometimes something can be done. If we can confirm that there ARE any survivors, we then track how they are being transported and rescue them." Hope flourished in Arthur's face as excitement rushed through his body.

"So Cratos could be alive!?" Arthur exclaimed frantically, but Delfer's face wasn't keen to match Arthur's enthusiasm. His expression was uncertain and uncomfortable.

"I'm betting on it," he answered with a grimace.

"Why is that bad?" Arthur challenged; he thought Cratos was Delfer's friend. Delfer sighed.

"We don't have the luxury of storytime right now. I will explain later." Arthur rolled his eyes; he hoped one day to meet a Werewolf that doesn't always say 'later.'

"Right now, we have to act fast, follow me," Delfer ordered before heading to the door, immediately going through it. Arthur followed behind briskly; the hope that Cratos could still be saved was keeping his faith going.

The room led to a long corridor, plenty of doors on either side stretching down to the end. The walls were the same as the room, grey concrete with nothing else. All other entries were metal, almost looking like the sort of doors inside a prison. Delfer was hurrying down the corridor quickly, Arthur following behind. Delfer was speaking as they walked.

"This is one of our communication stations Arthur," he began to explain.

"We see to it every meeting establishment for Werewolves, like that pub we were in, they all connect to one of these facilities for emergencies as well as for any new information arriving from scouts." Arthur looked at the rooms as they went down. He could hear people talking in each of them. The door at the end of the corridor had a sign on it, but Arthur couldn't see what was said from where they were yet.

"It is from places like this we keep contact on our war most of the time, Arthur. Orders were issued as well as tracking down Vampires and any rogue Werewolves. All information our people know going through places like these. We are like blood passing through the organs of a body, keeping it alive and functioning." Arthur nodded as they walked, keeping his ears open for any critical information he could use to help Cratos.

"Usually, if we think one of our hideouts has been spotted by Vampire scouts. We tend to alert the place and evacuate it or set a trap for our oncoming attackers. Today was a minority of what usually happens. It doesn't happen often, but it still does happen." Delfer was deadly serious, the look in his eyes murderous. It was like the joke glare he saw when he first met the man. The laughing friend of Cratos had vanished from his sight and had now been replaced with a vengeful soldier. Delfer then pointed at the door at the end of the corridor.

"From there, we will have clarification of whether or not Cratos is alive or not. So, prepare for the worst if it comes, Arthur." Arthur held his breath as they came to the door. The sign on the front said 'War' on the surface. Saying nothing else, Delfer opened the door, and the pair went into the room.

The inside of the room was like a beehive of motion. There were dozens of people walking and running around, talking to each other and always on the move. People were speaking on the phone. There were those with computer monitors, giving directions through headsets. The entire room was alive with action. The walls were littered with large wooden boards on all four sides, several of them. Pinned against the wood were different maps of countries and continents. Arthur noticed there was a large one of the entire world. On the maps were different colored pins. There were red and blue ones, pressed down in various locations for reasons beyond Arthur's speculation. It all meant nothing to Arthur anyway. Down from the boards were several rows of tables with computers, phones, and other electronic devices Arthur couldn't recognize. They all had wires running out of them throughout the room. To Arthur, it looked like veins inside an arm if you pulled the skin away. They were wrapped around the walls, the ceiling, and the floors like millions of snakes swarming around them. No one addressed the pair as they entered, and while Arthur looked around, Delfer went forward and towards one of the men at a computer.

"Any survivors from the attack on the bar?" he asked bluntly. The man clicked on the keyboard in front of him a few seconds before answering.

"At least four scouts have confirmed that at least five were left alive. The rest are all dead," Delfer winced; Arthur could see the veins rise against Delfer's skin in anger.

"Bloody scum!" he hissed. As Arthur looked around, he noticed all the people here had dark hair. Their hair was black or severely dark brown, and they also all seemed to be very tall wearing black clothing. They appeared highly focused on the screens in front of them and the maps they observed from the tables and boards.

"Was Shadow class Werewolf Cratos Mane among them?" Delfer then asked with little expectation. However, to his surprise, the man nodded immediately.

"Yeah, first one confirmed alive." Arthur smiled with relief; he was glad to hear Cratos was at least alive to be rescued.

"How long before a retrieval squad can be deployed?" Delfer continued to ask. The man typed into his keyboard again; Arthur was counting the seconds before he answered nervously.

"Assuming you want to go now, minutes. The prisoners are being transported in an armored black van, SWAT-grade quality. We are monitoring its route, but with Cratos Mane there, it'll be heavily guarded. You're in for a rough rescue, sir," he answered. Delfer nodded and patted the man's shoulder.

"Good work. Get me details ready. I'm going to suit up." Delfer then turned to Arthur and nodded at him.

"OK. The others and I will do what we can to rescue Cratos." Arthur smiled widely, ready to go along and help.

"You are staying here. I will arrange an independent escort to travel with you to Europe where you will be transported safely to our main base." Arthur's face fell, the tower of cards that was his hope falling into dust.

"Upon success, you will be told as soon as possible. Goodbye for now, Arthur Thorn," he finished firmly. With a brisk nod, Delfer then turned away from Arthur, leaving him to stand there shocked as Delfer went to leave the room.

"I'm coming too!" Arthur insisted angrily, chasing after Delfer as he walked out of the room and into another. Delfer shook his head.

"No offense, kid, but you would be a liability, not an asset. I would have enough trouble keeping myself alive than worrying about you." Arthur's face twisted angrily; they were now standing in a storage room filled with different crates and cases along with multiple shelving units. It was vacated for the moment, but Delfer didn't slow his pace. He shuffled through the boxes, sorting out a variety of different clothing. Arthur leaned his head forward to see. The containers had protective armor within them. They had solid and tough vests for the torso and padded trousers with shin-high boots on the bottom spaces of the shelves. There were also elbow and knee pads as well as plated masks and helmets to wear as well. Delfer continued sorting through the crates. He started pulling out the different sorts of armor to fit him.

"Don't get used to this sort of sight. Only rescue squads wear armor like this. The only reason for it is that we cannot change into our wolf forms in broad daylight. So, we must protect ourselves as human soldiers do. But this is mainly the duties of Shadow class, so you won't have to worry about it." He spoke as though the matter of Arthur coming had ended.

"The sort of world you will go on to see will be a lot of action, especially given your training ahead of you when you reach Europe. The guard going with you will be able to explain more, OK?" Delfer began to zip his vest and bent down to fasten the straps on his boots, not even looking in Arthur's direction. Arthur shook his head, glaring at Delfer.

"NO!" Arthur snapped in response. Delfer sighed.

"This is out of your league, boy. This work isn't for a Crimson. Let's say you were capable and knew what you were doing, which you don't. We don't need a front-line brawler getting in our way!."

"Fine, I won't go with you; I'll rescue him by myself if I have to!" Arthur shouted back, hands shaking in a combination of fear and rage. Delfer chuckled in Arthur's face, shaking his head in amusement.

"May the great wolf gods save me," he answered lowly.

"And how exactly will you find him, Arthur? Tell me, how will you stop the van? break him out. Fight off the guards. You don't know what you're talking about when it comes to these situations. We have procedures and strategies to follow, and you would only get in the way. Do you understand, boy? You can't help him; you know nothing of our ways, so don't go around pretending as though you do. You are a Cub; you do as you're told!" With that, Delfer turned his back to Arthur and began fitting himself for the rest of his armor.

"No," Arthur said with his voice now calm and precise. Delfer turned around and faced sternly at Arthur, who only glared back at him.

"Let me go, and I promise you this," Arthur continued, his voice more deadly than he had ever been in his life. The void of darkness that was his pupils bellowed into Delfer's own like he was trying to make them dissolve with his very gaze.

"I will kill more Vampires than you can count," he finished solemnly. Delfer saw the dreaded determination in Arthur's eyes and let him continue.

"You made me leave him behind once. That man was responsible for saving me from a horrible fate, the life I led was misery, and he saved me. It's now my turn to save him. I owe it to him. I am his friend Delfer, and I will NOT turn my back on him again, and I dare anyone here to try and get in my bloody way!" Arthur tensed his arms and spread his fingers, not blinking, waiting for Delfer to respond. Delfer smirked at Arthur, still amused, but his respect for the boy had grown immeasurably.

"I see why he chose you. You have a fire that is truly remarkable." Arthur didn't respond to the compliment.

"Delfer. I'm going to help rescue Cratos," Arthur said again, with no hint of hesitation in his tone. Delfer raised an eyebrow for a few seconds and saw Arthur wasn't going to let it drop. He rolled his eyes and sighed.

"They're going to collar me for this," he groaned, then nodded at Arthur and reluctantly gestured to the shelves.

"See if you can find some armor in your size, then stick to me like glue. Understand?" Arthur's face exploded with a blast of excitement; he nodded frantically.

"Right away," Arthur answered, scrambling around the crates with lightning speed, ready to rescue his mentor and best friend.

CHAPTER FOURTEEN

Cratos Mane dived straight into the thick of the attack. He turned his back and safely concentrated his attention on those at the door with the guns the second he heard the back door bolt. Cratos knew Arthur didn't want to leave him, but the boy wasn't trained for this kind of action yet. He also knew Delfer would look after him and keep him away from trouble. Gunfire was still hailing all around the room of the besieged bar. A swarm of bullet holes was scattered all around the back walls and sides of the entire area. Several red Werewolves were on the floor dead. The black-furred ones like Cratos were on the sidelines and the small gaps with their red brethren, striking like they had hands made of knives, severing hands and heads in seconds.

Cratos attempted to try and prevent the armed attackers from following Arthur. The second the Werewolves gave way and allowed the soldiers to enter the bar, they would circle them, and they would be doomed. Cratos had been trained to focus his hearing on whatever he decided to prioritize. He chose his most urgent priority, which was to focus on the opponents on the front line. The deafening gunfire around him was merely a blurred noise in the background to his refined and trained ears. Cratos roared at the black armored soldiers in front of him. In each of their hands were automatic firing weapons. Cratos observed that the Vampires must have called in the best for this raid. A soldier by the bar door, only just behind his fellow soldiers who were busy with the other Werewolves, noticed Cratos come to join the battle and aimed his gun at him before he could fight. Cratos snarled and ducked his head down low out of the man's sight for a split second. The soldier didn't react to Cratos's duck in time and had already fired dozens of bullets towards where Cratos used to be. Cratos only needed this moment. He snapped his body to the side as he continued running on his feet at the man, moving as fast as lightning from human eyesight.

Before the man had the chance even to reposition his aim, Cratos was already upon him. With a swift right uppercut, he severed the soldier's left arm up to his shoulder. Before the man even had the chance to scream in pain and fall backward, Cratos shot his other arm forward and lanced the man straight in the left breast of his chest, piercing his heart with his long sharp wolf claws. Cratos ripped his hand straight out of the dead soldier's body, fingers clamped together, dripping and sticky with fresh blood. The man dropped down to the floor with a clunky slump, dead before he hit the ground. Cratos crouched down low as he swatted his hand at another soldier now to his left who was shooting his gun pitifully at a red Werewolf in front of him who was taking the thick spray of the bullets directly. The red Werewolf yelped. He had taken too many shots in the chest. The centerline of his body now resembled Swiss cheese as blood poured down the sides of his mouth. The bullets fired at him had passed through the thick muscles of his torso and punctured his organs deeply. The red Werewolf fell to the floor, growling still but unable to move its limbs. It looked up at the soldier, and with a final pulse of life, it threw both his hands forward in a final strike. He grabbed the gun out of the soldier's hands and into his own. The red Werewolf broke the weapon into two pieces with his giant arms and tossed the pieces aside like a snapped twig. Then the Werewolf, with mere seconds to live, grabbed the soldier firmly by his arms, violently dragging him forward. Before the man could call for help, the red Werewolf threw his head forward and, with his entire mouth, crunched the man's skull with every fang along his jaw. The soldier's head flattened inside the Werewolves' mouth like a hydraulic press squashing a juice-filled jawbreaker. Brains and blood spewed from the sides of his mouth, flowing down his jaw like a thick crimson meaty slurry. The Werewolves' body then shuddered, and he instantly fell sideways, dead.

Cratos saw the gap next to him and took a hesitant step backward. The wolf to his right fell to the ground dead, and now Cratos was staring dead-on at five soldiers with their guns trained straight on him. Cratos looked over his surroundings. The second he moved, they would all mow him down like grass against a scythe, and unlike the red Werewolves, he didn't have the muscle mass to take the bullets for a few seconds before dying. He turned his head from left to right. Apart from him, there were only eight other Werewolves left, all the rest dead. The fallen Werewolves lying on the floor all around them were bleeding out of an uncountable amount of bullet holes. Their blood was soaking around Cratos's ankles like he was standing in a bloody shallow pond. The stench of human and Werewolf blood was pungent in the air as he stopped fighting. The stench of death bludgeoned his senses to an almost vomiting effect. Sadly, Cratos has been surrounded by many bodies covered in much more blood in his life. Compared to those times, this was nothing. Cratos took another step backward as he looked on. This attack wasn't his first Vampire raid, and he figured any second some commander would shout an order, and Cratos would be turned into a very holy statue of himself made of lead. The other Werewolves around him were snarling hatefully at the soldiers as they too stopped fighting and accepted that they had lost this fight. Like Cratos, they gazed at their fallen family, engrossed with a twisted feeling of rage and mourning combined with helplessness as they could only now await their fate. Most of them saw many of their close friends dead at their feet, leaving them no time to grieve properly. The only thing stopping them from leaping forward to their bloody death was that it would cause the massacre of the rest of the survivors. Then, as Cratos had predicted, from outside the bar, a woman's voice was heard.

"Have the mutts stopped barking yet?" she asked, her voice insufferably smug and cream-like smooth to the ears. Cratos could tell she was young. One soldier in the middle holding a gun at Cratos firmly replied, his voice deep and rough, like nails in a meat grinder.

"Yes, miss, there are nine hostile targets left in total." The voice from the outside laughed loudly. A few soldiers at the door parted for her to enter. A woman in a red silk hood with full black and red mixed color fancy silk clothing came from the outside light. Her face was young and smooth, with thin lips with bright, and red-colored eyes. She had long brown hair flowing from her head that looked soft and weightless, bouncing with every step. She casually walked forward and looked over the remaining Werewolves. Then her gaze looked over at the dead ones within the bar on the floor. Her smile lowered into a smirk.

"That's what happens to bad doggies. They get put down," the woman cooed mockingly as she gazed at all of them. Several of the Werewolves remaining roared at her. The soldiers pointed their guns at them. The woman simply laughed without flinching at their bellows, ignoring them as her eyes focused on Cratos.

"We've been looking for you for a long time Cratos Mane. And now we have you. Perfect!" she giggled, clapping her hands together a few times. Cratos snarled hatefully; he had been trapped.

The Werewolves were forced to revert to their human forms. They were gathered in a circle by the soldiers before being handcuffed in the middle of the room. They were ordered to keep their heads down as the soldiers swept the rest of the bar, tearing it apart. The other Werewolves struggled angrily at their handcuffs as the place they loved was ripped to pieces. The woman in charge was applying makeup to her face while the soldiers worked, using a handheld mirror. Catching sight of that made Cratos briefly smirk as he remembered the silly stories about Vampires and how they don't have a reflection. She then began fixing her hair with her hands so it looked correct.

"So sorry about this," she said with fake sincerity at the Werewolves, not even looking away from her reflection.

"In order for this much force to be authorized, we had to drum up that you guys were seriously dangerous terrorists, gun runners, and drug runners. So, we need to make it look like we raided the place for drugs and use what we have stashed in the black transport vans as what we found. Just procedure, give us a minute, and you'll be shipped off yourselves." Three soldiers finally broke down the door to the backroom, the sound of the wood snapping going through Cratos's ears with a hollow screech. He began silently, hoping Arthur was as far away from their pursuit as possible. One of the soldiers came out of the room after a few minutes.

"Miss, we found an escape tunnel. A few of the men recall seeing a number of the targets escape into the back room during the raid." The woman sighed angrily, as though she had just been told her coffee would be a few minutes delayed.

"I hate it when they run away," she whined like an impatient child would if refused sweets.

"Well, what are you waiting for!? Go after them! I want to know where their little tunnel leads," She finished pointing at the back room. The soldier, without flinching, nodded firmly.

"Yes, miss, right away," the soldier responded, saluting. The woman sighed; she knelt and leaned forward, so she was face to face smiling smugly at Cratos. He looked at her as though gazing upon an open wound. She was wearing some sort of fancy perfume which now smothered his body, its scent crawling up Cratos's senses like a spreading parasite. He simply remained silent, glaring back at her.

"Apparently, you came here with a boy. Do you think you got him to safety? I'll personally make sure you see him die before we finish you."

Cratos lost his temper; he threw his body forward, his Werewolf fangs sprouting from his mouth in an instant like a striking cobra intent on biting her smooth pale face off in a single chomp. Before he came within an inch of her, the butt of a rifle slammed hard against the side of his head, knocking Cratos down. The woman laughed at Cratos as he recoiled and recovered from the temple strike to his skull.

"You dogs are always so easy to rile up, I love it!" She giggled before laughing again. Her laughter was a painful high-pitched shriek, ringing through even the soldier's ears. She stood back up and looked down at Cratos like how a cruel child behaved when it had just pulled off an insect's legs to gaze at its suffering.

"You have much to tell us, Cratos Mane, and I promise," she then narrowed her eyes and squeezed her lips tightly together. She leaned down, so her lips were right next to Cratos's ear. She then spoke in seductive whispers.

"I will flay the skin from your body. You will be begging to be put down. I will make sure your agony goes on for weeks if I must, and when you have told us everything you know and have been repaid for every Vampire life you have taken, we will feed you alive to rabid wolves. We have a good dozen kept alive just for occasions, and I will enjoy watching you being ripped apart, you diseased, dirty, disgusting dog!" The woman's smile squirmed across her face, waiting for Cratos to say something. For a few seconds, Cratos said nothing; he remained on the floor entirely still. Out of nowhere, the floor began to shake like an earthquake. The woman stood up immediately, shocked.

"What's happening!" she commanded the room, but the other soldiers were just as confused as they looked at each other. The shaking then stopped suddenly, and a few seconds of silence filled the room. All the Werewolves in the circle began to chuckle softly before it grew increasingly into hysterical laughter. Even Cratos wailed, laughing like a madman, growing lost in the moment. The Vampire woman looked at each of the Werewolves with white-hot fury.

"Silence! You stupid mutts! What's so funny!" she screeched. The laughter died down into a few chuckles as Cratos lifted his head, now bearing a smug smirk of his own.

"I wouldn't bother waiting for the soldiers you sent down our tunnel to come back," he answered, beginning to laugh again. The woman's face twisted hatefully into a hideous sight. Her mouth opened, and her fangs sprouted from her mouth with flowing drool dripping from each fang. She then threw her leg forward, kicking Cratos hard in the stomach. He winced at the strike as it bared a slight sharp pain, but he couldn't help but hold his smile.

"But don't worry," Cratos continued trying to stop himself from laughing more.

"I'm sure their life insurance doesn't cover being buried alive," he finished with a wink. The woman shrieked again and began kicking Cratos several times; all the while, he continued laughing. The other Werewolves began taking up laughter again at Cratos's remark. Her rage passed after she saw her kicks did nothing, and she stopped. She breathed for a few moments, then fixed her composure, returning to the dignified presence she had before she lost her temper. The Vampire then turned to the soldier that struck Cratos and spoke calmly.

"Get these filthy mutts in the van now!" Her tone was sharper than any knife with merciless menace. She looked down scornfully at Cratos.

"I'm eager to get my interrogation underway," he finished with as much venom in her tone as she could muster. Cratos simply winked at her again mockingly.

"Hey, I always let the woman choose the first date; what's your favorite movie? Is it Dracula?" The other Werewolves completely lost it at that. Each soldier began to secure and bind Cratos like the other Werewolves before they were dragged and pulled out into the street and inside a large black van as they howled with laughter. Cratos was restrained with very thick, strong handcuffs. They tightly bound their wrists together behind his back, same with his ankles. Cratos knew these weren't ordinary handcuffs but ones specifically designed to hold Werewolves. Cratos was now left with the woman alone in the room for a few moments. She knelt and faced Cratos, staring at him curiously for a moment. She then leaned her face forward and sniffed the skin of his cheek.

"If only I could drink from you mutts," she whispered to him, sticking her tongue out of her mouth and caressing her still long and sharp fangs. The tip of her tongue writhed past her teeth and up and down Cratos's cheek.

"I would keep you as my personal blood slave. Your existence would be pure agony. I would make your life a living hell," she said with seductive breathy spite. Cratos pulled his head away, chuckling as he looked her dead in the eyes.

"Sorry, I'm not quite ready for a long-term relationship," he muttered in a whisper back to her. The next thing Cratos knew was darkness as another butt of a gun smacked the back of his head, knocking him out cold.

Cratos awoke later to the sound of knocking and the engine of a van. His head was resting hard against the cold floor, every vibration and bump burrowing through his skull like a nail gun. He tried to hold his head up, but he couldn't move. He struggled with his arms behind his back. He couldn't pick or break the locks that restrained them. Cratos then decided to stop struggling at such a wasted cause. In regular human handcuffs, Cratos knew he could break free laughing. But with Vampire handcuffs, there was no point even trying. His eyes opened wide as he threw his body upward with a significant heave, leaving him standing upright on his knees. He was then glad they didn't gag him. He then looked around the van. The other Werewolves sat against the metal of the walls with their heads held down, not making a sound. Their faces were beaten, and their expressions were defeated. They were reflecting on the fates that awaited them and the fates of their brothers and sisters, who they had just lost. Cratos assumed that escape must be impossible. Just like the handcuffs, these walls were built to contain Werewolves, and they were being transported. He guessed odds are the walls were just about impenetrable. Sighing, Cratos fell backward against the back of the van like his fellow Werewolves and bore a sad, sorry expression.

There wasn't much for Cratos to look forward to now. He knew he would soon be subject to Interrogation, torture, and execution, or he could be kept alive and suffer a worse fate, Vampire slavery. Cratos knew that some Vampires found it very amusing to keep some Werewolves as slaves. They would trap them and make them fight for amusement, keeping them as caged animals and torturing them for entertainment. Especially given his reputation, Cratos knew they were going to make quite the example out of him. The only reason Cratos hadn't already bitten off his tongue so he could bleed to death was the faint hope of rescue. He knew that once Delfer had transported Arthur to safety, he would try and stop the Vampires. There were many successful rescues in the past, so he had hoped he would survive this ordeal. But other rescues in history didn't have him within the bowls of a black van, and he had a feeling the Vampires had a few more tricks up their sleeve. The Vampires weren't going to hand over Cratos easily, especially without more blood to be spilled.

The sound of heavy breathing broke Cratos's train of thought from one of the Werewolves to his left. He was a young man, with shoulder-length blond hair with no tattoos or visible scars. His chest was heaving up and down with rapid, panicked breathing. It seemed Cratos wasn't the only one thinking about their fate, but this man was reacting to it a lot worse. Cratos shook his head slightly. He felt terrible for the kid. He looked as though he had only just passed his stages and was new to the fighting side of the war.

"That was probably his first strong drink as a full-fledged Werewolf in that bar, only to get captured in a raid," Cratos thought bitterly. He knew it was just the unfortunate bloody luck of their life sometimes. Cratos looked around at the other Werewolves in the van with them. They were all at a decent age and had passed their stages of the Werewolf many years ago. They had a chance to live at the optimal prime of their lives. This lad was the youngest and now faced his death before the best of his life had started. Cratos didn't like to be overly philosophical. He always thought there were lessons to know for life, and there were questions about life, and the latter didn't interest him at all. He didn't believe in fate exactly. Cratos liked to believe in the power of a person choosing their destiny; what happened to this lad was pure bad luck. It was that simple.

Cratos shuffled up next to the lad. The guy noticed Cratos shuffling next to him and nodded slightly with a thin tight smile, his eyes returning to the space in front of him. He was struggling to keep his body shaking along with his breathing. Usually, a Werewolf was trained to handle situations like this perfectly, hence why the others in the van were relaxed and remained still. They were controlling their fears and anxiety through years of mental and physical training. But it seems, despite his training, this lad let fear get the best of him. Cratos had seen first-hand in many different fights that no training can change a person's core, and this kid was scared to die. Cratos could see the pure dread in his eyes. Cratos had seen this look in many different people, Werewolves, and even Vampires in his time. Cratos had seen the vacant realization of mortality rush through someone's pupils a million miles a second in his past battles and travels. They were consumed with an enshrouding fear within themselves, screaming like a horrified banshee. They weren't cowards, most of them had fought bravely next to him, and he discovered in their war that courage could not exist without fear. Cratos knew more than most Werewolves that there is no shame in fearing death; sometimes, that can be your strongest self in the face of death. But in this case, it had hollowed out this young man, and he had become a glass being. Odds are, if those doors opened to some Vampire interrogation building, Cratos suspected the boy would freak out and try and run for it. The Vampires then wouldn't bother with his screams and hysterics and probably shoot him there and then. They had plenty of others to interrogate, and they wouldn't miss one kid. Cratos knew, though, it was a sad end for any life. Cratos had seen it in the aged as well, older Werewolves. Hard men and women who were moments from death's icy grip with smiles on their faces, were suddenly reduced to the sad whimpers and tears of frightened children, begging to some unseen presence or entity for more time to continue to live. But Cratos always heard the empty void never answer such pleas. They had always died. No one knew what was within the depths of themselves unless faced with actual deaths. Cratos had seen that some are heroes, who grin in the face of turmoil and try to get in one last punch, but then some are also cowards. Giants were brought down to their knees in seconds.

Cratos looked at the lad, who then looked back, nodding out of habit than assurance. Wanting to help the poor lad, Cratos offered a weak smile.

"How are you holding up, lad," he asked, friendlily. The Werewolf didn't want to seem weak in front of his brothers. He may have just spent the last few minutes acting like a startled kitten, but his sense of image suddenly returned as Cratos spoke to him. His face immediately sharpened into a severe frown.

"Fine, ready for anything," he replied with a tone as hollow as his eyes. His body stopped shaking, and his shoulders arched. Cratos sighed but didn't stop looking at the man. Cratos said nothing, waiting for the kid's brave mask to drop as he knew it would be any second. The Werewolf saw Cratos was looking straight into him and knew how scared he was. His face then fell apart, and tears began to form in his eyes.

"This wasn't the plan. There was so much more I was going to do. It's not fair. Why do we all have to die now?" the man whispered. The other Werewolves heard the kid and looked up, confused frowns on their faces. Cratos sent them a glare that made each of them turn their head back down; they knew to keep to themselves right now.

"Who told you we were going to die?" Cratos said in return, catching his attention. The man looked up at Cratos, his face now riddled with confusion.

"What do you mean? Don't the Vampires have us? We're dead..." Cratos shook his head. It pained him to hear such defeatism from one of his brothers.

"You can't give up that easy, kid. Do you know why the Werewolves have managed to exist for so long in our war without dying out?" The lad shook his head as Cratos shrugged.

"We're all too bloody stubborn to die, nature's biggest nuisance," he finished with a wink. The lad couldn't help but chuckle. The other Werewolves listening in couldn't help smirking. Cratos saw him chuckle and continued.

"Vampires don't scare me, kid; you know what's worse?" The Werewolf kept his smirk as he looked at Cratos now.

"What?" he replied soundly, a small flicker of spirit returning to his tone.

"Fleas! I caught the buggers a few years back. I had to shave all my fur in our form. I looked like a giant pink alien. I would rather face a hoard of Vampires than go through that again." The lad couldn't help but start laughing as he pictured a furless Werewolf, letting himself chuckle for a moment. Cratos smirked with him.

"Don't worry, kid, it would be worse." He looked at Cratos again, now looking like a different man than who we were five minutes ago.

"Oh yeah?" he laughed again with Cratos nodding.

"Much worse! We could be vampires!" he finished, and the entire van of Werewolves was chuckling and laughing at his comment. The van settled back into silence after a few moments, but the atmosphere had changed immensely, from night into day, as they all seemed in higher spirits. Cratos now saw a warm smile on the lad's face, which was good. Cratos enjoyed making others smile when they were down, ever since he was a boy. Despite his more hostile demeanor, he seemed to have a touch for it. The young man then looked at Cratos oddly.

"Tell me, back in the bar that woman seemed to know you, said they had been looking for you specifically, why?" he asked. Cratos sighed, looking down at the van floor for a few seconds.

"You probably haven't heard about me yet. You wouldn't during training and trials, I suppose. Maybe you'll know at the next eclipse celebration." The lad squinted his eyes curiously, but he allowed Cratos to finish.

"Let's just say I have killed a lot of Vampires in my time. Some were forgettable wretches, flaunting their power and money without discretion. Typical new young Vampires feeling it was their time to win the war before getting a large sharp bite of reality. Then there were others. They were smarter, more important, and much older. They were very high up in the ranks. Once even..." he trailed off and didn't finish. The young man was fixated on Cratos.

"Even what?" he asked, puzzled. Cratos hesitated, then looked at him with a stern expression, speaking calmly.

"I killed a Vampire Master," he finished curtly, letting that go through the air towards the young man. The young man's eyes widened with shock, feeling he wouldn't have been more surprised if Cratos's head had just exploded.

"Really!? A MASTER!? That's incredible. I thought no one had ever been near one of the Master Vampires in centuries!" the man spluttered. Cratos shook his head, though.

"I have. Even Cyrus himself hasn't fought against one, but I did. I got lucky, though. I was extremely lucky or extremely unlucky, depending on your point of view. Despite the circumstance, the result was still the same. I killed it, and the Vampires have had a special vendetta against me since." The young man grinned widely. He looked like a small child hearing about a superhero for the first time.

"Bloody hell! What did it look like?" he asked. Cratos raised his head slowly and eyed the lad thoughtfully, not blinking for a moment.

"It was the most terrifying demon I had ever laid eyes upon. It was a thing of great evil and ever greater power. I can only pray you never see what I saw." Cratos then took away his eyes from the lad and let them drop down like the other Werewolves. His mind was now cast into his memories. The lad turned his head away from Cratos and went silent. The man was no longer shaking in fear but no longer smiling either.

"Do you think we'll be rescued?" he asked casually, his being in a more formal or neutral composure. Cratos didn't lift his head but shrugged.

"I know they'll try, but I don't know if they'll succeed," he answered remorsefully. The lad didn't respond or speak again. The whole group sat in silence as the van drove them to their deaths.

CHAPTER FIFTEEN

Arthur's veins were flowing with anxiety and adrenalin. He felt like his heart was beating at the speed of light. His eyes were wide with excitement and fear simultaneously. It was a frightful combination for anyone to experience. Despite the intensity of the situation, Arthur did not forget the rules Delfer had poignantly given him. No matter what happened, Arthur was told he was to stay close to Delfer as instructed, and if he broke that rule, he would be sent back to headquarters immediately with no argument. Delfer even had instructed one of the Werewolves in the team to be the one to bring Arthur back on his order. Arthur felt the urge to just jump into action and save the day as he looked on. He knew better, however. He knew that was the same impulse any idiot with no proper training would feel. Arthur also knew that if he behaved unprofessionally in any way, he would be considered a liability and cause others in the rescue team to die. He didn't want that on his conscience. However, even with his kid-like excitement for the mission, fear still riddled its way through his stomach with unrelenting force, causing him to feel sick with horror at the mental image of Cratos's death.

The group was waiting silently upon a rooftop, watching the traffic roll past them on the roads ahead. The group was hidden away in the shadows, out of sight from anyone who could spot them. There were eight of them, including Arthur. The others in the group weren't happy about him coming along, but Delfer had sternly insisted, commanding greater authority that was not challenged. The crowds of humans were walking by below them, completely unaware and ignorant of the chaos that would soon be raining over them. Delfer had taken them to an area nearly on the opposite side of the city from the Werewolf bar's attack. Delfer had instructed the group that the Vampires made quick work on their damage control and managed to keep the attack publicized as a standard raid and for the public to carry on. Arthur was nervous about the plan at first, but Delfer assured him.

"Remember, we work to protect humans, not harm them. No innocents will be harmed if we can help it." It didn't make him happy, but it was the best

Delfer could offer. The traffic, the people, and the buzz of city life were still as loud as when he first arrived with Cratos. The entire group was wearing black heavy hard helmets, their eyes covered with black tinted visors, but the noise continued to ring through his ears, angering Arthur to no end.

They were forced just to wait. The whole group was utterly still, not one of them moving an inch. The blaring fullness of the sun was hammering down on the city. The rising heat boiled each of them intensely through their dark heavy armor. However, Arthur didn't even notice any of the others in the group so much as sighing from discomfort. Each of them refused to give in and break their focus. Arthur, however, was struggling hard. He hadn't gone through their training, and his need to keep up was straining him. But Arthur knew if he showed any signs of weakness, that he was slowing down the group in any way, or threatened a need to be treated differently than anyone else, then Delfer would send him back to the headquarters. Arthur knew he could not let that happen, there was a lot of payback he had to give to the Vampires, and he felt that even the surface of the sun itself wouldn't break him from his desire for revenge. Arthur recalled the encounter he had with other Vampires before. When Arthur punched the woman that attacked him in the alleyway and when he attacked the other Vampires in the warehouse. He knew the Vampires were monsters, murdering humanity and herding them like cattle. However, they still resembled a human form, and he felt uncomfortable with the notion that he might have to take lives in this mission without it being in direct self-defense. But he also knew that Cratos would fight for him and kill for him if he was being transported as a captive right now. Arthur always knew he would do anything for his friends, his true friends, and Cratos Mane had been the only friend in his life who hadn't let him down once. He felt he owed his mentor more than he could imagine. Arthur knew deep inside when the chips fell, and he needed to act, that he would do the right thing. He only hoped he wouldn't buckle and let his people down when that time came.

The armor he was wearing was also highly uncomfortable. Delfer had helped him strap it to his body before they headed out, and it was strapped onto him tight as though it was his flesh. But despite how uncomfortable it felt, the clothes being black were drawing in more heat than he could bear. That coupled with how heavy it was, Arthur was worried it might do him more damage than help him survive the attack. If he continued to melt in the unbearable heat, he doubted he would even make it to the fight. Despite the drawbacks of the heat, before they headed out into the world, Arthur couldn't help but feel so much stronger just wearing it. This amour felt solid upon him like he could fall from the building top they were on and just stand up and laugh. However, he had a strong feeling that he would just easily break his neck, so he didn't do that. Their target would come into sight any second now, and the group would have to spring into action. Keeping that readiness was proving an impossible task as his eyes felt like they were going to melt out of their sockets and his insides were in knots of anxiety. His stomach was a twisted ice fortress. Arthur was nervous, and he was scared.

Arthur was also slightly excited on the surface despite his present fears, eager to prove himself as a Werewolf, but his human side was screaming out in terror within his mind. It was roaring at him to tell Delfer he shouldn't be here and to go back and wait for Cratos. He had heard this human weakness within himself many times before. Arthur knew this was the same voice that controlled his every decision as an average human every day of his life. It was a voice telling him not to fight the bullies as they wailed at him. It was something scary, warning him away from anything that might put him at any risk. Since becoming a Werewolf, he felt he finally had the strength to say no to that voice. He felt like he had a new voice to listen to and trust himself in. However, he had learned the hard way to be wary of its seductive voice from when he went too far. He had now come to understand that if he controlled it, he would always be able to maintain control of his darker impulses. As Arthur stewed within his mind, his train of thought was abruptly broken when one of the Werewolves spoke quietly but sharply with no warning.

"Target sighted," Arthur snapped back into focus and looked at Delfer to respond.

"Where?" Delfer replied with a robust and serious tone in his command. Arthur could feel Delfer's worried distress as he attempted to remain in control of himself as the group's leader.

"They are down the far-left lane on the main road. A large black van with two confirmed Vampires in the front seats from the scopes retinal scan." Delfer hummed for a moment, then swore under his breath.

"It's a trap. They're waiting for us to act. They wouldn't have only two vampires guarding them even if Cratos wasn't there." The Werewolf to his left spoke but didn't move an inch, not even turning his head to Delfer as Arthur had.

"Sir, what are your orders?" Delfer sighed heavily, then looked at Arthur for a few seconds, who simply stared straight at him back. A moment passed between them. Arthur knew what this look meant. Delfer didn't have to say any words. This message was told in a single glance.

"Are you ready?" Without missing a single beat, Arthur gave a firm nod back, holding his gaze. Delfer smirked and nodded back at him, then replied.

"We take the target down and rescue our brothers. Get ready! It's time to play!" he grunted eagerly. Arthur remembered back to before they headed to this rooftop on the mission. When they were getting ready, Delfer was flicking through a dossier of information about the mission ahead. He remembered the small conversation he had before they left to rescue Cratos.

"How did the Vampires get away with attacking us without causing a major commotion with the public? You said this happens all the time, but I never heard of it on the news or anything like that?" Delfer had laughed then shook his head as though he had just heard a kid talking about Santa clause.

"Oh yes, you did Arthur. You heard about it every day in some way or another. Never forget the Vampires control the media, boy. They also have strong political and military ties. Nearly every time you hear of some gang den being raided, a terrorist group intercepted, or some militia group raided and taken out in foreign countries. Anywhere we are, all they have to do is give us some sort of label, and they are given the green light to take us down. Especially in less developed places like this, all they must do is report that we are holding drugs and guns or even some politician's child for ransom, and they get the OK to use as much lethal force as they want." Delfer then returned to his report as Arthur thought on Delfers' words for a moment. He would watch the news at home and see the front lines of newspapers all the time as a kid. Arthur remembered every other day that he saw what Delfer was talking about. He recalled people on the news talking about how violent militant armies and gangs were taken down by either their government forces or other countries' militaries aiding them in faraway lands. Arthur now knew that most of the time, that was their subterfuge, Werewolves were being slaughtered right under his nose, and all the public needed to be told was what they needed to hear, that they were dangerous.

"So, every time, it's just Werewolves being killed," Arthur voiced nearly tonelessly as realizations continued to spread through his mind. Delfer hummed, interrupting Arthur thought process.

"Not EVERY time. Bad humans do indeed exist in the world, Arthur. That's why they CAN pin that on us. They do certainly exist and do the horrible things they do. The Vampire leaders just take advantage of that and use their name as an excuse to get humans to kill us," he finished, not looking up from his notes. This information was no different from a weather report to him now, but it was near world-shattering to Arthur.

"So, humans are so easily tricked into killing us," Arthur replied with clenched teeth at the end. Unable to think of how humans are fooled so much by Vampires.

"Ordinary humans are not to blame, Arthur. They are carefully and diligently conditioned and brainwashed into believing everything they are told. However, most of the time, some humans oppose the stories and try to expose the Vampires for what they are. Sadly, those people are sent to the farms." That caught Arthur's attention.

"Farms?" he parroted back. Delfer pulled a dark expression. It looked pained as though horror was flashing over the softness of his eyes. For a moment, his voice went quiet and solemn.

"It isn't my place to tell you about them. Wait for Cratos to do it." Arthur noticed the seriousness in his tone. If it were horrible enough that Delfer did not want to talk about it, Arthur could feel that it must be too disturbing for casual conversation. Arthur then quickly backtracked the conversation.

"So, every time the Vampires want to take out one of our meeting places or bases, they just tell the human leaders that we are gun-bearing murderers to get permission to take us out?" Delfer pursed his lips then nodded.

"Pretty much. There have even been wars started now and then as an excuse to take us out. But I will explain that another day if Cratos will let me." Arthur nodded and left Delfer to his notes and reports to finish getting ready for the mission.

The black van was in the entire group's vision now. All eight of them followed the vehicle's move with their strained yellow eyes trained on it fiercely. Like the wolves, they were ready to strike at unsuspecting prey. They simply waited for Delfer to give the order for them to spring into action. Cratos told Arthur that the Werewolves weren't as rich as the Vampires.

"The bloodsuckers made their money through war, economics, as well as anything else profitable at the expense of humanity," Delfer explained thoroughly, words that rang similar to what Cratos had told him in the warehouse. He then explained that the Werewolves weren't exactly legitimate themselves regarding how they financed their war against the Vampires. They acquired their funds through, at the least, exploitable legal means. But despite that, they had enough to fuel their campaign against the Vampires, who themselves could spare zero expense when they wished to. To Arthur, he could gather this meant the black van was probably heavily armored, like the kind he had seen in action films. With Vampire money behind it, it would be the kind of bulletproof van that could fall off a cliff and still be intact at the bottom. The Werewolves didn't bother with gunfire for missions like this, but even the vehicle's metal would be incredibly resilient against their claws.

"Everyone stay focused and act fast. We won't have much time to break the others free once the attack starts. They are waiting for our move, remember that," Delfer said with a focused tone. Arthur saw a look in the man's eyes; it appeared as though he was running a thousand different simulations of the upcoming attack through his mind. Luckily Delfer had produced what Arthur felt was a solid plan. It gave them plenty of leverage to not only free their allies but also escape without an immediate chase, he hoped. But it was also temperamental, according to Delfer, who had explained there is no such thing as a full-proof plan. The key objective was breaking out the captives from the van. The group was firmly instructed to by no means purposely engage the Vampires unless they needed to. They would be able to call in more substantial reinforcements within no time of the attack if they needed, but that could only be used as a last resort given how much attention that would draw towards them.

"Bloody reinforcements! Half the time will only approve of a call-in only if the threat is a nuclear bomb being dropped on us, and even then, only as long as we can prove we can see it falling!" Delfer had grunted in the briefing, which made the others chuckle. It was heavily relayed that this was a rescue mission and not a revenge mission. The lives of their brethren in the van are the priority.

"If this plan goes haywire, Arthur, I want you to run. I will be forced to go down and try and help as I can, but I want you to flee no matter what. Our kind will track you and help you easily, but you must promise me, Arthur. If I give the order for you to run, you do so. Promise me!" Arthur could tell this was the unmentioned condition of him being allowed to help with the mission. There was no sign of negotiation in Delfer's tone or expression; it was hard and unrelenting. Arthur faced Delfer seriously and nodded.

"I promise. But you promise me you won't send me away on a whim. You only make the call when there is no other option left, OK?" Arthur knew it was very cheeky to throw his condition on the end of Delfer's command, but the Werewolf oddly respected Arthur's tenacity. With a smirk, the pair locked handshakes and spoke together.

"Deal!" they exclaimed proudly, with the same fellowship that he would have given Cratos himself.

The van was caught in traffic, irritating for the Vampires driving in the front who were only thinking of what they would eat after dropping off the prisoners. But one man's hell is another's heaven, as this was perfect for Delfer and his plan. The road they were stuck on was several feet away from the rooftop they were watching on. The people walking the streets down below were unsuspecting and being their usual noisy human selves. Car horns were blaring at each other as the traffic was refusing to budge. The Werewolf that spotted the van before spoke up again.

"Two Vampires are driving the cars are swearing at each other, arguing about the traffic, I think." The thought of Vampires experiencing 'Road Rage' made Arthur smirk despite how focused he was meant to be.

"Any second now," Delfer whispered. The other Werewolves were scattered along the edge of the roof, ready to act the second Delfer gave the word. The stifling air turned to numbness in Arthur's veins as time seemed to slow down around him. He took in his breaths slower and slower. This technique was something Cratos had shown him in his training. It was not just to calm his nerves, but it was something he had called the sixth sense.

"that's mind powers, right? Telling the future and moving stuff with your mind?" Arthur had asked. The forest was raining heavily that night. The pair's campfire had gone out, and they lay with the shelter of a tall tree with thick branches, swigging water together as though they were a pair of old friends reminiscing over whiskey. Cratos chuckled deeply to himself for a moment.

"I give you too much bloody credit sometimes, you idiot!" he continued to chuckle, then his face grew grave, and Cratos shook his head.

"Not in the way I am saying. This sense is crucial, especially in moments when everything is in chaos. It happens to some people without them noticing sometimes. When everything blows up around them, it seems to them as though time slows down. Sound drowns out all around them, and within a mere few seconds, they take in everything around them all at once." He turned to face Arthur with a stern look.

"If such an impulse could be used and mastered, it can grant a fighter his greatest weapon possible. Omnipresence!" Arthur only stared dumbly at a word that sounded like the name of a supervillain in his mind.

"What's that?" Arthur had asked, his face twisted with confusion. Cratos rolled his eyes but knew this was a good teaching moment, so he remained patient as he tried to explain.

"It is a sense of existing in more than the space that occupies your own being. You no longer just take in what your eyes present to you. Every sense is pushed to its maximum. If there is a fly a few feet away, you count every beat of its left wings as it flies. Anything that comes within inches of you, you instantly where it is, how big it is and how fast it's coming. In a simpler sense, Arthur, nothing can surprise you, and you can prepare yourself when all around you are bedlam." Arthur, at that moment, lent back and took that in for a moment. He thought about having the ability to sense everything around you within seconds and act upon it and wondered if such a thing could be possible.

"But how, how does one train themselves to use such an ability if it only happens when chaos strikes?" he asked after thinking. Cratos raised a finger and smiled faintly.

"That can be the problem. You need to prepare yourself for it when it happens. Be ready for the second it occurs, and you will know it when it happens. In those fleeting but precious seconds, you must be fast. See everything you can because you will only have moments to act. Remain calm and give your body completely to instinct when that happens. You must be willing to trust yourself completely at that moment. Understand?" Arthur nodded, saying nothing else for the rest of the night as the pair lay there, hearing the rain shower around them as they drifted to sleep, one of nature's most soothing lullabies for Arthur.

Arthur hadn't felt the sensation when he fought the tiger because that battle had been different. He hadn't the experience with this extra sense to the point he could make use of it in a one-on-one fight. But with mayhem erupting all around him, Arthur would try his best to seize any opportunity he could to wet his feet in the experience. He wanted to learn to fight, his training with Cratos had been informative, but it also has been frustrating. Cratos had fed his mind well enough for what he needed to know so far. Cratos taught him how to steel his nerve, control his emotions and guard his mind against petty, weak, humanly corrupt impulses. He had also trained his body physically; the exercises he did got his body in decent shape. He was strong and fit enough to take down a ferocious tiger. But he was no fighter yet. So far in combat terms, he knew he had only his rage to call upon if he wished to be any kind of threat. He was tactical with the tiger, but Arthur knew there was a significant difference between hunting an animal and fighting Vampires. Arthur knew he lacked combat experience, and in a widespread battle with an enemy behind you, he knew experience is what would save your life at every turn. That was why Delfer had said Arthur would be a liability. Arthur knew why he had to stay close to his new friend's side as though they were joined at the hip. It was all because none of the others could rely on him. Every time Arthur has fought, he has only had his intuition and instincts to guide him through it. He had no proper knowledge of fighting like martial arts or self-defense. Cratos had told him that he would be instructed in these things as he went through his stages as a Werewolf. When he joined their race more fully, he would be immensely trained to become a living weapon.

Childishly, Arthur enjoyed the idea of becoming a seasoned warrior who could be counted on in a rescue mission like this and not be seen as a boy who had only killed a mangy cat in some trees and who nearly failed his first full-moon trail. Yet here he waited. Arthur was waiting for the call to come. He awaited the panic and action to start. Since joining up with Cratos, he felt like he jumped headfirst into the deep end, and this mission was no different. But this was not only to save the man who had given him a great life to live. But it was also to prove that he deserved this life. To truly prove that he was no longer the weak boy who cowered before danger. He wanted this fight. He wanted to feel like an actual Werewolf, and he had a feeling he would never be accepted as one among his peers until he went through the initiation that all true wolves of the night had. He knew he needed to spill Vampire blood. Not as a boy acting within the moment with a lead pipe but as an actual full-blooded Werewolf.

So as if it were happening in slow motion, he saw Delfer's lips slowly say the word 'NOW', shouting for the whole group to hear. Within seconds, the Werewolves swung their arms wildly and then proceeded to launch gas canisters through the air. Black smoke sailed from the rooftops as they spun through the air, hitting the ground in the middle of the road around the black van. People began to scream in the street as black smoke smothered the area quickly and thickly. Dark smog filled the air around the black van; solid objects were now only visible within sight to the other Werewolves. Just then, as Arthur expected, complete chaos erupted. The sound of the people shouting for help, the sound of them running, crying, and panicking was alive in the world around them. Once the smoke was thick enough, every

Werewolf in the group jumped off the rooftops, diving into the thick of the black smoke, and darting towards the black van. The rescue mission had begun.

The second Arthur's feet hit the ground hard, a shock wave of force bolted through his legs like a dozen hammers had struck every point below his waist. At that moment, Arthur was immediately grateful for his Werewolf muscles and bones preventing him from instantly shattering into pieces. As he landed, he entered the black smoke with the others. He could hear the people screaming and panicking all around him. Those around the black van were running out of their cars and fleeing in all directions. To avoid inhaling the smoke, Arthur had a black lower face mask with special breathing filters fitted within them to inhale air without problems. His eyes stung from the smoke as the dense fumes struck his eyeballs, but he wasn't blinded, and he began to ignore the pain after a few seconds of it. He could feel the smoke against his face as he ran forward with the others. It was a smooth sensation, as though it was oddly caressing his skin. His armor was fixed firmly to his body like it was his very skin as he leaped over a car hood, dashing towards the black van like a bullet fired from a gun. Despite the smoke affecting his eyes, it felt as though every other sense was his to command, that the entire world around him was in his complete comprehension. A regular human would only be able to see the smoky blackness as they scrambled in a blind panic in some random direction, smacking into anything in their way without seeing it. But with Arthur's eyes, he saw beyond the thickness of the smoke and sensed the physical objects within the smoke. It was all clear in his sight. He couldn't see the delicate details of what was before him, but he could see the overall black shape. It was difficult to tell the difference between a person and a car, but Arthur locked his sights on a large van straight ahead of him, looking like an enormous black shadow-like object.

Arthur saw the front doors of the van open as two hissing Vampires emerged from their seats to meet the Werewolves. The other Werewolves were snarling in deep dark animal tones as they approached the van, morphing their legs into their Werewolf legs so they could run faster, all dashing ahead of Arthur. He was running as fast as his untransformed legs could carry. They were each running in motion together, their arms spread, their mouths roaring fiercely. Pulling from the sides of their waists were long daggers clutched tightly in their hands. They began slashing through the air toward the Werewolves with expert precision. Arthur wondered why they weren't using guns themselves so they could kill the Werewolves more easily with bullets than needing to get close with knives. Arthur could see the several

Werewolves in front of him, closing in upon the two hissing figures ahead with their arms ripping the air before them with deadly near-invisible slash attacks as they closed in. They stepped in with ferocious speed, then all together, the Werewolves embedded within the depths of the gray smoke all leaped upon the two vampire figures, merging their physical forms in the mist with the other two, proceeding to savage them horrifically. The two Vampires screamed as the Werewolves made short work of their bodies, completely eviscerating them in a mere few seconds as a group. Delfer grabbed Arthur by the wrist and hurried the pair of them away from the two dead Vampires, and moved quickly to the back of the van doors.

"We have the move quickly. The smoke will dissipate in only a few minutes," Delfer said through the chaos at Arthur; his voice sounded almost mechanical and emotionless. Arthur remembered his orders and stuck close to Delfer. He focused his mind on what he might see, preparing for anything. Delfer had been concerned before that this was a trap for them, and so far, the attack had gone well, too well for Delfer's comfort. Delfer had planned for the smoke bombs to prevent anyone from picking them off with guns, but he was still on edge that something seemed off. The pair came up to the doors of the black van. The metal of the doors was now visible because they were inches from its surface. Delfer gave a quick look at the lock of the door. He stuck out his right hand, and it grew three times in size within seconds, followed by long sharp nails piercing out of the glove's tips. With a swift speedy slash, the lock of the van collapsed into pieces, and with both of his arms, Delfer swung the doors open with a feral roar.

Delfer's pupils shrank with a hollowed disbelief at what he saw as he gazed into the back of the black van they had just fought their way to reach. It was far worse and far more insulting than anything Delfer could have thought up. Arthur swatted the black mist away from his eyes and investigated the van himself. Nothing. The inside was completely vacant of anyone. All that lay before them was a small white piece of paper. Arthur picked up the paper as Delfer remained still, looking into the empty space inside the van. Arthur unfolded it and read the words aloud.

"Do you dogs think we only own ONE van?" Arthur let the note slump by his side as his arm lost feeling, and he assumed the same stance and expression as Delfer.

"A decoy," Arthur heard Delfer whisper. But Arthur's brain was a few steps ahead of Delfer's shock. The Vampires wouldn't bother wasting all of this just for an insult, especially now that they were all around a meaningless van in the open. Realization hit Arthur, and he whirled around on Delfer and spoke.

"It's not just a decoy; it's the bait!" Arthur shouted. Delfer's head snapped up as he caught what Arthur had meant. But the pair of them realized too late, that the sound of gunfire ripped through the black smoke as it slowly began to face. The sound of their fellow Werewolves' screams hallowed Arthur's heart as he could tell just from the sound that they were being ripped to pieces. Delfer acted fast; he grabbed Arthur by the scruff of his neck and threw him into the van with one arm. Arthur shouted with shock as Delfer jumped in after him, slamming the doors shut behind them. The sound of their brethren dying out was still fresh in Arthur's ears. They had been tricked, and now they were going to die.

CHAPTER SIXTEEN

Arthur fell sharply on the van's floor as Delfer quickly scrambled past him to the driver's seat. Quickly regaining himself, Arthur felt the gunfire shatter hard against the walls of the van all around him. Thick indents pounded inward towards Arthur's very face all along every border of the van as he froze with shock.

"If those damn bloodsuckers made one mistake today!" Delfer said with sullen urgency.

"It's their attention to detail! This van will be just as impenetrable as the real one. Their gunfire will not pierce this shell!" Arthur sighed with relief, a feeling that was quickly overtaken with deep pain for the other Werewolves who had just died outside. All for this mission to save others, they were cut to pieces by gunfire before they had a chance to jump to safety with them. Delfer fastened his seat belt at the front of the van and quickly turned the key, causing the engine to fire up. He looked over the pedals and buttons on the dashboard with confusion. Arthur frowned at the sight of Delfer's confusion.

"Have you ever driven before?" he asked cautiously. Delfer nodded his head a little.

"Yeah," he answered, then coughed discreetly.

"Once," he finished sheepishly. Arthur winced.

"And how did that go," Arthur reluctantly asked back. Delfer chuckled uneasily.

"I crashed," he said blatantly.

"My instructor refused to teach me again after he came out of the hospital," he added. Arthur rolled his eyes, looking around him, noticing there were no seat belts in the back of this van. Delfer moved around the gear stick and grinned.

"But don't worry, though; I'm nearly sure I knew what might have gone wrong at the time." The black smoke cleared so Arthur and Delfer could see through the glass, and right outside of the van were several thickly armed solider with their guns aimed straight forward.

"Hold on!" Delfer yelled into the back of the van.

"Oh, fu-" Arthur began before being hurtled backward through the van as it charged forward towards their foes Delfer slammed his foot as hard as he could on the accelerator.

The guns held by the human soldiers fired straight towards the oncoming van driven by Delfer. The dozen bullets that flew forward at speeds that even Werewolves couldn't match hit the glass of the van and bounced off without even leaving a scratch, each of them. The soldier's gazes exploded as they roared with shock. They attempted to scramble out of the way of Delfer, but the van was rushing through space at full speed. The van struck against the soldiers harshly, sending each of them flying under and around the van like bowling pins struck by a cannonball. The sounds of their anguished screams sent a vicious grin up both sides of Delfer's face as he continued forward eagerly. His gleeful face made it seem that he was racking up points for each hit inside his head. The van swerved and dodged the deserted cars people had left after they heard the attack in the area. Delfer drove down the road as fast as possible from the chaos and away from the Vampire ambush. Arthur managed to sit up in the van finally and dragged himself towards the front seat, scrambling like he was on a derailed train going up a mountain. Arthur quickly hurried to the front seat behind Delfer, gripping his chair as he watched the Werewolf badly drive around the city.

"What now?" Arthur asked, trying to hold himself from falling aside as Delfers' sloppy driving made him feel like a battered ragdoll. Delfer's face hardened, and thorough determination replaced his joyful expression as he squeezed the steering wheel with his hands.

"We are going to complete our mission! We will rescue Cratos and the other captured Werewolves," he vowed with fire in his tone

Arthur sighed and slumped back, sitting on the floor looking at his feet, an odd pang of despair seething its tendrils into his mind as the adrenalin of the past moment began to wane.

"But it's too late. We already fell for another van. For all we know, they have already driven the other van to where it needs to be already."

"Not a bloody chance!" Delfer growled as his grip on the wheel of the van tightened to breaking point.

"If the van were that close to their headquarters, then they wouldn't have bothered trying to bait us in the first place! I strongly wager the bait was ALSO purposeful misdirection!" It didn't take long for logical strands within Arthur's mind to quickly link together.

"Therefore, while we go for the decoy van," Delfer continued, leaving the rest of his sentence unanswered for Arthur to finish.

"The other van travels safely without being attacked," he whispered.

"Exactly!" Delfer said with triumph.

"We will find that other van, Arthur. Odds are with interference, but we have lost too many Werewolves today for them to have died in vain now." Hope slowly returned to Arthur's eyes as he sat back up next to Delfer's chair and looked onward with his friend. His mission was far from over yet.

Delfer's driving was horrific; Arthur would have sooner trusted a blind man to handle this van than he would this Werewolf. He couldn't help but vice grip his fingers around Delfer's seat. He felt if he didn't, then otherwise, he would be flying around the van like a bouncy ball. If the pair didn't locate the other black van in this vast city, this van would soon turn into a hearse for them both. People were shouting as Delfer was dodging other cars going down the road. He was changing streets at every turn, bouncing around the city, trying to cover as many routes as possible in hopes he would sight the other van by luck. Delfer figured the other van would be notified that their decoy failed, and they were now being hunted, so he knew they would change their route, which meant they could be anywhere. Arthur then quickly heard the blaring sound of police sirens that was now following them. Arthur listened to the sirens and looked out of the back door a little, seeing more than five or six cars following them. A man with a megaphone said something to them in a language that Arthur didn't understand. Arthur retreated towards Delfer.

"What's the problem? Did I not signal at that last turn?" he asked with a chuckle. Arthur smirked himself back towards Delfer.

"What should we do? They'll roadblock us eventually, right? Won't be long before we're either trapped or they shoot our tires." Delfer sighed and nodded.

"You're right, we'll have to abandon the van eventually and search the black van on foot if we don't spot it soon, but if we don't at least know where it is or going to start with, it's lost. Just hang tight kid, I may not be able to drive, but I can wing it pretty well!" Arthur pulled a face and rolled his eyes, and chuckled.

"Very comforting," he commented back dryly and continued with Delfer as they drove through the city, praying that they spot the black van soon or it would be all over.

Arthur didn't bother to check if more police had joined the chase. He and Delfer were transfixed in concentration. Delfer slapped the steering wheel with both his hands suddenly.

"THERE!" Delfer shouted, nodding towards a black van not far from where they were a few lanes ahead. As soon as he saw it, he slammed his foot on the accelerator, roaming through the streets as fast as he could. The screeching and noises of the cars as Delfer forced them out of his way were deafening. It wouldn't be long before a driver went nuts and happily let Delfer charge into him in a fit of road rage, sending the pair of them through the windscreen to their deaths. More than a few minutes later, Arthur was looking at Delfer's eyes. The man seemed possessed to complete this mission, his pupil dotting around literally every inch of everything that was before him. Delfer was adamant about missing nothing in his vision as he charged through this city as though he was wielding a massive bulldozer. Arthur remembered as the pair were talking back in the raided bar, laughing and joking with each other like old friends. He couldn't help but wonder if Cratos would have been just as much determined to free Delfer had he been the one caught. Arthur then realized that this was the reason he was allowed to come on the mission. Arthur saw that Delfer shared his strained determination to help his friend entirely because he felt the same. But his train of thought was broken as Delfer made Arthur nearly jump out of his skin by roaring.

"We're close!" His left hand pointed to the far top right of the road as a crosswalk. The black van was a replica of the one they were driving. Arthur spotted it and nodded.

"Are you sure that's the right one? There could be loads of them out here for all we know!" Delfer sighed with frustration.

"We have to take the chance, Arthur. If this isn't it, then it wasn't our lucky day, and Cratos is dead!" Delfer pressed forward with all his might, speaking as he drove these final few feet.

"Not everything is within our control Arthur. Sometimes you just must accept reality when given to you. Sometimes, fighting it can only drive you mad," Arthur thought about it, and while he didn't say it aloud, he disagreed with Delfer. He would always keep fighting no matter what. Arthur wouldn't give up on his mentor if that black van didn't hold Cratos and his teacher was held elsewhere. He would find him no matter what.

"So, what's the plan?" Arthur asked. Delfer was silent for a few seconds, thinking hard.

"That's a tad more complicated" he finally said.

"Oh........good plan!" Arthur replied sarcastically. Delfer breathed heavily, exhausted.

"The police are tailing us in the middle of the road, and we're in a large black van. If we jump out of it, we'll be cut to pieces by gunfire, and the other van knows we are too close, and it'll fight back at us like hell, so if you have a plan, smart ass! Please enlighten me!" Arthur thought for a few moments too. They were a tricky situation, and he needed to consider his options. He could continue to tail the black van and wait for the right opportunity to strike. Too dangerous, they could be blocked off by the police any minute or have their tires shot out, as well as the danger of the Vampire driving the other van to flee at top speed. Try and abandon the van to chase the black van on foot. It was better than the last plan, but sadly, just as lethal, they could be shot on sight the second they were within view of a policeman holding a gun, or other Vampires could be lying in wait to strike. A third option popped into his head.

"Can we call for any more backup?" Arthur asked. Delfer hummed for a moment.

"It would depend on what for. Headquarters aren't going to send anyone else out just to be bullet fodder. They don't want to sacrifice any more lives needlessly if this mission is a lost cause. If we can, do you have a plan?" Arthur shook his head.

"Not really. I thought backup could be a distraction so we can escape the van without being seen." Delfer shook his head now firmly.

"A lot of eyes are watching us kid, escaping unseen is not an option. For you at least, you're not fast enough yet." Arthur thought on it a moment, then he shook his head angrily. He realized he was trying to approach this situation as a human. Arthur knew he needed to try trusting his instincts.

As the car zoomed through the streets, he briefly closed his eyes and focused. He blanked his thoughts and waited for the first impulse to strike him. After a few seconds, a command shot through his mind in a dark and grizzly manner. Arthur's eyes snapped for, and he darted away from Delfer's front seat.

"Hey! What are you-" he began, but before he could finish, Arthur kicked open the back doors of the van and jumped with all his leg strength forward out of the van and towards the police cars chasing him, the roar of his inner Werewolf bellowing from his lungs.

The first thing Arthur heard as he flew through the air was the sound of Delfer roaring after him. Then suddenly, Arthur began to become engrossed entirely in the moment as his feet slammed hard onto the bonnet of the police car that was right behind the van. As he landed, his feet heavily dented the metal hood of the vehicle. Arthur gazed into the windscreen before him and saw two completely startled policemen staring back at him. Arthur stared at them awkwardly for a moment before he refocused his mind and his face twisted into a monstrous snarl. Swinging his arm far back behind him like an archer pulling his bow in the air, Arthur shot his arm forward, his fists shattering the glass of the car's windshield around his arm. The two police cried out with surprise as the vehicle began to swerve and turn and lose control. Arthur felt his body nearly fall from the car in the momentum. He rapidly pulled his arm back out, his hand ripping away from the gaping hole in the car's window. Arthur then crouched, his head turning from side to side as he planned his next move. With a second bellowing roar, Arthur soared into the air forward onto the car behind that one. As the vehicle Arthur had leaped from ran out of control, it swerved off the road and crashed violently into a wall. A rush of adrenaline unleashed itself from within the depths of Arthur's heart as his eyes ran wild as he glided through the air as though held aloft by wings. The noise around him was simply scrambled into a gargled hum of noise. The screeching of cars, the sound of the car he punched crashing, and people and police shouting in panic and fury turned into feeble whimpers. It all merged, allowing Arthur to drown out the distraction and focus on what he was doing.

This time he landed straight on the roof of the car. However, this car had witnessed what this strange kid had done before them, and this police force acted swiftly. The second Arthur's feet once again inhumanly dented the hard metal of their police vehicle; the driver began to shake the car's wheel from side to side, instantly attempting to send Arthur flying to the ground. Arthur toppled backward for a moment. Fear shot him through his heart like a bullet as he signed over control of his body to his instincts. Without thinking and with all the strength his abdominal muscles had, Arthur flung his body forward and jammed his fingers down on the back of the roof of the car. His now wolf-like long and sharp claws shot through the metal like a nail gun, holding him in place as the rest of his body swung from side to side like a lifeless doll.

Being securely in place as the car continued to try and shake him off, Arthur quickly thought of what to do. The car was still shaking, but he couldn't hold onto the roof forever. Tensing his right arm, Arthur snapped his hand free off the top and completely rolled his body over as far as he could until his body was hanging from the left side of the car. He had to twist his hand still gripped to the vehicle to reposition his body, the metal morphing with the strength of his fingers with enormous effort to contort the solid mass. His other hand was still firmly in place, keeping him from falling off the car. He then turned his head and stared down hard at the road before his face. Arthur spotted the back left wheel of the vehicle. Arthur threw his free arm forward and slashed at the tire's rubber with his hand in a slicing motion as though his fingers were replaced with razor blades. The wheel made a loud snapping sound with a thick pop as it was shredded open. The car's driver no longer needed to swerve the vehicle as the vehicle now began to twist and turn on its own with the damaged wheel. He used his one hand still attached to pull himself back onto the roof, followed swiftly by his other hand; he pulled himself back on top of the car. He looked straight ahead as the car was losing control. With the unrelenting speed that the vehicle was going, it wouldn't be able to make the next turn that was coming up and would crash harshly into the wall of a building up ahead.

Arthur looked behind him and saw the other police beginning to slow their speed so he wouldn't be able to leap onto their cars. The second they could, the remaining four vehicles fled into desperate directions elsewhere down different roads, or they just stopped chasing the van outright. He couldn't help but chuckle as they vanished from his sight, raising a mocking hand to wave them goodbye. Returning to the immediate situation, Arthur turned his eyes to survey what was around him and saw the car about to pass an alleyway. Arthur had no other choice. He quickly released his fingers from the security of the car roof, and then with what balance he could muster, he stood onto his feet. Arthur then crouched down one more time in a squat position. Arthur then jumped from the moving damaged police car straight into the cover of the alleyway with a single leap. As he landed hard on the ground from the speed and momentum he had been traveling at, Arthur had his eyes closed for a few seconds to endure the impact. He was now suddenly glad he was wearing every inch of the tight, uncomfortable body armor. A second went by then the air suddenly filled with the sound of the police car crashing violently against the wall. With such ferocious force behind it, a few seconds later, the loud noise of an explosion soon followed the car's crash. The thick flickering flare of fire sailed through Arthur's ears as smoke began to surround the area from all the chaos and damage caused. Arthur wanted to look around the corner of the alleyway and peak to see how it looked, but he knew he had to remain focused. Opening his eyes, Arthur immediately stood to his feet and looked around where he was. He was unsure where Delfer had driven to, but hopefully, now that the police were gone for the moment, the black van could be pursued. Arthur knew, however, that every second was precious. Delaying no longer, Arthur set off down the alley towards a direction he hoped the black van would be. The last thing he wanted was to be stranded in a city on his own after destroying two police cars.

Arthur ran through the streets and alleyways as fast as possible, still exploding with energy after attacking the two cars before. Those events were still racing through his mind. The way he did all that carnage was incredible; he had never felt more capable. He dashed forward through several different alleyways in a wild frenzy. Arthur did his best to keep to the shadows as best as his stealth could allow him. Despite the light of day, he quickly moved himself to the shaded areas that buildings blocked, so he wasn't standing in nature's spotlight. Arthur was moving as quietly as he could, but he was still making noise as he moved, thanks to the solid concrete grounds. Yet people treated him like an unappealing stray animal going past them; in their minds, he exists, but they numb their eyes instinctually away from addressing him.

Arthur froze dead several times as he cleared the area, running at breakneck speed. He didn't stop for a person noticing or even the flash shots of startled cats darting into the garbage. Every time Arthur heard a police siren, he stopped and slapped his back against a wall. He felt it wasn't long until police cars would be swarming the entire area and pin him down like a trapped rat. Arthur figured it wouldn't take long for police to begin cramming down every other alleyway and would cut him down with a hail of bullets on sight. He knew he needed to find the Vampire van. As he came upon another alleyway, he noticed a fire escape comprised of multiple stories of ladders leading up to the roof of the building with a ladder end just out of his reach from the bottom hanging off the side of one of the buildings. Crouching down, Arthur then jumped into the air, throwing his hand forward and firmly gripping the ladder's bottom around the metal bar. With little effort, he hauled himself up the ladder in seconds, one arm in front of the other as fast as he could. Arthur quickly climbed up to the metal landing and began going up to the roof, hopefully away from any police sight. He rose with ease despite the physical trauma he had just gone through. From the minimal training he had completed so far, Arthur felt he was stronger than he ever thought possible and would only become stronger from here on.

As he reached the rooftop from the fire escape, he went to the edge and began scouting the area below. It felt like he had been running through those alleyways for ages. He prayed the black van hadn't gotten too far, especially with Delfer still tailing it. He could still see the two rising clouds of smoke from the two damaged police cars he had left in the wreckage. He scouted his eyes in the other directions, checking the roads carefully so he didn't miss a thing. He hoped Delfer wouldn't lose track of the van after Arthur risked his life getting rid of the police chasing them. Within moments his eyes finally set upon the pair. Both vans at once came into his sight, and Arthur moaned with distress. He witnessed the two cars racing through the streets, one right behind the other as they twisted and turned through multiple streets. Arthur trained his eyes hard on the two vehicles, focusing on the pair intensely, seeing where they were, and making sure not to lose track as they moved. They were two streets over, more than two buildings ahead of Arthur, and it would only be minutes before they were right in front of the building ahead of him, so he did not have much time. He snapped his head up and looked at the distance between the buildings and groaned.

There were two full roads with two pavements separating him from the next rooftop. He remembered his jump from the car and analyzed the distance. He wasn't trying to use his full power then, but they were right behind each other, so there wasn't a considerable distance at the time. Arthur smiled slightly with confidence. He took several steps backward until he was at the edge of the other side of the building. Kneeling slightly, Arthur sharpened his eyes and focused himself, tensing his leg muscles tightly. His grin increased as he quickened his breath, getting the blood flowing through his body. Now, as a Werewolf, Arthur relished the challenge. Without delay, he set off in a dash straight towards the edge of the rooftop, getting his speed to a full-fledged sprint in a second. Arthur then reached the edge of the roof. With a sharp bend of his knees, he leaped with all the strength and might his legs would grant him. Arthur had hurled his entire being off the rooftop and towards the flat floor of the following roof ahead.

Arthur pitied the residents who occupied the room at the top of the building as he landed. He felt the thunderous vibrations of force he created echo downward. Arthur saw the cracks in the floor where his feet had landed, and he couldn't help but smirk. However, he didn't waste time on his victory against gravity. He quickly crouched again, now feeling immensely more confident of himself this time, and once again, without hesitating, he dashed in a sprint as before and launched himself into the air. Arthur was soaring forward as though he was thrown from a catapult. Arthur didn't tempt fate by looking down while he was in the air. He was only half-hoping no one saw him making the jumps. Delfer had specified, as well as Cratos a few times, how serious it was for the Werewolves to remain hidden from the human world. He had mentioned before that the Vampires could control media and publications to twist any event to their liking to conceal the war. Still, Arthur felt even that had its limitations. The Vampires wished to avoid human persecution and genocide that would inevitably follow being discovered. Regardless of where he was in the world, Arthur noticed that this city seemed reasonably modern, so he half worried his leaps of faith would end up on the news or as a picture in a newspaper. Some nut would snap a photo somehow, and his kind would risk exposure. If that happened, he would not look forward to having to explain to Delfer this when it was all over.

No sense of immense triumph as he landed this time, the excitement of making the jump was greatly lessened after a second time. He landed on the floor of the roof intensely again, but he didn't bother to contemplate whose ceiling he just dented this time as he instantly shot to the edge of the building edge and threw his head over to the far left to see if the vans were heading down. The sounds of human screams and car screeching were a good sign as Arthur faintly saw the two black vans turn a corner at a fast rate. Delfer's van had nearly pulled itself on two wheels at the sharp turn around the corner of the road. Arthur observed the situation steadily; he lowered his body down as far as he could on the off chance the Vampires driving the car might see him on the roof and prepared for his last leap. He saw he would have to time it correctly, especially given how fast the Vampire van was trying to flee. The two vans were closing in; Arthur was crouched as low as he could, his legs poised like a predator ready to spring on its unsuspecting prey. The vans were far away now, and Arthur was only guessing, but he assumed he wouldn't make it if he didn't jump directly. So left with no other option, he gave one final leap. He jumped into the air like a frog darting upwards. Arthur carried himself down towards the road as the first black van zoomed within his range. In a matter of seconds, Arthur's feet slammed hard on the bonnet of the black van. His body nearly tumbled down the side of the vehicle and fell to the ground, instantly knocked onto his side from the momentum of speed the van drove. As Arthur regained his poise and crawled to his hands and knees, he looked up a little bit and stared directly into the window of the Vampire's black van. On the inside front seats, one man was dressed in black-built special soldier armor, and there was a stylish red and black dressed young vampire woman with long hair next to him in the passenger seat. As Arthur knelt on the hood of their van, before either of them could blink, he held his arm back as far as he could go and pulled a snarled face towards the Vampire woman, then mouthed the word to her.

"Hello," he spoke, shooting his clenched fist forward into the windscreen. In the heat of the moment after his success in attacking the police car, Arthur had forgotten something Delfer had said when they first entered the van.

"It's their attention to detail. This van is just as impenetrable as the real one would be. Their gunfire will not pierce this shell." All those words flashed through his mind as the knucklebones in his hand shattered into tiny pieces underneath his skin like a leather bag of glass slamming against a concrete wall. Within mere seconds, Arthur's entire hand was utterly annihilated against the reinforced bulletproof glass windscreen. The sounds of dozens of cracks rippling past his ears as the van moved forward down the road made Arthur's entire body freeze solid. Slowly Arthur moved his head down to see his hand, which held still against the unscathed glass. He then looked past the glass inward at the two in the car.

The woman was smirking at him, trying to stifle herself from busting out laughing. Then in an instant, the pain hit Arthur. The agony smashed against his nerves like a flaming wrecking ball plummeting upon his hand. His teeth clenched together as he tried to suppress the pain. The immediate threat of the van he knelt on was still the central part of his attention. He quickly ripped it away from his hand, the shattered bone moving around each other as he moved it like a water balloon filled with ice. At that moment, the pain was screaming at total volume at Arthur in a deafening pitch. Arthur felt he was nearly going to pass out from shock. His eyes started to suddenly grow woozy, his breathing becoming strained as the only thing that occupied his mind was the horrific pain blazing from his ruined hand. The world around him began to grow darker. The sound of the traffic and the wind rushing through his ears on the moving van slowly vanished and drowned out. He felt he was about to topple and fall for all to see.

"I don't think so!" growled the voice of the Beast in his mind.

CHAPTER SEVENTEEN

Arthur's pupils shrank to a point they were nearly gone from visible sight. His Body froze utterly still for a moment. Then his shoulders heaved upwards, and his head was flung backward while still on the hood of the moving van. His body began to shake irreparably, as though a thousand eels suddenly possessed him.

"What the hell is going on!?" the Vampire woman cried in confusion to her comrade. The driver next to her shrugged as he was focused on looking past Arthur while he drove so they didn't crash. Arthur's torso began to throb physically. With every heartbeat, his body mass began to rise and fall rapidly, his arms expanding in size along with his chest, stomach, and legs all growing larger. His body only took a few seconds before stopping its convulsions, leaving Arthur's body three times the size it was a second ago. His body armor was not even straining against the expansion in his size. Arthur assumed it was because it was designed for Werewolves and was meant to grow with him. His muscles had now become rippling huge in their expansion. The woman had only time to glare with uncertain shock as Arthur's head then jolted straight up, making her jump in her seat, the driver as well. His pupils were no longer shrunk; they were huge, with a sizeable bright color around the black hole. It was a vibrant, piercing yellow. Arthur was staring at the two once more with near-insane glee that nearly splits both sides of his face. He then opened his mouth to reveal razor-sharp rows of fangs shining out back to them. Before either Vampire could react, roaring began to flow out of Arthur's mouth. It was a dark evil deep bellow as both his eyes were fixated on the female Vampire, who could only look at Arthur bewildered. Fear was strangely beginning to work its way through her spine. Arthur leaned his body backward once again, his head swinging back as far as he could to the point that his body was nearly lying on his back as he leaned.

"What the hell is he doing!?" the woman asked. The driver could only shake his head as he drove. Then, just like before, Arthur shot himself upward. But this time, he did not simply stop when he was right up straight. With a massive heave, he threw his body forward and power-charged his forehead straight into the glass of the windscreen. However, when his skull connected with the windscreen surface, it didn't crack. The screen didn't even dent with the strike from his head. As Arthur stuck the glass, it shattered massively into the van as though a tiny explosion had just detonated on the supposedly invulnerable surface itself. Arthur's face was now on the inside of the van; his hysterical laughter was ringing out over the surprised screams of the driver and woman.

Shards of glass flew into the front seats of the van, straight at the pair. The viciously thin pieces of the glass plummeted straight into the soft, smooth pale flesh of the Vampire woman deeply, causing her hands to fling to her face as she screamed in horror and pain. The driver was also subjected to the glass shooting into his face. Three pieces alone had drilled straight down to the back of his left eye. The man bellowed in pain and hit the van's wheel to the far left in a panic. The van flew sideways as Arthur's grinning, sadistic snarling face turned into a burst of harboring laughter while the driver and woman continued to scream from the shards of the windscreen that were now nested within their faces. Arthur looked at each of them and settled his gaze on the woman. Feeling his eyes burning through her hands, she took a moment out of her pain and lowered her hands to look at him. Her blood was dripping down the cracks around the wounds of the glass; her face was cut to ribbons. The two had a moment before the van crashed through the metal railing of the roadside. They had been driving across at that moment to which only a wall lay ahead. Time then slowed for all of them. Just as Arthur had been told before, the slow motion between the two only lasted a brief span of a few secular moments. Arthur whispered words to her with a twisted dark grin before the van smashed into the brick of the nearest building.

"If I ever see you again, I won't just kill you; I will eat you." The woman had only a moment for her eyes to widen in shock, and then the van smashed into the wall of the building. Arthur had only the propulsion of the crashing, sending the rest of his body into the van's front seat area as the entire thing became scrap against the brick in the space of a second. Before there was only blackness in Arthur's eyes, he fell unconscious to the sound of his hysterical laughter. Then there was only darkness.

Arthur's eyes snapped open, revealing him to be in a world of complete darkness. He immediately stood to his feet quickly and defensively. He looked around the shadows frantically, his head snapping from side to side in awe. He couldn't believe it. He thought this was impossible, but he knew he was now standing within the realm of the world Arthur had fought the Beast within his mind. He was back within its domain. Arthur lifted his hands and held his head, trying hard to think. The last thing he remembered was being on the front hood of the black van. Arthur recalled he had then fallen into a strange unconsciousness, and then, he woke up here. He pulled away from his hands and looked around once again. Arthur recognized that this was the world within his mind where he battled his inner Beast before. He couldn't understand why he was here, though.

"Because you lost focus!" growled a dark, hateful but familiar voice. Arthur instantly clenched his fists, ready for anything.

"Oh, don't bother!" the voice shouted again, but Arthur held his ground. In front of him, materializing from the black floor a few feet away from him, was the enormous figure of his inner Werewolf. Out from the obsidian ground Arthur stood on, rose thick liquid-like pieces of flowing shadows that sculpted themselves as they rose to nearly ten feet tall, assembling the figure. Its head morphed into a giant wolf with a long mouth, tall ears, and piercing bright glowing yellow eyes that stared down icily at Arthur. He, in turn, looked up at the Beast fiercely.

"What do you want?!" Arthur snapped. The Beast shook his head and curled its lip like Cratos did whenever Arthur had asked a dumb question.

"If I hadn't stepped in," he began as his left arm swung upward, his long, sharply clawed finger pointing straight at Arthur.

"You would be dead. I saved your pathetic, miserable life," it snarled.

"You liar!" Arthur responded in confused spite.

"Like you would ever miss a chance to see me dead!" he spat in response. The Beast sighed again.

"You are a foolish child. If you die, I die! You were going to give up, so I was forced to step in." Arthur frowned, confused by his phrasing.

"What do you mean 'step in'?" Arthur asked, causing the Beast to chuckle darkly at Arthur's ignorance.

"When your willpower had evaporated after your hand shattered, I assumed control of your consciousness and saved us both. It resulted...differently than I had planned, but we WILL live. You're welcome, your weak swine!"

Arthur looked away from the Werewolf and thought for a moment. After a moment of thought, he faced the Beast again, his emotions more under control as he spoke.

"How did you do any of this? I thought after I won our last encounter, I wasn't meant to see you again until the next full moon." The Beast sneered at the context of his question.

"Next time, you might not be so lucky in our fight." Arthur narrowed his eyes suspiciously as the Beast continued.

"I won't always be able to step in and save your worthless hide. It took a lot of effort for me to do that at all. I am weakened for now. You need to be careful, boy. I plan to have this body for myself one day, and I won't have you ruining it!" Arthur spat towards the Beast.

"I will slit my own throat before I hand this body over to you!" Arthur replied coldly. The Beast squinted at Arthur and shook his head.

"You're a fool. Eventually, you will have to accept me. Only then will you truly be powerful. Until then, you are doomed to struggle and die like a weakling dog!" Arthur snorted at his threats.

"You'd know," Arthur retorted back immaturely. The Beast roared savagely at Arthur.

"Leave here, stupid child!" it snarled. The Beast held up his hand and snapped his clawed fingers. All feeling suddenly was lost in Arthur's body as he slumped to the floor like a sack of bricks. As he hit the ground, darkness began to swallow his body like he was sinking into quicksand.

"Train hard, boy. There is much more fighting ahead and twice as much pain for you to endure." That was the last thing Arthur heard the Beast say before he went into unconsciousness once again.

"Wake up Arthur! Wake up! Dammit, Arthur, wake up NOW!" came words that shouted Arthur back into the real world once again. His eyes slowly widened to see Delfer's face staring at him angrily, a piercing glare drilling straight into Arthur's pupils. Arthur frowned with confusion and tried to move. His body screamed back at him like a bellowing parent forbidding their child from leaving a corner. He immediately felt jolts of pain that rained through Arthur's entire body, halting his moments back into stillness. His teeth gritted against the sharp horrific pain until it subsided while he lay still once more. He tried to lift his head to examine his condition, but that was too much for him to bear. So, he decided to simply stare up at Delfer, who looked over him, hoping he would at least be able to speak.

"What happened?" Arthur asked; his voice was dry, and it ached to speak, but he was glad he could at least talk. Delfer sighed angrily and answered.

"You disobeyed my orders and jumped out into the city, nearly getting yourself killed! Then once, I thought you were dead. I saw you leap from a building right on top of the damn Vampire van hood!" His teeth were clenched as he spoke, and Arthur could feel his rage like a fierce heat against his face. Arthur pulled a sorry-looking face but tried to defend himself.

"I had to act! We were trapped back there, and I had to do something; otherwise, we would have lost the van." Arthur winced again as he tried to move, but the pain was ever vigilant to return him to being a statue.

"Am I going to be OK?" he asked with a shaky voice. Delfer snorted indifferently; Arthur could tell he didn't have an ounce of sympathy for his pained state.

"Despite the fact you don't deserve to be, yes. Your body is healing fast, but nothing was broken beyond repair. Bones were only severely fractured. A few hours and you'll be walking like before," Delfer answered bitterly. Arthur sighed with relief. Delfer was furious with Arthur as he lay there, but Arthur didn't care for the moment. There was only one person in his mind he wanted to talk about right now.

"Where's Cratos?" he asked. Delfer's frown burrowed deeper into his forehead as his arms tensed.

"Him, as well as the others, are currently also sleeping off their injuries. It's a bloody miracle none of them broke their necks and died, you know!" Arthur winced after hearing that. Whatever the Beast within him did when it took control of his body, it didn't consider that the whole point of this adventure was to rescue what was in the black van and not hurt them. But before Arthur could feel guilty, something odd struck him.

"Wait," Arthur said as his eyes looked side to side in their sockets.

"Where are we?" he asked. He felt a hard floor under him. It was cold and solid, but the only direction he could look was up. Delfer once again gritted his teeth as he was forced to recall his struggles of fixing Arthur's recklessness.

"When the van crashed, I signaled for backup to move all of you to the closest safe house. You're currently lying in a storeroom while the others are lying on beds in a medical wing." Arthur felt it was his turn to frown now.

"Why didn't I get a bed," he growled, followed by Delfer immediately snapping.

"Because you nearly got yourself killed and everyone else along with you! Seriously boy, what were you thinking?!." Arthur looked away for a moment. He was not sure if he should tell Delfer about his inner Beast and what happened. He certainly planned to tell Cratos, but he wasn't sure how Delfer would react. Delfer noticed Arthur's hesitation immediately and saw him look away. Now suspicious, he persisted.

"What is it?" he asked firmly. Arthur sighed and explained everything to Delfer. He told him how he blacked out, awoke within the place where Arthur fought the Beast within him during the full moon, and what the Beast had told Arthur before he awoke. Delfer listened quietly, waiting for Arthur to finish, and when he finally did, Delfer hummed oddly.

"What you're describing is not completely unheard of. It happens to small minorities of the clan. The Wolves within us sometimes develop a form of respect, or at least some sort of bond with the being it shares a body with, and in dire situations, it would act as you have described. But here some factors disturb me greatly." Fear reared its ugly head in the pit of Arthur's stomach as he shot his body upright despite the pain, held in place leaning against his straightened arms being him.

"What factor?" Arthur asked fearfully.

"One," Delfer began; the anger disappeared from his face. It washed away and was immediately replaced with a disturbing expression of worry.

"You are too young. This phenomenon NEVER happens to a cub. Only to Werewolves that have had their beast live with them for years. It especially has never happened after just one meeting!" Delfer seemed almost unable to contain his disbelief; to him, it was as though someone had just displayed genuine magic in front of his face. Arthur didn't interrupt and let Delfer continue.

"Two, the fact it had taken full control of your body without you knowing about it. That is even rarer, and Three, the most confusing and scary of all," Arthur's eyes shook with anticipation as Delfer paused before finishing with his tone gritty.

"What is it?" Arthur pleaded strongly. Delfer eyes narrowed as he looked on at Arthur as though he was staring at an alien itself.

"Thirdly, the fact he gave your body back to you." Delfer finished with an ashen, hollow voice.

Delfer left Arthur alone to recover after their talk so he could check on the other Werewolves. He had left explaining nothing else about his worries about what Arthur had told him. But Arthur remembered the fearful look on his face. Arthur himself didn't know how to feel. He was left by himself without the others and his Beast to bother him. If the Beast hadn't taken over his body, then he probably would have died. The Beast acted ferociously and may have killed Cratos and the others in its action, but it's through its action that he can continue right now, so he thought he couldn't be too bad that it happened. Arthur would remember to bring up to Cratos when the next full moon was so he could more thoroughly question his inner Beast. But thinking about that drew Arthur's mind to his actions not long before. His body had healed very quickly, and having been left alone for a few hours, he was now standing. The room he was in was a simple grey cement square room. It was virtually empty except for a thick metal door. His joints, bones, and muscles were still throbbing with an aching, but at least he was mobile now. He stood up high and leaned against the wall thinking hard with his arms crossed. He felt that even if he feels sorry for himself now, Arthur will just forget this sad feeling when the next crisis happens, and he will go off the edge repeatedly until the Werewolves have no choice but to deal with him or worse, perhaps even kill him.

A couple of hours later, Delfer returned; Arthur had fallen asleep and was resting down on the concrete floor where he had first woken up. The Werewolf walked over and knelt close by Arthur, studying the boy while he slept. Delfer couldn't wrap his mind around how the Beast within Arthur took control the way it did and why it gave power back to him upon having its freedom which all inner Beasts within Werewolves sought so severely. In his entire life among the Werewolves, he had never heard of such an occurrence, especially for a cub. Delfer wondered if he should tell Cratos about Arthur right away. He was sure the boy would tell him the truth, but if Arthur honestly didn't want to, he thought it wasn't his place. However, despite that, he would most certainly tell Cratos that Arthur had disobeyed him, given that the boy nearly died and then almost killed the others. Delfer sighed as he stood up and pulled an uneasy face; he wasn't used to a situation like this. Dealing with children wasn't his strength. He could tell Arthur didn't mean to crash the black van; that was the Beast's fault, but he still jumped out of the van in the first place and leaped onto the police cars.

Delfer wondered just how much influence the Beast within Arthur had over him. He walked out of the room, closing it behind him when Cratos suddenly approached him on the other side. His old friend smiled fondly at him as he came. The pair themselves had been through many adventures in their youth together when they were first Werewolves. Delfer recalled a similar time Cratos was in trouble during their training, and he couldn't help but smirk. Cratos looked tired, and Delfer had a feeling he hadn't fully recovered yet, leaving his resting space to come to check on Arthur.

"That better be sleepwalking, I'm seeing," Delfer said with a raised eyebrow, mimicking a motherly tone of voice. Cratos smirked but shook his head.

"I just wanted to see if he was OK," he replied with a strained smile. His face had somehow looked even paler and aged as he faced his friend. Delfer rolled his eyes and chuckled.

"He's fine. The laws of both nature and physics are probably insulted by that fact, but he's recovering, as you should still be!" The edge in Delfer's tone genuinely made Cratos smile, and he put a hand on his friend's shoulder.

"You don't have to worry about me; we've both been through worse," Cratos chuckled but his worried face looking past Delfers' shoulder at the door betrayed his concern.

"But he hasn't," Cratos finished firmly, the resonating authority slowly returning to his disposition. Delfer sighed as he knew he had to tell his friend what he had learned about his student.

"Cratos, there's a problem with Arthur we need to discuss." Cratos noticed a genuine regret in Delfer's expression, and fear swept across Delfer's face.

"You said he was fine!" he quickly snapped, more eager to go past Delfer than ever. Delfer took Cratos's hand off his should and looked into his eyes for reassurance.

"He is fine physically. I mean, there is a problem of a different nature." Cratos saw the discomfort on Delfer's face and nodded somberly, less panicked.

"Very well, let's speak elsewhere." The pair then walked down the corridor away from the room where Arthur was resting.

"That's impossible, Delfer," Cratos snorted dismissively. Delfer had finished relaying to his friend what Arthur had told him, and the Werewolf only rolled his eyes at his friend. The pair was sitting casually in one of the eating areas in their safe house building, sitting across from a steel desk on steel chairs. Each of them had a drink of beer in their hands.

"He was confused somehow," Cratos stated simply as though that ended the matter. Delfer shook his head.

"You know he couldn't have made that up. It does actually happen to our people Cratos; you know that," Delfer argued.

"Yes, but barely ever, and when it does, it's only to people who have been fighting their beasts for decades, not days!" Cratos countered erratically. Delfer sighed with resignation and spoke quietly to Cratos. Cratos finished his drink with a sharp snap.

"He wasn't lying Cratos. I know when someone lies to me. We are both trained to know that. The beast within Arthur took control of his body and then handed it right back to him." Cratos's eyes narrowed intensely as though he was looking for a needle in a haystack simply with his vision alone.

"That's what irks me the most. Why would a Werewolf's' inner beast ever do that?" Delfer said nothing; he had no answer to that one. The pair sat in silence for a few minutes before Cratos broke the silence.

"Either way," Cratos began, his voice sullen as he tried to distract away from that last question.

"Even if the beast in Arthur was responsible for the van crashing, I shall have a very stern word with him for disobeying you and jumping out of the van in the first place. Foolish child!" he finished, nearly snarling. Delfer, though then, couldn't help but chuckle.

"I recall you being rather reckless yourself when we were training together. I remember when you got drunk in America and tried to play chicken with an oncoming train. You nearly turned yourself into railway jam." Cratos's face went red a little as he puffed up his cheeks, embarrassed.

"Firstly, I wasn't THAT drunk, and secondly, I knew full well what I was doing." He paused before saying anything else. Something from the entire story had popped up in his head, and he was now frowning at Delfer.

"By the way, Delfer. Why exactly DID you let Arthur come with you? I stayed behind in that attack for him to escape safely, and you take him to even worse danger straight afterward." Rather than Delfer growing angry or ashamed from the question, he simply gave a warm smile as he looked at his friend.

"Because he was so dead-set on rescuing you, if I didn't take him, he would have tried to on his own. It was rather inspiring to see I couldn't help but let him come alone. I must say, you have quite the loyal cub there, Cratos." Anger washed away from Cratos at that moment. As Arthurs' mentor sat back in his chair smirking, losing himself in thought about their travels together up to this point.

"He does have a lot of tenacity, doesn't he? I saw it straight away. He has so much potential." Delfer nodded back to his friend, glad to see him smiling after the ordeal they had gone through.

"Think of it this way. Yes, he screwed up a few times, but if he hadn't, odds are, we would all be dead. Both the rest of the team and me would be in an unmarked grave covered in bullet holes, and you would be in the heart of the Vampire empire right now being tortured in their cells. The kid messed up, but he also came through at least." Cratos returned the nod but kept his look stern.

"Yes, you are right. However, Arthur will not be told that, understand?" Delfer nodded, and the two continued to drink and speak, Cratos not noticing the crossed fingers Delfer had behind his back as a joke.

Arthur awoke to see he was no longer in the concrete room. He moved his head to look around and noticed he was now in a smaller enclosed space. Arthur could hear a running engine, and he realized he was lying in the back of another van. His heart stopped beating as fear immediately screamed inside his head that he had imagined everything. He thought that Delfer must have knocked him out, and they were looking for Cratos still before he was tortured and killed, and the entire rescue had been a dream. Arthur sat upward sharply in a blind panic. He felt very foolish as he saw the front seat and noticed the person in the driver's seat. It wasn't the face of Delfer desperate to find his captured friend but instead the concentrating face of his mentor Cratos Mane, who was not bothering to react to Arthur's sudden burst as he woke. Arthur didn't hesitate for a second.

"Cratos!" Arthur cried out in joy, scrambling across the floor of the van they were into the man, hugging him as he drove forward.

"I can't see the road," Cratos said casually in response. Arthur let go of his teacher and looked out the window in front of them. They were on a giant stretch of road with hundreds of other cars around them.

"Where are we going?" he asked, calming down now, knowing they were safe. Cratos didn't answer right away. He instead just nodded towards the seat next to him, signaling for Arthur to sit in it. Arthur crawled across into the second front seat without saying anything else and waited for Cratos to speak. Arthur felt odd about how stoic Cratos was acting, and it was starting to put Arthur on edge.

"Seat belt," his mentor commented. Arthur pulled his seat belt across his body and clipped it in place. A few moments of silence went by before Arthur spoke again as he couldn't stand the silence.

"Did you speak to Delfer?" Arthur asked nervously, starting to catch onto why Cratos was quiet. His mentor nodded, but his face remained unmoving like a statue as he spoke sternly.

"Yes, he told me everything. Tell me, is it true?" Arthur looked down for a moment and nodded himself.

"Yes, completely true. The Beast within my mind took control of my body." Cratos didn't look away from the road as they continued.

"Do you know how?" Cratos responded; his tone and expression were unreadable. He was looking as though he was simply focusing on the road without a care in the world. Arthur was very unsettled by Cratos's disposition but did not want to turn it from neutral to angry so he answered promptly.

"The Beast itself had told me. I had tried to break the windscreen of the black van, forgetting how reinforced it was, and my hand had shattered. I felt faint and was about to pass out. Right at that exact moment, as I gave into the unconsciousness, it came forth and took charge of me. I then remembered nothing and woke up to Delfer." As Arthur finished, Cratos sighed heavily. He had hoped Arthur would have mentioned a detail Delfer had not. He was hoping to hear something that would have explained the problem clearly. But to Cratos' dismay, the explanation was the exact same as Delfer had described to him the first time.

"Usually, in the small cases where this has happened, the Werewolf always knew its other half was taking over. The fact you didn't know until the beast itself told you is...different," he finished hesitantly. Arthur turned his head and frowned in confusion as Cratos.

"Is that bad?" Arthur asked in return. Cratos didn't answer for several moments before finally saying.

"I don't know...but I know someone who will." After those words, both

Cratos and Arthur were silent. They were going on the road somewhere going to someone Arthur didn't know who might be able to shed light hopefully on what happened to him.

A few hours had gone by as they drove. Cratos was still angry at Arthur for endangering himself by going with Delfer on the rescue. But at the same time, he couldn't help but begrudgingly respect the boy for his loyalty towards him. As the silence began to drive Cratos to near madness himself, he finally broke his silence and began speaking to Arthur again. After a few minutes, Cratos had forgotten why he was even mad at Arthur to start with, and they were chatting to each other as they had before they entered the city. Arthur didn't speak of the Beast or the situation himself while they spoke. He felt it was a topic for darker conversations, and he didn't want to ruin his reunion with his teacher after being terrified he would lose him. Arthur had almost lost his teacher, and he didn't know what he would have done being in the Werewolf world without the only friend he had left in his life. Arthur asked who they were going to see once the point of this trip came back to him. Cratos thought for a moment, choosing his words carefully.

"A doctor...of sorts," he answered vaguely, shifting in his seat uncomfortably. Arthur frowned at his teacher's response.

"Why are we seeing a doctor? We'll heal ourselves naturally from the crash, right?" Arthur asked cautiously. Cratos nodded and groaned slightly; it seemed like he did not want whatever he was about to say to be used against him in the future in any way.

"Yes, that's true, but that is not why we are going. Usually, I would wait until we were inside the Wolf Kingdom to have you looked at for your look-over. However, after this recent incident, the situation has become more urgent and hence, requires a more...refined eye to see what exactly happened to you." Arthur continued to frown. Now he shifted with discomfort in his seat. Arthur hated going to a doctor; they were always poking and prodding him like a puppet with strings to pull. It always creeped him out ever since he was little. Cratos saw his discomfort and chuckled to try and reassure him.

"Don't seem so worried. We were going to have someone look at you either way. This is routine for all new cubs. It is usually just to make sure you're ship-shape and ready for training. There just happens to be a stronger agenda for this visit, but I'm sure everything will be fine. The person we're going to see is very...good at their job." Arthur caught the pauses in Cratos's tone and confronted it.

"OK, what's wrong?" he challenged. Cratos took a large and deep breath.

"It's tricky to explain. And I don't mean that in the way I usually do. You will actually have to see what lies ahead to understand because I'll be damned if I say anything that's not accurate." Arthur merely rolled his eyes and looked out of the window in resignation. The weight of the endless riddles and puzzles Cratos spat at him was becoming quite heavy on his shoulders.

A few more hours passed as the pair were no longer amongst other cars on a long road, but now, they were being thrown around the front of the van as they drove on a bumpy dirt road. Nighttime had descended upon the pair as Arthur could see nothing around him outside the windows. Only the light of the headlights showing a few feet in front of them could be seen. Even with his Werewolf eyes, he could only make out shapes of trees in the far distance and nothing else. To Arthur, it seemed like they had taken themselves in the middle of nowhere. All else around him was complete darkness. As Arthur stared out into the void of black nothingness, he looked up into the skies and tried looking for the moon, even a half-moon or crescent. Nothing could be seen. There were only the dark black clouds that plagued the sky like a wave of pestilence as it covered every inch of the skies. Arthur sighed with disappointment; even nature itself was hiding from him. Then out of nowhere, Cratos commented.

"Better cross your fingers it doesn't rain; this road is treacherous enough as it is." Another look into the skies, seeing how dense the black clouds were, and Arthur figured it probably was going to rain, but he didn't care. He felt his eyes growing heavy then. Despite how much Arthur had slept after the crash, he was how in the welcoming grip of sleepiness. Arthur then yawned loudly.

"What time is it?" he asked casually, thinking some form of conversation would keep him awake. Cratos hummed for a moment as he continued to drive, the bumps and jokes from the road not affecting his rigid concentration.

"Around one-thirty," Cratos then answered plainly. As Arthur grew more tired, he let his mind drift and just waited for his train of thought to grip onto a passing idea to catch his focus. The first one that came to mind was Delfer as he thought about everything that had happened when he got ripped apart from Cratos, how Delfer made sure Arthur got out of the bar attack without a scratch and took care of him during the rescue. Arthur felt genuinely thankful to the man for all the help Delfer gave him when Cratos was taken. He was then upset that he didn't get a chance to thank Delfer or even say goodbye properly. He figured since he and Cratos were such good friends, he would run into the man again soon, at whatever this 'Eclipse festival' was; he remembered Cratos had mentioned it in the bar before it was raided. His tiredness finally won over Arthur as this time his eyelids dropped down entirely, not rising back or even twitching in resistance. Arthur then quickly fell fully asleep once more.

Arthur found himself walking along the landing floor inside his house. He went along the corridor which led to the top of the stairs. Arthur looked around the place he used to call home. He saw torn wallpaper on the walls on each side of him; his eyes focused on the dents and scratches against the brick beneath. Arthur then stopped as he came to the stairs. He looked down to the bottom, seeing the same front door he walked in and out of for years. His eyes then looked at the hanging light bulb with no shade hanging from the ceiling above him. Arthur then looked back down the stairs again and saw the light from the kitchen casting a glow on the carpet ahead in his vision. He tried to sniff the air but couldn't smell any food cooking. There was no smell at all. There wasn't even the familiar scent of dust or mold clouding his nostrils like always. Here there was nothing to hear but complete silence. There wasn't a sound in the entire house. No sound of Alice playing with her toys or any of her kiddy music. He couldn't hear the television blaring downstairs in their living room from one of his father's idiotic shows. That was something that frightened him greatly. The house was NEVER silent. He looked down at himself then. He was wearing the regular clothes he wore back when he was at home before leaving with Cratos. It was a plain black shirt with similar colored trousers and shoes, which was nothing immediately out of the ordinary. The only problem he noticed was that his regular home clothes were ruined in the accident with the black van, and he was given a grey shirt with black trousers and large heavy black boots. Yet here he was wearing the same outfit he wore nearly every day before he became a Werewolf. What Arthur found stranger was that he didn't seem to care. He wasn't processing that information as he usually would and merely shrugged, beginning his descent down the stairs of his old family home.

With every step he took down his stairs, the space around him seemed to grow dead. The walls around him were slowly decaying with each step. The mold and rot chewed their way through the brick, turning the white walls around him into savage green and black-filth shades. The decay was smothering around his home interior like a dozen fissure cracks, spreading

221

as he walked like live tree vines possessed to infest his house. The walls weakened and even began to crumble as he walked on. He stopped for a moment and looked behind him. He couldn't see the top of his stairs anymore. There was nothing left. There was literally a void of nothing itself. He looked down and saw that even the steps he trod upon were beginning to feel weaker and unstable, like stepping into wet and treacherous swampy mud. The world behind him faded, and he was unable to turn back. Fear punched Arthur violently in his stomach as the threat of falling into the rotting nothing with the rest of his house raced through his mind. Arthur then ran down the stairs as fast as he could. The stairs and walls behind him, rather than dying slowly of rot, had now collapsed angrily. They came crashing down behind him as he reached the bottom of the stairs. Arthur looked behind him now, and even the first step of his staircase was no longer visible. Behind him now was only nothing. Even darkness of shadows would be something, but Arthur only felt a feeling of nothingness as he gazed at it. Turning back, the ground floor of his house was still alive and present. To his left was his kitchen. He peered in a saw no one inside. There was only the table, chairs, sink, cooker, and everything else. It all looked the same as he remembered.

"YOU BLOODY INGRATES! I'LL SHOW YOU WHOS BOSS AROUND HERE!" came the horrendous thundering roar of his bellowing drunken father from the living room that lay to his right. Arthur froze with fear. The scream of his father was fresh in his ears. Even after his fight with his inner Beast, he still trembled at its quake. Not moving a muscle, now Arthur hoped nothing behind him would swallow him with the rest of his house so he wouldn't have to face him. He closed his eyes and waited for it to be over, only for him to then hear two screams following the roar. In the depths of his soul, Arthur listened to the high-pitched shriek of his mother and the wailing cry of his little sister. Arthur's eyes then snapped open, his arms tensed, and he darted towards the living room as though he was suddenly possessed, his face twisted in murderous fury.

The inside of the room was a horrible, gut-wrenching, and demonic sight but still familiar to him. The table was knocked over on its side, and several chairs had been thrown around the room. Vases were knocked over with spilled drinks and food on the floor. The lightbulb was hanging from the ceiling, swaying side to side as though knocked in the commotion. Sat down crying with her legs crossed and her hands gripping her tiny knees was the sobbing face of Arthur's sister Alice. A few feet away was his mother. Her mascara was streaming down her face from her tears of fear. Her eyes were alight with horror as her entire body trembled like a human earthquake with the towering shadow cast over her. He was standing like a mighty enraged giant; his nostrils flared with a red face resembling that of a demon. His arms tensed, and fists clenched into solid hammers of steel. Arthur screamed out at all three of them, but their heads didn't even turn towards him, faces not responding to his call like they couldn't hear him. Arthur tried to scream out again, but not a sound echoed around the room. They were ignoring Arthur's presence entirely. His mother wailed in utter distress.

"Please, honey, don't! I'm sorry, I'm so sorry!" she cried out hysterically. Alice, with tears running down her cheeks, cried out as well.

"Yes, daddy, we're sorry!" Arthur's dad didn't even respond; his shoulders were heaving up and down as his breath was coming out of his nose like a thunderous bull. His bloodshot eyes narrowed like piercing needles on Arthur's mother.

"You wretched, bloody ingrates!" he hissed through clenched teeth. His mother knew what was coming and closed her eyes as Arthur's father shot his fist forward, slamming all his nail-hard knuckles straight into her stomach. Her eyes exploded open as she was knocked backward hard against the wall. She gasped like a dying fish for a few seconds before falling to her knees. Her body was shuddering as she collapsed entirely on the floor.

"Mummy!" Alice screamed in terror as she dashed forward to help her mother, who still hadn't taken in a breath yet. Arthur's father acted quicker, though. Turning his arm around to face the other way, he threw it outward, backhand slapping Alice across her face and throwing her to the floor. She screamed with pain as half her face went red instantly, then quickly becoming purple before Arthurs' eyes. Arthur's father snarled down at Alice,

"The boy isn't around to coddle you any longer. You better learn your place, young lady! Or else!" Alice cried her eyes out as Arthur screamed and leaped forward at his father, fully intent on using every shred of his Werewolf-given powers to tear his father limb from limb and leave him as a bloody pool of ripped-apart flesh.

Arthur's leap, however, was rapidly cut short. The impossible slammed him in the face as Arthur seemed to hit his body against an invisible wall that stood between him and the living room. His face was crushed against it as he fell to the floor, smacking his fists forwards, striking against the unseen force field that was keeping him from saving his family. Alice's crying little face rose slowly. She stared into the fire-lit eyes of her father.

"Yes, daddy," she sobbed, her lower jaw shaking.

"I'm sorry, daddy," she finished, her small hands rubbing against the mark on her face. Arthur was roaring uncontrollably like a madman in a straitjacket. He was throwing his entire being at the invisible wall, which blocked him. Arthur was screaming his sister's and his mother's names and cursing his father's with all his might. Their father spat on the floor between them and stormed away from the living room and into the kitchen. Sobbing her eyes out still, Alice crawled over to their mother.

"Mummy, are you OK?" she croaked in a low, shaken voice. Their mother lifted her head, taking short rapid gasps of air, her face bright red and soaked in her tears. She nodded her head and took Alice into her arms, hugging her tightly as they both cried on the floor together. Arthur fell to his knees further, nearly in a fetal position with both his hands flat against the wall, separating him from running over and saving them both. Arthur was now crying himself. Tears were rolling down streams of his pain like a newborn baby. Alice nuzzled her little head into her mother's shaky embrace and whimpered a few words, which Arthur heard all too clearly.

"I miss Arthur," she said softly and continued crying. Their mother nodded and hugged her tighter despite her injury, making it hurt.

"I know, sweetie...I do...too...but you have to be...strong baby...he left us alone..." At those words, Arthur felt his heart was virtually ripped out of his chest. A
Arthur called out their names again, over and over. The utter nothing that had devoured the staircase behind him was now smothering the living room. The room began to cast a shadow over his mother and sister, who were still crying in each other's arms. Then before Arthur's eyes, they were quickly swallowed out of sight and into nothingness. Arthur screamed for them both one last time before all around him were shadows, leaving him alone in the void. His house around him vanished in the blink of an eye. Arthur was still crying uncontrollably. He lifted his head. Arthur looked to the left and saw nothing, only nothing. He then looked to the right and saw the same emptiness. He turned his head forward, and his eyes then were met with the sharp-fanged demon head of the Werewolf inside him, staring deep into his eyes with its hellish yellow ones. Before Arthur could scream in surprise, its jaws opened and shot forward to consume Arthur's head.

CHAPTER EIGHTEEN

Arthur cried out as he snapped awake in the front seat of the van. His eyes were on fire with fear and despair, and he looked around himself. He saw the inside of the van and Cratos driving next to him. It was all gone, Arthur realized; it had all been a dream. He then relaxed, sighing deeply.

"Nightmare?" Cratos asked with a caring embrace in his voice. Arthur slowly nodded before he spoke.

"It was horrible. My family...they needed me...I... couldn't help them...I..." the words then turned into the air in his mouth. Cratos simply nodded back.

"That's understandable. I take it you tried to stand up for your family often." Arthur turned his head and looked at Cratos, who was focusing on the night's darkness still surrounding them as he drove. He remembered that Cratos mentioned his father when he had been following him and how Cratos saw what sort of man he was to Arthur.

"Not that it ever did any good. I was always too weak to make a difference," Arthur answered morosely, haunted by the words of his mother and her cries. It was too real for an ordinary dream. Every single tear they shed was still fresh in his mind as though he had witnessed it for real.

"And now you're not. Now you have strength. You have incredible strength. I don't know what you saw in your dream, but if you had been able to do something. What would you have done?" Cratos asked pointedly. Arthur didn't feel the need to lie, and besides, he knew his mentor knew him too well either way.

"I would have killed him," Arthur said with his eyes facing outside the window of the van, not facing Cratos. For a few moments, Cratos was silent, then he finally sighed and nodded.

"I understand how you feel," his mentor answered. Arthur was shocked. Cratos had scolded him for striking against Gary; he had expected a long lecture on not giving in to the dark impulses of our hearts or something profound like that. Cratos noted Arthur's confusion and spoke softly to him.

"There's a difference between hurting someone for vengeance and protecting those you love," he explained with a voice that made Arthur feel he was speaking not from simple logic but more experience. Arthur nodded in agreement. He did want to leap to his mother's and sister's rescue. But Arthur knew if he were honest with himself, he wasn't sure he could trust himself to let his actions be that pure. It would be to protect them, but he knew he would enjoy it as well, that he would also turn that protection into vengeance.

"Family is the ultimate flaw for any human's heart where right and wrong are concerned," Cratos continued.

"Loyalty that we bare to those who raise us, our blood. Those who show us a love that is utterly unique to the world...such an existence to some people. To preserve it, they would tear the very world apart...more often than none, they end up tearing themselves apart over it." Arthur didn't respond; he didn't have anything to say. He had no answers himself, and he knew Cratos could tell what he was feeling. After a few more minutes of silence, his mentor spoke up again for the last time for a long while.

"I can't tell you what is right and wrong...not for this situation Arthur. I will always give you advice and support, but this is a matter that could not be any closer to your heart. I know you want to protect your family, but when you take the blood of your own family to do so..." Cratos's eyes grew dark and mournful. His gaze was harrowing as his pupils disappeared to show images of some painful memory he wouldn't bring to the surface.

"It leaves a stain, a stain so deep and so dark that you can never wash it off...no matter what..." Arthur leaned back in his seat and thought about his nightmare and then thought about Cratos's words. He hoped his dream was wrong, and he hoped his father took his threat that night before he left them to heart and left Alice and his mother alone. Arthur thought about the day when he would be able to return home. He wondered if he found out that his father had continued to hurt them and the sort of state he would find his family in, then what would he do in response. Arthur's eyes drifted out of the window into the darkness, he knew full well what he would do, and that side of him scared him beyond comparison. Right at that moment, he had a strong feeling about why he saw the Beast before he woke up.

Hours later, with a sudden screech of the van's tires, the pair came to an abrupt stop. Arthur was pulled out of his train of thought as he looked out the window next to him. The same scenery as the last endless dozens of miles they had driven past. It was just the same empty void of darkness. There weren't even any trees around them. It looked as though they had just stopped on a dirt road in the middle of nowhere. It was hard to tell if there was a field around them or just damp, dry earth. Arthur groaned.

"Please tell me we haven't run out of petrol," he groaned. Cratos chuckled as he unfastened his seat belt.

"No, we've arrived at our location," he announced. Arthur frowned, taking another look out of the window and seeing only the utter blackness of the night.

"How the hell can you tell?" he asked. Even with his Werewolf eyes, there was still nothing but the darkness of the night all around them. Cratos shook his head, bewildered.

"You kids today, no sense of direction," Cratos laughed again as he opened the door and closed it behind him. Arthur raised an eyebrow and undid his seat belt.

"Old people," Arthur muttered, opening his door.

"Always have to be bloody right." As Arthur began to close the door behind him. Then Arthur heard Cratos reply as he entered the frosty night air himself.

"I heard that," Cratos grumbled back to him.

The pair walked away from the van and continued down the dirt road for a few meters. Arthur's eyes slowly began to adjust to the darkness with every few steps. He could now discern the world around them more accurately, distinguishing shapes and physical objects like trees and certain rock formations. He quickly came to realize that where they were was utterly deserted. The ground around the dirt road was paired with a field. But there was nothing in the space around them both; Arthur saw nothing around for what looked like miles. No trees, bushes, or any sign of a building; it seemed utterly lifeless. The night air alone was chilling Arthur to the bone; Arthur guessed it was freezing given his breath was a thick mist in front of his eyes. He was shivering, but he wasn't feeling as cold as he thought he would have been back home. He assumed that it was his wolf blood somehow keeping him warm. The skies above him were still blocked out by black throbbing clouds which threatened a storm any minute. The land around them seemed to be completely devoid of any wildlife.

"Who could live out here?" Arthur asked, wholly puzzled at the idea of how someone had both food and water or even adequate shelter in an area that doesn't seem to have either a stream, wildlife, or any plant life. Cratos chuckled again in his usual know-it-all way.

"You'll see. This area is very discreet. This person doesn't even go to the Eclipse festival. Any Werewolf that wants her, has to go to her, even Cyrus himself." Arthur sighed purposely loud to lament his exhaustion at Cratos's lack of explanation.

"Care to tell me what the Eclipse festival is, or who Cyrus is?" Arthur asked with an attempt more out of habit than expectation. Cratos pursed his lips in thought as they walked.

"Cyrus, I can tell you is the leader of our race. He is the current Alpha Werewolf." Arthur thought about that for a second. The Alpha Werewolf of the entire race of Werewolves.

"He must be immensely powerful," Arthur muttered, which caused Cratos to nod thoughtfully.

"You'll know when you see him," Cratos continued with Arthur trying to pry now that he had a foot in the door.

"And I'll see him at this Eclipse festival?" Arthur asked.

"Yes, but I will explain more about that once we are within the Wolf Kingdom. It'll be simpler there, OK?" Cratos asked. Arthur nodded as they continued walking, happy to at least get half a response from the answer vault that was his mentor.

"Why did we get out of the van only to continue walking up this damn road?" Arthur grunted as the night continued to grow colder around them.

"Rules," Cratos answered, simply saying nothing else. A few more yards away, Cratos then stopped walking and looked around. Arthur did the same, and everywhere he looked, he was nothing different than when they first got out of the van. Now the van was a tiny dot in Arthur's vision. Cratos started stamping on the ground, stomping his foot in different spots.

"Should be around here somewhere," he grunted as he continued to rest the ground. Arthur watched his mentor stamp on the brown dirt road around him until finally, he heard a loud metal bang.

"Aha!" Cratos exclaimed gleefully. Arthur frowned as his mentor bent over and dusted his hand over the spot, then he heard the sound. Cratos quickly began brushing away the dirt. Arthur watched on until he eventually saw the thin outline of a sizeable hatch-like square. He then remembered that Cratos had told him the Werewolves had built their kingdom under the earth in Europe. He guessed this person must have done the same with their home, and that's why they live in the middle of nowhere. Cratos smirked as his hand gripped around the indent of an inverted metal handle at the far end of the hatch. He pulled on the handle, and the metal square lifted, revealing a metal ladder bolted to the earth leading downward inside the hole the hatch had shown. Arthur leaned over and peered down the hole. He couldn't see the bottom from where he was standing.

"Are you sure this person won't mind us just dropping in without asking?" Arthur cautiously murmured. He was strangely unsure of going down the hole and into the darkness of the earth.

"We are already expected. Now, after you," Cratos gestured impatiently at his student towards the ladder leading down the hatch. Arthur sighed as he moved into the open manhole and began moving down the metal ladder one step at a time. Cratos waited a moment, then climbed in after his student, closing the hatch entrance behind him from the handle, both of them then descending deep into the body of the earth.

The pair ventured down into the depths of the earth. To Arthur, the ladder leading them seemed virtually endless given how long they had been descending. Arthur began counting the seconds in his head as they climbed in silence. The clinking and clacking sounds of their feet and hands were almost like clockwork in his ears, nearly maddening. He counted to ten minutes before he couldn't handle it any longer.

"Does this person happen to live in the earth's molten core?!" Arthur snapped. Cratos sighed, too exhausted to bother chiding Arthur for his impatience.

"Just keep going; we're almost there," he responded as they both returned to silence again before Cratos quickly added hastily.

"And lose that attitude! Nothing but respect while we are here. Understand?" Cratos then snapped. The sudden sharpness in his tone surprised Arthur, catching him off guard. His mentor hadn't been that hard on him even upon hearing he destroyed two police cars in the city. He figured this doctor must carry a lot of weight in the Werewolf world. That idea opened the gates to his curiosity about what kind of being this person was. Arthur tried to imagine such a person when his vision instantly changed around him. The end of the tunnelway vanished before his eyes as he saw himself climbing from the ceiling of a large space tunnel down onto the hard concrete floor at the bottom. He was now within the bounds of a giant-sized cavern tunnel.

The spacing looked like a gigantic tunnel passageway but twice as large as a standard sewer size. The ceiling, rather than only normal earth, was paved entirely in concrete, with large and small pipes littering the space around them like a million snakes glaring around him on every side. Along the walls around the pipes in a symmetrical row were large green lights illuminating the space around them. The green light was turning the surface of Arthur's skin to make him look less like a Werewolf and look more like a lizard man. The floor they walked on was wet, and there were puddles scattered along all over as they walked. What they were puddles of was something Arthur was afraid to ask in case he stepped in one. There was also a dense smell of mold and flesh-like stink that felt like it was constantly rising and stagnating in the air. Arthur coughed as he continued to breathe it in, the scent horrifying to the senses. Arthur saw as they walked a turning corner several feet ahead. The sound of constant rushing liquids running through the pipes over his head and on both walls at his side was constant. Arthur looked around, breathing heavily and heaving as though he was inside the stomach of some mechanical giant. Cratos patted his shoulder, making him jump.

"Relax, your perfectly safe," Cratos assured him. Arthur looked up at his mentor, who seemed to be calm himself, not even reacting to the smell of this place. Before he could nod to his teacher, the sound of footsteps was heard ahead of them. They were quiet at first, then grew louder as the echo grew closer to them. Arthur froze in place as the shadow of the figure approaching hit the side of the tunnelway they were facing. It was growing massive in size. The figure ahead was now growing closer and closer. Cratos leaned in closer to Arthur and whispered in his ear.

"Remember what I said, Arthur, nothing but respect!" he finished desperately. Arthur's breath caught in his mouth as the approaching fabled Werewolf doctor that lived in the bowels of the earth in a lair that was in the middle of nowhere revealed themselves, or rather, herself.

Arthur had thought Cratos himself was immensely tall when they first met. Even the other Werewolves at the bar back in the city were of impressive height themselves. However, it seemed that the woman approaching them was just about twelve feet tall from Arthur's eyes. She seemed dangerously thin, like a skeleton covered in clothes. She wore a long white lab coat, which must have been specifically tailored to her as it reached down to her ankles with a green shirt and combat trousers on the inside with black boots on her feet. She had fiercely long purple hair that stretched down to behind her knees, and from the front, two separate thick long strands of braided hair swung down from her face to her upper thighs with large blue orbs at the ends of each one. She wore green-colored gloves with the fingertips cut off, revealing exceptionally long fingernails that were several inches long and filed into sharp points on all fingers. Arthur noticed with his keen eyes that there was a distinct color of nail polish for each finger. The top half of her face was unseen as she was wearing some strange apparatus. It was a sizeable metal-looking helmet with several different-sized glasses and round glass scopes all around it with several microphones by the sides of her mouth. Her lips were razor-thin, with dark purple lipstick smothering their surface. The tall woman approached with her thin lips smiling warmly at the pair. Arthur focused his eyes again as he tried to look past the glasses which were currently over her eyes from the helmet, but they seemed to be mirrored; he couldn't see anything but her nose and mouth. She spread her arms wide as she came a few feet from the pair.

"Cratos! It's been far too long," she announced happily. Her voice was smooth and creepy to Arthur's ears. It didn't sound threatening or croaky. It was the complete opposite, like a soothing melody used in a lullaby. But there was something about the tone behind her voice that made Arthur's spine shiver for a reason he could not explain. Arthur looked at his mentor and saw the same reaction on Cratos's face. Cratos nodded and waved at her rather awkwardly.

"Hello, Siren. I trust you have been well," Cratos replied formally, his body rigidly tense. She chuckled in a deep tone as she approached Cratos. Her height to his looked like how Arthur looked when he stood up against Cratos in height. She patted Cratos on the head, messing up his hair like he was a child.

"Silly little Cratos. Of course I've been well," she gleefully replied. Cratos bit hard on his tongue as he forced himself to remain silent. Arthur couldn't help but grin as he watched his teacher look helplessly embarrassed. The woman called Siren then moved her head and turned her hidden gaze on Arthur, her grin extending further along her face.

"And whoooooooo is this?" she asked with great disturbing euphoria, turning Arthur's stomach to ice. Cratos coughed uncomfortably as he gently took Siren's hand from his head.

"Siren Glacier, this is my current student, Arthur Thorn. Arthur, this is Siren Glacier, the top physician, and scientist of the Werewolf race," Cratos answered formally. Siren chuckled a little.

"I would say the world is more than just the Werewolves, but whatever," she muttered before leaning down and looking Arthur over. Her head began moving around his form without much focus, eyes darting side to side, then up and down. She brought up his hand and began poking and prodding his face, humming without rhythm as she did it. She grabbed his arm and squeezed it slightly, then tapped a finger against his stomach. Arthur's eyes looked at Cratos, who commanded him with nothing more than a striking look to remain completely still. Siren released Arthur from his grip and sniffed his person for a few seconds.

"He's passed his first stage, I see," she muttered below her breath. Arthur had no idea how she figured that out from any of the observations she just made; even Cratos had to ask himself, but he remained silent.

"He's also been in a bit of a fight; I take it he was involved in that mess from the city several dozen miles from here," she asked. Cratos nodded grimly, his expression reducing.

"Yes, another hideout was busted into by the Vampires. Arthur here assisted with the rescue and got himself a little banged up in the process." She hummed again, not looking in Cratos's direction as she continued to scour her gaze over Arthur. He felt like she was an antique dealer evaluating his worth.

"An odd choice to bring a Crimson on a rescue mission," she muttered again. Siren then stood up straight and looked at Cratos oddly as her head tilted a bit left.

"You wouldn't bring the boy here for just a few mission injuries. What's the reason you're here Cratos, interrupting my important work?" Cratos sighed as he cast a brief look at Arthur and then back to Siren. His gaze again was plagued with worry.

"Ever since he passed his first stage, certain problems have arisen. Problems especially where his inner beast is concerned," Cratos answered hesitantly. Siren's smile exploded up her face as she squealed gleefully with a high pitch.

"Fascinating, tell me more in the lab." She then waved a hand at the pair as she turned her back on them and began walking back the way she came.

"Follow me now, hurry up," Siren ordered as she then speed-walked off back down the tunnel way. Arthur and Cratos exchanged glances of uneasiness and then followed on after Siren to her laboratory with considering effort given one of her leg strides for two for them.

The strange doctor known as Siren led the pair down the tunnelway towards her lair. They had been walking for what felt like to Arthur had been more than fifteen minutes. Fifteen minutes of endless tunnels with their pipes and green lights and rushing sounds. There were several left and right turns, like he was in a gigantic hedge maze. Arthur was amazed how someone didn't get lost; he wondered if Siren had built all of this herself. Arthur mentioned the size of the tunnel to Siren, and she laughed.

"Little lesson in women, boy, we prefer our privacy," she answered, giggling. Arthur smiled at that even though it didn't really answer his question. Cratos then stepped in a finished the answer.

"That and the work Siren does for us is extremely vital. Even if the Vampires came across her, we couldn't risk her capture or death," Cratos said with an almost proud expression. Arthur then waved a hand across the tunnelway they were walking along.

"What are all the pipes for?" he had to ask now, having seen them stretched to seemingly no end around him since he arrived. He had been subjected to the sound of liquid rushing through them constantly at a high pace, and his curiosity couldn't be higher. Arthur didn't know how Siren could stand being around it all the time. He had been underground now for what felt like more than an hour in total, and it was driving him insane.

"Very inquisitive, isn't he?" Siren voiced curtly, which made Cratos grimace.

"Yes, but I assure you it is not insolence, just a lack of tact!" Cratos responded with a cutting edge in his last few words, glaring at Arthur. Arthur then rolled his eyes; he saw nothing wrong in the question. After a few seconds, Siren answered, her voice prouder than she intended.

"These pipes are instrumental to my work, child. Not only do I require the constant use of the dozens of different chemicals that most of these pipes carry for me, but they also act as a distracting noise for any sort of radar or sonar detection from outside sources. They detect the noise, but that noise hides me, but then it would only be observed as average geometric patterns. Without them, I couldn't do my work, and I would become more easily located from hostile visitors." Arthur nodded and looked around again at all the pipes along with the ceiling and walls surrounding him. He wondered what different chemicals were going through them each and where exactly they ended up. Arthur then wondered what sort of work this doctor does that would require such immense secrecy.

The three continued through the tunnels for more time. Arthur had asked a few more questions since the noise coming from the pipes with no talking to mask the sound was driving him up the heavily piped wall. Arthur asked about the foul smell that smothered every inch of the tunnels they walked through. Arthur noticed that the scent hadn't lessened no matter what part of the tunnels they were walking in, and despite his attempts to ignore its bile, his Werewolf-fueled nostrils wouldn't let him. Cratos had winced as he asked it, and Siren had turned her head back to look at Arthur.

"What do you mean? What smell?" she asked with a playfully innocent yet underlying threatening tone. Arthur's breath caught in his throat as his face froze with no answer. A few seconds later, both she and Cratos burst out laughing, making Arthur scowl.

"What's so funny?!" he growled. Cratos finished chuckling.

"The gullibility of the young for one," he answered. Siren stopped laughing abruptly and then spoke.

"It's for any unwanted guests in my home. For humans, the mixture of gasses would knock them out unconscious after a few minutes of inhalation for me to then place them elsewhere, unless I'm experimenting, that is. In which case, they can very well wait." Arthur's eyebrow raised at that strange off-note, but he didn't interrupt.

"And for Vampires, if THEY breathe it in!" she continued, pausing to giggle for a moment with anticipation, which gave Arthur further uncomfortable shivers.

"Should this chemicals mixture get into a Vampire's nervous system from inhalation of the lungs, into the brain and such, it kills them DEAD! For Vampires, this entire tunnel is riddled with deadly nerve gas! Isn't biological warfare fun?!" she finished with a few more giggles. Arthur sniffed the air again. It was a horrible stench, but he didn't feel any pain or even dizzy from it. From his point of view, it was merely just uncomfortable.

"So then why doesn't it hurt Cratos and me?" Arthur asked blandly. Siren looked towards Cratos at that question.

"Do you teach this boy anything? Or do you just throw rocks at his head all day?" Cratos simply shrugged.

"He's only just passed his first stage; I don't have twenty hours to set aside to explain every inch of our anatomy." Siren snorted at that and frowned.

"Fools! Education should be your first priority. Werewolf biology alone fills in for any sort of fitness." Cratos shook his head at Siren.

"Such thinking would weaken the constitution of Werewolves as a race. We train for a strong mental state, first achieved through a well-honed and strong physical state. It is our discipline that keeps us strong psychologically," Siren snorted at him again.

"Bloody foolish pride," she mumbled, then spoke to Arthur directly to answer his question about why the gas didn't harm him.

"The prime senses of Werewolves develop immeasurably. As I'm sure you know, boy, from when you awoke as a Werewolf for the first time. Our sinuses have an incredible resistance to harmful gasses. Human-made means like tear gas or sleep gas would have no effect. Thus, neither do my gasses. Unless I wanted them to, that is. Any time I want, I can release a specially concentrated mixture of my own concoction which would make you think you've grown nineteen heads." Siren then turned her head back around and pulled her helmet up a tiny bit, exposing her eyes. Arthur noticed from the side that her left eye was a bright, vibrant green color and the right was a deep, almost glowing purple color. She winked with the purple one at Arthur and smiled.

"So, make sure to stay on my good side, boy," she said with a menacing smile as she turned back away and continued walking as freely and gleefully as ever.

"Come now Cratos. You may as well tell me the situation while we are walking. It'll save time," Siren announced out of nowhere as they once again turned what Arthur had felt was the millionth corner. Cratos was about to answer when he noticed the annoyance on Arthur's face and nodded at him.

"Let Arthur explain; it'll make more sense from him," he answered, nodding at Arthur to go ahead. Siren said nothing as silence filled the air for a brief moment. Cratos widened his eyes, signaling for Arthur to start speaking. Over the next few minutes, Arthur went into as much detail as he could about what happened in the city. He started when the Beast took over his body on the van finishing after he woke up from his dream meeting with the Beast within himself. Siren was silent during his entire explanation. Hearing this again made Cratos's face shift into discomfort. As he finished, Siren hummed for a moment as she thought.

"How about it Siren? I've never heard of something like this happening to any one of our race, have you?" Cratos asked without realizing his voice was rife with fear. After another hum, she answered.

"Possibly," she muttered. Her voice didn't sound as though she was uncomfortable or scared the way Cratos was. However, to Arthur, she seemed almost suspicious of the news. When she spoke again, her tone was now serious and firm.

"If this is what I think it is, then it's extremely rare. However, if it's something else, then I have no idea." The three finally turned another corner only to see a long hallway with a large steel round vault door at the far end. As all three of them came to the door, Arthur saw it had ten different safe-like dials with numbers the size of an ant's pupil upon them. Without saying anything, Siren began to turn the dials, and with each number she pressed, a loud, metal-clicking bang sounded.

"Siren, what exactly do you think is the problem?" Cratos asked impatiently. As Siren was on the last dial, she turned around, still twisting the dial with her hand as she faced Cratos.

"That is not for me to declare yet; there are many tests to go through," she replied cryptically. She then looked down at Arthur and eyed him as though trying to stare his body into a puddle. The final dial on the door clicked as the door slowly began to swing open. The three of them took a few steps back as Siren Glacier's laboratory was revealed before their eyes. Arthur stared back at her, finally seeing past the mirror of her glasses and into the incredible color of her eyes; they both seemed to be glowing as they gazed at him.

"Follow me, Arthur Thorn. It is time to see what destiny has in store for you." In that word, the three of them entered the fabled laboratory that belonged to the doctor of the Werewolves.

CHAPTER NINETEEN

If Cratos and Siren were not right next to him on each side, Arthur would have sworn he had been knocked out somehow, and he was now living within a nightmare that even the Beast within himself could not conjure up during their battles. During his years, he had seen a few horror films. Some were cheesy, some dark and scary. They had evil scientists and insane murderers with their weird lairs that contained disgusting sights for the human eyes. Such images were now considered fond nostalgia to Arthur as he stepped into this twisted, bloody place, looking like it had been directly modeled from a room in hell.

The stench, as it slithered like solid slime up into his nose, made Arthur gag for a few seconds before he could recover himself from experiencing the rest of the room. He had thought the tunnel on his way here was terrible, but the inside of Siren's laboratory was something else entirely, something inhuman. It smelt like rotting flesh had been burned by acid, then set on fire and put out to dry, drenched in moldy vinegar. That stench radiated around the entire room. It was vibrant and warm and smothering his whole face like a monstrous fog. Arthur felt as though he was going to throw up because he couldn't handle it. The room was truly putrid. Even Cratos was straining not to show any signs of discomfort, his eyes watering as he tensed his face solid and held his breath for as long as he could. Siren looked at both of them and chuckled. She inhaled deeply, then breathed out with her mouth open as though she had just sampled the fresh new air of spring weather.

The inside of the laboratory was enormous. After walking through the medium-sized tunnels, Arthur wasn't expecting the laboratory to be this big. The entire floor beneath him was some sort of black steel that was thick to step on like dense concrete. The room was littered with tables and countertops. There were tall ones, small ones, and even some hanging in the air from wires attached to pulleys. On their surfaces were dozens of different-sized beakers and bottles along with test tubes and different-sized funnels with endless dozens of sealed glasses of various acids and other liquids inside of which was every color imaginable, littering the entire room. Hanging from the ceiling was what looked like one single giant ventilation system, an enormous grate nearly the full length and width of the roof with a massive rotating fan behind it. Hanging down from the many grates were dozens upon dozens of green, bright light bulbs and dozens of lamps and other stage-looking lights decorating the entire room, which all also had the same green light. At the far end of the lab and in other places in the room were different workstations and worktop desks right next to what looked like large empty tables with straps at both ends. Some of the tables were caked in blood. Some of the blood was brown, which meant it was dry, but at least two tables bore fresh blood. If that alone had been all the room had inside, Arthur could have felt fine being here. The equipment seemed excessive and eccentric, but it was nothing insane. However, what also occupied the room made Arthur feel faint. There were body parts among nearly every workstation, next to almost every beaker, littering the sides of the long blood-stained tables, and even right next to him in jars on shelves within an unknown green liquid. There were severed hands, feet, heads, and a vast array of different organs and bones. They were all openly on display in jars and upon metal stands to be observed for study. Some pieces were cut open on the tables. Many hands and heads were hanging from the ceiling on large thick butchers' hooks hanging from the ceiling all around the room like a gory collection of flesh wind chimes.

Arthur noticed some of the heads were human; he could see the typical facial features. Some heads had longer hair than others, which meant there were both men and women. There were also Vampire heads among them too. He could see their signature red eyes inside their heads, and he investigated the open mouths which exposed their long fangs. Arthur also noticed many Vampire fangs on display in the thin metal apparatuses. There was also something else with them in the collection of limbs and pieces, Werewolves. There were transformed hairy parts preserved within the jars among the Vampire and human vats. Their thick fur littered the preserved limbs, hands with claws, and heads with fangs and yellow eyes. Arthur noted there were all assorted colors of hair on the pieces as well. Some with black coats of fur, red, golden, and even a few white furry limbs Arthur had never seen before. Arthur was snapping his neck from right to left, seeing everything all at once and feeling like a tiny piglet that just stepped into the slaughterhouse. All the carnage around him, felt as though every severed head had its lifeless eyes planted straight at him where he stood. Arthur's breathing became rapid, and he panicked. He instinctively took a step back, fully intent on turning around any second and fully happy to spend the rest of his life running through Siren's labyrinth than spend another second in this severed hell. As he was about to take another step back, he felt Cratos's hand against his back. He instantly looked up at his mentor, his terrorized face looking up at only an uncomfortable gaze looking back at him. Arthur felt his knees go a little weak, but he continued to look at his mentor and friend, saying nothing with words but his eyes speaking a language to him that Arthur had seen many times.

"Stay strong! You can do this!" to him. Arthur saw the same look as he gazed at Cratos now. He then gulped deeply and nodded at Cratos to signal he was ok. He strengthened his posture and again looked forward, trying to ignore the pure carnage ahead of him.

Siren looked at Arthur with confusion and rolled her eyes, walking behind the pair and closing the vault door behind them, the sound of all ten locks clicking back into place as she closed it.

"Such silly boys," she cooed as she walked back in front of them, waving a hand at her laboratory with a prideful relish.

"You people spend your lives avoiding real physicality! You glorify the body, choosing to ignore what's truly inside it! You are always remaining ignorant of the incredible machine that pumps life through you every millisecond of your existence. I say it's insulting personally." Arthur looked away, feeling a strange embarrassment. He still thought this was all an incredibly horrible sight, but he had a peculiar urge inside him that wanted to impress Siren, and he now felt like he had somewhat disappointed her. Since joining with Cratos, Arthur had always pretended to seem more mature than he was to separate himself from who he was as a human, but Siren had thrown him entirely out of his Werewolf body and back into that of some dumb human kid. He remembered in science class back in school when teachers were going through sideshows of people being cut open and such; he felt fine at the time. Other students had to leave the classroom to be sick, but his stomach never even twanged at that moment. Now it was as though a hammer was slamming against his body for him to run, hide and then cry. He felt once again afraid he had made a wrong impression on Siren. Arthur then heard her giggle as her hands clasped around his chin, pulling his head back up to see her mouth smiling.

"Now, Arthur, don't let it get you down. Everyone reacts the same way when they first see my home! Even small, dark and handsome here still gives out a face that looks like he just sucked on an old lemon still to this day." Arthur felt a slight smirk appear on his mouth then, feeling a bit better by Siren's reassurance. Cratos rolled his eyes.

"Anyone's discomfort is expected, Siren, even natural. You doctor's with your weird agendas about life, trivializing how unnatural these sights truly are," Cratos challenged like a begrudged child. Siren chuckled cutely for a few seconds, letting go of Arthur's chin and staring intently at Cratos, her nose left no air between hers and his own as she leaned down to his level, almost looking like she was at a right angle. Her eyes were more expansive than ever before as she stared at Cratos.

"Biology is nothing more than one of the many instruments to science, my dear Cratos," She raised her hand slowly towards Cratos's face. Siren then began bringing one of her long, sharp nails, slowly down the side of his face, scratching it at first as it slowly descended. Cratos's face was frozen with a fear that Arthur had never seen his teacher facially display before.

"And I," she continued without blinking once, the menace in her tone strong enough to make steel cry.

"I am nothing more than a fellow musician. Making whatever body I wish to play all the songs I want. Even writing a few of my own melodies when properly motivated." She then brought her nail back to the top of his face and did the same thing again, bringing her finger down his face, but this time her nail was scratching harder. As the fingernail went down his skin, a small line of blood began to descend his face, creating an extended open cut.

"And my dear sweet Cratos, every specific body has its own unique song to be played, a song to be carved out of them and heard by all! Tell me, Cratos, shall I find YOUR melody? Hmmm?" She then released her nail from his face and let her hand hang in the air to its left, all her fingers spread out like a claw. Blood was dripping down to his chin and then dripping on the floor. Cratos was still frozen with fear, saying nothing for a moment but then shaking his head slowly. Siren finally blinked several times and smiled motherly at Cratos.

"That's what I thought. For the rest of your visit, I recommend you keep your opinions to yourself about how I do my job. Do you understand, sweetie?" she asked calmly. He then nodded slowly in response again. The menace then dropped from her smile, and it turned into a genuine smile like when she first greeted them.

"Good to hear," she then leaned in a kissed his cheek with the bleeding cut with a loud smacking sound. As she pulled away, the small cut she made was now entirely gone. It had vanished, fully healed without even a tiny mark remaining on his skin. She then turned her back on the pair and began walking away into the depths of her lab, gesturing her hand for them to follow as she strode on. Cratos gave Arthur a terrified look as the pair quickly walked on after her. Arthur then made sure to remember strongly not to comment on anything regarding Siren's work or her home carelessly.

Cratos was firmly silent from that moment on as they trailed after Siren through her lab. Arthur didn't notice the fear still afire in his eyes like he was a traumatized child after being roared at by a dragon. As he walked along, Arthur's eyes were drawn to the tables and shelves they walked by. Each jar along the rack had a different label, some in English and lots in other languages with strange-looking symbols. Arthur now looked at all the various organs in jars and on the shelves in display racks. He saw all the hearts, brains, and kidneys in graphic detail. Arthur even saw particular parts of people that made Arthur feel increasingly embarrassed to see. Arthur quickly scoped past, and after seeing what happened to Cratos a moment ago, he decided not to comment. Arthur was curious about what was inside the different jars and vials, which weren't filled with a clear see-through liquid, and their contents couldn't be witnessed from the outside. However, he had a feeling that if he stopped Siren every half step to enquire about something, it would probably irritate her. In the science corridor, similar-looking chemicals were kept for teachers to use and gather supplies in his school. He remembered all the different experiments he did and learned while there and pondered what sort of experiments Siren did. He spotted a few Bunsen burners and ovens with pots and beakers bubbling away above their flames casually without Siren interfering at all. Arthur now knew that Siren was far more than just a simple doctor for the Werewolves. As they continued walking past the different ongoing experiments all around him, Arthur noticed on the sides of the walls were all the openings and endings of the endless pipes he saw on their way here. Not every single one but dozens upon dozens were stretching out of the wall, and the ends had something attached to them looking like the taps for sinks he had at home. Arthur observed it, intensely fascinated. Siren was right; all sorts of different liquids were pouring from them into her mixtures. Some taps ran constantly, and some ran with nothing emerging from the end, bone dry.

"Um, Siren?" Arthur said quietly. She didn't slow her pace, and Cratos was still holding the side of his face, acting like a disciplined child.

"What?" she said in a tone that made it sound like she had been waiting for

Arthur to start asking questions.

"All the pipes on the way here lead to this room where you get your liquids, right?" he inquired as his eyes gazed at the different liquids that were spewing from the pipes and into other contraptions that never seemed to overflow.

"Uh-huh," she answered plainly; neither sounded interested or uninterested in wherever Arthur was going with this question.

"Where do they start from, and where is all of them coming from constantly?" She giggled again.

"That's a good question! No one ever asks me that. Nice to have someone with more than just a one-digit IQ around here for once." Arthur smiled at the compliment and let her continue to answer.

"This is my main laboratory, but there are many other rooms around the entire complex if you know where to go in the tunnels. There are a few private studies that I do more personal work within and a basement below all of this here. Through there, I receive my supplies yearly and simply connect them to the pipes that start there, and they then feed upwards through all the tunnels and come here and in other rooms then travel more and more like veins in a body carrying blood all around us constantly. I like to think that my laboratory is the heart of my home." Arthur thought for a few seconds about that answer.

"Then how large exactly is your entire home?" he muttered in a marveled expression under his breath, it wasn't directed at her intently, but she answered it anyway.

"The construction took over ten years to perfect to my exact specifications, and I wouldn't allow even the slightest compromise in effort and efficiency. Only I will ever know how large my home is, and it shall stay that way." Arthur nodded and looked around the room again, wondering what rooms in this place are above or below him. He figured it must have been the Werewolves that built it for her. Arthur found the idea of all those enormous scary-looking people he saw from the bar back in the city being ordered around during the construction to her exact will a bit silly and that they wouldn't let anyone boss them around. Then again, he remembered how scared Cratos was of her and how he reacted to her being even the tiniest bit displeased with him. Arthur figured this woman must be capable of amazing but horrifying feats to get the entire Werewolf clan to build a secret underground lair for her.

Finally, the three came upon a far end of the room from where they first entered. All of them were standing around one of Sirens' worktables with dozens of draws surrounding its body. On the surface, at the far-right side of the worktop were countless different tools. There were scalpels, tongs, scissors, and all other kinds of different devices and instruments that Arthur couldn't identify. There was also a much more extensive assortment of items that looked like they belonged more in a garden shed than an operating table. Out in the open were hack saws, different-sized hedge clippers, even some tiny hand shovels, and various stabbing items as well. Arthur didn't know the names of half the tools he saw before him. His eyes drifted onto the worktable, this one with the same leather straps at the top and bottom end, caked and stained in dry blood.

A lump exploded in his throat as he then instantly pictured himself tied down on the table, an image of Siren laughing with an almost cartoony evil laugh as she cut him open and pulled out his heart in front of him. Arthur felt a hand grab his shoulder, giving it a reassuring squeeze. Arthur looked up and saw Cratos smiling at him to help him keep his center. His tension began to drop a little as he watched Siren dart from draw to draw all around the area, pulling out all sorts of different tools. Once her arms were full of various implements, she then laid them all out on the table, looking them over and humming in thought, checking if she missed anything.

"Right, let's get started. Remove your clothes," Siren said without looking Arthurs' way, picking up an item he did recognize, a stethoscope. Arthur's stomach tightened as he hesitated and looked at Cratos.

"Siren is still a doctor, Arthur. There is no need to be shy," his teacher reassured him. Arthur nodded but still felt unsure, especially with Cratos there. Even when they lived in the wild, he bathed separately from his teacher. Siren chuckled at Arthur, still not looking his way and preparing for her examination mentally.

"If you're shy about a simple physical examination, kid, you're going to end up traumatized when you go to Europe and meet the rest of the Werewolves in action," Siren chuckled. Arthur looked up at Cratos, confused who pulled a face at Siren.

"Don't frighten the kid, Siren; he's just never done this before." She sighed impatiently, looking at Arthur with a raised eyebrow, then her head snapped towards Cratos.

"Fine then. You go elsewhere and feed Demise for me." Cratos nodded, he patted Arthur on the back and turned to leave.

"Who's Demise?" Arthur asked nervously. Siren turned her attention back to her instruments.

"My snake," she answered blandly, then facing Arthur sharply, she had entered a strange mode of concentration that somehow made Arthur tenser than he already was.

"Now, let's get this over with. For the sake of your modesty, we can skip some of the tests I had planned, and you may keep your trousers on if you must." Arthur sighed with relief a little inside and removed his shirt and shoes, keeping his bottoms left on. Siren looked Arthur over for a second and patted on the worktop. Arthur gulped as he sat on the desk and waited for Siren to begin her examination.

Arthur had never been to the doctor much growing up. When he was little, he had been for a few injections and other shots he needed to get. Siren started off her tests with the usual actions doctors in the past have done to him. She checked his heartbeat, tested his reflexes, and then his breathing as well. She attached several rubber square patches onto his chest with wires streaming out of them into some machines with screens that displayed figures and graphs only Siren could make sense of. Siren read through each result without saying a word through the examination, just telling Arthur what to do next and not saying a word to him. She put some weird device into Arthur's ear and looked deep into his eyes and down his mouth in his throat. After those tests, she finally spoke.

"Regardless of any different situation, your development is going at an excellent rate. You shall start to notice distinct growth and change in the coming time very soon in both body and age." Siren continued to scribble on her papers as Arthur frowned.

"Age?" Arthur echoed, confused. Siren looked up from her board and looked at Arthur oddly.

"Yes, boy, age." She then saw the blank expression on Arthur's face, and her eyes widened.

"Did Cratos not explain how Werewolves age?" she asked wearily. Arthur shook his head.

"He said things would be easier to explain as I grow and develop, rather than going through it all at once." Siren's teeth clenched for a few seconds as the pencil in her hand snapped in two. Her anger unsettled Arthur.

"Why is that bad?" he asked worriedly. Siren looked at Arthur for a few seconds, then sighed, taking another pencil from her desk and returning it to her paper.

"It doesn't matter right now. It's not my place to tell you; it's Cratos who needs to say it," she answered in a tone that reminded Arthur of Delfer, who said a similar thing to him. Her hands tensed a little again.

"And he WILL tell you when you two leave; I promise you that!" Siren finished firmly. Arthur nodded, saying nothing. Siren then moved on to other tests at a frantic pace. She took his blood after that, the prick off her needles barely making Arthur flinch as they pierced his skin. She filled over ten vials of it before turning her back on Arthur to study and experiment with them on different workstations leaving him to sit on the table silently.

He leaned to the side to try and look past Siren's side as she worked with his blood. She dropped different tiny droplets of other mixtures into his vials of blood. She was carefully watching the dark red liquid react with each drop in each vile, then writing down words on her pad as she did. He saw his blood fizz up in one and turn bright pink in another. What caught his eye the most was Siren's reaction. Through the first nine vials, her face was plain and stoic, as though she didn't see anything new. Then she came to the tenth vial of blood and looked at it for a moment longer than the others. Arthur saw Siren reach into her pocket and pull out a small, tiny bottle that was completely black, so he couldn't see what was inside it. She looked at the bottle for a few moments, then back at the final sample of Arthur's blood. Siren unscrewed the top of the bottle and slowly tipped it over the top of the vials. A few droplets fell into the blood before she pulled the bottle away from the vial. Arthur saw the liquid itself look like a dark red color, almost blood-like. Siren re-screwed the bottle and placed it back into her pocket, and leaned over the tenth vial as close as she could. Her left hand then went to her head apparatus as she clicked a button on her helmet with her finger a few times, causing several different glass scopes to fall in front of her eyes as she monitored the sample like a still statue. Arthur counted the seconds that went by in his head when finally, Siren gasped loudly. She rapidly stood straight back up and took a couple of surprising steps backward, her hands raised like she was in front of a rabid animal, staring at the tenth vial.

"Impossible!" she whispered fearfully.

"Absolutely incredible...but it does explain it... I suppose." Her hand then dropped to her side, and she went silent, the tenth vial from Arthur's eyes looked no different than before she experimented on it at all.

She trailed off, not looking at Arthur. She walked back over, took the tenth sample of blood, and placed a rubber cork over the top. She then proceeded to open her coat and place the vial within an inside pocket, closing her coat again instantly.

"What is it?" Arthur asked, feeling the mood of the room that something wasn't normal.

"Is something wrong with my blood, is that why the Beast took over my body?" he asked Siren desperately, his thirst for understanding reaching its peak. Siren simply smirked; her face of shock vanished, but she still didn't turn around.

"On the contrary, Arthur Thorn, there is nothing wrong with your blood," She began placing her equipment away, saying nothing else, leaving Arthur on the table still to be more confused now than before they started. She finished putting away her tools in their drawers and the pads with her papers she had written on away to return towards Arthur, smiling warmly at him. She leaned in forward so that Arthur could once again see past her eye scopes and gaze into her amazingly odd-colored green and purple eyes. Arthur found her smile unsettling, feeling the wolf part of him grow impatient. He produced some flicker of confidence and looked straight at her.

"Siren, what is it?" Arthur asked desperately. She leaned her head in closer, and for an odd moment, Arthur was scared she would bite him. She moved her lips to the side of his head until her lips were next to his right ear.

"You, Arthur Thorn, are an incredibly unique Werewolf. Within your body is a potential that has only ever existed in the legends of our race. That is why the beast within your body acts the way it can. I had a small inkling of this possible outcome of this when I first heard it given how ungodly rare it is, but it's confirmed now." Arthur clenched his teeth angrily, he needed to know.

"Siren! What. Is. It?!," he said again sharply for her to only giggle like a schoolgirl. She then pulled away from him and stood up straight, staring back down at him. Sirens eyes examined Arthur's body once again, her new understanding adding new questions to her thoughts about him. She thought for a few seconds and nodded.

"Listen to me very carefully, Arthur," she began, her voice serious again. It had once again become a terrifying, commanding, dread-inducing tone that completely evaporated Arthur's confidence in a second. Arthur nodded as she continued with a confident smile.

"You will not tell Cratos what I have told you. You will not tell him about any of the tests I conducted on you, especially with your blood. I will speak with him privately and inform him of a different answer about your inner beast that will satisfy his own confusion. You, on the other hand, keep this to yourself for now."

Arthur felt he couldn't have been any more confused if he had just spontaneously grown an extra three heads.

"WHY?!" he franticly spluttered out; he could only muster that one word in his mental dissolution. Siren's expression, however, did not change, and neither did her commanding tone.

"Because you are not ready to hear the information yet. I am usually the last person to agree with Cratos's methods of experience before understanding. Usually, I believe that all new cubs should be told everything the second they are bitten, but this is not an ordinary situation." She then sighed, putting her hands on her helmet. Her fingers pressed buttons on the opposing sides of her ears in a specific sequence. After a few seconds, a dozen clicks sounded, and Siren then lifted the helmet off her head and placed it on the worktop. Arthur gazed at Siren's entire face, seeing it whole for the first time. Arthur couldn't help but think her eyes were amazing. Their shine was captivating in a clear cosmic way that Arthur had never seen in his life. Her face was without a single scar or blemish; it was simply very pale and smooth. She looked only in her late twenties, which was strange as she sounded a lot older when she spoke. Arthur noticed her hair that flowed down from her head resembled almost silk in texture as the balls that hung from the bottom of the two strands at the sides of her face were swinging from side to side as she looked at Arthur. Siren smiled kindly.

"Do you trust me, Arthur?" she asked sweetly.

Arthur almost answered yes purely on instinct. He knew if Cratos were here, he would have snapped at him immediately for not answering yes. Arthur opened his mouth but caught himself before sound came out. He had only just met this woman, and while Cratos vouched for her, he didn't want to just trust her based on what is still his first impression. As Arthur failed to answer right away, her warm smile turned into a sinister smirk up the side of her face, the right side of her face rippling as her smirk sailed up.

"Smart boy," she chuckled, nodding at Arthur with genuine respect.

"Be wary of trusting anyone right away. Take your time before you judge someone, boy. When you do say you trust a person, make sure it is someone worthy of your trust who has proved themselves to you first." Arthur smiled back at her. He couldn't help but feel she had a point.

"But trust me or not, I am telling you the truth, and if you listen to me, I will make you this promise as thanks," she continued, gripping his attention stronger.

"Telling you this information now would only hurt you mentally, possibly even preventing you from winning your next encounter with the Beast. So, for everyone's sake, just go on as before, OK?" Arthur nodded at her request, waiting for the promise she mentioned.

"If you can wait patiently, I promise the next time we meet, I will explain a lot more to you. Perhaps I can't say everything but more than I can today. Deal?" Arthur sighed; he had a feeling that no matter what he said, Siren would end up getting her way. Given how Cratos acts around her, Arthur guessed that she often gets her way, and he wanted to stay on her good side.

"OK," Arthur agreed reluctantly, though he knew it wasn't much of a deal, especially since she was asking him to lie to Cratos. But Arthur doubted she was lying to him; there would be no need for her to toy with him for no reason. The point also stood that this woman held a prominent level of respect among the Werewolves, and Arthur had a feeling it would play better in his favor to do as he was told for now. The feeling of lying to Cratos still didn't bide well with his morals, but Arthur then figured, given his teacher's fear of Siren, he would at least understand if Cratos ever found out why Arthur had lied to him. Siren saw his expression and raised an eyebrow, humming again.

"Arthur?" she called, grabbing his attention back from his contemplation. Arthur looked back into her face as her smirk was gone, and her regular smile was back. Arthur had a weird moment then where her smile strangely reminded him of Ashley back from school and how she used to smile at him. There seems to be a genuine sweetness from the look that Arthur was not used to seeing from people.

"Don't fret about it, OK? You're going to be fine. By the way, you can put your clothes back on now." Arthur, having just thought about Ashley, blushed as Siren stood back up straight and began putting the rest of her tools aside away from Arthur. He hastily put on his shirt, feeling embarrassed about blushing in front of Siren. He knows she saw his blush, and while facing away, Siren spoke about it.

"Don't feel too silly, Arthur," she voiced, her voice plain now.

"The first time I gave Cratos a physical, he tried to seduce me." Arthur couldn't help but burst out laughing.

"Really? What happened?" he asked back excitedly, all feeling is discomfort vanishing upon the opportunity to have something to tease Cratos about. She turned around, her face adorably smug.

"He tried to make an adult move on me during an examination, so I knocked the little pervert out, of course," she answered, grabbing her helmet back off the table and placing it back on her head; several metallic clicks sounded as she let go of it and it had reattached back onto her skull. She looked past Arthur back down the lab.

"Speak of the devil," she muttered, smirking. Arthur turned around to see Cratos walking back to them. Arthur tucked in his shirt, and he thought about his physical as Cratos approached them. Arthur didn't know what Siren wasn't telling him, and he decided he would keep his promise to her and not tell Cratos. Arthur wondered what was ahead of him from here. Siren had told him he had immense potential inside him, but he couldn't wrap his head around how he was exceptional in any way. His mind drifted to the small bottle that Siren had poured into his blood on that last vial. He could almost swear that it had been blood when he looked at it too. He wondered what was in that bottle that could have told Siren anything about his own blood. Cratos smiled at his student as the pair faced Siren, who nodded at Cratos with a stern look.

"I need to speak to you in private," she announced. Cratos nodded and turned to face Arthur.

"Arthur, wait outside the laboratory entrance door for us," he told him. Arthur looked at Siren and then at his mentor. Arthur said nothing and turned away from the pair towards the vault door of the laboratory to wait outside. Once Arthur was out of earshot, Siren snapped her finger and thumb sharply around Cratos's ear, making him yelp in shock and pain.

"Come with me right now, you bloody idiot!" she growled. Siren began walking, pulling Cratos along as she walked, looking like an angry mother taking her difficult child away.

Siren's library was a complete archive in every definition of the word, with dozens upon dozens of shelves crammed with books on nearly every subject any person could want. Siren dragged Cratos past each row of bookcases down the long hallways until the pair reached her desk. On its surface, along with lamps, were various papers of diagrams, calculations, and text filling the pages scattered and disorganized everywhere with books, open and closed all around. Siren let go of Cratos's ear as she sat down on her oversized leather chair behind the desk with him in front and looked him dead in the eye as he rubbed his ear, looking over the room.

"Is it me, or have you added a few extra wings since I was last here?," he asked casually, not sensing Sirens' blatant fury. The smell of dust and books littered the air around them, the room itself lit by Siren's green lamps attached to the walls. She clicked her fingers sharply again, catching his attention.

"Why didn't you tell Arthur about how Werewolves age?" she said darkly, her fists clenched. Cratos's eyebrow rose as he looked at her oddly, confused at her frustration.

"What does it matter?" he replied idly with a shrug. Sirens eyes blazed wide.

"I told you, he learns as he goes forward, his body won't be affected by that for a while yet." Siren's teeth now clenched as she struggled to contain herself.

"You should have told him, Cratos! I think he would be interested to know given it's too late to change his mind now, and this is his fate!" Cratos leaned in closer to the desk.

"Speaking of interest, what is wrong with him? What did your tests come out with?" She exhaled loudly to calm herself down, then leaned back in her chair and intertwined her fingers, closing her eyes.

"Nothing major. It turned out to be just an irregularity with his blood in terms of the bonding to the Werewolf gene. His blood type was struggling to adapt to the changes the Werewolf bite introduced to his system. His body's natural defenses were fighting them off to a point the beast within him was able to do as it wished once his consciousness vanished. Nothing to worry about; he may lapse again now and then, although he is aware of the problem now. Therefore, lapses would be highly scarce. My advice is just to go forward as though everything is normal." She waited for Cratos's reaction, hoping her elaborate bluff worked. She felt it was convincing; she almost wanted to believe it herself. Cratos smiled, looking relieved.

"Fair enough then. I'll brief Delfer on your diagnosis. We are both heading to Europe straight away so he can begin his training as a normal cub." A smile came to Siren's lips for a moment as she opened her eyes before they snapped away, and she scowled again.

"Cratos!" she said firmly, not letting him escape her first problem.

"You need to start telling him things. The longer you put this off, the harder it'll be for him to accept." Cratos sighed and rubbed the back of his head with his hand.

"I understand," He muttered, turning his back on Siren as he began to walk out.

"Cratos," she called out again. Cratos turned around to see Siren without her helmet on, smiling fondly at him.

"It was nice to see you again," she said with a deep voice winking at him with her purple eye. Cratos's face blushed as he quickly bowed his head at her and then hurried out of the library to meet up with Arthur. As Cratos vanished from her sight, Siren reached into her lab coat and pulled out the vial of Arthur's blood, holding it in her fingers and eying it carefully, once again humming.

"There's no doubt about it," she whispered under her breath ominously.

"Arthur Thorn, you don't see a specimen like you every five hundred years sometimes. Though the last person I saw with that blood wasn't too long ago either. You have the making of either a legend or a monster, Arthur." She nervously bit her lower lip as she placed the vial back in her lab coat, remaining in her chair as worry flashed across her green and purple eyes as she puzzled.

"This boy's future is very dire indeed," she finally whispered before falling into silence, brooding over a discovery that she knew she could tell no one, hoping with all her heart that Arthur will be able to contain the beast within himself as he progresses through the world of the Werewolves.

CHAPTER TWENTY

Arthur thought over what Siren had told him while he waited for her and Cratos to finish talking. He was leaning against the vault door as he painfully learned the pipes that ran across the walls got extremely hot at random times. Arthur stared into the palms of his hands, wondering what the next stage of his Werewolf life would bring him and how he would change. If this fantastic potential Siren saw within him would be released, then he could change beyond recognition. Siren had promised she would explain everything to him when they next met, but Arthur felt she wasn't missing out on anything herself in this deal. He wondered when he would cross paths with the eccentric doctor again. Arthur then thought about the next fight he would have with the Beast within himself; during the next full moon, he would be thrown back into the depths of his mind once again to battle against all his hidden fears. The last time he only made it through because the voice of his younger sister saved him at the last moment. He then remembered the dream he had in the van on their drive here. His father continued to be a bully and monster to his mother and sister, and they couldn't see or hear him. There was the invisible wall that stopped him from being able to help them. He hated the irony that dream presented to him. As a human, he was too weak to help his family, always tossed aside when he did try and intervene. Now Arthur had the strength to defend his loved ones; he cannot be anywhere near them for who knows how long. He clenched his fists angrily.

"So strong," he muttered to himself, closing his eyes, trying to fight back a few tears.

"Yet still so helpless," he finished. Thoughts of his sister and her terrified face filled him with anger and regret. He felt the compulsion and the need to save them no matter the consequences. He wondered what would happen if he ever returned home to face his father. If it would accomplish what he hoped it would. If he killed his father, he would make his mother a widow and his sister fatherless. The house would have no income coming in, and his family would then become homeless. All of which would be caused by his actions. With or without the strength and power of a living Werewolf, Arthur knew he couldn't change anything the way he was right now. Despite whatever unique potential Siren saw within Arthur, he felt no more relieved of his troubles than when he first stepped into this tunnel.

The vault door locks began to click one by one suddenly, making Arthur jump a little. Arthur stood away from the door as it swung open, revealing his mentor smiling up at him.

"Hey there, champ, ready to go?" Cratos called out. Arthur returned his smile and nodded as the pair walked back through Siren's maze and back to the surface world. Though Arthur made a mental note that he would return here alone and get the answer from Siren that she promised him as soon as possible. Arthur only hoped he would be able to lie to Cratos in the meantime as she had asked. They walked back through the tunnel to leave with Cratos assuring him that he knew the route.

"I've been visiting Siren for many years," he muttered dryly. Arthur, for a moment, thought that he meant to say more, but when nothing else came, he simply nodded and carried on walking. Arthur thought more about the Wolf kingdom as they walked. Now that a Werewolf doctor had looked at him, Cratos was going to take him to the home of the Werewolves for further training. He wondered if he would see Delfer there. He still didn't get a chance to say thank you or goodbye to him for everything he had done. Thoughts of Delfer made Arthur remember being back in the bar; he heard that Delfer and Cratos were friends during their training. It made him think about what kind of people he might meet during his training. He wondered if it would be like some sort of wolf school like the human one he had left. Given his experience with school so far in his life, Arthur had sincerely hoped it wouldn't be anything like that. He asked Cratos about his thoughts, who only laughed at his notions.

"You really should have led a life on the stage, boy," he said, still laughing. Arthur's face twisted as he regretted bothering to speak to him about it. After a few more seconds of Cratos laughing at Arthur, he finally answered his question correctly.

"Your training will not be education formally. It is a series of tests and preparation. You will spend a lot of time underground for a while, but there will also be many field tests as well." Arthur nodded, wondering what sorts of tests he would experience.

"Sort of like the ones you've done?" he asked, making Cratos shake his head instantly.

"For Crimsons? Not a chance. Do me a favor, please, Arthur, keep your level head. The lessons I've taught you will serve you so much better than anything those muscle heads will show you." Arthur squinted oddly at Cratos; he was still dying to know about this Crimson and Shadow class thing his mentor kept referencing. Arthur also noticed a small edge in his teacher's voice as he gave that warning, sensing a small note of disapproval at whatever these Crimsons were going to teach him. He was about to ask further on the matter when a more troubling thought sprung up in his head.

"Wait," Arthur voiced weakly. Cratos turned his head at Arthur and saw a troubled expression.

"What's wrong?" Cratos asked. Arthur turned his head to see his teacher and only friend in the world.

"Does this mean you won't be my teacher anymore when we get there?" Arthur asked desperately

Cratos turned back to face front as they walked and thought for a moment. He wasn't producing an answer but more trying to word it the right way.

"Yes and no," his mentor answered after several seconds of thought.

"What does that mean?" Arthur asked in exasperation, this being one of the few times he wouldn't let Cratos give him a vague answer. The last thing he wanted was to be separated from the only person in his world who knew him, only to be suddenly ditched like he was being abandoned at a Werewolf boarding school.

"It's not exactly a boot camp, Arthur. I'm not going to drop you off and pick you back up when you're done. We are both going to be living there for the duration of your training. Odds are the Eclipse festival will happen during that time which should be interesting for you to see." Cratos suddenly stopped when he noticed a growing red angry face of Arthur grow intensely, a not very subtle hint for him to get to the point. Cratos put his arm around Arthur's shoulder and patted it reassuringly, seeing the worry of being abandoned present on his student's face. He made a mental note to work on the boy's composure. Cratos knew learning to hide his immediate feelings would come in handy for him.

"I'm not going anywhere, Arthur. I will watch your training, and work with you in private to keep your ego in check. You'll still be stuck with this ugly mug for a long while yet." A smile went to Arthur's face as he nodded back with relief. Cratos removed his arm and chuckled.

"You never know; you may make a bunch of friends and forget about poor old Cratos." Arthur couldn't tell it was a light comment and instinctively snorted with contempt in immediate response.

"Make friends? Me? I doubt it," he grunted dismissively. Cratos frowned at Arthur as he turned back into a scolding teacher.

"Hey, hey! None of that Arthur. I know you have had bad experiences with friends as a human but don't judge someone before you know them." Arthur sighed, looking away from Cratos. He had told his mentor about Jack and his other friends who always abandoned him in their time together. All the stories about how they would leave him when Arthur needed them most. He knew Cratos was right, but he couldn't help his instincts at this point. Arthur doubted he would easily make friends with the other cubs in training, being the cautious introvert he is now. He wouldn't be able to trust them easily. He looked back at Cratos and nodded.

"OK," he replied blankly, saying it more just to appease his teacher than genuinely agreeing with him. Cratos noted then that if his student didn't honestly agree to that information, he knew better than convincing Arthur otherwise. Cratos understood that trust is a lesson that must be learned, not taught. It was up to the other students Arthur is to work with to change his opinion about trusting others, not his teacher. Cratos knew Arthur trusted him, and despite his experiences, he could tell the boy put his complete faith in him. Cratos had confidence in his student to see in the other Werewolves what he saw in his teacher; it would just take time.

"How are we getting to the Wolf Kingdom, by the way?" Arthur asked as they climbed the ladder back to the surface. Arthur didn't bother to take a last look at Siren's home as they began climbing the ladder's metal. Once again, the tapping of their feet on the ladder rungs began to drive him mad again. Cratos was rising above him, so he spoke loud enough for Arthur to hear in the black enclosed space they traveled in.

"As we threw you into the back of the van, Delfer handed me the necessities for the pair of us to get us to Europe." Arthur decided to ignore the 'thrown in the van' part of that answer and touch on something else.

"You're always so bloody vague. WHERE in Europe?! It's a pretty damn big place!" he snapped. Cratos only laughed at Arthur as they continued to climb.

"It doesn't matter where we are; we'll be under it in no time. It would be best to stop acknowledging the lines that squabbling politicians, kings, and emperors put around what they consider their land next to some other countries land. There's nothing like that within the Wolf kingdom, Arthur. We have our system of living, and the silly playing of human politics doesn't matter. I don't bother telling you the names of countries, let alone what country we're in, because it doesn't matter. It is one earth we live on, not a series of countries, just one earth."

Arthur thought about what Cratos had just told him for a little while as they climbed up to the top. He figured they would hit the surface any minute now, judging from how long it took for them to climb down. He thought about the concept of there being no more individual countries in the world anymore. That is the idea of the lines that separate countries vanished and left just one solid piece of land everyone lives in. It sounded weird and insane to him, but he didn't know why he thought that. He knew a lot of people who were proud of their country and place. From geography class back in school, he knew each land had its own flag, history, and contribution to the world. He didn't think he could so easily just detach himself like Cratos was suggesting. But he knew now not to mention countries to his mentor anymore.

Given that man used the term Europe, continents must still be OK with him. It was all so confusing to him personally anyway. He then thought of the bar in the city. There were probably Werewolves of all different ethnicities and cultures from all around the world there. He noted at the time how diverse he found the Werewolves. The way they simply mixed as one single person. He remembered back home that the area he lived in had its share of prejudiced people who would blame unpleasant things in their own lives on people from other countries who emigrate to theirs. Or they would even just regurgitate what they had heard and been told themselves growing up without utterly understanding why. To Arthur, it had never made sense when he heard them say those things, and he grimaced at the idea of himself ever sounding like someone so horrible.

Arthur puzzled further as he continued to climb the ladder. Comparing what Cratos said about his own home, small thin lines of logic began to come together. Eliminating meaningless territorial lines, Arthur thought maybe that's how people are more easily able to come together. He thought it made sense but felt it probably had more complexity beneath the surface than just that. Arthur had never thought about that kind of stuff before anyway. He knew the world was filled with horrible racism, wars, and many people dying throughout history because of it. Arthur compared that information to how the Werewolves operate. It seemed that the hierarchy of the Werewolves didn't judge those based upon anything superficial or national, just on how they were as people. Arthur liked the idea, but he realized he was still more human on the inside than he first thought. After a few weeks of training with Cratos in the jungles and forests, he felt he was no longer human and was now one hundred percent Werewolf. In that life, Arthur woke up, thinking like a Werewolf. He hunted, ate, and slept like a wild animal like his teacher trained him to embrace. But Arthur noticed that he was still reacting as an ordinary human would sometimes. He would let his temper flare and feel the same insecurities that he carried with him every day to school. He guessed what Cratos was trying to say when he was speaking about the countries and how humans make up the lines between lands and the names of those lands. Arthur then roughly shook his head on the ladder; these thoughts were giving him a headache. He didn't think he fully understood such ideas yet as he was. He would focus on what's ahead for now and come back to such thoughts when he was older and more experienced in life. His resolve was then met with the sound of Cratos pushing against the door of Siren's tunnel hatch. A bright beam of light shot down straight into Arthur's eyes, making him roar in surprise and pain. His eyes then took a minute to adjust, the rays of light feeling like lasers shooting directly into his eyeballs. He smiled as he climbed out into the world once again, feeling a lot more excited to head to the Wolf Kingdom to meet his new family than he was before.

The light of the sun had never been more painful and mortifying for Arthur in his entire life. He thought his eyes had adjusted by the time he climbed out of the manhole while Cratos resealed the door on the ground. Even the blue of the sky made Arthur snap his eyes shut for a few moments before he could reopen them. His hands were smothering his eyes entirely as he clenched his teeth against the pain. It felt like two lit torches had been jammed straight against his pupils.

"How long were we in that damn lab," Arthur groaned at Cratos, who was getting up, chuckling as though nothing was bothering him.

"A fair few hours, maybe four or five," Cratos mused casually, pulling his hands away from his face and walking past Arthur, whistling merrily. Arthur then very slowly opened his eyes gradually to the daylight blaring at him. With the light of day smothering the earth in its hellish bright beams, Arthur saw the lands the pair had arrived within. As his eyes blurring began to vanish slowly, he now saw the clear open fields stretching out for endless kilometers all around him. The dirt road Arthur was standing on seemed to run nonstop in both directions. Arthur looked behind him back towards the direction where Siren's door was and focused his eyes to try and see something in the distance, but it just seemed to keep on stretching into the landscape. In the other direction, Arthur could see the faint dot that was the van they were driving. He still didn't get why they couldn't have driven straight to Siren's ground door entrance. As Arthur walked on after Cratos, he found himself able to appreciate the environment around him. The wind was blowing a cool gust against Arthur's face, lightly brushing his hair as he walked against its breeze. The air around him was warm and clear as he breathed in. He found himself oddly enjoying the scent of the outdoors in a way he never thought possible after spending time in the stink of Siren's home. Going from her literal toxic gas-filled home to the vast outside was night and day in comparison, and it was an enthralling state of euphoria Arthur was put in as he walked on.

They were reaching the van quicker than Arthur realized as they walked towards it. Arthur figured his mind was too focused on enjoying the sunny day than the minutes of walking. The near cloudless sky was a smooth, light blue with the whole round sun shining strongly on the pair of them. Arthur noticed that his pale skin was open to the sun's bright rays as he was walking. Growing up as a ginger kid, Arthur knew his skin was near deathly pale, and his skin burnt fast without sunscreen. He looked over his hands and forearms for signs of his body pinking slightly.

"What are you doing?" Cratos asked, noticing his student examining himself.

"Did Siren inject you with one of her experimental serums?" He asked Arthur worriedly. Arthur shook his head without looking at Cratos.

"No, nothing like that. I was just checking to see if –" Arthur began to answer when he suddenly snapped his head towards his mentor.

"What serums?" Arthur quickly rebutted, now not sure if she did or not. Cratos shrugged uneasily, but then Arthur noticed he was suddenly standing a new distance away from Arthur.

"Siren performs a lot of work for the Werewolves. She likes to experiment with Werewolf biology the most. She tests our endurance, our strengths, and weaknesses as well as our inner defense systems." Arthur was only slightly following what he was saying. He knew of similar things in certain places in the world; some scientists pay people incredible sums of money to test their experimental drugs.

"Why would she try me? I'm still going through the stages, aren't I?" Arthur muttered. Again, Cratos shrugged, and Arthur couldn't determine how much exactly he knew about this woman he had just trusted his entire being with not long ago. He could tell Cratos had more history with Siren than even she had told him; it was another chapter of Cratos's life that he hoped his teacher and friend would share with him one day.

"Her reasons are her own. I thought she might have taken a special interest in you, given your irregularity with your inner beast. We have Werewolves across the world that comes to Siren to test her insane concoctions." Arthur then remembered all the other bottles and glass beakers with the vast array of different colored chemicals in them.

"Like what?" Arthur asked, intrigued.

"Well, Siren has synthesized these super adrenalin shots. They're chemicals to increase our energy and maximize our strengths to sadly near-fatal levels. Those are more to be used last resort, though, and Siren does not give them out to anyone in the clan. She is very protective of her work." Arthur nodded at Cratos but didn't say anything, allowing him to continue. He found all this amazing. Arthur sometimes enjoyed science class back in school, but the things Cratos described reminded him more of the mad science experiments from movies.

"She has also worked on trying to eliminate sleep for the body entirely so we can operate full time." Arthur thought about that for a moment. The way Werewolves operate is almost like demigods in the feats they can accomplish. To then combine that capability with never needing to rest would make them unstoppable.

"Is that possible?" he asked in disbelief. Cratos hummed uneasily before answering uncomfortably.

"Yes and no. Siren discovered she could force a body to stop sleeping. That was easy, apparently. The tricky part for her, which she is still working on, was stopping the user from either going insane from brain function overload or dying outright from sleep deprivation." Arthur's eyebrow nearly hit the clouds in the sky.

"People have died in her tests!?" he asked, shocked.

"Yes, but Siren forces no one to take her tests. They are all volunteers," Cratos explained clearly. Arthur couldn't fathom the logic.

"Why does any Werewolf sign up to do it if they can die," Arthur asked quietly. Cratos's tone shifted before he answered, feeling like this answer would be necessary for Arthur to understand.

"Because if the test on them proves successful, then by acting as a test subject, they have provided a substantial service for the entire Werewolf race. That service then moves us one step further to gaining an advantage in the fight against the Vampires." Arthur thought on that for a moment. He did like the idea of taking some 'magic' liquid and gaining additional super strength and other extraordinary powers. But with the risk of his body dying from it, he wasn't sure he would ever want to take such a risk.

"There is also one flaw of our biology that Siren has been working on since she began her work," that snapped Arthur out of his inner thoughts.

"What is that?" Arthur again, casually. Cratos looked Arthur seriously in the eye for a moment and sighed.

"How we age?" he said ominously, and before Arthur could say anything else, he spoke ahead of him.

"And that is something we need to discuss in the van." Arthur was confused at first; then he remembered vaguely letting Siren know that Cratos hadn't told him something specific about how they age, and she had been furious about it.

As the pair began driving back up the dirt road and onto the main roads, Arthur didn't know what to say. The tension in the van was borderline lethal as Arthur was just sitting in intense silence waiting for Cratos to drop what he was worryingly assuming would be a bombshell about himself. Arthur felt like a regular human in a doctor's office, waiting for the doctor to return to the room and give him the bad news. He looked at Cratos, who was focusing intensely on the road ahead; Arthur could see his teacher's pupils going from side to side as he tried to work out in his head what he was going to say. Arthur looked away from his mentor and out of the window next to him. He suddenly realized he was hungry. Arthur felt his stomach rumble, and he was amazed at how long he had gone without food until now. He thought back and figured he and Cratos hadn't eaten since they first entered the city. Arthur wondered if this was part of the Werewolf metabolism somehow. He hadn't worked as hard since he left the jungle, even when rescuing Cratos despite his attack on the police cars. Arthur thought perhaps that the Werewolf body could conserve its energy more. Although he knew he was only speculating, anything to get away from the silence in the van. Cratos then suddenly began his explanation out of nowhere.

"Werewolves are amazing creatures, Arthur," he began with a solid and severe tone. The pit of fear that burrowed deep into Arthur's bowls suddenly began commencing a crippling turbo drill with that mere opening line. Arthur had no idea what surprise was in store for him now, putting his whole life in perspective.

"Our bodies are put through immense pressure in our lifetime. That pressure and stress are mainly from when we change into our wolf forms and exercise our strength and speed as normal people. While the bite we receive mutates and changes our blood to that of a Werewolf, our body itself is still partly human, and our brain now must accommodate the extra functions and powers, working harder and harder constantly to keep us ticking." Arthur nodded along, following what he was saying. The sort of things he did in his training in the jungle would probably have made a human Olympic athlete pass out from exhaustion. Cratos continued uneasily.

"With these powers, we are given, and I still believe this no matter what, we are given the opportunity for an amazing life as Werewolves. There is not just fighting the Vampires but also the chance to experience amazing things and achieve feats of strength and power that are impossible for any human." Once again, Arthur agreed. Still, he felt Cratos was trying to put a bucket of sand on the quickly approaching fire about to hit.

"So much pressure on the body, so much more work for the brain to do, and the Werewolf form we transform into only triples anything we do." Cratos turned his head. He looked at Arthur with unease, trying to figure out if his student would be able to take this information or not. Sighing, he continued looking back at the road.

"In this world, Arthur, there is rarely anything gained without something lost. To get, you must give, and there is no place that better proves that right than the Werewolves' body. They say people who have too much stress are driving themselves into an early grave...our existence is similar, Arthur." Arthurs' stomach clenched at that line, fearing, and anticipating the following sentence.

"Arthur the Werewolves life is only half the life of a human. We never make it past the age of fifty sometimes" with the truth finally said, Arthur sat back in his seat in silence, processing the fact Arthur was just told he only had a few decades of his life left.

"I don't understand," Arthur finally murmured as Cratos also sat in silence, understanding that Arthur would need to think this bombshell over.

"Some of the people in the bar looked older than fifty," Arthur recalled some small groups of men sat by wooden tables away from the main bar itself towards the back. He saw from the table where Cratos and Delfer were seated. He saw men and women with these wrinkled old faces, clearly showing advanced age. They still had blonde and brown hair, but it was very balding. Arthur thought they must have looked about in their mid-seventies. Cratos just nodded.

"We don't die looking our age. You will see yourself age at an alarming rate as the years go by. Think of it this way, for every year you age, your body will age two years." Arthur's breathing grew faster as he calculated that in twenty years, he would have aged forty years. He felt trapped at that moment; his stomach was a swirling vortex riddled with shards of ice. Arthur never gave it much thought, but he was hoping to live a full, long life. He wanted to have enough time to see the world change around him. Now Arthur was going to die before all his friends back home and probably even his parents. He was barely a teenager as it was, and now in a few years, he would look like he was in his twenties.

"So ever since you bit me, have I been aging as you've said?" he asked fearfully, frantically filling in any empty gaps of information he could muster. Cratos shook his head.

"No, you don't begin to age as much until your next few stages of becoming a full Werewolf commences, and then it goes from there." Cratos looked at Arthur and hummed for a moment.

"By my guess, by the time you've finished your training and become a full Werewolf, you should look in your late twenties, I would say. Siren will be able to explain the specifics more when you see her next." Arthur nodded and returned to his thoughts. Nothing more was said for a while as Cratos drove the pair of them to their next destination. Arthur's mind, now feeling like it was working faster than he realized.

As the hours went by, the initial shock of the information had now passed, and Arthur now felt surprisingly underwhelmed considering his panic before. While he was still upset that he wouldn't get to live a long life, Arthur considered what kind of life he might have lived if he did have that chance. Arthur thought that if he had remained a human and carried on in his previous life, he would have eventually finished school. Then, he would have got some tedious job that he probably hated, followed by a house of his own somewhere. Arthur felt the odds were that he might have just gone into the same work as his father rather than anything he liked. Maybe he would have a wife and kids, and then he would just do the same things day after day until he was ninety and finally die. But as a Werewolf, everything was different. He had been a Werewolf for only a brief time so far, and already he had experienced adventures that he would never have as a human. He had gone through Cratos's training, hunting the tiger, fleeing the Vampire attack, and then joining the rescue mission to save those captured. So far, he has now lived better than most who could reach the age of even a hundred. Arthur understood that he wasn't given some death sentence. Even if he had been told he would only live another year, he would wager it would be quite a fantastic year. After a few hours of thought in the van, a smile came to Arthur's face. This revelation, while shocking, had changed nothing for him, he decided. As far as he was concerned, he was still experiencing the most incredible opportunity to live, and he refused to squander it by worrying about his death. Cratos noticed Arthur smile, and he smiled himself.

"Accepted it?" he asked, and Arthur nodded with a sense of clarity.

"I realized I haven't lost anything, given what I have ahead of me," he answered, keeping his smile. Cratos nodded fondly at Arthur.

"That is exactly the point, Arthur. The horizon ahead of you is always brighter than sunset behind you" The pair then continued their journey in the van as they headed to the next major step in Arthur's new life as a Werewolf.

CHAPTER TWENTY-ONE

"Stop acting nervous, you idiot! You're going to make us stand out," Cratos snapped under his breath again to Arthur.

"I thought our pheromones disguised us," Arthur whispered back to Cratos, barely moving his lips. Cratos exhaled with frustration.

"Yes, but it doesn't make us invisible, you idiot! It would help if you still acted natural, at least. It's simple, just stop looking like you're hiding something!." Arthur sighed, and he continued walking close to Cratos. The endless crowds of people walking around the pair were constantly making his anxiety spike to jittery levels of discomfort. As they walked, Arthur was afraid that every other person would be a Vampire and another attack would jump at them like the soldiers in the city bar. They were both walking through the airport on their way to their terminal. They still had a few checkpoints to go through with their bags before they could get on the plane. Because they were traveling to another country, Arthur used the fake passport Cratos had given him. He pulled it out of his pocket again and gazed at it. It was an accurate picture of him, but the name was different and where he was born. It even said that Arthur was a year older. When he first got it, he challenged Cratos on how he had his picture.

"We took your photo when you were unconscious and edited your eyes as awake." Arthur found that idea immensely creepy but said nothing else. Delfer had given Cratos passports for the pair of them and enough money for them to make it to Europe. Arthur, however, couldn't help being on edge the second they arrived. Being around this massive crowd of people was making him increasingly nervous by the second. He was never claustrophobic because he was always surrounded by people like this back in his school. But since the bar was attacked back in the city, he didn't want to let his guard down. Cratos had told him Werewolves fly across the world constantly, and Vampires never like to ambush people in airports anymore. Humans who use flight as travel take their safety very seriously, and the Vampires care more about the stability of their control a lot more than capturing the odd flying Werewolf.

"I don't think it's my worried face that will give us away anyway," Arthur muttered with sarcasm.

"What are you whining about now?" Cratos responded sharply.

"Look at us!" Arthur exclaimed in a low tone. He gestured at Cratos's long black trench coat and clothes along with his own black attire himself.

"We look like freaking assassins!" he grunted, still trying to barely move a facial expression making his face turn a bright red. Cratos could only chuckle as his student.

"You often overthink Arthur, just act calm and natural, and we will be fine." The pair reached one of the checking points at the airport. They had to walk past a metal detector, and this was the first place Arthur had to use his passport. Cratos had mentioned they don't usually present them here, but it seemed this airport was different for reasons he didn't know. As Cratos went on ahead, brandishing his passport, his expression was calm and relaxed, however as he came even slightly closer to the gate, Arthur felt his pulse begin to rise and panic set it.

"They're going to know. They're going to capture me! They're going to take me; I need to run! I need to run!" he roared in his head. He tensed his body, trying to focus his mind on something else. He then remembered the pit of the snake's test. Arthur then tried to see this situation as the snakes around him, and like then, if he acted wrong here, he would be bitten. He first started to regain his composure by controlling his breathing with slow inhales and exhales. However, his pulse refused to lower as Arthur came upon the security guard at the gate in the line, leaving him frustrated and petrified now. He placed his bag on a conveyor belt to go ahead of him to collect on the other side. He then handed over his passport to be inspected, trying to look as neutral as possible. The airport guard was wearing a blue and black generic security outfit with a bland uncaring expression on his face. He couldn't care less even if Arthur did look suspicious; he was just sending people through until his lunch break. As he nodded at Arthur to go through and handed his passport back to him, Arthur began to smile with confidence flowing through him as he took his steps forward and grabbed his bag on the other side. With the fourth step, all sense of safety burst into flames inside his brain, and his feelings of fear and panic skyrocketed. The arch doorway he walked past beeped loudly at him as he passed through the metal detector, and within a few seconds, Arthur was approached by frowning security guards. Arthur's eyes widened, and his breath caught in his lungs.

"FIGHT! THEY'RE VAMPIRES COMING TO SWARM YOU, FIGHT NOW!" he screamed inside his head as the two guards approached him with their stern expressions.

"Sir, do you have any metal on your person you did not hand in?" the one on the left said. Arthur's heart was still pounding with fear; he couldn't answer. The second guard narrowed his eyes at Arthur.

"Are you OK?" the second one asked, his tone sounding different. Arthur caught the difference in the man's voice. It seemed familiar somehow. Arthurs turned his head to look at the second security guard and noticed an instant flash in the color of his eyes for a moment. They had flashed yellow for a second before returning to normal as he looked straight at Arthur, smiling. Arthur caught on immediately.

"He's a Werewolf!" he gasped in his head. The guard, seeing Arthur catch on to what he was, spoke again.

"Sir, did you forget any metal on your person?" the man said formally. Noticing a Werewolf as one of the security guards calmed Arthur down very quickly. Even the tone he spoke in seemed strangely reassuring. Arthur instinctively checked his pockets for anything metal, keeping his eyes on the second security guard, who slightly nodded at Arthur. His hand gripped around a metal pen he used with his drawings. Arthur had been so focused on acting normal that he had forgotten to check his pockets when handing in his metal items. His heart rate instantly returned as he brought the pen out and handed it to the Werewolf guard. He smiled at Arthur and nodded for him to walk back and go through the detector again. They walked away as Arthur did as he was instructed, and this time he passed through with no problem. As he and Cratos recollected their items, his mentor leaned over and whispered to him.

"Learn to check your pockets next time! Had that been a Vampire, we would have been detained!" The angry edge in his tone hurt Arthur harshly; he didn't mean to panic. He hated it, but Cratos was right. If the second guard hadn't been a Werewolf to reassure him suddenly, he would have stayed frozen and might have been taken aside. Arthur refilled his pockets, grabbed his backpack, and quickly followed after Cratos, holding his head down, pretending he didn't exist.

A short while later, after the two had gone through what Arthur had felt had been all over the entire airport to reach their flight gate, they were sitting within rows of metal chairs waiting for their flight to be called. They sat together still in silence, both counting the seconds in their heads. Arthur was eating a sandwich Cratos had bought from one of the stores inside the airport. There were many people around them waiting for this flight, but none were paying Cratos and Arthur any notice as they kept to themselves. Arthur finished his food and his pop drink with it, then decided to strike up a small chat with Cratos to help pass the time. Arthur mentioned to Cratos how he noticed he hadn't eaten in a while though he kept his voice low, so it didn't arouse suspicion. His mentor nodded.

"It is a survival instinct. Despite the energy, we use our bodies to stave off hunger and thirst, so it doesn't distract us for lengthy periods. We are sort of like nourishment camels in the way of how long we can go without necessities. You've only noticed that since passing the first stage, right?" Arthur nodded; his hunger and thirst were very apparent while hunting the tiger, but it didn't concern him after his first encounter with his inner beast. He was surprised he didn't notice until recently. Ordinary people had to eat three times a day, often with snacks and the like in between, and Arthur never caught on that he had gone endless hours without it even fazing him. That thought made him wonder how much of his brain was changing without him noticing. The Werewolf stages transformed a person's body and mind through a prolonged process, according to Cratos. He told Arthur that he'd develop physically, and as Arthur only recently discovered, he will age dramatically. He was now thinking about how much of his brain would change along with his body and whether his personality would be altered. Arthur wondered if he would even become more savage and animal-like. Cratos said to him once that it was dangerous for a Werewolf to remain in their wolf form for too long without reverting to a human at all. At first, Arthur assumed it was because it would increase the chances of discovery or that perhaps it would put too much pressure on the organs. Now Arthur thought it might change a person's mind if they stayed as an animal for long strands of time. Maybe if he were in his wolf form for too long, he would forget being human and become a homicidal savage.

There was the fact that his inner Beast could assume control of his body without Arthur stopping it. But this was the reason he was going to Europe, according to Cratos. He would be trained physically and especially mentally. He remembered Delfer and Cratos talking to each other back in the Werewolf bar. They spoke like regular old friends. If a human had been in there, he would have just seen a bunch of incredibly strong-looking people. No one had been grunting at each other like thugs without mental capacity. He was sure that if he stuck to his training with Cratos, he would be fine. A woman's voice came over the lobby through a speaker, telling them their plane was ready. Cratos sighed and faced Arthur.

"Let's get this over with," grunted Cratos uncomfortably. Arthur frowned but stood up regardless, throwing his rubbish from his meal in the bin and following the line of people onto the plane. From here, his next stop was Europe, where he would begin his training to become a full Werewolf.

Arthur had never been on a proper big airplane before. He had known people who feared flying, and they couldn't get on a plane without having a panic attack and needing to get off. Much like how Arthur didn't understand people who had a fear of needles, he felt perfectly secure as he sat in his plane seat. He looked across from his seat at the aisle across from him and saw a man gripping the sides of his armrests stressfully. Arthur smiled as he lay back in his seat comfortably and sighed with relief. After the stress of walking through the airport and the heart attack he nearly suffered at the metal detector, this closed-in space of peace and quiet was very welcome. It was just snug for him, and he felt more comfortable here than anywhere else he had been since he joined up with Cratos. Arthur had always enjoyed enclosed spaces, even when he was growing up. He recalled when he would sometimes hide in small, tiny crawl spaces that he could find. Sometimes Arthur even preferred sleeping in closets now and then for a bit of fun when he was younger, loving the idea of having walls all around him sort of like a coffin. Although such an idea was associated with Vampires, therefore Arthur figured if he told Cratos, his teacher wouldn't be impressed at the notion.

They had boarded the plane with no trouble, and once everyone had settled in, the flight attendant explained the safety procedures followed by the plane taking off without any delays or problems. This smooth beginning to a flight was something Cratos told him was nothing short of a miracle. Cratos himself was next to Arthur, sleeping. Just like Arthur, Cratos hadn't caught any sleep since he woke up from being rescued in the city. Cratos had told Arthur before that Werewolves didn't need much sleep, that because of their body's ability to heal well, they only need a few hours of rest at a time here and there to recharge their internal batteries. So, since they were handed a few hours of uninterrupted peace, his mentor caught up on his rest hours. Arthur, however, couldn't make himself sleep; he didn't even feel remotely tired. When he told Cratos this, his teacher only chuckled as he closed his eyes and shuffled his body into a comfortable sleeping position.

"Yeah, get used to that. As you go through the stages, you will not see much sleep for a while. As your body keeps changing, your energy levels will randomly maximize for long or short times. Next time bring a book to read," Arthur snorted and mumbled to himself.

"Like I could ever be that bored!" he mumbled in response. With that said, his mentor had fallen asleep and said nothing else, leaving Arthur to simply just stare around the plane for however many hours this long flight was.

Arthur spent a lot of time picturing what he thought the Wolf kingdom would be like in his head. It had been built up by Cratos and Siren a lot, and his curiosity was killing him. He wondered if it was anything like Siren's laboratory and tunnel way. If that were the case, he hoped it would be without the smell of Sirens home with it. He wondered how many Werewolves there were at any one time. He assumed there had to be endless thousands worldwide, living their own lives and fighting the Vampires or whatever else they had to do. From what he saw in that communications room with Delfer, they kept themselves busy. Arthur recalled the people in the control rooms and all the equipment they had in the storerooms. Delfer had said they acquired their funds through legal and illegal means, but he didn't go into specifics. There was so much more about the Werewolf world he wanted to know. Cratos always kept the information on a need-to-know basis. That always angered Arthur to times of near madness. Sometimes, he couldn't tell if Cratos was treating him like an equal, a partner, a student, or an idiot. He was grateful to the man for everything he had done for him. From saving him from that Vampire woman, to begin with, then teaching him to live and now up to here. He knew Cratos cared about him, but he just wished that Cratos was willing to share more information with him and trust him more. Arthur looked over at his mentor, who was now soundly asleep. His teacher's chest was barely rising as he breathed, looking as though he was a corpse. His long black hair covered most of his scarred face, with his black clothing covering everything except his hands. The knuckles on Cratos were rough and reddened the same way a lot of bare-knuckle fighters had their hands. He remembered Delfer talking about Cratos when they were together in training. Arthur recalled Delfer saying his teacher was some sort of ladies' man, according to Delfer at least. Arthur thought about the campfire when Cratos seemed to be talking into the flames more than to Arthur. How Cratos he would speak of his inner beast with some sort of deep darkness haunting his eyes. Arthur knew nothing about Cratos Mane entirely. Arthur knew he didn't know his teacher's past or the relationships he had with other Werewolves. Arthur only knew what the man had shared with him since they met, and Arthur could only work on that knowledge alone. Yet strangely, Arthur knew he trusted the man completely. To the point, Arthur had willingly leaped out of a moving van and onto police cars to save a man who he had met only a month or so before. Turning away from his mentor, Arthur chuckled at himself a little. He felt a strange sense of enjoyment at the oddness of throwing such much loyalty to his new friend so fast. Then Arthur knew, despite what he didn't know about Cratos and what his teacher didn't tell him about the Wolf world, he knew Cratos was a true friend to Arthur, and he also knew that was something he had never had in his entire life.

As the hours went by, Arthur began to lose his patience of waiting still in his seat, wide awake. Cratos was still sleeping soundly, and Arthur had read the safety instructions on the back of the seat in front of him a hundred times. He looked to his right and checked on the guy who was scared witless before the plane took off. The man wasn't in his seat any longer, and the older woman who sat by the window next to the man was snoring loudly as she slept. Arthur frowned; he didn't remember seeing someone in the corner of his eye get up and leave. He wondered how he did not notice the guy going. The plane itself was quiet. There were no crying babies, and only the faint whispers of people talking to each other in their seats were barely heard. Though Arthur knew with his Werewolf hearing, he only had to focus on the whispers, and he would know what they were saying, he didn't want to be rude and eavesdrop if he didn't need to. The pilots now and then would speak through the plane's speaker system to tell everyone of the weather conditions, how much longer it would take to arrive, and other essential safety instructions they had to repeat. This constant lull was like an unscratched itch to Arthur, who now really wanted to stretch his legs. He couldn't fall asleep, so he thought he could walk around a bit, at least. Arthur decided to use the bathroom on the plane if he was getting up either way. He undid his seat belt and got out of his seat, then headed down the aircraft aisle.

As he walked through the body of the plane, nobody in the other seats bothered to look up at him as he walked past them. There was a usual mix of different people who were on the plane. There were men and women, some were young, and some were old with a few children he saw in a couple of seats either sleeping or speaking to the adult sitting next to them. Arthur noticed people were reading books, and newspapers, or watching films on portable machines that he had never seen before. A bit further up, Arthur saw more children looking nearly as restless as Arthur was a few seats ago. These kids were whining to their parents for snacks or just being annoying in general to amuse themselves. Arthur couldn't help but smile as he walked past the whining children. He always thought little kids were hilarious to watch, especially with his little sister, and the random mad things she would say always cracked him up. While walking, he looked at the plane around him. The overhead compartments were all solid in place, an average dull white color with all the passengers' luggage inside them probably. Some of the people had the odd bag by their feet, but he wasn't sure if that was allowed or not. As he saw the restrooms up ahead, Arthur noticed one of the blue-uniformed flight attendants approaching his direction. She smiled at him as he turned to his side to let her past.

"Thank you," she said friendlily. Arthur nodded and continued walking before stopping dead as he got to the door of the toilet. His nose caught a strange scent. It was familiar, but he couldn't place it somehow. He wondered if it was the flight attendant's perfume she was wearing. He couldn't imagine why he would recognize it so much unless it had been the same scent his mother used to wear. But that didn't seem likely, but the scent was more recent to him in memory. He couldn't think of it, but the smell made him feel uncomfortable. He shook his head and went into the bathroom.

After he had finished, Arthur washed his face by the sink in the bathroom, taking his leisurely time. He had washed his hands correctly and was taking a small quiet thank you to the universe for being able to use proper toilets after all those weeks in the jungle and traveling in the wilds with Cratos. As Arthur splashed the cold water on his face and then dried it with a towel, he took a small look at his features for a moment. He seemed different in his eyes. He jokingly thought it looked weird he didn't have a bruise to see healing for once, but once his smirk about that disappeared, he noticed a lot more subtle changes. His skin looked somehow rougher and more resilient. Before, it looked like normal skin that was pale with a weak softness. But while it was still pale, it seemed stronger somehow to him. His hair was still its intense ginger color, and he strangely noticed tiny wisps of hair along his lip and chin if he looked incredibly close with his enhanced eyes. Most boys his age would squeal with joy at such a discovery, but it only made Arthur ponder. He wondered if this was the effect of his Werewolf blood that was finally starting to age his body. Or was it the result of his recent adventures, and his skin and face had grown rougher from his experiences with the

DYLAN ALTOFT

Vampires? With either answer, he smirked a little bit. Despite the reason, he liked that he did look older as well as stronger. He squinted his eyes a little bit to 'play' looking tough for a moment. He scowled with his eyebrows, then focused an intense look with his eyes to see how murderous he could appear. Holding the look for a moment, he relaxed his face, laughing a bit, then finished with a wink at his reflection. At that moment, the plane began to shake like an earthquake. Everything around him was rumbling and bouncing around. The noise became a growling hum as everything shook. Arthur didn't panic. He remembered that the captain said to everyone before they took off that turbulence was to be expected. Arthur did what he could to level himself with the plane while it shook and then left the bathroom to head back to his seat.

Arthur returned to his seat to notice that Cratos was still sleeping soundly and hadn't moved an inch. Arthur smiled and sat back in his seat. He quickly fastened his seat belt, followed by a flight attendant with a trolley of drinks and food appearing before the pair.

"Anything to eat or drink?" she asked with a smile. Arthur smiled back; his grin met with a quick strain as that unappealing scent he was met with before appeared to him again. But this woman wasn't the same attendant he had walked past earlier. Strangely, Arthur still smelled the unmistakable unpleasant but familiar aroma. Cratos was deep asleep, and he didn't have any money in his pockets, so he just shook his head.

"No, thank you," he replied. The lady then held a jug of water up.

"Would you like some complimentary water?" she followed up. Arthur found that strange, but he figured Cratos might want some when he awoke, so he nodded his head this time.

"Oh, yes, please, thanks," he responded uneasily. The flight attendant's smile widened as she filled a plastic cup with the water and handed it to Arthur before moving on to the people in front of them. Arthur placed the cup on the plastic tray table before Cratos, turning his mind back to the smell. He knew he had smelt it before and began racking his brain, trying to figure out where. This sense made him feel nervous and on edge, almost like it resembled something terrible that he couldn't yet decipher. But Arthur noticed there was nothing around that could hurt him. He thought that maybe it was just his wolf sense going weird now as he was growing. Cratos did tell him aspects of his senses would also rise and plummet at random points. He shrugged it off and sat back in his chair again with his eyes focused on reading the instructions on the seat in front of him.

A bit of time had passed since then. The plane was going through turbulence again, but Arthur tried to ignore it as he tried to look out the window next to the still sleeping Cratos. It was night again now, and all he could see were the faint bulges of the black clouds in the night sky and the wing of the plane. Arthur noticed the weather was quite strong outside, which made him connect that to the turbulence, but he swore he also saw a flash of lightning at one point. But he couldn't tell if the noise around him was the sound of thunder or just the noise of the plane shaking. Arthur then spent the next several minutes just staring out of the window, waiting to see a second flash to see if he was right. Just as he turned his head away to give up, he swore he saw another flash in the corner of his eyes. Like before, he snapped his head around to see nothing. He sighed angrily, feeling like an idiot. This continued further as Arthur refused to give up, but it was the same every time. Arthur felt it was as though the lightning itself was waiting for him to give up before flashing again. Before he decided his eyes were playing tricks on him, the largest growl of thunder bellowed around the entire plane. The sound of a few surprised adults and happy squeals of children could be heard at the reckoning blast of thunder seethed loudly for several seconds before disappearing. Arthur found the noise worrying to him. Without even thinking, he made a slight whining noise at the sound of the thunder as it raged through his heightened Werewolf ears. Arthur quickly put his hand over his throat and frowned in confusion.

"That was weird," he muttered to himself.

"It's common, the same way most animals fear thunder; it also makes us dislike it as well. Instinct," muttered Cratos, making his first noise in hours. Arthur snapped his head sideways to see his mentor still motionless with his eyes closed.

"When did you wake up?" Arthur asked. Cratos answered, sounding drowsy as he yawned, but his eyes didn't open.

"Just now. That thunder is fearsome to our entire race. Just keep an eye on yourself if it happens again; that whine can be a bad giveaway in public to the wrong ears." Arthur nodded as he saw Cratos's eyes slowly open. Cratos yawned again and properly sat up in his seat, stretching his arms as he woke up the rest of his body. As his teacher settled back in his seat, he saw the water in front of him, still half asleep.

"The flight attendant came by earlier and offered it; I figured you would want a drink when you woke up." Cratos nodded with a small smile.

"Thanks," he mumbled, yawning again. As the turbulence continued, Arthur decided to ask Cratos about the weird scent that bothered him earlier. He explained he thought it came from the flight attendants as he smelt the same thing from both. At first, Cratos shrugged, uninterested.

"Who knows, maybe they all trade the same deodorant or something," he mumbled in response, not properly listening. He leaned over and picked up the cup of water to drink. His hand then stopped dead in its tracks as it reached the brim of his mouth. Arthur noticed his mentor freeze as he then saw Cratos's nostrils bunch up several times. Cratos sniffed intensely at his drink. His eyes shot out wide awake as he frowned thoughtfully.

"You got this from the flight attendant, right?" he muttered in a quiet voice. Arthur nodded nervously.

"And she had the same unpleasant smell like the one you walked past before, right?" Arthur nodded again. Cratos took another sniff and placed the cup back on the tray table. He half-turned his head to Arthur, his eyes serious and half scared.

"We have a problem," he declared in a lowered, grueling voice.

"What is it?" Arthur asked, catching into Cratos's worry instantly.

"Shh!" his teacher snapped. Cratos then slowly but firmly turned his head, looking around their area for anyone listening in. He quickly looked at either side of them, from the seats in front of and behind them.

"Keep your voice down. You panic, and we're dead," he muttered calmly. Arthur frowned as he glued his lips together, thinking.

"Oh yeah, tell me that, now I won't panic!" he grunted in his mind. Arthur then leaned closer to Cratos and lowered his voice so only a Werewolf could hear clearly.

"What is it?" he whispered gently. Cratos sighed and whispered in return.

"Our fellow friends of the night." Arthur's eyes widened in shocking disbelief. He knew Cratos was avoiding using the word, but Arthur caught on instantly. The smell the attendants had now clicked with him. from that night when he was within the grasp of that woman before he killed her with Cratos. That strange scent, he smelt it stronger now with the attendants because of his Werewolf nose.

"They're Vampires!" he roared in his head. Upon that realization, he looked at the water for a few seconds that the flight attendants gave. Cratos had smelt it before he drank it. Arthur nodded towards the cup at Cratos then mouthed the word.

"Drugged?" without speaking. Cratos slowly nodded his head and looked around to make sure no one had approached them yet. Cratos then whispered as low as he could, Arthur's sharp wolf ears struggling to hear the turbulence still raging.

"I can't see anything around me. Very discreetly, lean your head over and tell me if you see any of the flight attendants in the aisle and tell me where they are." Arthur nodded and did as Cratos instructed. Very casually, as though he was just leaning over to look around out of curiosity. Arthur looked ahead first at the end of the row of seats, and there Arthur could see two of the flight attendants. As he looked, he noted them more carefully this time. They were two women, one blonde and the other with light brown hair. They looked young like they were in their early twenties. They had flawless faces that looked slightly pale, but they were purposely wearing lots of makeup to hide it. They were blocking the exit in that direction. They didn't notice Arthur as they were chatting, giggling at each other's words in their conversation. As slowly and casually as he could, Arthur then turned his head around to see instantly in front of him the uniform of a similar young-looking dark-haired attendant staring down at him, with a pleasant wide smile.

"Is there anything wrong, sir? Can I get you anything? Some water perhaps?" she asked cheerfully. Arthur nearly froze from shock. He was shocked he didn't hear her footsteps approaching him before he leaned over to look. He tried to control his breathing as he turned to look at Cratos to see him back in his previous sleeping position, probably pretending. The cup of water sitting on the tray in front of him was still untouched. Arthur turned around to see the attendant's face hadn't changed an inch, and she wasn't even blinking with her smiling face. Arthur caught the smell again. That bloodsucker's scent infested his nose, making his spine tingle and stiffen inside him. Now that he recognized the scent, a defensive rush burned inside his body. It was an instinct to attack her right now. But he controlled such impulses and smiled back at her as though nothing was wrong. He hadn't been this close to a Vampire since that night he first met Cratos. The Vampire woman he saw in the van was behind bulletproof glass away from him; plus, with the speed they were going, he could barely smell his own sweat at the time, let alone her stench. But with this woman right here, Arthur only needed to use his nose with a single sniff to smell the blood on her breath as she breathed out.

It was faded from other foods and drinks, but Arthur was looking for it now, and his instincts made it clear to him. Catching the smell on her breath made him angry. He didn't want to get himself killed by ditching his composure, but the person in front of him right now was a Vampire, and the Werewolf side of him wanted to kill her. The impulse to kill was pushing hard at him on the inside, begging for him to give up and attack. Arthur felt his hands clenched as he struggled to suppress the killer's instinct and contain himself. He instantly loosened his hands; if there was ever a time to control himself, it was now. He shook his head at her, whose smile hadn't budged an inch.

"No thanks, just stretching the body out a bit," Arthur answered with a forced smile. Her face didn't change as he declined her offer. Almost robotically, she replied.

"Are you sure sir? It's been a long flight so far." She held out a hand, her eyes still not blinking or looking away from Arthurs' pupils. Arthur caught a faint, tiny twitch at the corner of her smile. In her hand was a cup of water exactly like Cratos's.

"You must be very thirsty, right sir?" she said again, her voice sweeter than honey in his ears. Arthur got the slightest hint of a feeling that she wasn't going to give up until he accepted the water. Nodding at her, Arthur took the glass and placed it on the tray table in front of him.

"Thank you," he replied with forced courtesy. The attendant stayed still for a second, waiting for Arthur to drink from it. Arthur saw this, then took the cup and allowed a small sip in his mouth, and swallowed. She finally blinked and immediately stood up to walk back in the direction she had come from behind Arthur and Cratos. As she left, Arthur put the cup back into his mouth, spat the water he pretended to swallow back into the cup, and put it on the table. He turned his head to see how far the attendant had walked. What met his head was the attendant standing attention no more than several feet back staring directly at him, nodding her head sweetly at him with her smile unchanged. Arthur sat back in his chair quickly and faced forward like he was fused to his seat. Cratos was still pretending to sleep.

"What's the situation?" he asked quietly. Arthur thought for a moment and said softly.

"We're trapped." Cratos nodded in pretend sleep, saying nothing else. Arthur sat back in his seat. The Vampire flight attendants were now guarding them in front and behind. Both were now stuck thousands of miles in the air with the enemy all around them.

Arthur took a moment to collect himself as he had no idea what they could do to escape this trap. He wanted to panic. Arthur wanted to rush out of his seat and get away from the Vampires in a blind, violent attack. The problem was that he knew if he made a commotion, the attendants would scream or panic themselves. They would just announce that Arthur was probably some sort of terrorist, and he would be shot down, or the entire plane would attack and kill him and Cratos. He thought his only chance to keep their identity as ordinary people was to sit calmly and quietly like everyone else. Arthur looked at Cratos, who was still pretending to sleep as his chest rose and fell slowly more than when he was asleep before. As a Werewolf of experience, it looked to Arthur that Cratos's nerves were not on edge, and he was remaining calm. Arthur saw this and steadied his breathing to follow In Cratos's lead. Arthur focused hard to try to think clearly of some way out of this. He knew his time was limited at this point. If the water were drugged, the attendants would find it strange that the sip Arthur took had no effect. Arthur knew they would then realize they were caught out and would attack. Once the attendant realized Arthur recognized her as a Vampire, he and Cratos were doomed. He pretended to stretch and leaned over to whisper to Cratos.

"What can we do?" he pleaded, no ideas coming to his mind. The pair had a ticking clock over their heads.

"Still thinking," Cratos responded without moving an inch; only his lips twitched.

"Remember that our priority is also the people on this plane as well. They are innocent. We cannot act rashly and put them in danger." Arthur nodded in agreement. He had a feeling that would be his answer. Arthur tried to think of something more subtle. The pilot might be warned to land if Arthur made up some sort of emergency. But he would have to go past several rows of seats first, and if he were seen by the flight attendants going past the toilets, they would realize what he was doing.

"I have an idea," he whispered to Cratos, who nodded for him to continue.

"I just need to get to the pilot; I'll make up an emergency, and he'll land and –"

"Won't work," Cratos said, cutting him off. Arthur frowned but tried not to shift his body.

"Why!?" he asked desperately.

"Look out the window," he responded softly. Arthur leaned over his mentor and peered out the glass. The storm outside was powerful, thunder was still sounding around the plane, and there was nothing but blackness all around them. The aircraft was clearly caught in a place where it couldn't make a landing, even for an emergency. Arthur sighed mournfully.

"Keep thinking," Cratos mumbled. Arthur slunk back in his seat; even by the tone of that, he could tell Cratos couldn't think of anything either.

More time passed, and Arthur saw the flight attendants frequently walk past the pair of them. Arthur noticed how they slowly watched the two as they passed. Arthur knew that any moment now, they would realize he didn't drink the drugged water. Arthur then sighed in frustration as quietly as he could. Arthur thought about pretending to pass out or request medical attention. But then he realized they would probably just take him out of the public eye to murder him in secret. If given enough time, Cratos might be able to act and save him. It was a terrible plan, but he couldn't think of anything else at this point. Arthur leaned over to tell Cratos his plan, to see what he thought. Then he froze in place. His pupils began to shrink rapidly, his body solid as a statue.

"Oh...no," Arthur croaked in a strained voice. Cratos frowned with his eyes closed but kept his form for the moment.

"What's wrong? Did you actually drink some of the water," Cratos asked rapidly, his mind already forming a solution plan if Arthur had.

"N...o," he answered in a strained croak. Cratos opened his right eye and saw Arthur's petrified still face; his jaw was wide open with his pupils nearly invisible as his body slowly began to shake and convulse. Cratos turned his head to see what Arthur saw out of the window, and then his breath caught in his throat before he groaned. Out of his window, the clouds of the storm had cleared slightly, revealing a solid half-moon blaring its white light directly at Arthur's face. Cratos snapped his head around, abandoning his facade, and grabbed Arthur with his hands.

"Relax, Arthur, you must resist, calm yourself," he pleaded helplessly. Arthur couldn't respond. Cratos felt his students' arms tense like they were blocks of steel. The muscles began to throb and expand in his grip. Cratos cursed and attempted to keep Arthur calm, but he knew any physical efforts were in vain.

"It's the stages," he said in his head, looking at Arthur regrettably.

"He's more vulnerable to the light of the moon now more than ever.

Dammit!" Cratos thought. He knew he couldn't repel this. Arthur's body was growing; his previous blue eyes were now completely white from his transformation. Cratos undid his seat belt and nearly leaped over Arthur into the aisle. However, the second his feet hit the floor, he was immediately met with the twisted smile of one of the attendants who heard the commotion.

"Is something wrong, sir?" she asked sweetly. Cratos knew what she was but knew he had to lie for the humans around them to stay safe.

"My son is having a fit. He needs to get out of here," he pleaded quickly. The flight attendant didn't change her face at Cratos's plea, but her eyes looked at Arthur changing in a fit of anguish, fighting a losing battle and causing her smile to drop. Her face immediately morphed into twisted hate, thinking that the Werewolves were fighting back. She screamed for her friend. A second attendant ran forward after seeing her colleague's expression ordering the other passengers to remain in their seats. Her hand straightened like a blade ready to strike Cratos. The second attendant came up behind Cratos and shot her hand forward. Out of instinct, Cratos spun his body around and caught her hand midair with his own, then sharply twisted her wrist to the right, snapping it like a tree branch. She roared with pain then screamed as loud as she could.

"Hijackers!" The other passengers nearly all simultaneously screamed and began to panic as the first attendant threw her hand towards Cratos while he was distracted. But her hand wasn't stopped by Cratos's sharp reflexes this time. Instead, what stopped the Vampire claw in its tracks was the hairy vice-like monstrous grip of Arthur, who, with an effortless squeeze, wrenched her hand horribly, crunching the flesh and bone beneath its grip like it was rotten fruit. She turned her head and saw the twisted, red-furred half-wolf features of Arthur Thorn and screamed in terror.

"Stop resisting!" growled the dark, booming voice of Arthur's inner Beast. Arthur's control began to fade the second he saw the moon.

"Don't do this!" Arthur pleaded. His body was shaking rapidly. All the noise around him was turning into white noise as Cratos's pleas for him to resist fell on deaf ears. The mere shine of the moon was sending rippling shivers through his entire body like ghostly electrocution. He could feel every cell in his body howling up at the glowering rock in the night sky, bellowing for his wolf to rise.

"Stop acting stupid, boy," the Beast inside his head continued, its voice sounding more like a teacher's scold.

"You're past the point of plans now, boy. Release me, and I will save you from this flying deathtrap!" Arthur thought it for a moment; his body was beginning to expand and grow against his will. He was losing this fight and realized he had little room for negotiation here.

"How can I trust you?" he said in a weak struggle, internally replying to the Beast in his head.

"You're...a monster..." The Beast sighed in his mind with exhaustion, like how Cratos would respond when Arthur had asked him a dumb question.

"I am a monster boy," it admitted. The Beasts voice was growing into a more seductive whisper.

"But I am YOUR monster. Let. Me. Out!" Arthur felt his hair grow from his body.

"One condition!" Arthur growled back at the Beast. While there is no way he could have seen it, Arthur could have sworn blind he felt the Beast within himself had just smiled at that.

"Which is?" it asked with a purr. Arthur saw Cratos was in trouble out of the corner of his eye. He turned his head, and one of the Vampire attendants screamed. He needed to help.

"We do it together!" he growled darkly. The Beast laughed maliciously.

"With pleasure, boy. Now let us play!" it answered. Without hesitation in a half-transformed wolf body, Arthur then lurched forward with his morphed claw to save Cratos.

Arthur's body did not look like his inner Beast in his mind, nor did he even slightly resemble the body Cratos possessed when he transformed too. When Arthur had first gained his abilities as a Werewolf, he had only received muscle definition rather than an increase in size. The only time the Beast had surfaced since then was when he was in the jungle with the tree vines against the tiger and then fighting to save Cratos in the city attack. But right at this moment on the plane, his physique was nearly double his previous size. His clothes had stretched and ripped around his arms and legs. The surface of his hands was overrun with thin red fur accompanied by long steel strength nails at the end of his fingers. His teeth grew into several different fangs, four protruding from his mouth, keeping it open for comfort. His face had patches of red fur in sharp spike streaks shooting from the sides of his face across his cheeks. His ears were even slightly more pointed in an upward position. He hadn't fully turned into his full beast form. Instead, it looked as though he was stuck in a mid-way state. In only a few minutes of basking in the light of the moon, he was taller and more robust, with his physique only half that of a powerful Werewolf.

Yet somehow, Arthur was fully conscious and in control of his body. His eyes were blaring with a mighty, striking golden yellow. He was snarling like a mad beast, wide awake to witness the unbearable face of the attendant. The Beast within him was present in this form. It felt to Arthur as though the Beast was a ghost lying against the back of Arthur's body right now. It was moving its limbs with Arthurs' own in perfect sync. The Beast's mouth was constantly at his ear, guiding him as a second pair of eyes. The sharp screech of the Vampire from her crushed hand stung Arthur's ears at close range.

"Silence that miserable wretch!" The Beast snarled. Arthur felt more prone to doing as the Beast asked. His conscious voice of reason and restraint had vanished. He was now just angry, and he wanted to shut her up. With his other arm, he shot his other hand forward and gave the exact vice grip he had put on the woman's hand, on her throat. With the second clench of his claw, he mashed her windpipe and throat in a second with little effort. The face of the Vampire was aflame with insane panic for an instant before the snapping sound of her neck breaking into pieces caused her entire body to go limp. Her death didn't bother Arthur. He simply released both his grips on her dead body and let it slump to the floor of the plane like a discarded rag doll. The other screaming passengers on the plane saw what had just transpired, and they all left their seats and began to run away down the aisle, panicking at the sight of Arthur, heading for the back to be as far away from the grotesque monster as possible. The noise of the frightened humans was irritating him as well. He turned his head with the idea of advancing on them to silence the others like he did the Vampire.

"No boy, keep your eye on what matters," came the voice of the Beast, diverting his attention to Cratos next to him, who finished off the other vampire flight attendant with a quick speedy martial-art precise neck snap, causing her to fall to the floor dead with her friend. Arthur's arms tensed as he struggled to try and ignore attacking the other humans. Cratos turned to face Arthur and eyed him carefully.

"Are you with me, Arthur?" he asked skeptically, not sure if the Beast hadn't taken over. Arthur didn't speak, but he nodded at Cratos directly, smiling viciously at his mentor. Cratos nodded back cagily. The Beast wasn't behaving like Arthur, but as long as he didn't go on a rampage, it was the best result he could hope for.

"OK then, stick with me. We need to find a way out of here. I'm afraid everything hit the fan," Cratos grunted. With the entire plane in panic, regular humans witnessing the murder of two flight attendants, and currently seeing an inhuman monster among them, the two Werewolves were now in a world of chaos in the sky.

CHAPTER TWENTY-TWO

The Beast continued to cling to Arthur's wolf-like body like a child receiving a piggyback ride as he and Cratos moved through the plane. Arthur was struggling to maintain his urge to lose control. In this wolf-like transformation, his mind felt much more primal and untamed. This plane journey was his first time in this kind of form where he was in control, and he felt his mind slowly unravel as his craving for slaughter and bloodlust was rising. The only voice keeping him in the realm of sanity was the very Beast that Arthur thought would try and encourage him to go on a rampage of mindless slaughter the most. However, contrary to Arthur's expectations, the Beast continued to speak to Arthur, making sure he behaved normally for Cratos.

"Why do you even care?!" Arthur finally roared internally at the Beast as it felt like it was holding a dog leading to Arthur.

"Because, your body is also MY body as well you idiot! I won't let you ruin OUR life by forcing Cratos to put you down if you kill any innocent humans!" That retort would usually have driven Arthur into a rage forcing him to claim his body was his own and the Beast was an unwanted possession within his soul. However, in his simpler mental state, Arthur simply went silent at the Beast's reply. Therefore, Arthur tried to ignore his homicidal wish to murder these loud flailing humans crying and screaming around him and focus on any real problems ahead. The pair was now close to the cockpit at the front of the plane, where the pilots were seated. Arthur recalled hearing the pilot's communication through the plane's speakers. He was calmly telling the passengers to relax and assured them everything was under control. However, it seemed the grisly appearance of Arthur coupled with the brutal deaths of the plane's flight attendants were more convincing than their confident announcements. Cratos saw ahead after they passed a few more screaming passengers was a man dressed in a blue pilot's uniform standing between them and the door to the pilot's room. The pair of them stopped dead a few feet away from the man. Cratos narrowed his eyes at the man and noticed his red eyes as well as catching sight of the tiniest hint of a fang from his toothy smirk. Arthur stood behind his mentor, still heaving his shoulders, and smelling the bloody scent of the Vampire ahead of them well before Cratos had spotted it with his eyes. Arthur spread his clawed hands and snarled hatefully, wanting to dash forward and destroy the Vampire and turn him into a fleshy puddle.

"Wait," Cratos said quietly. The fanged predator raised his arm and waved at the pair. His mentor was disturbed by the calm smugness of the Vampire ahead of them.

"I trust you passengers are enjoying your flight," he called out with a sick chuckle. Cratos's frown burrowed deeper, but he kept his calm as he tried to assess the situation. Arthur was not even listening. The Beast roared inside through his head as he stood idle in his half-wolf-like form, struggling to contain himself much longer. The pilot brought up his right hand to reveal a handgun pointed straight at Cratos.

"Not another step, you filthy dogs, one more step, and you'll be put down permanently!" Cratos clenched his teeth, trying to think fast. Arthur rolled his eyes at the man. He spoke to the Beast that clung to his body.

"What now, smart guy," he grumbled at it. The Beast hummed enjoyably.

"You heard the man, not another 'step'," it purred back at Arthur, trying to guide him through suggestion.

"So, get creative," it finished, then the Beast went silent to see what Arthur would do.

"What is this?!" Cratos roared at the pilot as his confusion took over his senses in a lapse moment of panic. The Pilot looked at Cratos with evil glee and laughed.

"My partner behind me in the cockpit is quickly fulfilling our mission! You insects actually think our masters didn't know you would be taking your new mongrel to your worthless pit of dogs!" he laughed crazily with his right eye twitching.

"At this point, after all the destruction you have caused us, you two dogs have your own bloody satellite tracking your movements!" The Vampire snarled. That caused Arthur's mind to switch to a thought of Siren. A small bolt of fear revealed itself as he pictured the Vampires knocking down her vault door and filling her with bullets.

"The rest of the people here are innocents! Leave them out of this!" Cratos shouted in desperation, his eyes flickering yellow as his body began to shake into his wolf.

"Ah, ah, ah! The boy is one thing, but If I see a single strand of fur sprout on you, and I start shooting mutt!." Arthur was only half listening as his mentor and the pilot Vampire exchanged words. The Beast told him to get creative, so he decided to eye the space around him. The only things around him were the emergency door off the plane to his right and one more window to his left. Everything else in their near vision was regular metal-plated walling and the lights above them. Arthur scowled as he saw nothing to throw at the bloodsucker.

"Cratos seems to be in your way," the Beast muttered again, quietly. Arthur frowned for a second and then grinned excitedly as he understood the meaning. Arthur immediately threw his arms forward and latched tightly on Cratos's steel thick arms. Cratos roared in surprise, but he didn't have time to say anything as Arthur hurled his body backward, pulling Cratos back with him looking like he was performing a wrestling move on his teacher. Arthur released his grip as his mentor was in the air, throwing Cratos several feet backward away from Arthur and the pilot. Cratos landed hard on the floor unscathed as Arthur brought himself back upright and locked his eyes on the Vampire, who was aiming the gun straight at him shakily. The Vampire was utterly taken aback by Arthur's attack on his ally. Arthur then leaned back up and faced the Vampire with his eyes trained murderously on him.

"Stay back! Stay back, you filthy mutt!" The pilot threatened as he trained his gun straight towards Arthur's head. With a beastly roar, Arthur darted forward with both his arms raised forward, intent on grabbing the pilot, claws first. Arthur, however, heard the fear in the back of the Vampire's cry, and it excited his viciousness.

Without blinking, the Vampire fired his gun at Arthur. The sound of the gunshot ripped through Arthur's extra sensitive ear, which made him painfully wince at the sound. As it sailed through the air, the first bullet struck his chest, but it didn't stop his pace as he charged forward even by an inch. The Vampire stepped backward until he was dead against the cockpit door behind him. His back now against the wall with nowhere left to go, the Vampire unloaded his five remaining bullets straight at Arthur, which merely embedded themselves deep in the flesh of Arthur's torso. Despite the six bleeding holes on his emblazed chest, not one of the bullets slowed

Arthur's warpath towards the man. Arthur's temper only rose further with each shot. As the final scrap of lead burrowed itself into his thick pectoral flesh, the pilot continued to pull the trigger on the gun with the clicking noise echoing in Arthur's ears pleasantly as he focused his pupils on the shaking, scared Vampire. With a demonic snarl, Arthur latched his claws on the upper arms of the Vampire. Arthur didn't even blink as he gripped the man, his mind lost in the rage of being shot; his claws instantly snapped the arm bones of the vampires swiftly, then he lifted him into the air. The Vampire screamed out as the shards of splintered bone sliced apart the insides of his arms, leaving deep indents from Arthur's claws crushing his arms. Arthur grinned maliciously, hearing the man cry out and enjoying every pained second of its sound. Sparing the man no further seconds of life, Arthur opened his mouth, ready to bite the pilot's throat out.

"Arthur, stop!" called Cratos behind him. The wolf instinct in him caused him to halt as his mentor's voice penetrated his ears, bringing Arthur back into further control. Cratos came up behind Arthur and stood next to him. He looked into Arthur's eyes and saw the blazing death glare fixed on the vampire as he struggled to obey his teacher's command.

Cratos looked over his pupil for a moment. He knew that because of the stages Arthur still needed to pass, and because the moon was not yet at its strongest, Arthur hadn't fully transformed into a Werewolf. This form was advanced for him but commonplace during training. But despite being typical for new cubs, this amount of self-control was odd. He was constantly watching Arthur since they began going through the plan, expecting him to be a raging beast. Not to mention Arthurs' immense strength concerned Cratos as well. Arthur had operated with a full Werewolf's relative speed and power, which Cratos felt should be impossible. Cratos was beginning to think Siren knew more about Arthur than she told him. A sharp growl from an impatient Arthur struck Cratos out of his train of thought as he nodded at his student and faced the crying vampire who was shaking in agonizing pain. Blood seeped from his limb wounds as he hung in the air entirely at Arthur's mercy.

"You... fools!" the Vampire gasped meekly. Tears flowed down his face, but he tried to appear scornful as Cratos stood next to Arthur, who held him grinning.

"Killing me means nothing...you...and everyone else on this...plane...are already...dead!" Cratos sensed danger like a light switch being flicked and rapidly answered.

"How is that!" he snapped, fearing whatever answer would come next. Despite his pain, the Vampire managed a pained chuckle.

"This plane is going to...crash into the side of a mountain...any minute now...neither of you will survive...there will be no wreckage...or evidence either...the whole plane is...wired up with C4...rot...in... hell!" he finished with a vicious hiss. Arthur had heard more than enough. He threw his head forward and sank his fangs deeply into the throat of the pilot. The Vampire screamed before his voice was cut out as his body shuddered in Arthur's grip, going still in seconds with flesh and blood rained down from his hanging corpse. Arthur ripped his head away with chunks of the Vampires flesh and throat filling his mouth. Blood sprayed out from the Vampire's now gaping hole for a neck, drenching Arthur with blood in seconds and painting the floor beneath them both. Arthur dropped the dead Vampire to the floor as emotionlessly as he did the attendant before, letting the still bleeding corpse slump to the ground beneath him like a broken, discarded toy.

Adrenalin slowly began to weaken within his wolf body after dropping the pilot's body to the floor. Other senses started to return to him slowly. Out of all the senses to return to Arthurs' state of mind, the first sense that exploded upon him like a wrecking ball was his sense of taste. His mouth was riddled with the flesh and blood of the Vampire. The disgusting taste in his mouth was like rotting poison festering and bubbling upon his tongue like a putrid acid smothering his mouth. With a retching heave, Arthur vomited out the Vampires flesh and blood onto the Vampire's corpse, an odd way of returning his remains to him. His body was rejecting every scrap of Vampire flesh that Arthur had put into his body by continuing to throw up and heave until even the blood that had run down his throat had left his body. Arthur was whining and growling as he did this for a few moments. Cratos walked past Arthur, he knew this would happen, and he instantly began working on trying to open the pilot's door to prevent the pilot inside from crashing the plane. He started by simply turning the handle, only to see it was locked. He then attempted to pick the lock open with his wolf nails, but they didn't work on this lock. It was more complicated than other doors. He looked around the door frame, thinking quickly, but he knew, given past events with hijackers on planes, that the pilot's room would probably be the most impenetrable part of the plane for protection from brute force.

"Arthur!" he snapped towards his still retching student. Worry began to weigh on Cratos's shoulder as he thought about how every life on this plane was their responsibility for saving. Despite the disgusting taste still alive around every inch of his mouth Arthur rose and stared at his mentor.

"Did you hear what he said?" Cratos asked, met with Arthur nodding in response but saying nothing.

"That means we have limited time. I don't know if the bomb is on a timer, but if there is a detonator, it's behind this door, and I will need your help to open it. Do you understand?" Arthur again nodded, getting increasingly irritated at his teacher treating him like a mindless simpleton. Cratos turned towards the cockpit door and pointed straight in the center of the metal.

"I need you to use all the strength you can, Arthur, Then punch the door inward as hard as you can. Once the steel around the edges is pried open enough, I can take it from there." Arthur again nodded and walked towards the door, then looked it over. He smirked as he tensed his arms and clenched his fists. The Beast again purred into his ear, its ghost-like claws massaging Arthur's shoulders like a champion's coach.

"Breathe in deeply," it advised slowly. Arthur paid close attention to the Beast's words.

"Ignore the pain of your knuckles when they hit the metal. That door is like pure steel, but you're a Werewolf! You have the strength to tear this flimsy piece of scrap apart. Your bones will fracture and bruise, but you will heal. Fight on Arthur. We will survive this, but only if you succeed!" Arthur felt excited by the Beast's words. Adrenalin once again began to flow through his veins like liquid fire fueling his arms, tensing them into pieces of indestructible power. Hunching his shoulders, Arthur squared up to the door and growled deeply. He brought his left arm back behind his body, squeezing his fists into a solid ball. Then with a mighty roar, he charged it forward, slamming his row of knuckles fiercely against the door, ignoring all feeling of pain as the bones of his fists struck against the solid surface. Cratos's eyebrows soared in shock by the sheer force of that first hit. As Arthur pulled away from his fist clear of his mark, it revealed a near-perfect indent of his fist deeply embedded into the door. Small ripples and wrinkles around the crater of the strike formed as he pulled his hand back. Happy with his first result, Arthur grinned, ignoring that the skin around his knuckles was nearly completely shredded away. The white blobs of his bone that shone through were also visible, but he continued to ignore it all. He was blinded by the endorphins now pumping through his body which numbed him to the pain. Arthur then continued his work and hurled his right fist forward directly. Pulling back his fist to see the same result as before, Arthur then unleashed a mountainous flurry of strikes against the door unrelentingly without stopping.

The seemingly impenetrable door was slowly crumbling in seconds before the immense strength of Arthur's strikes against it. The edges of the doors were as Cratos had hoped, crumpling inwards. Its figure grew wider as Arthur's punches' indent continued to push the metal forward into the cockpit. With a slight tap of his teacher's finger on his shoulder, Arthur's body instantly went still. His chest was heaving like a grizzly bear as he caught his breath after stopping. He was exhausted, and his hands were shaking and bloody from his punches.

"Good work, Arthur, I'll take it from here," his teacher said with an unnerved tone. Arthur's vision refocused as he witnessed his work before him. Cratos stepped towards the door, which looked as though a dozen cannonballs had just been launched at it.

"Impressive," the Beast purred smugly. Arthur couldn't help but smile dumbly at how well he had thrashed the door in just over a minute, even as the feeling and pain returned to his decimated knuckles.

Cratos straightened his hands like blades, and with a low focused grunt, his hands blew up in size like balloons. The veins on the surface of his hand looked like visible pythons writhing under his skin. His nails were several inches longer than when he tried to pick the lock and razor-sharp. Arthur squinted for a moment before remembering Cratos's telling before during his training that Werewolves who have completed maturing through all their stages can transform only a single part of their body into that of their Werewolf form. Closing his eyes, Cratos then breathed in sharply and slashed his arms down both sides of the weakened door, slicing through the steel like it was wet paper. Cratos then jumped and slashed his left hand sideways at the top connecting the cut lines from the side of the door. As his arms came by his sides, the door swung forward, slamming on the floor, revealing the pilot's room entrance. Cratos breathed out as he opened his eyes and let his hand shrink, returning them to their original size. The pair looked in to see the pilot with his back to them. He was casually steering the plane. As both gazed at the man, he chuckled.

"Your efforts are adorable but pointless. My fate, your fate, and everyone's fate on this whole plane are already decided." He then nodded his head forward, gesturing out the window in front of them. The storm was still raging, but Arthur could see the faintest shadow of an oncoming giant mountain they were heading straight towards through the black clouds.

As the mountain came into clearer view, the pilot's hands sharply moved forward, and the pair felt the effect of the plane sharply turning downward. His finger was hovering over a small red button clasped in his hand tightly. Cratos shouted in fear and dashed forward before the pilot's left hand released from the controls to grab a small item from his side and held it up to them, both freezing Cratos in place.

"I take it my co-pilot informed you about our explosive option. Don't think for a second that I won't do it, you mongrels. Either way, we go up in flames; it's your choice on how soon!" Cratos glared at the man but couldn't think of anything to do. Arthur was beginning to feel the skin around his knuckles scream at him with agony, but it didn't distract him from the pilot's words. Arthur had a feeling his current approach of biting out throats wouldn't work in this case. Right now, if he made one wrong move, the entire plane would blow up.

"Any ideas?" he asked the Beast in his head. The monster growled in a humming way as it thought.

"Nope, good luck," it finally answered, going silent.

"Useless," Arthur grunted out loud in a hollowed deep tone. Cratos turned his head at Arthur before shaking it and refocusing on the situation at hand. The pilot's finger hadn't budged away from the button, and the plane was nearly nose-diving towards the mountain, which after a few moments was no longer a mere blur in vision but now in full chilling view. The pair was only minutes from certain death.

With the insane Vampire pilot only a few feet away from the pair, Arthur and Cratos didn't have the time to map out a plan together that wouldn't tip their foe off. Arthur briefly gazed at his mentor, whose eyes were continuously switching from the pilot to the window. He was desperately trying to think fast before the mountain became his tomb. Still, in the hairy grip of his wolf form, Arthur was struggling to think logically at all. His most loud instincts were roaring at him to throw the pilot through the airplane window. The only fact preventing such a suicidal yet appealing alternative was the Beast on his back reminding him of the sensitive red button the Vampires finger hovered over. Despite his struggle to think in the almost mechanical way, Cratos felt, that one slight advantage was at his disposal. The Vampire was focused entirely on the mountain he was steering the plane towards without stopping. Meaning he wasn't looking at either Arthur or Cratos, which allowed them to act if they remained silent. According to Cratos, as he explained, Vampires had excellent hearing, far greater than a Werewolf cub during his training. However, much like Cratos himself, trained Werewolves could move in complete silence, which now seemed to be their only chance of survival.

Arthur had taken each lesson and every second of his training with Cratos seriously. He attempted to think for a second about how a stealthy approach could save his life. Arthur knew that even if he sneaked up on the Vampire, any attacks would cause his hands to clench, which would cause him to press the button. He couldn't go for the hand itself as that was within the Vampires sight. He clenched his teeth in frustration. This in-depth thinking while in his current form was hurting his head. He just wanted to roar and start ripping limbs apart already.

"Stop thinking like a cornered prey and think more like a predator," growled the Beast in his ear, stealing his attention.

"Oh, decided to contribute now," Arthur replied sarcastically. The Beast ignored the jibe and continued speaking.

"This form we are in now is only a means, not an end, you foolish child. Rule it! Don't let it rule you; steady your mind. You can control it and think of a solution. You know it." Arthur wanted to yell at the Beast. He wanted to roar and tell it to shut its hairy trap. His body and muscles may have been near twice their standard size with his body smothered in dark red fur, but deep down, he was still Arthur Thorn, and he knew who was in charge here. Steeling his nerves and narrowing his eyes now, Arthur began to change his focus through his mind to think of a plan. He wouldn't allow his first temptation to be his death.

Arthur observed the Vampire pilot for a moment. The plane was only a few minutes from hitting the side of the mountain. Cratos had started to act a cunning scheme already running through his thoughts as he crouched and began to advance slowly. Not even with Arthur's hearing in his transformation did he hear the slightest ping of the metal floor from his teacher's feet. He felt that his mentor might as well be a ghost floating through the air with his near-supernatural light feet. However, his teacher's advance gave Arthur a small idea of how to deal with their problem. While Cratos moved slowly forward, Arthur assumed he would try and strike the Vampire and instead stepped backward. Arthur attempted to lighten his approach as much as he could. Despite his efforts, he simply didn't have the mastery over silent footwork that Cratos did. His training in the jungle and his hunting of the tiger fast-tracked his skills immensely, but he was still a novice and not adept. His third step made a ting noise that the pilot heard, but he didn't look back at them to see what was happening.

"No point trying to run away. There's enough C4 to send every inch of this place up to the heavens. From what I have seen from the security cameras, all the remaining passengers are cowering at the back of the plane. Feel free to feast on them if you wish, dog. Think of it as a final meal," the Vampire chuckled before laughing scornfully, his voice riddled with spite as Arthur took another step back. He didn't hide his noise as much this time as the pilot had no problem with Arthur moving away from him, which couldn't be more perfect for Arthur's plan. Cratos was nearly within striking distance of the pilot now, and he was about to make a considerable gamble which meant Arthur didn't have much time to execute his part of the plan.

Outside of the door frame, Arthur saw the dead body of the co-pilot he killed. His blood had smothered the floor around him, and its stench wretched into Arthur's nose. His body was already decomposing to the near skeletal rotting husk that all Vampires turned into upon death. He saw the empty gun in the dead Vampires hand and picked it up within his ghastly red hairy wolf hand. He looked away from the gun and started fumbling around the dead pilot's clothing. Arthur checked the front pockets of his coat, which were empty. He grunted, annoyed, and then he checked the pockets of his trousers, which also had nothing inside of them. His head turned, and he saw Cratos inches away from the Vampire now. If he failed in his attack, Arthur would be blown to pieces. A thought crossed his mind, which he acted on with furious speed. Arthur then unbuttoned the co-pilot's jacket and saw there was an inside pocket. With one last shred of hope, he plunged his hand within, and with a ferocious stroke of luck, his fingers clasped onto a piece of metal.

Pulling it out, Arthur saw it was a spare bullet the pilot forgot to use in his state of panic. A sickening smirk slithered up Arthur's hideous wolf-like face as he harshly slammed the shell into one of the empty holes of the gun barrel and slapped it back into place. He then rotated the barrel so the bullet was ready to be fired. It was a struggle to hold in his inflated muscle-bulging hand, but after a few seconds of fumbling, it was held in his hand well enough, so the end of the gun was at least pointing forward with his finger on the trigger. While he had no experience with firearms, he had a good idea of what he expected to happen, especially given the multiple bullet slugs still embedded in his chest. He stood up straight and turned back to face the open cockpit. He then pointed the gun straight forward at the pilot. Cratos was right behind him now as he raised his hand to strike the pilot in an attack, which Arthur was hoping would kill him instantly. Arthur closed one eye and aimed carefully. He then moved the sight of his gun, so it was in what Arthur prayed was the correct position, and then he fired the gun. In a flash of noise, the bullet flew through the air and shot straight through the glass of the plane's front window right above the pilot's head. The Pilot was shocked, he hadn't expected a gun to be fired, and stupidly his finger left the red button for a fraction of a second in his surprise. Cratos took instant advantage of the distraction and swung his arm around the pilot chair using all four nails on his fingers to instantly slice open the vampire's throat like a ripe tomato.

The Vampires body shook without stopping as blood sprung forth from his neck with powerful ferocity. His blood began painting the front window of the plane its ugly ruby color like a full-powered garden hose. His hand slowly tried to return to push the red button in a final act of spite, but Cratos had already caught it in place, then he promptly twisted his wrist nearly a full circle, severing all forms of movement. The sounds of the pilot hatefully choking to death on his blood now filled the air as his gurgling voice spat out blood as it freely flowed ferociously down his body, drenching his clothes and puddling on the floor below his chair. Cratos moved in front of the Vampires' slowly dying body and looked down on the shuddering creature with a look of total contempt. Saying nothing, Cratos spat onto its face. His lips curled as his saliva ran down the rage-ridden face of the Vampire. In a sudden jump, the pilot's body eased its shaking and went utterly still. His blood continued to pump from his severed throat for a few more seconds before it slowly stopped, its body beginning the process of its instant decay before its eyes.

Arthur approached, not bothering to look at the pilot, and instead grabbed the steering control of the plane. At the same time, Cratos continued his piercing stare at the Vampire, temporarily letting his mind become lost in anger. Arthur had no idea what any of the buttons on this control panel did, but he gripped the wheel tightly and pulled it back towards him as quickly as he could with considerable effort. The plane slowly began to pull upwards back into the skies as he did allow a breath of relief to escape Arthur's lungs. Cratos snapped back into reality and grinned with ecstatic relief as the mountain disappeared from their view.

"That was a close shave, eh?" he said with a nervous chuckle, his gallows humor almost ringing hollow as the dread in his tone was alive. With a happy grunt response, Arthur slowly nodded but kept his hands on the wheel. He was not sure what would happen if he let go. Cratos looked at the bullet hole Arthur had made. Cratos knew, given the plane's cabin pressure, it could be any second before the entire window crashed, and they would be sucked out to their deaths. The only reason it hadn't so far Cratos mused was because of the Vampires.

"They planned this entire ambush since we went to the airport. They must have made sure the cockpit was more durable than most planes. But we don't have long regardless!" Arthur thought for any ideas in his head desperately. The rushing noise of the air on the glass windshield in the cockpit escaping through the minimal vacuum was sharp and growing louder by the second.

"Good thing they make the glass too strong otherwise, we would have been sucked out like ants," Cratos continued to muse aloud. Arthur grunted again in agreement as Cratos knelt over the Vampires' dead body, which was still slowly dissolving.

"Let's unstrap this worthless cur so we can think of a plan on how to land this thing somewhere and get going." Arthur then watched his mentor fumble around the pilot chair, looking for the release of the seat belt when his body froze completely. He looked under the pilot's chair and came across a device that made his smile drop and his heart stop. Arthur looked at Cratos's face, which looked as though he saw his face ripped off staring back at him. His teacher was frozen in place as he stared at something.

"Arthur, we need to get off this plane now," he said in a hollowed whisper. Arthur frowned at his teacher. Arthur knew that since they had regained a clear path in the sky, he allowed himself a few seconds to release the steering wheel and crouch down to see what was going on. As Arthur looked under the chair with Cratos, his eyes were greeted by the long black box with several colored wires sticking out of its sides going down to the plane's floor. On the face of the box was a digital clock with a timer going from one minute exactly and continuing to count down. Arthur's fear expanded rapidly to the point he thought his eyeballs were going to drop out from sheer shock alone. Cratos shot up like a possessed man and frantically looked around the cockpit.

"There's no time to disarm it Arthur, we need to go!" Cratos said in a frantic strain, making it clear he had no idea how. Arthur looked at the clock as he heard his teacher go out of the room and grab something from the wall next to the emergency exit door. Before he had a chance to look up and see what I was, he felt Cratos's arm reach around his neck and tightly lock around his throat, dragging him backward. Arthur roared in his beastly voice as Cratos pulled him to the emergency door. He saw Cratos's arm grab a parachute that was next to the door as he quickly put it on and strapped it to his body.

Arthur was unable to ask what was going on as the sheer force Cratos used was almost mechanical. Cratos firmly but mournfully said.

"Hang on! Things are about to get a little windy!" he warned. The grip around Arthur's throat was tensing even more, nearly wholly cutting off air circulation. Cratos snapped up the release handle, and the door exploded open. The air was being ripped out of the door madly around them in a sudden violent vacuum. All Arthur could hear around him was the chaotic rushing of air hamming through him. Without another word spoken, Cratos hurled himself backward, dragging Arthur with him. The pair descended into the ferocious grip of the raging storm in the open air and straight into the mercy of gravity as the plane continued through the skies to its inevitable doom without the pair of them anymore.

CHAPTER TWENTY-THREE

The wind battled like a thousand sharp whips against the half-grown red fur surrounding Arthurs' entire body. The ferocious winds force was assaulting him with the below zero temperature cold of the night air, complementing its physical trauma. His ears were plugged with the rushing thrash of the air as he and Cratos plummeted down to the ground with increasing speed. The storm of the night still bellowed its thriving rage around them as thunder howled its fury as they fell. Great flashes of lightning illuminated their bodies through the air in milliseconds. Arthur even found himself struggling to breathe as they fell, finding truly little oxygen as he tried to take in short gasps as often as he could in the madness surrounding him. Arthur couldn't help but stare back up at the plane, which was slowly becoming smaller in his vision.

A terrifying blast of regret dug deep in his heart as everything else around him, which would have been deemed chaos, turned to nothing in his mind. He thought about all the terrified innocent people who were flying to their certain death now with no one steering the plane and possibly even sooner when the bomb went off. He wanted to close his eyes and roar in his head, so he didn't know what was coming, but his sad efforts were in vain. Arthur witnessed the fiery orange and yellow eruption of the plane's abrupt explosion appear in the distance. The magnitude of its combustion echoed through the air with its noise meshing into the menagerie of the storm, intertwining their bellow together almost harmoniously. As the glow faded from the air in a few seconds, Arthur pictured every single life that was just instantly lost, and his heart sank faster than they were falling. They were innocent people who had nothing to do with him and just died. The Vampires wouldn't have destroyed that plane if he and Cratos hadn't been on it. It was his fault, and he couldn't argue in his head that he killed them. Arthur's mind then went utterly blank again, and all his thoughts of guilt vanished. His eyes widened again as he turned his head to the side to see once again the pale white brilliant blaze of the moon's light upon his being. It had once again managed to pierce a sneak point through the black clouds which raged around them. His control over his more conscious mind dissolved and through Arthur back into the mindless beast he roared into when he first changed.

"Oh, bloody hell!" Cratos shouted as they fell. He was now fighting to keep an arm around Arthur, who was shaking and struggling from within his embrace from the moon's direct light causing him to further convulse and react with energy and power. His pupil's body began morphing further into a carnivorous creature as more of the moon's surface shone down on Arthur. He was uncontrollably growling and snarling and could not be contained much longer as he was. Cratos's most significant fear right now was that his student would fight him and wrestle himself out of his grip, sending him to his death. Cratos looked down to the ground and saw that they were going to hit the earth soon. He judged it right and used his other hand to grip the chord of the parachute he was wearing lightly. The top of the backpack released open and sloppily sent the contents out into the open rushing air, expanding in seconds and halting their quick descent. They were now hovering over the ground in the storm, which was no picnic. The winds were still bashing against them like moving cars, but Cratos put his entire being into steering safely and holding Arthur firm for as long as he could. Cratos's face for a moment was ashen with grief from the passengers on the plane. His priority was to save humans, but he knew he couldn't have done anything to stop their deaths. His mourning was cut short by the back of Arthur's head slamming hard against his chest in his animal-like state. The moon rays were blaring illuminating strength down on Arthur's skin, regressing his mind into that of a savage animal. Cratos knew he had no choice but to try and bear with the creature until they were on the ground. A small part of him wished his student wouldn't change back as he knew once the night was over and Arthur had his mind return, he would be utterly consumed by guilt. Cratos went over the experience in his head as they continued to drop to the earth gradually. Every time he ran through it, he still couldn't think of a way he could have saved the passengers. Cratos looked down below and saw that the pair would drop in the middle of cold, harsh snowy lands. Given where they were heading, he had a reasonable idea of where they might be. However, Cratos knew he would have to think of a plan quickly; otherwise, he and Arthur would freeze to death.

As the pair hit the ground, the icy winds only worsened their bodies. Cratos released Arthur from his embrace, which prompted the boy to dash

off in a random direction like a charging bull through the snow. Cratos
sighed as he stood up and detached the parachute from his body. He then
saw Arthur's state as the boy continued to run aimlessly in the blistering
storm. He knew how to sort the boy out, and luckily for him, it coexisted
with his means to survive this frozen wasteland. His head moved round
to see if there was anything distinct to head towards in any direction. The
cold winds were blowing straight through their bodies down to the bone,
feeling like they were dipped naked in an icy lake. Even with their Werewolf
DNA, they weren't wholly immune to the elements, and the cold could kill
them quickly if exposed for too long. They had a better chance of survival
than normal humans, but their bodies would eventually give out to the
cold, and they would become frozen corpses. Cratos saw the ground was a
barren sheet of white snow which he couldn't even guess how deep it ran,
but the thickness felt like a solid brick on his feet. There was no wildlife
or signs of vegetation in sight. It felt as though the pair were trapped in a
winter purgatory of endless nothingness. The sky above them was black and
throbbing from the lightning storm that now seemed to pass slightly. There
were fewer lightning flashes and the noise of thunder appearing further
and further away after the bursts of light, which Cratos knew meant the
storm was moving away from the pair. However, with the thunderstorm
passing, they were still stuck with the blind thrashing of the intense windy
snowstorm ever-present. The mountain they had just avoided hitting was
in sight behind Cratos, but he decided not to turn his back as he knew he
would only mourn. Cratos then looked to the sky with his eyes locked on
the moon's shade that had caught Arthur. If he wished, he could utilize the
rays of the moon himself, but with his training, he could ignore the call of
the rays of the moon and remain focused. The white beams rested gently on
Cratos's being as the chilled winds sliced against the pale flesh of his face.
The monster within the depths of his mind was clawing at the barriers of
Cratos's mind. His beast was awoken from its slumber by the moonlight and
raged for release.

Cratos knew this beast well by now. He closed his eyes and slowly allowed
his body to transform. His black fur sprouted from his body, smothering his
hands and face in seconds. His chest and other muscles began to expand,
but his clothes didn't rip. They were specially tailored for this exact thing.
His skull morphed into a black, snarling wolf head with his mouth long
accompanied by several rows of glistening sharp teeth. His transformation
into his complete wolf form finished with his eyes which now boasted the
classic Werewolf bright yellow gleam. He looked up at the minuscule slither
of the moon and crouched slightly. With a sharp but strong inhale, he

howled towards it. The deep bellow of sound charged through the air like a beastly foghorn.

The second Arthur hit the ground, he started dashing off wildly. The voice of the Beast was nothing but a faint whisper in his mind as he thrashed around chaotically. Arthur felt the cold winds racing across his thin, not fully formed fur across his body. He shivered slightly and snarled at the cold as though he could somehow intimidate the weather itself. Arthur had changed direction multiple times, thinking going a different way would solve his problem. He found himself looking for something to eat. Arthur was hungry, and he wanted to feast on something meaty. He remembered not long ago he was in front of plenty of fresh meat, but Arthur didn't eat it then, and he couldn't remember why. Arthur then stopped dead in his tracks. He was on all fours, and Arthur snapped his head around wildly before circling his body, trying to catch the scent of something for his nose to latch on. The cold made him shiver again. His fur provided much protection, and his clothes were now in tattered rags barely hanging onto his body. Halting him in his tracks was the bellowing howl of Cratos several feet away from him. Arthur's instincts instantly recognized the howl as another Werewolf. His senses were snapping him strangely to attention like a trained dog for some reason. He straightened his back and arched his head upward, twisting his neck to face Cratos. His eyes were fixated, and he felt like he was reacting without thinking; it was like that howl alone demanded his unquestionable obedience.

Arthur was now walking on all fours with his shoulders hunched submissively, feeling like he was awaiting orders from Cratos. His head turned as he looked upon the still fully dressed standing upright body of his mentor Cratos in his complete wolf form, looking down upon him with his bright, yellow-crested eyes. The black-furred face of Cratos with only his wolf-morphed hands and blade-length claws bared clearly for Arthur to see, glared intensely at his student. His teacher condensed his throat and growled in a deep underlying tone. However, Strangely enough, the sound of the mere growl is not what Arthur heard. Through Arthur's ears, he heard something beneath the growl.

"Follow me," the sound seemed to say to him. Arthurs' ears pricked up as he understood the words within the sound. Cratos turned his back on Arthur, then knelt slightly and dashed off in the snow. Arthur snapped his legs instantly in Cratos's direction and ran after his teacher, still on all fours as the pair now ran through the twisted snow-ridden wasteland they had fallen within.

The cold winds felt like razor blades whipping against Arthur's face as he dashed off after Cratos. He kept a steady pace behind his teacher, who never slowed his speed for even a moment, running like a speeding car on only two feet. The ground he ran on was bursting all around his body as his limbs pelted the ground with each step. Arthur snapped his head from side to side but saw nothing distinct as they ran. All around them was the storm and snow for miles, like when they had arrived outside Siren's home in the dark. There was nothing but the floor beneath them and the black sky above them as a thrashing blizzard hammered against their bodies every second. Arthur wasn't yet transformed into a fully evolved Werewolf like his teacher, so his small trim of red fur was thinner and only barely shielded him from the freezing weather. His attention was fixated entirely on following his teacher through this frosty land. He had no idea where they were going, and he doubted anything was around for them, especially no shelter. He hoped Cratos could handle this situation despite the trap that was set for them. Arthur felt like he couldn't hold out in the cold for too much longer if his teacher didn't have a plan for them. He also was unsure how long his wolf form would last. The bright moon's glare was still shining through, but the clouds around it could block it away once more, putting Arthur on a timer. The biology behind the wolf stages was still a mystery to him, and Werewolf blood or not in his human form, he would have died by now. He only hoped this form would last for him a bit longer.

The Beast hadn't said a word since Arthur had landed on the ground and remained silent as he began following his mentor. The pair had been running endlessly for what felt like nearly half an hour, Arthur thought. However, with the storm still raging around him, it was difficult to accurately tell any sort of time. Arthur's human senses began to return to his conscious mind as he ran slowly. The adrenalin and danger of being on the plane were running thin as he was now. The Vampires were now far away from him, and he was now able to breathe without a gun pointed in his face or explosives threatening to blow him into tiny pieces. He now feels more like himself even though his physical appearance remains unchanged. His body still adorned its huge extensive muscle change and his minor hair growth with its uncanny red color. His hands and feet were thick with what felt like solid steel-like claws replacing his fingernails several centimeters longer than expected. He felt his long nails dig into the snow as he continued to run on his hands and legs. The thickness of the snow felt nearly frozen solid.

Arthur now had the chance to wonder if this was his wolf transformation.

He had defeated his inner Beast in his mind, which meant he should have the freedom to use his wolf abilities at his will. He still wasn't sure how to change into the wolf by choice yet, but here he was running as a giant red Werewolf nearly twice the size of his previous body, feeling as though he had the strength to rip a person in half. That then made him remember back on the plane with the Vampire flight attendants. He recalled that without blinking, he murdered one of them, as well as the co-pilot, literally biting the man's throat out and retching on his flesh a moment later. He knew his inner beast egged him on at the time, and he had also temporarily lost his senses, meaning he wasn't acting like himself. But oddly enough, Arthur didn't feel guilty about killing the Vampires in such a savage fashion. He instead felt the opposite. Arthur was still enraged after what they did to all those people on the plane. He wished he could kill more of them, a lot more.

Arthur wondered if it was a good feeling to have that sort of instinct. Killing Vampires to protect humans was expected and had any Vampires gotten in his way during his rescue of Cratos, odds are he would have killed them as well. But now, this was a different feeling. He knew that in the middle of a fight to the death, it's either do or die. He had found that taking a life is a lot easier in the moment when you ultimately must. He came to understand that when you're fighting for your life and instinct takes over, it's your hand that makes that choice and not your head. But in the aftermath, when all the fighting has ceased, and it's time for a killer to reflect, Arthur thought he would mourn. Just like he did when Arthur had knocked down Gary that day in school, and he felt guilty for hours, but he still felt no regret despite his reflection.

"Gary hadn't murdered a plane full of innocent people just to kill you," he thought to himself. It made sense, and it was a completely different scenario. In a way, he was fighting to protect the humans and not make himself feel better. His logic calmed the shaken nerves that were sprung up by his sudden blood lust, but it hadn't vanished completely. He thought that he would have to keep an even closer look at himself in the nights to come to make sure that he didn't become the monsters he fought against constantly. On the plane, he wasn't in the frame of mind he is right now; he was a beast. Before Arthur could reflect further, Cratos had stopped running and stood dead still in his tracks. Arthur saw this and slapped his heels and his palms dead in the snow, which caused him to lurch forward and plummet his face into the snow. Cratos looked back over his shoulder at Arthur. His teacher's wolf face saw what happened to Arthur and chuckled slightly.

Pulling his face from the frost, Arthur looked up at his mentor like a startled pup. Cratos was standing upright on both his legs. Arthur saw all his clothes were still completely intact. They weren't in tattered rags like his own, with his night dark fur smothering his face and hands. Cratos growled in a low specific tone to Arthur. Like before, no words were uttered, but Arthur picked up on what his mentor was saying. Before, Cratos growled a command telling him to follow, and with this growl, he said.

"Are you yourself now?" Arthur wasn't sure how to communicate in this manner, so he instead nodded briskly in response, hoping it would suffice. Sighing with relief at Arthurs' answer, Cratos's body slightly began to deflate in its size. The fur that covered his face began to recede into his skin as he reverted to his human form. Through his eyes, it looked as though the hair was just vanishing into nothing. Only if you stuck your eyes up close would you see the fur return inside his skin. His form regressed, and in less than a few seconds, he was his normal-looking mentor once again. He had the same long black hair, a tough-looking face, and black clothes though he was barefoot. Cratos snapped his neck from left to right, and loud cracking noises followed. Cratos smiled down at Arthur, and he spoke loudly against the winds.

"Good to hear. You did well. Are you OK? Feeling alright?" he asked, remembering the bullets that plummeted into his pupil's torso on the plane. Arthur noticed the slight worry in his mentor's tone accompanied by that odd question, and he began to observe himself for anything wrong. His chest did still have the holes from where the bullets struck him. The bleeding had subsided both from the cold and the Werewolf's ability to heal. The pieces of metal seemed to be still embedded within his flesh. Arthur wagered that if it had been the automatic rifles used on the Werewolves at the bar and not some small pistol he had been shot with, he would be dead. He also wondered if his muscles were more resilient than they would have been because of his transformation. Sniffing around himself, he noticed nothing wrong that would prove fatal and looked back to his teacher and nodded quickly again.

"Alright then. Just making sure. We'll double-check when we get to safety and make sure you're patched up properly," Cratos said with a calm smile. Arthur caught a forced smile from his teacher, it looked strained, and his eyes carried a heavy, near unbearable weight of pain behind them. Arthur knew then that Cratos was suffering from their failure on the plane as much as he was. Kneeling, Cratos began to fumble around on the snowy floor. Arthur frowned and watched his teacher silently, not sure what he was doing. After a few more seconds of Cratos's hands digging deep around the snow, they suddenly went still, and a grin raced up the side of his mentor's face.

"Found it!" he declared. Both his arms tensed as he heaved himself backward with all his strength. As he walked back, a sizeable square-like panel of the snowy ground rose backward with him. As it was pulled up, Arthur looked to see it was a hidden passageway with a ladder leading down a long hole just like when the pair had gone to Siren's home. Cratos let the hatch hang in the air on its hinge and waved a hand at Arthur.

"Go on ahead Arthur. I need to close this thing behind me," his teacher said. Arthur nodded, then walked over to the opening and looked over the hole. He turned around and began to put his legs down the ladder, his hands moving down the rungs of the ladder as he began to descend once again into the depths of the earth. Arthur only hoped he was now escaping the perils of the snowstorm outside and the memory of the horrible plane attack behind him.

Arthur traveled down a long ladder again, hoping it didn't take longer than the descent into Siren Glacier's labyrinth of a home. As Cratos slammed the metal opening shut above him and followed down after Arthur himself, the pair were immediately plunged into complete darkness. There weren't even any light beams from the edges of the opening hatch above them. They were sealed entirely in without a single light. Arthur was never scared of the dark, especially not now with his new, improved eyesight, but he couldn't recall the last time he was awake in absolute darkness; not even his handheld right in front of his eyes made any difference in what he could see. Not wishing to seem disturbed to Cratos and look like a scared child Arthur simply closed his eyes and continued downward. He had fought against the inner Beast inside his mind, and after confronting that harrowing embodiment of his greatest mental fears, there was no way he was going to let a slight lack of sight spook him into looking like a scared infant. To his luck, though, this ladder did not go down as far as before in Siren's home.

His feet hit the ground, and Arthur took several steps backward until his back was against a wall. He still couldn't see anything but felt safer with something solid behind him. Now that Arthur could know whatever was behind him, he thought that he only now needed to know what was in front of him. He could hear Cratos shuffling onto the ground a few moments after him sighing with relief.

"So good to be out of that bloody cold!" Cratos exclaimed with forced positivity.

"Now to just find that damn light switch," he chuckled jokingly. His right hand began slapping the sides of the wall around him as Arthur heard him start to shuffle around the walls. Arthur sighed himself with relief. It was good to know that wherever they were, they would have some light in a minute. As Cratos continued to search, Arthur began to feel strange. His stomach was churning slightly and making him feel very nauseous and sickly.

Arthur's head began to feel very heavy, his muscles also feeling like they were being pulled to the ground. His arms dropped by his sides like wet sacks of cement. His torso began to feel like stone, with the sick feeling in his stomach spiraling, causing him to groan loudly. His voice was a mix of his wolf-like growls and oddly slipping back into human-like moans. Without warning, he was leaning back against the wall, positive he was about to throw up. Cratos was saying nothing despite Arthurs' pained cries. He was sure his teacher could hear his moans as his body slumped down to the cold floor beneath him. His hands gently brushed the ground he sat on; it felt ice cold and dusty. He didn't understand what was happening to him. It felt like he had been drugged somehow. He felt like if he could lift any of his limbs, he would panic. If he could say anything other than belching up a horrible moaning feeling like he would vomit up his internal organs, he would call out for help. It was as though suddenly the world's gravity, just by stepping down here, had been doubled. As his head slumped back against the stone wall, he felt his eyelids now growing heavy.

"See you in a bit," Cratos chuckled cheerfully as he continued to look for the switch. Arthur wanted to ask what he meant, suddenly panicking and trying and move, but he couldn't. The sickness felt like a million hissing snakes surging all around his torso with its slithering bile reaching every inch of his body. Arthur felt as though every individual organ inside his body was melting. With one final wretch from his throat, his eyes slammed shut, and he fell into black unconsciousness, lying with an unmovable body in the shadows of some unknown pit under the hailing snowstorm above.

Arthur woke up sitting upright in a comfortable chair. The first thing his eyes saw was the back of an airplane chair in front of him. He turned to his right and saw a small window with nothing on the outside. There was only complete darkness. There weren't any clouds or sky or stars. It was just a seemingly endless black void. He turned away from the window and looked to his left, seeing the other seats on the airplane across from him with regular people sitting in their seats. They were reading books or watching movies as they calmly waited for their journey to continue. No one was in the seat next to him as flight attendants were going up and down the plane, going right past him without stopping. Arthur sat back in his seat and said nothing, staring at the chair in front of him.

"Was it all a dream?" he thought to himself briefly.

"Maybe the Vampires didn't strike. We're all fine. No one is dead because of me." He smiled, wondering where Cratos was and suddenly feeling strangely vulnerable without him. He laid back comfortably in his seat with his mind drifting; he seemed unable to latch his mind into a thought strangely. He never thought to ask Cratos if any of the other cubs would be around his age or anything like that when they got to the Wolf kingdom. His mentor hadn't told him if there were any age restrictions to recruiting new Werewolves. He would ask him that when he got back to his seat, hoping to get a straight answer. Just like always, he felt his teacher would shake his head, or what was most infuriating for Arthur was when he wagged his finger at him like a smug fox and spoke.

"You'll see for yourself." Arthur wondered how long he had been asleep. He doubted it was that long as he didn't feel drowsy or anything. He slightly recalled Cratos mentioned how Werewolves didn't need to sleep very often. He wondered why he had such a strange dream, especially with the Beast within himself coming forth the way it did. He remembered working along with the creature in the dream and how it didn't seem evil at that moment. It acted and spoke to him as though it was on his side and helping him survive. Arthur then chuckled to himself at the ludicrous thought of that monster trying to help him. In his peripheral vision appeared the body of a flight attendant.

"Excuse me, sir, would you like some water," came a polite, sweet voice. Smiling, Arthur turned his head to say no when his smile vanished like a fond memory before him. The flight attendant was leaning over with a plastic cup of water in her hand, her face smiling at him. Arthur looked only a few inches down to see her throat was completely ripped apart. The inside of her entire throat was completely open and bare to the world and in blood chunks and pieces. Her blood was flowing heavily out of the gashed raw wound. It was pumping out her inner red water down her uniform onto the floor by her feet. Several individual droplets were swinging from her collar like falling rubies. The sound of each drop splashing on the floor rang through Arthur's ears. There were multiple thick, burrowed indents on the sides of her eviscerated throat that resembled giant claws. Arthur's eyes shook with horror as he stared deep into the pulsing red torn flesh of the flight attendant's gored vocal cords.

"Is something wrong, sir?" She asked sweetly, her voice not slightly affected by her completely shredded throat.

Arthur began to breathe rapidly, as though he had just woken up in a coffin buried in the ground. The demonic sight in front of him made his eyes spread wide as he pushed himself back into his seat, suddenly finding himself unable to move. His legs suddenly felt dead, and his hands were vice gripped on the armrests of his chair, fusing him in place. Arthur looked through the flight attendant and suddenly realized all the other people in their seats had their eyes dead set straight towards him. Their bodies were suddenly charred. They were blackened, and bloody, and their visible flesh melted from head to toe. One man had his entire torso cracked open with their ribcage on display; behind the ribs were red and black ash organs. They were staring directly at Arthur, their eyes not blinking and all bloodshot with their sockets split and bloody. The sight was horrific. A minute ago, they looked normal, and now these inhuman forms were staring at him hatefully, death smoldering within their pupils. Without saying another word, the flight attendant's head suddenly shot sharply to the left.

The sound of her neck snapping smacked Arthur's ears painfully. Her mangled body immediately slumped to the floor with the water in the cup she had offered, merging with the puddle of blood below her dead body. Her eyes were still open, and her friendly service smile plastered across her face without waning even the slightest. Arthur stared down at the now-dead flight attendant when his attention was once again grabbed by the sight of all the other passengers standing up from their seats, and then they all began to move towards him slowly. The charred crooked passengers stumbled towards him with their arm and leg bones snapping like the flight attendants' necks with each sharp movement. They moved closer and closer, beginning to raise their arms towards Arthur, who was still molded to his seat. Their burnt fingers curled and shook as they grew closer.

Arthur could only watch in stunned fear as the corpses made their way to him. He was trapped, and there was no escape. They would swarm him and tear him to pieces. They hated him. From the two seats in front of him came into sight from the top of the chairs were the upper bodies of two small children. On top of the left chair was a young boy who looked only about eight years old. The right half of his face was utterly obliterated. His skin and flesh either melted or disintegrated, revealing the entire white dry bone of his skull underneath. Arthur saw a black empty eye socket with blood-stained cracks throughout the visible skull. The rest of his poor body was the same as the other passengers. Arthur saw broken bones with horrible, charred skin. To the right was a small girl. Her face melted nearly off entirely. The skin on her face looked like molten plastic, frozen in place before falling off her skull. There were barely a few patches of blonde hair on her head, which was heavily singed and short. Unlike the little boy next to her, both her eyes were firmly within their sockets. They were bloodshot but very much wild with sight, staring straight at Arthur unblinking. Her cold child eyes were dead set on his own. Arthur's breaths became slower and heavy, paralyzing his entire body.

The two children extended their arms towards Arthur, their bones snapping and disjointed at several angles as they came within centimeters from Arthur's face.

"You...killed...us," the little girl cried softly. Her voice was a sharp, twisted whisper, riddled with sorrow and pain. Her words reached Arthur's ear with the tone of a lost and scared infant moaning for its parent, lost and alone. Arthur felt his heart stop in place. The tiger cubs were one thing, but this disfigured little girl blaming him for her death was soul-destroying. She whined slightly before speaking again; her voice was a saddening crater of despair.

"My mummy...my mummy is dead...I want my mummy back..." The girl continued to try and reach forward. The up-close features of her melted face became more visible in Arthur's eyes.

"My mum died next to me," the boy said. His voice possessed an unnervingly calm tone.

"I saw her explode next to me before I died...all of her insides went all over me... it was your fault," he finished with a sudden twist of spite. Arthur had nothing to say back to the two dead children. It was his fault. The Vampires wouldn't have destroyed that plane and its passengers if he hadn't been on it. The blood of all these innocents was on his hands. He gazed around. The other passengers were now also inches from smothering his body.

"You killed us," they all moaned at once. The children and the adults were chanting together in unison. They were all dead and destroyed. Their melted forms were casting the blame for their diseased existence thoroughly upon Arthur. The feeling of panic erupted back into Arthur as they came within, grabbing distance from him. Arthur roared out in terror. But instead of his human voice came the powerful blast of his inner Beast, which roared a harrowing snarl, halting all the passengers completely in place like statues.

The people had stopped moving, and they stopped moaning or even talking now. They were just completely still. Arthur watched them completely motionless, standing in place. Every one of them was neither blinking nor breathing. His breath slowly returned to a regular rate. He was still immensely uncomfortable with how close they were, but now he felt slightly safer. He still stared with inner disgust at the passengers. Not at their appearance but with himself. The guilt of their lives stained his soul unbearably.

"Don't be a fool, boy," whispered the Beast inside him from his mouth. His jaw and tongue began moving on their own without Arthur controlling it. Arthur's face turned back to the window, but he no longer saw his reflection. Instead, the head glaring back at him from his still human body was the massive demonic head of his inner Beast. Arthur felt his own eyes widen with shock, but the Beasts piercing yellow eyes remained strained and focused on Arthur in his seat.

"These humans' deaths are not on your hands. You know who is truly responsible," The Beast spoke again with Arthur's mouth. Its voice was coming from his throat with the look of his long wolf mouth moving in the reflection along with Arthurs' lips. His head swung from the window, and he looked back at the passengers. Their bodies are still statues from the Beast's roar, but their disfigured bodies were so graphically detailed to his eyes. The children's voices from their seats began to return to him, but they were sharply cut off before they could start.

"Listen to me!" the Beast snarled attentively, sensing that Arthur was allowing the voices to distract him again.

"You tried to save them! Don't let their lives destroy your own!" it growled again, even louder than before. Arthur was struggling to believe the Beast. He wanted to, but he was so sure of his guilt. Arthur turned away from the passengers and back to the Beast, whose gaze was a pure embodiment of contempt for Arthur's sad face.

"ENOUGH!" the Beast roared. Even though he felt his limbs remain firmly at his sides without budging, in the reflection, he saw both the Beasts' arms spring upward with his fingers spread and shoot forward towards him. The window of the glass broke entirely in his face as the arms came through the glass. The window shards shot past him in an insane rush as the air suction tried to pull him forward out of the hole. Out from the window's hole, shot two muscular hairy wolf arms with their claws the width and length of butcher knives. Those claws clasped tightly around Arthur's throat. Arthur choked on the hands as the wolf's body slowly emerged out of the rest of the window. Arthur feebly tried to pry the wolf claws off his neck as the nose of his inner wolf slightly connected against Arthur's own. The Beast's yellow eyes watched Arthur struggle against its claws, his own eyes looking back at the Beast. Arthur found his strength had vanished. He felt even too guilty to give the Beast his usual scowl of hatred.

"If you allow yourself to weaken inside as well as outside, you will die! Accept this tragedy as wrong, boy. But also accept it is not your mistake! Focus on something more productive that you can actually do to right this wrong!" the Beast spat into his face viciously. The Beast was failing to mask his anger at Arthur as his growls mixed with his words.

"W... what's...that then?" Arthur asked back, his voice muffled in the choke. The Beast smirked at him before tensing its massive hairy arms.

"Vengeance!" the Beast hissed in response. Before Arthur could respond to that, the Beast roared once again as its body was suddenly sucked backward out of the plane window. However, the Beast did not release his grip and dragged Arthur with him. Arthur found himself ripped out from his seat and forced somehow out through the small window hole of the plane seat. The pair, Arthur, along with his inner Beast, had left the plane filled with the dead and into the darkness of the outside.

CHAPTER TWENTY-FOUR

Arthur's eyes exploded open. His entire body jolted all at once as though he had been electrocuted. His hand instantly went around to his neck as he still had the feeling of the claws of the Beast around his throat like a phantom strangling him still. Arthur immediately jumped to his feet and edged backward sharply until his back was against a firm cold solid wall. His chest was rising at a fast rate through his quick, fearful breaths. He looked down and saw his entire body was covered in sweat. His hands went to his throat again for a final time to first confirm that the claws were gone. Feeling that they were gone and there was no actual damage to his body, Arthur realized he was safe. He gulped, then slightly relaxed, taking in many large breaths as he tried to calm himself down. Arthur then made himself aware of his surroundings. He saw he was in what looked like a prison cell. The space was only a few meters apart. He had been lying on a grey concrete floor with little room to move around in. All around him was solid concrete as he looked around, not just the floor but also the walls and ceiling above him. It was all grey and unscathed. A few blankets folded together in the middle of the floor to form a small bed and a final more oversized blanket that had covered him while he was sleeping. On the wall facing him was a large steel door that looked sealed shut tight with no handle on his side. A strongly lit lightbulb was hanging from the ceiling above his head, giving him more than enough light.

The air around him smelt dusty and reeked like a building site somehow. It was irritating to his senses. He looked over his body. He wasn't wearing a shirt or socks, and his black trousers were ripped to pieces but only around the legs. The waist was intact but had been wretched to its limit. He felt like something was wrong with his body. He felt physically fine, there was no pain, but he thought he was different than he remembered. His well-defined muscles were normal as he looked at them, but they almost looked bigger through his freshly woken-up blurry eyes. Not the size they became when he transformed on the plane but larger, even just a little bit. He scanned his eyes over the rest of his torso and noticed a similar change. While having his nightmare, his entire being seemed to grow a small fraction.

"How long was I sleeping?" Arthur thought, having no idea how this could have happened. He shook his head, knowing Cratos would be able to explain it when he next spoke to him. He slowly sat back down on the blankets, his heart beating much faster, complimented with severe hard thumps from his panicked rush as he then began contemplating his dream.

It wasn't like his normal dreams. Whenever Arthur had dreamed before, the existence he experienced wasn't like everyday life. Not just the fact he would be in different situations, nearly all of which he didn't recognize, but that one he just had seemed like actual reality. Dreams to him always seemed strangely fuzzy, as if Arthur weren't moving correctly. He couldn't recall reacting or feeling any pain if he got hurt. To Arthur, it felt like being a ghost. He thought it was like experiencing some form of reality through a half-human existence. Arthur, however, believed he was himself at the beginning of the dream. He felt that he had just woken up from a dream while having one. He never had that sort of presumption or deductive thinking while dreaming before. The dream where he saw his family and couldn't help them because he was trapped behind an invisible wall as reality around him faded away only for his inner beats to strike him awake. That thought left Arthur frowning, perplexed.

The Beast had appeared on the plane with him as well. Its roar halted the dead passengers from swarming him. For some reason, when it spoke to him, it tried to ease his guilt and ripped him out of the plane. The Beast only appeared once everything had dissolved around him in his dream of home and then slapped him awake. Even Delfer himself said after explaining when Arthur was on the van, and the Beast took over, how shocked he was that the Beast gave his body back to him. Siren herself thought that whatever was wrong with him was incredibly rare. Arthur knew the Beast within himself had an agenda of its own that seemed to go beyond just acquiring Arthur's body. The way it acted as though it was his ally, he guessed there must be something else it wasn't saying to him.

Arthurs' train of thought was interrupted by several knocks on the large metal door. The door didn't budge an inch after the echo of the knocks died away, and Arthur was left in silence staring at the door for a moment. He figured he had to answer back in some way, so he stood up on his feet and walked to the door. On closer inspection, Arthur noticed that the exit was several inches of thick steel from the gaps around the edge. He helped up his hand in a fist and knocked it back three times. There was no reply for a few seconds, and Arthur wondered if he had just been hearing things. Then just like the door of the Werewolf bar, Arthur heard multiple clicks of locks unfastening. He took a few steps back in case the door swung open on his side of the room. The clicking sounded ceased as the door slowly began to open. The figure of his mentor was revealed to Arthur in the light above him. Cratos was staring uncertainly at Arthur.

"Are you OK?" was the first thing his teacher had asked. His tone was warm and calm like he was trying to soothe a stray dog he had just found. Arthur looked behind Cratos and saw a narrow hallway. The walls along it were the same Grey concrete as inside his room, with several bulbs going down the hall lighting the way. The scent of raw dust and dirt was still alive in the air around him as though he was back in that warehouse; he fought the Vampires with Cratos before. The now glowering presence of his mentor Cratos was still staring down at him uncertainly like he wasn't sure Arthur was completely present with him. So as not to trigger a bad reaction, his face was stone solid in a neutral expression.

Arthur stared up at his teacher. He was not sure if the man was angry with him or not. He took several steps forward until he and Arthur were face to face. Cratos was still saying nothing. Out of nowhere, Arthur felt tears begin to well in his eyes as he stared at his mentor's unblinking stare. The passengers on the plane had all died. The thought of that just by looking at the rock expression of his teacher struck him like the highest note on a piano. He remembered their screams as they ran and how they had to jump out of the plane to safety. But all the innocent people died from the explosion. Tears flowed down Arthurs' face as his shoulders began to shake, struggling to keep his feelings inside. However, that feeble crumbling wall preventing him from breaking down was shattered as Cratos opened his arms to Arthur to invite comfort. Unable to hold back, Arthur burst into a hysterical cry as he hugged his teacher and friend Cratos Mane. Arthur was crying now like a normal person of his age. Any pretense of acting like a powerful Werewolf capable of handling anything had dissolved, and he was now mourning the lives that were murdered because of him. He thought of all the families he knew would be stricken with misery. The thoughts of all the widows created and children orphaned. Arthur cried aloud and ridiculously hard. It didn't matter what the Beast within had told him. The reason his nightmare had felt so real was that he blamed himself, and that was a shame he would be carrying for a long time. Cratos embraced his student and let him cry his pain away. Cratos understood more than Arthur would ever know how he felt, but he also held Arthur firm because he knew this was just the first of many innocent casualties Arthur would have to bear witness in his long war against the Vampires. Compared to what Cratos knew of the bloodsucker's capability, that plane was a drop in a vast ocean of blood.

Arthur recovered from his crying after several minutes. His teacher said nothing to him after he stopped. Cratos simply just offered Arthur a piece of cloth to dry his eyes before gesturing down the hallway for him to follow. The pair then exited the holding room Arthur awoke from and began walking through this strange underground complex. The only sound that echoed through the enclosed space was the sound of Cratos's boots slapping the cold stone floor as they walked. Despite his tears ceasing, Arthur still felt riddled with blame. His stomach was a panicked writhing chasm of guilt, making him nearly throw up. He remembered feeling bad when he was a transformed Werewolf, but the feeling was nowhere near this level. His animal instincts forced a reduction of his pain to keep him focused and conscious but not fully comprehending the situation. Now he was back to normal, awake, and aware of everything he had done and especially caused. He knew that he had to try and harden himself because if Arthur let it overwhelm him again, he would just burst into tears once more. Arthur never thought death would hit him this hard. After years of watching films with people dying, he didn't know it would be so horrible to be around in real life. Even the main hero in the movie would spend only a few moments feeling bad and then move on without blinking to continue onto what was important ahead. While he knew he needed to now focus on his training ahead, he couldn't shake it off so quickly. It wasn't like a heavy coat he could simply pull off and hang up. This guilt felt more like his skin had absorbed liquid steel, then it suddenly turned solid on the inside, forcing him to keep dragging around the weight endlessly. All the Werewolves had probably suffered in their lives with their endless fighting as well as seeing plenty of innocent people die. Arthur knew innocent lives were lost as a result of their failure on the plane. But despite that, Arthur knew they had to continue fighting. That they needed to grit their teeth and hold back the tears because deep down inside, Arthur knew that he would have to be stronger than his pain if he was able to keep going. That If he allowed his sense of guilt to cripple him inside, then not only would the Vampires win, but he would just wallow in his misery for the rest of his life. Breathing in sharply, Arthur raised his head high to try and act stronger than he honestly felt. He made his eyes focus and his stare determined, walking on forward with Cratos.

Arthur desperately wanted to work past what had happened and fight on as a creature of strength that doesn't let tragedy defeat him but evolves him.

"Cratos," Arthur finally spoke, his voice ordinary and controlled. Cratos looked over his shoulder and noticed the relatively sudden change of composure from his student. Cratos assumed that his pupil would be stricken with his grief for much longer, and he had planned to work Arthur through these feelings if he needed any help. But Arthur was now looking like he was ready for another fight after such a brief time. He hoped the boy wasn't burying his feelings as that would just cause him further agony the longer he pretended to be ok. Cratos then decided he wouldn't prompt Arthur about it as that would just cause Arthur to deflect defensively. He hoped Arthur knew that if there was anything he wanted to talk about, he could come to him when ready.

"What is it?" Cratos replied casually, as though nothing was wrong.

"Where are we? I hardly remember anything after we left the plane," he asked. Cratos raised an arm and gestured around the enclosed hallway they were walking around.

"This is one of the Werewolves' many safehouses we have secluded throughout the world. This one is currently unoccupied now, and we will rest up until we are ready to resume our travels." Arthur looked around and hummed as they walked.

"How are we going to carry on? We're trapped in a frozen wasteland," Cratos sighed impatiently.

"I do sometimes wish you would take a moment to think before speaking," he muttered, annoyed. Arthur, however, only shrugged at his teacher's exasperation. Sighing purposely loudly, Cratos answered Arthur begrudgingly. Despite sensing his teachers' frustration, Arthur knew if he had never asked any questions, no matter how dumb they sounded, then Cratos would tell him next to nothing.

"All of the bases have a distress signal we can send out in case of emergency. We have to report this incident as well and get ourselves transportation to the Wolf kingdom." Arthur nodded as he understood.

"Will we be in trouble for not being able to save the plane?" he asked. His teacher didn't answer straight away. He thought for a second with a frown burrowing down his face.

"Probably not," he murmured in an almost judging way.

"Sadly, events like this happen a lot. Some things are just out of our hands, and it is not labeled our fault if we have done our best to prevent them. Still, though, best not to bring it up to others unless directly asked. It is hardly a tale to be proud of." Arthur nodded once again. He doubted he would ever want to tell others about what had happened. He just wanted to move past this tragedy as fast as he could, and the last thing he needed was people constantly bringing it up to him.

"So where are we going now then?" Arthur asked in a follow-up.

"To do some training while we wait for the reinforcements to arrive," Cratos answered firmly. That piqued Arthur's curiosity.

"What sort of training, more tests?" he asked, but Cratos sharply shook his head.

"No, the tests before were a matter of preparing you mentally. After the incident on the plane, it's time you were given a quick crash course in other affairs vital for self-preservation." The pair came to the end of the hallways to be met by another door, the same as the first one in the underground stronghold. Cratos swiftly opened it, and the pair stepped through, out of the hallway, and onward to whatever was ahead of him next. Arthur thought about what this next step with Cratos could be, but if it could mean he would never repeat what happened on the plane, he would give it his all no matter how hard it was.

Cratos's fist sharply connected with Arthur's jaw delivering a powerful strike. His mentor then held his pose like a frozen statue with his arm stuck out with it bent slightly at the elbow. Arthur himself flew backward through the air smacking against the cold gray concrete wall behind him from the power of the punch. Luckily, none of his bones didn't break. Arthur knew precisely how strong Cratos could be; he knew that his teacher was holding back his power immensely and distributed his strikes in controlled doses so that he didn't just outright kill Arthur. Though neither did that mean they were feather-soft punches either. The lower half of Arthur's jaw was now feeling numb and slowly beginning to swell. His body slumped down against the wall like a dropped sack onto the floor. Arthur could do nothing else but cough as he inhaled the air back into his body. They had been at this for an hour now. They had entered this empty room with a vast amount of space, and Cratos simply instructed Arthur to attack him. He said nothing else except for that one simple command. Cratos said just to attack him, and since they started, his teacher had blocked every one of Arthurs' strikes and then sharply countered him before Arthur even had the chance to blink. He didn't need to look under his clothes to check his condition because he could feel every bruised part of his body that had been used as a punching bag by his teacher.

"Rise," Cratos said to Arthur with emotionless authority. Each time Arthur fell and paused before standing back up to attack again, Cratos always said the same thing. He gave no words of encouragement or criticism on his technique. Cratos just said that single word to Arthur, and he would say nothing else. Arthur was breathing heavily with exhaustion as he struggled to stay conscious. He was drenched in sweat all over his body while clenching his teeth against the pain in his now throbbing jaw. Arthur moved his tongue around the inside of his mouth, checking to see if any of his teeth were loose. Luckily, they were all fine, for now. Arthur raised his head as he struggled to move to his hands and knees. He kept his eyes squinting at Cratos, who was only returning Arthurs' look as he patiently waited for his student to stand up properly once again. Cratos's gaze was unyielding and cold. Arthur couldn't explain it, but something about that look made Arthur want to punch it straight off his face. It wasn't a look of hatred, but something through its features that made his blood boil. He had never seen Cratos give him that look since they met; however, since they started this training session, it was as though his teacher was treating Arthur like he had just killed his childhood pet in front of him.

"Rise!" he repeated sharply. The mere sound of that word now felt like a drilling poison in Arthur's ears. He tensed his arm muscles in anger. He was feeling a hazy mist cover his eyes like it had done so in the past when he couldn't contain his rage. Arthur breathed heavily and tried to remain in control of himself. He knew if he just lashed out like a child having a tantrum, then Cratos could probably one-shot him to the floor again. His chest began to grow heavy. He was suddenly much more aware of the pain in his arms and legs like they were pleading for him to just drop to the floor and give up. But Arthur refused to listen; he couldn't. Rolling over on the floor and surrendering was something the old Arthur Thorn would have done. Giving up was something he did every time bullies outmatched him. So, seizing all his strength, Arthur struggled to his feet. His knees were shaking as his torso slowly rose. His left knee rose into the air in front of him until he was now kneeling. With beads of sweat pouring past his eyes, his body trembled with every effort and struggled further as Arthur didn't stop moving. Little by little, his body slowly rose into the air and back onto his feet with his arms rising shakily. He then held them out in front of him, slowly clenching his fists. Arthur held his head up straight and locked his eyes onto Cratos's cruel gaze. Arthur then clenched his fists even tighter and tensed his arms as brutally as he could. The entire top half of his body felt like a battered stone statue that was brittle and chipped but still standing. Cratos said nothing as his student stood there with his body shaking from exhaustion and injury. Arthurs' stare was as solid as steel and unblinking as his face continued to redden and bruise from attacks. His hair was drenched with his sweat hanging down over his face like dead seaweed.

As Cratos observed his student, he knew full well how much his 'rise' line had been annoying Arthur immensely. He wanted to provoke one last burst of reaction from Arthur before giving the boy a break. Cratos inhaled deeply and smirked. He saw his students' lips curl with now blind fury because he felt like Cratos was mocking him. To put a cherry on top of that cake of rage, Cratos sharply winked at Arthur with his left eye. Arthur didn't go into his wolf form, but it seemed as though his eyes went completely white with pure wrath following that gesture. Arthur then forgot all pretense of caution and strategy as he then surged forward like a red charging train.

Cratos didn't judge his student for his impulse. It was a common thing for the Crimson class. He knew they were the front-line force for the Werewolf race and known for going berserk in battle. Cratos had done his best to try and steer Arthur's way of thinking to the Shadow side of strategy. For the most part, he had been successful. He was molding Arthurs' mind with test after test to make him a careful and calculating strategist. He remembered watching his student's progress as he hunted the tiger and how he kept a level head on the plane when they discovered the Vampires. Cratos knew he couldn't completely change the boy's nature. He knew Arthur was naturally hot-headed and easily angered. There is no changing someone's natural state. But with these tests, he merely hoped he could create a student with a strong feeling of self-belief so he wouldn't have to think that fighting like an animal was his only solution to problems. He knew there would be lapses in his senses, and this right here and now was going to be an example. There would be plenty of brutal battles ahead for Arthur, and Cratos didn't want to be around still to see his student die. So, he would train him now and train him hard. Cratos knew he would always push Arthur to his limits and closely observe him as Arthur went past them every time. It was on that night the two had first met that he sensed something incredible within Arthur. No ordinary boy would lunge headfirst toward a Vampire trying to kill them. Repeatedly, Arthur displayed acts of unreal courage and strength. If such potential weren't nurtured, it would only be a waste to the world.

The roaring Arthur came a meter away before he slashed wildly and aimlessly at Cratos. His arms were thrashing in every direction with his hands wrenched into claws plunging forward at his mentor's face. However, Cratos was in firm control of the situation. The way Arthur was injured, this would be his final charge before collapsing. Cratos remained calm and calculated the situation. His body snapped from side to side as each hit was dodged in the blink of an eye. His expression was uninterested and bored as Arthur relentlessly attacked. As the attack continued, Cratos happily remained within Arthur's reach, waiting for the right opportunity. Cratos also noticed the distinct difference in his student's body mass as he attacked. He knew it was due to his transformation on the plane. Arthur was going through the stages, and this minor increase in his muscle mass was just the first of many alterations to his physical form. Despite having larger muscles than before, Arthur had not grown much faster with his punches, and one of the first lessons Cratos had instructed in his combat training was that a fast strike will always hit harder than a strong strike. Arthur, lost in rage, continued slashing his hands towards Cratos with futile fury. His precision was sloppy and unfocused. Arthur was striking as though there were four of Cratos lined up next to each other, and he was trying to kill all of them. Cratos could tell he was reaching his limit due to being both injured and overtired. Cratos decided this would be enough fighting for now. Arthur swung his left arm back like a master archer aiming his shot before immediately shooting it forward like a fired bullet.

Cratos didn't even flinch. He ducked his head downward instantly in a flash that looked to an ordinary human's eyes as a blur. Before Arthur could react to his missed strike, Cratos clenched his hand into a fish and shot it upward, arm fully extended with his knuckles striking the bottom of Arthur's chin. A deafening cracking noise echoed through both their ears as Arthur flew into the air. Cratos and Arthur launched into the air high towards the ceiling. Arthur's body was bending backward with his eyes closed, struck unconscious before he was even an inch off the ground. Maintaining his balance as his body glided upward like a fired rocket from his uppercut strike, Cratos simply drifted a few inches backward from his knocked-out student before he landed back on the floor with both feet. Arthur fell to the floor with a heavy slam. He wasn't even twitching as he hit the floor because he was knocked out cold. Cratos casually walked over and observed Arthur, making sure he wasn't too damaged. With his Werewolf healing ability, he knew his student would recover from anything broken, so a few fractures or snapped bones weren't a big issue. This observation was especially true while Arthur was going through the stages because his Werewolf fast recovery ability would spike constantly. Cratos noticed a small amount of blood seeping through the cracks of his mouth and forming around his body on the ground below his head. Closing his eyes and focusing, Cratos could still hear the breaths of his unconscious body and knew he would be ok. Cratos then reopened his eyes and chuckled at his unconscious student.

"One session down," Cratos muttered pleasantly underneath his breath towards Arthur.

"With plenty more to go!" he finished smirking before picking up his student and carrying him away to sleep off the fight in the holding room he had woken up in before.

Arthurs' skull was pounding as reality returned to him. He felt as though someone was banging pots together right next to his eardrums at the same time an earthquake was raging all around him. The pain caused him to wince and tense his body. Then the absolute agony struck him like an unforgiving burst of flame. Every fiber of his being was straining from even the slightest twitch. He had woken up to his body aching before from training in the wilds with Cratos, but he had never woken up to this kind of agony previously. Even when the van had exploded in the city, and he woke up to Delfer, he could barely move, but this feeling was like his every nerve had been torn apart somehow. His jaw especially felt like it had been put back together piece by piece with glue-like a shattered window. He attempted to remain as still as a statue. His breathing was seemingly the only thing that didn't set off the chain reaction of his fight's aftermath. Arthur then thought about what had happened, and he recalled his recent training with Cratos. It had been ruthless. He didn't even remember landing a single punch on his mentor. Cratos had effortlessly blocked or dodged every strike thrown at him, and he had then countered Arthur with strikes that felt like he was being hit by an iron statue come to life. Arthur exhaled that last thought heavily. An experienced and trained warrior like Cratos Mane would never have fought Arthur at his full strength, and if he had, Arthur would be dead five times over. Arthur figured his teacher must have been ashamed of his poor performance. Even though he had managed to track and kill a tiger, he couldn't even strike Cratos once. The last thing he could remember about their training was feeling almost fatally exhausted. Cratos had utterly flattened him, and he was growing more enraged by the second in the fight. Then his teacher did something that simply pushed him over the edge. After that happened, his memory was blank. Arthur felt that it was just the first fight of many battles before the rest of the Werewolves would rescue them from the frozen wasteland they were hiding in. Arthur knew if he was going to meet his teacher's expectations, he needed to show more promise. Arthur would need to hit faster and harder, and if he didn't, Arthur feared his teacher would not bother to keep training him.

"Perhaps then I can be of assistance, hmm?" suddenly muttered the growling voice of the inner Beast from inside his head.

"Go away," Arthur snorted back. He was in no mood to speak to his Beast while recovering in agony. Though he knew that even if he could move his body, it wasn't like he could storm off from his own mind.

"I will handle this myself, thank you!" Arthur said proudly. The Beast only chuckled inside his head. The sound of its deep cackles rattling inside his mind drove Arthur into a quick rage.

"Yeah, because I haven't helped in the slightest this whole time, am I right?" the Beast replied with smug sarcasm. Arthur rolled his eyes. He was expecting his inner Beast to make quick work of mentioning its appearance from the plane when they next spoke. The Beast itself said it would be involved more ever since he was told he saved Arthur on the Vampire's van.

"So what? It wasn't completely selfless. You said so yourself. You're only preserving this body for yourself. You don't care about me," Arthur spat spitefully in reply. Sarcasm turned quickly in exhaustion as the Beast then sighed.

"One of these days, you'll have to trust me, you know," it muttered quietly.

"I didn't have to pull you out of that nightmare before, but it would have seriously scarred you had It continued." That mention made Arthur's eyes widen. He once again tensed his body, causing him to gasp out in pain. He had almost forgotten about his dream of the plane. He recalled the nightmare he had with the dead passengers returning to blame him and then tear him apart. He remembered their burnt faces and the mutilated, charred children. The Beast had appeared in the plane window and ripped him away from it, causing him to wake up.

"Why then? Why help me? Do you want my body for yourself or not?" Arthur challenged. The Beast was silent for several seconds as Arthur eagerly awaited an answer. This question was something he had been curious about ever since Siren diagnosed him in her lab. She said he was somehow a different kind of Werewolf. She had confirmed to him that something was undoubtedly abnormal about the Beast's behavior. Even Cratos and Delfer found the way it acted strange and unnatural from other cubs in their training. From when it took over to the most unbelievable part about the Beast giving his body back to him.

"Yes, I do," it finally admitted blandly before continuing before Arthur could snap angrily.

"But not the way it is," he added scornfully. Arthur's lip curled, and his teeth clenched, but he said nothing in response for the moment.

"Right now, it is weak. You are weak. Mentally and physically, and you still do not understand who or what you truly are." That last bit struck a nerve with Arthur.

"What do you mean?," he inquired, but the Beast didn't respond to him. At that last question, the Beast fell silent and didn't speak any further, leaving Arthur alone once again.

Arthur's training with Cratos commenced again the following day after Arthur was back to his full strength.

"I could get used to this super-fast healing," Arthur boasted as he flexed his arms and grinned at the lack of pain after his rest. Cratos said nothing in response. He and Arthur ate food silently before starting their next session once again. The strange bunker base they were hiding within was well stocked with canned food that didn't expire for years to come. It always was well stocked with clean water kept cold and drinkable. It also had a ventilation system with air grates all over the complex that, if Cratos wished, could also warm the base. However, Cratos never seemed to bother putting the heat on, and Arthur had a feeling he wouldn't put it on if he asked. Cratos had said there was a power generator that kept the lighting and other devices powered. He also explained that these generators were only maintained a few times a year.

"Not the most sought-after job in our world. If you ever decide to transfer from the front lines and become an engineer for the Werewolves, don't piss off your boss, or they'll put you on maintenance rotation for a year," his teacher had warned when he explained the complex. Arthur nodded, but he had no interest in that kind of work, he thought and continued to eat the food Cratos had prepared for them. He oddly found himself devouring can after can of nutritious food, sometimes meat, sometimes vegetables, with his appetite unending. Arthur had even eaten more than Cratos did during their mealtimes. Arthur hadn't explored the entire facility yet, and his nearly always present teacher hadn't given him a chance. He was already more than familiar with the room he had first woken up in because it was there that he would rest and sleep after his training. There was also the room at the end of the hallway Cratos was leading him to. That room was just a simple room filled with boxes of different assorted supplies. There were several doors around that room, but he had only been through the far one to the left, which led to the room they did their training in and one next to it was a bathroom where he washed and took care of his other bodily needs. Cratos said the other rooms were none of his concern but that only made his curiosity stronger. The canned food wasn't too bad tasting either. At first, he was hesitant as Cratos prepared each of his meals for him out of sight in a different room Cratos had said was minimal cooking facilities, but there was a good assortment of other foods to enjoy. There were plenty of assorted meats, vegetables, and carbohydrates. It was all plenty enough to keep his body ticking as they continued to train. As Arthur downed another bottle of water, he calmly reflected on how much he missed other drinks he used to enjoy as a human. Since joining Cratos, the only liquids he had consumed was water or the odd juice from fruits. Arthur used to have a solid sweet tooth like an average human, and he missed fizzy drinks and sweets immensely. Arthur then made a mental note to himself. He decided that the first chance he got a little freedom in a regular city without supervision, he would separate from others and indulge in junk food.

Arthurs' training this time was a little more concentrated than before. Cratos ran him through a couple of punching techniques as well as a few blocks for him to use. Arthur tested them repeatedly and continuously for the first few hours. The endless repetition was agonizingly dull. He had to move or block multiple different angled strikes. This system continued until Cratos was satisfied with Arthurs' competency of the moves. After that, he was only then allowed to put the actions himself into practice. Cratos didn't explain why he was forced to go over the same move a hundred times each, but Arthur didn't challenge or criticize his teacher and went about his training with his expected focus. Cratos had not let him down before, so he wouldn't begin questioning him now. So, for now, Arthur gritted his teeth and continued to try and focus on what he was doing, repeatedly without any end in sight.

This time in their sparring match Cratos was on the offensive rather than before when he would just counter Arthur's attacks. He didn't warn Arthur when he was going to attack or what attack he would use. Instead, Cratos would just lunge at Arthur and expect him to react. Before Arthur could even blink, his mentor disappeared from his sight quickly and then instantly reappeared in front of him. His right arm held out by his side, bending as his fist swung inward for a right hook strike to the side of Arthur's head. In an instant, without Arthur's knowledge or even having to think, his left arm shot up and curled behind him. Now the bulk of his arm was making a shield covering the left side of his skull from the attack. Cratos's fist struck the side of his arm, knocking Arthur aside mildly, but his skull remained untouched by the strike. Arthur flinched slightly at the strike, it only stung a little bit on the muscle of his arm, and he wasn't knocked off his feet like the punches his teacher was throwing in their last session. Taking the strike in stride, Arthur then whirled to face his teacher and darted forward, bringing his left arm down and throwing it forward, remembering the technique Cratos had shown him. He didn't wholly stick his arm out entirely and kept it lightly bent at the elbow, leaving it loose and only tensed his muscles upon impact with his target. Cratos saw the punch heading toward him, so he reacted by slapping its side with his right hand, causing Arthur to redirect his attack and hurl himself forward with his right shoulder for a backup. However, Cratos also saw this and quickly turned his body to the side, dodging the attack, then he slammed his whole being against Arthur, knocking him to the floor. Though Arthur had hit the ground with a rough crash, he recovered quickly by rolling away as he landed. Arthur then jumped to his feet and leaped backward to gain some distance from Cratos to plan his next move. Arthur had a feeling that now he knew how to defend himself and fight back, his teacher wouldn't ease up in the slightest. If he didn't stay sharp, he could get seriously hurt.

Cratos ran forward rather than vanishing out of sight this time. Luckily, Arthur had a series of new movements he was looking forward to trying. Cratos held his arms out in front of him at equal positions, flying punches out with insane speed toward Arthur. Having no other option given their speed, Arthur threw up his arms with his forearms facing Cratos held close together. The punches were beating hard against Arthur's skin, feeling as though the hardness of Cratos's knuckles would quickly begin to tear through his flesh if he didn't act fast. Arthur couldn't help but be pushed backward on foot as Cratos fired his barrage of punches at Arthur's sturdy arm guard, which quickly became weaker with every strike. Arthur couldn't even see Cratos's arms as he threw them forward. His punches were just a blur of movement. Though Arthur couldn't see the fists, he felt every single solitary strike that hit him. Each one sent powerful radiations of force through his entire body to the point his arms began to feel numb. Arthur was closing in against the room wall, and he knew that letting himself become cornered could be his defeat. Arthur, however, couldn't help it even if he wanted to because Cratos was utterly overwhelming him. The urge to panic was taking over Arthur's senses.

Then suddenly, like the sound of a large dry branch snapping from deep within his mind, Arthur's eyes became a thick blanket of white. He roared at the top of his lungs, his usual human scream running several seconds through the air before it turned sharply and deafeningly into his beast's bellow. With fierce anger and rage, Arthur threw his arms apart, exposing his torso openly as Cratos fists plunged forward with nothing in their way now. Both Cratos's right and left fists struck with intense force against Arthur's face. The left fist struck his cheek, and the right connected with his lower jaw. The cracking sounds of his skull crumbling into pieces beneath his teacher's fists broke through the air like brittle glass falling onto a floor. Arthur didn't even flinch as the lower part of his skull felt like it had turned into wood chips. His mouth was now hanging open as veins along his neck and face bulged out thickly like rising angry pythons. Cratos's held his hands in place in Arthur's face. He was shocked that Arthur dropped his guard and let him strike him. Before he could read what his pupil was going to do, Arthur's arms swung inward. Then his hands wrenched on both sides of Cratos's neck like a bear trap. Cratos was taller than Arthur, so he managed to get Cratos to step within his reach for his hands to strike close. Arthurs' arm muscles slowly swelled in size as Arthur tightened his grip on Cratos's throat. He squeezed his teacher's neck and pulled him down towards him, so the pair were face to face. Foam began to excrete from the sides of Arthur's open-slacked mouth as shiny red hairs started to sprout from his face as he throttled him. Cratos gritted his teeth against the vice grip of his student and sharply latched his own hands onto his student's wrists, trying to pry them loose.

However, Arthur was hanging on as though his life depended on it. Arthur's body continued to change in size, with red hairs appearing from his pale skin being quickly joined by thousands of others forming into a blood-red colored coat of fur. His legs began to grow in both widths of muscle and height as his torso was heaving outward into a vast, mighty shape of pure domination. Cratos realized that Arthur had lost control and tapped into his Crimson class specialty. It was the Berserker trance. Cratos knew that his student would unintentionally kill him if he didn't fight back to his fullest abilities. Cratos attempted to take in a vital breath of air as best as possible with his windpipe being crushed. Then in a struggled heave, he growled deeply as his face quickly sprouted black hair. His face was quickly morphing into his wolf form to fight against Arthur's.

CHAPTER TWENTY-FIVE

Cratos kept a close eye on his student's progression as he first entered the stages of being a Werewolf. The first sign of his inner Werewolf coming through was that night in the jungle when he fought against the vines. The second sign was during Arthurs' fight with the tiger. When Cratos was told about what happened with the police in the city, Arthur's development then came into an unsettling question. Cratos saw that Arthur was progressing unusually quickly. It was much faster than others his age. Though every person progressed with tiny individual differences, Cratos knew from speaking with Siren that in all his years as a Werewolf, how much of a difference in a Werewolf's development depended on the person and how their body assimilated the wolf genes into their system. So, when Siren told Cratos that Arthur would be fine despite his inner Beast acting in ways impossible for someone within their stage, he had left it at that. That was until he changed on the plane. When a cub is going through the stages, the moonlight severely affects the body and mind, and it was never an exact science on how much it would alter them. Some cubs find themselves running around the woods naked until morning, and some feast without pause until they pass out. Arthur, however, had changed nearly entirely into a fully-fledged wolf transformation. He had entered a mid-way state that he wasn't supposed to go into until halfway through his training. Not to mention current strength and abilities were more advanced in that state. He didn't understand how this was possible. Even for an exceptional cub, he almost didn't believe it was some abnormality in his blood, but he didn't dare question Siren. At least he wouldn't question her for now.

This new development had now become a different situation entirely. From Cratos's vision, it was as though Arthur was going further than before when the moonlight had hit him on the plane. The red fur of a Crimson class Werewolf was more apparent and vibrant here than previously on the plane and in the snowy wastelands where they landed. It wasn't as long or thick as a fully transformed Werewolf, but it was thicker and nearly resembled a full coat. It seemed now that his student was between halfway and a fully complete Werewolf, and he had achieved this form without the moon's gleaming glow upon his skin. This new form was not entirely without reason either. This form, as Cratos knew, was also the first instance of Arthur entering a known mental existence for Crimson class Werewolves referred to as the Berserker trance. Cratos knew that because the Crimson class was primarily the front-line fighters of the Werewolf race, they were the ones to take the heaviest damage. This case was especially true now in the modern age of advanced weaponry. The Berserker trance allowed a Crimson class Werewolf not only to ignore any physical pain that is inflicted upon them, but it also maxed out their strength to its full potential. The only drawback was that this trance put any Werewolf around them in danger of being ripped apart from those in the mindset, as they would struggle to differentiate friend from foe in their killing frenzy. The Berserker trance is taught to be a last resort to use in the last man standing situation. Though Cratos knew all he had to do was knock Arthur out cold, and he would wake up completely fine. This fight was the first time Arthur had entered the Berserker trance, so Cratos wouldn't give Arthur any more chances to fight and now planned to end this quickly. Regrettably, in Cratos's mind, he now had to be extremely tough on his poor student.

Cratos's transformation into his black-furred wolf form was nearly instantaneous. His skull structure morphed into its standard wolf head as quick as a blink, and his body arched and grew in its size, typically at a similar speed. Cratos also grew taller, which strained Arthur's grip and dominant position on him too. Within a few seconds, the last of his fur coat was fully developed, and his yellow-eyed piercing Shadow class wolf form was born in full view against Arthur. In his form, he was now within the vice grips of his students' near-complete Crimson class form. Arthur didn't loosen his grasp throughout his teacher's transformation, even as he felt his mentor's throat swell and grow tougher within his claws. The sudden natural pushback in defiance against his strength only encouraged Arthur to squeeze harder. Thoughtless rage was flying through his mind like blood through his veins. Bearing the black fur of the shadow class, Cratos roared out at Arthur. His Werewolf howls rang down the boys' ears. As Cratos thought, the screech caused Arthur to wince in pain, which made his grip loosen for a moment, but that was all Cratos needed. Cratos's arms shot upward with a sudden swipe, slapping away Arthur's hands, leaving his body wide open. With that advantage now before him, Cratos immediately jumped backward through the air, giving himself some distance from any attacks by Arthur's raw strength. The power of even his simple back-jump landed Cratos against the wall on the other side of the room.

It took only moments for Arthur to regain himself and see now that his opponent had slipped out of his strangling embrace and fled across the room. With no pause for thought or planning, Arthur roared back at his teacher with a deafening snarl of fury. The pain from Cratos's roar was still present in his ears and only fed his growing wrathful warpath. Cratos lowered his legs slightly and turned his body, facing sideways. He then held his right arm out in front of him and his left closer inward, stopping just under his chin. Cratos then waited, readying himself for Arthur's imminent attack. Like a charging bull in a vast arena, Arthur dashed forward roaring. His overgrown legs were propelling him quickly and heavily towards Cratos. His arms were held outward with his hands spread into open claws, ready to tear and rip.

Cratos remained calm and entirely still as Arthur approached. Cratos observed Arthur closely as he stampeded forward without pause. Arthur was only inches away from eviscerating Cratos's being as his teacher immediately ducked down in another blur of speed and agility, which was immediately followed by Cratos twisting his body sharply before stabbing his knee fatally into Arthur's stomach. With the added force of his student's charge forward, Cratos tensed his body with an intense effort to remain stable as he felt his kneecap bury itself deep within the thick iron-strong layer of Arthur's abdomen. Arthurs' eyes bulged with surprise. His body from the neck down suddenly stood still, like a statue. Arthurs' mouth then hung open while he struggled to take in breaths of air as his body began to shake from the shock. He felt as though he was just stabbed in his stomach by a large blade. The edge of Cratos's knee was deeply buried within the bowels of his gut. Both were utterly still for a moment as though they were each frozen in time. Cratos held his position expertly. He was balanced firmly on his one leg with precise poise. He was bent down below with his body twisted diagonally and his knee still pressed against his student's stomach, using Arthur's weight to keep him steady. Then as a moment passed between them with no warning, Arthur's hands clenched into fists, and his left hand swung down upon his mentor. The front of his knuckles collided powerfully with the top of Cratos's skull.

"Impossible!" Cratos thought to himself as his entire body was sent to the ground like a dropped sack of bricks. A powerful ringing spluttered through his skull from the impact of his student's surprise punch, causing him to lose consciousness for a split second. He heard Arthur's body heave a pained inhalation of air as Cratos also hit the cold ground. Arthur raised his right hand to go for a second punch while Cratos was on the floor. Reacting quickly, Cratos rolled his body to the left of Arthur, quickly gaining distance as his student's strike embedded itself deep into the grey, hard concrete floor. Its surface cracked and broke sharply as Arthurs' fist buried into the surface. With barely any reaction to what was now probably a few broken knuckles, Arthur pulled his hand out of the earth and snarled as Cratos rolled himself quickly back onto his feet. Once again, Cratos jumped backward away from Arthur, though this was with mild panic than strategy. Cratos was sure he would have been able to end this fight quickly. In his time in the clan, he had fought more than his fair share of Crimson class Werewolves, and when they entered their Berserker trance, they were easily outwitted. This flaw was why Arthur didn't notice his subtle body movements or even try and protect himself from the knee strike. Yet somehow, within that trance, Cratos saw he had the presence of mind to not only switch tactics and punch while Cratos was within his striking range but also not telegraph it, catching Cratos entirely by surprise. It was nearly an exact tactic a Shadow-class Werewolf would employ to take advantage of an unsuspecting opponent who thought they had the win. Cratos knew it was a tactic that demanded some train of thought process.

"It's Impossible!" he thought to himself again as he allowed his skull a few seconds to properly recover from his student's punch. Giving no further time for Cratos to ponder, Arthur snarled spitefully. Somehow, despite all evidence to the contrary, it seemed that Arthur was fighting tactically now while in his Berserker trance. Arthur raised his arms in the air and tensed them manically. His bicep muscles expanded outward, becoming even more prominent than before. Cratos snapped to a ready position as he had been before. With another roar, this one louder than the last, Arthur took a menacing step forward. He didn't run at Cratos this time. Arthur set his eyes firmly on his mentor with a wicked grin as he held a clawed hand in front of him towards Cratos, ready to maul to his heart's content. Arthur then collapsed on the ground before he could utter another single solitary snarl.

Arthur was writhing in pain on the floor, groaning in agony as his arms began to relax and shrink in size back to normal. His hands were clutching his stomach as he lay on the ground, defenseless and looking like his usual self once again. At first, Cratos speculated that Arthur was possibly faking this to get his teacher within his reach. After that last punch, he now didn't want to take any chances. But Cratos then noticed Arthur's body beginning to shrink and return to its original form. He could then see his eyes snap shut as he gritted his teeth against the pain. The red hairs on his body began to slowly recede away as his body returned to before he transformed. Cratos relaxed as he saw the fight was over.

Sighing with relief, Cratos closed his eyes for a few seconds and transformed back into his human form as well. He reopened his eyes a few seconds later and he appeared normal again. Cratos walked over slowly to Arthur, realizing that when Arthur had struck Cratos with that punch, it was the last attack he was able to make. When he took that step forward at Cratos, his body couldn't muster the will to continue. The fallout from the strike on his stomach went into full effect. With his gut strike rippling through his body at once, Cratos thought it was no wonder Arthur fell like someone had pushed the off button in his head. Cratos slowly walked over to Arthur, who was entirely normal again. Arthurs' gasps of pain sounded more human than animal. Now, he took a moment to take note of how impressed he was with Arthur right now. Cratos did not hold back any power when he struck Arthur in his stomach. So, for Arthur to continue fighting after such a devastating attack showed real strength and willpower. Cratos also noted that Arthur was able to have an active thought while in the Berserker trance, which was something awe-inspiring. Too impressive for someone of Arthurs' current level. But for this session alone, Arthur had performed exceptionally well. Cratos, however, knew that strike to Arthur's stomach wouldn't come without repercussion. Even with his advanced healing properties, Arthur's body would be gravely injured for some time while he rested. There was a limit to even Werewolf abilities, and Cratos knew first-hand the power of that knee strike could have dented thick steel. Cratos knelt and gently patted Arthur's back to reassure him.

"You OK there?" he asked warmly. Now that he was out of the heat of battle, Cratos hoped he didn't do more damage than he thought. Arthur didn't reply immediately. His teeth were still clenched as he took in struggling breaths of air. After a painful exhale, he nodded at his teacher. Arthur then began opening his eyes and turning his head to look up at him. Cratos smiled back at Arthur proudly.

"You did pretty damn good, Arthur, well done," Cratos said proudly, which immediately brought a flicker of a smile to Arthur's lips before he was forced to return to his pained scowls as he retched in agony. Cratos chucked at his student.

"You think it hurts now? Just wait until you wake up tomorrow. Catch your breath for a bit and have a rest. We're done for today. I'll make us some food, and you get yourself washed up, then come join me when you're ready." With that said, Cratos gave Arthur another friendly pat on his back as he stood up and took his leave out of the room, leaving Arthur to regain himself. Their training today was complete, and Arthur Thorn was once again beaten to pieces.

The pain in his stomach was a throbbing avalanche that was washing through the rest of his body. The deep, dense throbbing pain kept Arthur glued down like a curled, kicked dog on the floor. His breathing was slowly becoming easier as time went by, so he knew he just had to wait it out for now. The wrenching pain in his gut felt worse than when he had woken before their first fighting session. Arthur then gave a silent thank you to his wolf side, knowing he would heal fast from this injury. He tried to recollect the fight mentally as he lay on the ground, given Arthur knew he had little else to do while still unable to move. He attempted to remember the end of the fight, but it was blurry. Arthur could recall he had transformed his body. It was like what he became on the plane, but it was different for him. This time it felt more natural. When he was on the plane, he was aware of his inner Beast once he transformed but not once had Arthur heard a single whisper from the Beast as he fought with Cratos. However, he also sensed he wasn't entirely himself as he gave in to his rage and thrashed around like a mad animal which Arthur also felt was what had led to his defeat. But Arthur also felt much more robust in that battle. He thought he was larger physically and much more capable than ever. Arthur felt he was slightly less animal-driven than he was on the plane, but the impulse for slaughter wasn't completely gone either. His senses were a mess when transformed, but towards the end of the fight, he recalled himself growing angrier and angrier until he blacked out in rage before waking up on the floor in the state he is in now.

Arthur then struggled to recall from memory precisely what he was doing. It was fuzzy and unclear. It was like he was there but as a passenger in his body. He simply recalled summoning all the strength he could, and then he went completely all out. At that moment, he wasn't thinking or planning but working on his immediate instincts. It felt strange to think about in hindsight. It was like recalling a time when you were small and trying to remember your exact actions in a single memory. He didn't recognize himself clearly at that moment. But as Cratos had struck him with that knee attack, he didn't remember coming out of that wolf-like phase as a passenger. No, he instead just recalled changing his approach. He was still enraged but more aware of what was around him, like being shaken out of a sleepy state when he first woke up. He was slowly learning to control his more beastly instincts with every transformation. Arthur then smiled and remembered before Cratos had left him to recover, that his teacher expressed that he was pleased with him. Arthur took considerable pride in that despite his pain. He was petrified before fearing that if his skill didn't live up to his teacher's expectations, then Cratos might abandon him.

Deciding he had been lying down long enough, Arthur sharply inhaled and attempted to push himself onto his hands and knees. His stomach protested immensely, driving its pained existence hard into his attention like a basket of vengeful dragons, demanding for him to resume his fetal position until they say otherwise. But Arthur refused to be a slave of his pain any longer. Arthur gritted his teeth and continued to try to push himself into a kneeling position. Every second felt like an eternity as he slowly started to bring up his right leg. Arthur breathed deeply and painfully as he moved. The agony from his stomach was making him think he would pass out. Summoning what strength Arthur could from his legs, he gently pulled in his other leg and pushed down on his knees with his hands to lift his body. This straight felt like trying to raise a car. However, bit by bit, Arthur managed to raise his torso upwards, so only his knees were on the floor. His body felt heavy and tearing from within, but he held himself up, trying to suppress the pain with futile effort. Arthur then sharply brought up his left leg again, so he knelt. Then breathing quicker and quicker, he slowly raised himself until he was standing upward on his feet. But Arthur had been too ambitious, and his torso quickly lurched forward, creasing his body rapidly. He was standing up now but still hunched over. He decided this was the best he could manage right now, so tiny step by step that he began to walk out of the room as Cratos asked.

Since staying in the underground base and using its limited facilities under snow lands, Arthur was also reminded of another luxury he missed dearly from the civilized world, which was hot showers. When he first started training with Cratos, he had to wash in rivers. Since then, Arthur had not been in a regular building with hot running water unless the taps he used in the airport before his flight counted, which Arthur felt it certainly did not. Arthur couldn't help but think that this underground base was the coldest yet, and given Cratos's hygiene rules, it was unbearable standing under what felt like literal hail showers washing him clean. There was regular soap and a sink for brushing his teeth and whatever else, but no hot taps at all. At first, it was the same as usual when Arthur washed. The freezing torture wanted to make him do nothing else but jump out and towel himself dry to escape to his warm clothes. Even though there were facilities for clothes to be washed and dried, he never got the chance to wear any of his clothes that came fresh out of the dryer when they were at their warmest. But after a while, the cold showers almost became a welcome experience. His body quickly began to numb when he first stepped into the water, and he felt the pain in his stomach a little less than before. He then proceeded to wash normally. The whole part of his lower torso was already turning a dark shade of black and purple, making it sensitive to the touch. He knew he would have to be extra careful as he washed his skin along there. Arthur then chuckled at the idea of longing for something as simple as just a hot shower, and he wondered when he would next get a chance to enjoy one.

Arthur remembered not too long ago; that he was longing for the idea of junk food because of what they have been eating recently. He pictured his old school friends and where they were right now. He knew if it were the weekend, they would be gorging themselves on sugary drinks and sweets. They would rest in beds comfortable with thick duvets on bouncy mattresses. Arthur found the memory of those things joyful; however, they never made Arthur regret where he was now. His rough living since he joined Cratos wasn't unbearable; it was just uncomfortable at times. It wasn't a lifestyle for everyone, and each of his friends would have probably cried out like children long before now.

Arthur knew not one of them would have made it as far as he has. As he got out of the shower, dried himself, and got dressed, Arthur chuckled again to himself. He felt his friends could have their soft beds and sweets galore, and Arthur knew he was happy to stick with his training and life lessons that made him a much stronger person than they could ever be in their entire lifetimes. He looked down at himself as he dressed and thought about the man he was slowly becoming. Then he remembered, given the way he would soon age, that he would become that man sooner than later. Now he knew Werewolves age faster than ordinary people; he would soon have the appearance of a fully grown man in just a few years. But while the idea was scary to some, Arthur welcomed the thought with open arms the more he thought about it. As his body grew and shaped itself, he knew so had his mind grown with it. The real exciting prospect was what would be awaiting him In the Wolf kingdom. Cratos had already told him about the specialized training that would be the true making of him as a Werewolf. He finished dressing and walked to eat with Cratos. His pain was barely any different than when he first stood up, but Arthur refused to let himself slouch and carried his head held high towards his teacher.

The pair ate in silence as usual. Both Arthur and Cratos's jaws were mechanically chewing as they swallowed their food as though they were in a feeding trance. Arthur came to a point where he was even barely noticing the taste of his meal anymore. The meat, veg, and other foods went down the same as each other as he quickly dispatched portion after portion to replenish his strengths. It now all seemed to him as trivial refueling like he was a car at a petrol station. That little thought made him chuckle loudly. Cratos looked up with his mouth full, so he raised an eyebrow in response. Just like with personal hygiene Arthur quickly discovered that table manners were equally crucial to his teacher. Arthur swallowed his food and explained for a moment why he chuckled. Cratos smiled and swallowed himself, nodding.

"You're not completely wrong. Though our sense of taste improves more than a human, it's not a matter of you no longer tasting the food, but rather you no longer taste any food you don't like anymore." Arthur frowned and then thought for a moment. Since becoming Werewolf, he didn't recall turning his nose up at anything in front of him. Mainly because Arthur had gone from hunting in the jungle to multiple strongholds, with barely any option for choice, he just thought he couldn't be picky and ate whatever he was given. Cratos continued speaking as Arthur thought.

"Humans tend to be very picky eaters, and sometimes their aversions are reasonable. Humans have allergies or something biological that prevents them from eating certain food types, but most turn down food just because it doesn't taste nice. Werewolves don't carry that distinction. Our taste buds change, so we can eat whatever we want as long as it's not poisonous." Arthur thought further on that.

"So, there are no Werewolves that have allergies or other things?" he asked. Cratos tilted his head.

"Yes, there are, though it is scarce. There are those in the clan that can't eat certain foods because it will kill them. Still, when a human first turns into a Werewolf, the Werewolf blood usually eliminates such biological factors. It varies." Arthur nodded and began eating again. He didn't recall being an overly fussy eater himself as an average human, so it mattered little to him. Sure, like any other kid, he didn't want to eat his vegetables, but he always stomached it down mainly because of what would happen if he did complain.

"However," Cratos continued. Arthur had a feeling that something was about to be turned on him.

"For you, until you complete the stages, your opinion of food being bland and tasteless WILL be more apparent. With your body changing and morphing, it will like your energy shall rise and fall in its severity. This effect becomes more potent when you change into your Werewolf form. Your senses will go in and out of flux at random moments. It's just a matter of your body adapting to the massive changes especially given how you will age now as well." With that said, both returned to their meals in silence, left to their thoughts. Arthur's aging was something he would go in and out of excitement for whenever it crossed his mind. He remembered when taking his shower that the prospect of looking like a fully grown man in only a few years was fantastic but to think about it now at this moment. In a matter of a few decades, he would probably look like an older man if he somehow managed to live that long. Cratos told him not to worry about growing into an older man because the Werewolves rarely lived that long anyway. They are always living exciting lives, and the repercussions of such excitement are dangerous. But those were things he would have much more time to process, and he figured he would eventually come to accept them. However, the prospect of death itself had been something he didn't process.

Arthur figured it was because of his age now that death wasn't a concern for him. Through his training, Arthur had come close to near death several times. Even when he was human and helping Cratos fight the Vampires on both those occasions, he had danced with death and could have quickly fallen to it then. He wasn't overly religious growing up. His father had scorned the idea when it was brought up. He would call anyone who believed what he declared were 'fairy tales' idiots, and his mother never mentioned the subject herself. Most of the other kids in his schools were of the same religion as their parents and didn't choose what to believe. Arthur frowned as he chewed his food more carefully. His contemplation grew into speculation.

It wasn't that he agreed with his father. He doubted such an occasion would ever happen, but neither did he feel that such a thing could exist either. However, before he met Cratos, the idea of Vampires and Werewolves was also impossible in fairy tales, so Arthur then didn't know what to dismiss as impossible anymore in his present state. Arthur looked over at his mentor. The man, during all their travels and lessons, never once mentioned anything religious. Cratos meditated often, but Arthur thought that was always something more mental than spiritual. Arthur swallowed his food and shook his head. This sort of thinking while eating was foolish and would only distract him. He pushed such thoughts away for now but decided to revisit them when his stomach didn't feel like a bowling pin against a thousand cannonballs. The thought of his stomach then reminded Arthur of what he wanted to ask Cratos.

"So, what will be tomorrow's training?" he asked Cratos before taking another bite, almost finishing up his food. Cratos thought for a second without looking at Arthur.

"Preferably, I would just carry on with the combat training, but today has put an interesting spin on it for me," Cratos answered ominously. Arthur caught Cratos suddenly speaking very cryptically, which threw off his guard.

"How so?" Arthur asked carefully.

"When you transformed in our fight today, that was one thing," he began with an uncomfortable cough following before he continued.

"But then you entered a state briefly known as the Berserker trance before the fight ended." Arthur nodded thoughtfully as he was glad that he now had a name to give whatever happened to him.

"Is that a bad thing?" he asked his teacher, who frowned at the ground for a moment as he chose his words carefully. Humming for a few seconds, Cratos finally answered.

"Technically no," he muttered formally as though he was speaking under duress.

"When you go to the Wolf Kingdom in Europe, other Crimson class Werewolves, as well as your instructors, will applaud you for having this ability this early on, and then they will encourage you to embrace it. They will have you rigorously train the ability so you can use it on demand whenever you wish." Arthur narrowed his eyes again at his mentor. This Crimson thing was becoming annoying to hear without an explanation. He would have happily interrupted to enquire about it, but his curiosity about this Berserker trance was more substantial, so he let it go again for now.

"But what do YOU think?" Arthur asked more directly, finding his teacher's hesitation strange. Cratos sighed in response.

"It's an immensely powerful technique to have. It makes you feel as though you are invulnerable and pushes your body to the max of its potential," he declared. Arthur's eyebrows nearly hit the ceiling with amazement from hearing of such powers.

"That there is the problem!" Cratos snapped, startling Arthur.

"It's too appealing for an ability. I know so many others that depend on it, and I can guarantee you, Arthur, it is more than likely to get you killed if you can't do anything else but use it!." Arthur found his teachers' strange dislike of this trance discomforting.

"So, what then? I shouldn't bother with it?" he asked almost accusingly, wanting Cratos to explain his disdain for it. Cratos only shook his head.

"Of course not. Like I said before, for your class, it's your most essential asset for staying alive when the odds are against you." Cratos stared into Arthur's eyes with a severe gaze. He turned his body to face Arthur as he wanted his student to listen to him very carefully.

"But remember all the lessons I have taught you, Arthur. You must remain self-dependent with your own skills. I want you to help yourself when you're in a dire situation and not just rely on the Berserker trance to bail you out. It's about using the ability in moderation and not just as a crutch because you lack skill."

Arthur contemplated his teacher's words for a moment. His mind was flying back to recollections of his training in the jungle and the forests. He thought about all the tests he was put through. They were tests and exercises that trained and developed his patience, temperament, and ability to think and react under pressure. Cratos put him through all these things to make him into a person who could rely on themselves when his luck turned on him. It was to make sure he wouldn't panic or become scared with no options left. They were to create someone capable enough to figure out solutions that wouldn't mean his death.

"So, it's like -" Arthur began grabbing his teacher's attention. Cratos focused hard on how Arthur processed his words.

"It's like with our powers themselves. This Berserker ability is something I can become weak on if I don't hone and respect it properly?" Cratos's smiles nearly knocked into the lobes of both his ears, and he nodded at his student with pride.

"Exactly Arthur! You hit the nail squarely on the head!" Arthur returned the smile as Cratos sighed with relief.

"Since you've been developing and since we took off on our journey to where our people live. I have been very worried." Arthur's smile then faded slightly.

"Worried about what?" he asked, confused. Cratos grimaced slightly.

"I don't mean this to sound bad, Arthur, but part of me was worried that once you undertook the training of your class. I thought that all the lessons I taught you would have been forgotten, and you would end up becoming a hubris drunk muscle head like the rest of the Crimson class." Arthur's smile did drop fully now, but he wasn't sad. He understood why his mentor would have such concerns, especially after Arthur's behavior when he went to school with his Werewolf abilities. But Arthur's understanding was knocked away when Cratos put his hand on Arthur's shoulder and sent him a smile of reassurance.

"But what you just said there proved my fears wrong. What you just said made me realize you will go there and do me proud!" Arthur nodded at his mentor modestly as the two finished their meals. Cratos was smiling fondly with his newfound respect for his pupil and close friend.

CHAPTER TWENTY-SIX

"DAMMIT, CRATOS! THIS ISN'T FUNNY! LET ME BACK IN!" Arthur howled in bludgeoning fury as his fist banged on the metal manhole cover. The freezing wind was flying in what felt like every direction cutting through his bare forearms like icicle razor blades. He had been banging on the cover since he had been tricked outside of the base by Cratos. Arthur hammered continuously on the cover, demanding to be let back inside the stronghold. It had all happened so fast, the way he was left outside.

"I'll be back this time tomorrow morning; good luck!" said Cratos in a chirpy voice as he darted back inside the cover once both were outside. Arthur barely had time to turn around as the sound of the cover locking behind him as Cratos slammed it shut. Arthur was shivering wildly as the freezing wind enthralled his body. Arthur's hands then began rapidly rubbing his body which was only covered by a black shirt, thick Grey trousers, and standard black boots. To Arthurs' dismay, his shirt was a short-sleeved top leaving his arms and hands to the mercy of the unforgiving chilly nightmare that now surrounded him. Luckily, because of his boots' density, Arthur took solace that at least his feet were able to escape the cold outside.

Arthur considered summoning his Werewolf strength to rip the hatch cover off by brute force. Then he figured that Cratos would know he would think of that, and Arthur realized that for a safe house for Werewolves, it must be heavily reinforced, and his strength would barely scratch the metal no matter how long he tried. Sighing with defeat as Arthur knew Cratos would not listen to his cries, Arthur stood back up from the hatch cover and looked around the area where Cratos had stranded him. The last time he gazed up at this sky, it was a nightmare of weather, and he was still barely transformed. Night or day, Arthur felt it made little difference right now to him as he could see nothing for miles even without a vicious storm in his face. No matter where he looked in every direction around, Arthur felt like he was stranded to die in the cold wastes with miles of snow everywhere. He quickly assumed it must have been another test, like when he left to hunt the tiger in the jungle.

"Survival," Arthur grunted coldly. He rubbed his arms again as the cold felt like it was turning his very bone marrow solid. Arthur felt like his teeth were close to chattering. Arthur thought forward and guessed that he dreaded how worse it would become at nightfall if it were cold now. The night's rest he had before being thrown out in the snow was a small bonus as he had healed significantly. His skin on the surface still carried a dark bruise in places, but Arthur had recovered well enough. He could move around with ease which could save his life before this test was over.

Arthur doubted he could hunt anything in this wasteland because he couldn't imagine any creature would be able to survive out here without a concrete underground fortress to keep it safe. The wind's ferocity began to grow more intense as the snow around him was being upheaved into his face as though the land was trying to bury him alive. The frost shards flying around him were carried by air, looking like a tribe of snow spirits moving about the land. This breeze wasn't the same blizzard he experienced when he jumped out of the plane. The snow in the wind was thick, growing stronger and becoming thick enough to blind a person. The breathable air around Arthur was quickly becoming cold enough to turn a human lung frozen solid. Arthur figured the only thing that hadn't stopped him from catching fatal frostbite already was the Werewolf blood within him. Arthur knew he needed to find shelter, and there was nothing that could save his life where he was now, but if he didn't find somewhere soon, he would die. Then his frozen dead body would be forever buried under the snow, never to be found by anyone.

Arthur shook his head angrily at himself. Now wasn't the time for morbid thoughts and dwelling on what would end up causing his death. He survived in the jungle by hunting the tiger, so if he made it in extreme hostile heat, Arthur knew he could survive in the brutal cold. He knew Cratos wouldn't put him out here if there weren't some way to survive. Cratos must have known about a cave somewhere or even possibly a hidden cache with supplies for him to use. Worst case scenario, Arthur figured he would find some sort of earthen crevice where he would be able to hide his body from the worst of the cold winds while rubbing his body warm to survive. Cratos gave no specific instructions or rules for this task. Arthur understood mainly that he simply said he would return tomorrow, leaving Arthur with all the room for improvisation that he wished. Sadly, he knew nothing about how to survive in snowy wastelands. Here Arthur was at the mercy of needing to think on the spot, and so far, he didn't like his odds. He had only been out here a short time now and still hadn't thought of a plan yet. Taking another look at the manhole cover, he sighed and began traveling the snowy wastelands to look for what would either be his salvation or his damnation.

It didn't take long for Arthur to lose track of time in his journey. He had no idea how long he had been outside after Arthur had looked behind him, and he could no longer see the opening hatch anymore. Since leaving the base, Arthur couldn't tell if ten minutes had passed or, at this point, even an hour. As his boots slowly trudged through the snowy void with his arms wrapped across his torso like a carcass inside a casket, he quickly began to doubt his chances of surviving this test. There were no signs of any caves in any distance regardless of where he walked. There didn't seem to be anywhere still that would lead to his survival. Arthur looked on only to just see the endless white abyss that lay all around him, slowly trying to swallow him whole. Arthur's breathing grew heavier as he continued walking. The cold was chilling his lungs as the air became denser in the wind and its icy blaze. Sharp gusts were shrouding his vision with snowflakes. After multiple times he eventually gave up brushing his eyes clean at this point and just allowed the snow to fall where it may on his body. He continued to keep checking his hands, looking for any signs of frostbite or anything out of the ordinary, so he knew he wasn't beyond the point of survival yet. He wasn't a doctor, but he was taught in science about hypothermia and the warning signs about when his body would be in a dangerous state. He knew if his limbs began to feel warm despite the cold, then he would be in trouble. Surprisingly so far, his body was holding together better than he thought. Even his fingertips were still the same pale color of skin as the rest of him was. He knew soon, though, they would turn black or even blue. Arthur walked onward still, undaunted by the weather's endless smacking of his face, which was becoming more ferocious, making Arthur feel that it was almost seemingly to spite him for not being dead yet. Arthur had a worrying feeling there would be another blizzard tonight, and it might just be the end of him if he didn't think of something fast.

What felt like hours later, Arthur still came across nothing that could save him. He walked across a few steep hills with his feet sinking nearly knee-deep into the snow itself, but nothing lay at the other side than just more blanket of white. Despite the feeling of time drifting away from him, Arthur could tell he was growing closer to sundown. The light around him was disappearing gradually, and the wind, as he feared, was blistering at a near-fatal level. Arthur was nearly walking blind as he willed himself to keep trudging along. He was only able to withstand the blasts of the storm on his eyeballs for a few seconds at a time as he walked. He felt he could walk off the edge of a cliff any second, and he would never have seen it coming. The thrashing winds around him were blowing in every direction against his body like he was in a boxing match against the weather, and it was winning. Arthur felt like he was underwater with the amount of snow piling on his body like white armor. It became heavier the longer he left it on his body, which now began to feel numb. The cold was unbearable as mentally as it was physically. He felt like there were still no signs of hypothermia, but he was shivering like a madman. Now his memory was utterly blank of what warmth was or what it had felt like within his body. There was now only the writhing existence of this cold presence to Arthur, turning his blood from red to blue inside his veins.

Finally, after a little bit more walking, Arthur collapsed. He wasn't sure how far he had even managed to get since starting his expedition. It came more slowly than he was expecting. The first thing that happened was his legs stopped walking him forward. For so long, he felt as though his legs were carrying him forward on autopilot; then he figured they just gave up and stood him standing completely still for a few moments. The wind continued slapping his body with determined hatred as though it was now furious at him for giving in. But Arthur now felt numb inside and out, and by this point, he gave no reaction. His eyes were not wincing from the pain of the cold, slowly freezing every nerve in his body. The entirety of his face was unmoving as he stood motionless. Arthur stood in the wastelands for what felt like an eternity with his arms slumping dead by his sides. He was no longer trying to cover his torso for warmth; he was too tired. His muscles ached, and the movement only tripled the pain as Arthur tensed. His knees buckled, and he slumped down hard onto them into the snow. His head raised, and his face looked upward into the sky. The night was nearly upon him. The blizzard was growing wilder into chaos. The gusts of snow were showering his body from all sides and brutally entombing him. It was becoming like a placed blanket around him, trying to soothe him to rest. His breaths were becoming short and rapid. He was feeling pain in his chest with each inhale and exhale. His eyes were strained and aching as well as he no longer closed them to be shielded from the cold. Arthur now found himself welcoming the icy peril as he gazed out into the sky, watching the stars emerge into sight with a strange euphoric awe.

Death's cold, unforgiving hand was beginning to wrap its boney hands around his heart and slowly started to squeeze. Arthurs' breathing became strained and nearly made it impossible to breathe further. But none of that bothered Arthur anymore. His body was now nearly completely covered in the snow, but Arthur chose to focus on the sky above him. The blizzard was rushing around his ears and other senses gradually, trying to swallow the boy completely whole, piece by piece. Arthur simply continued watching the heavens, letting the snow slowly take him. One by one, his pupils noticed each little star that came into view as the night turned black for him. Every one of the stars was an individual spotlight casting down upon him for his final moment on the snowy stage. The odd clouds were beginning to expand in size and width, but Arthur still saw all that the open heavens had to offer. Before him, Arthur thought that nearly no other human being had witnessed what he saw right now. It was only the true expanse of the night sky for him and him alone to gaze upon with the fading life withering within his cold eyes. With every light in the night before his near-frozen view, a small flicker of a smile emerged on Arthur's face. Weirdly, he felt completely at peace. He was no longer feeling the cold of the land, the pain of the blizzard, or even the enclosing fear of death. All those concerns were swept aside as he felt utterly whole in this singular moment of his life.

Arthur's head turned as his pupils fixated on the divine illumination of light upon his face. Something was revealed from the corner of his eyes by a sneaky and unforgiving cloud, which was a familiar luminous glow. Arthurs' pupils shook wildly for a few moments before expanding outward. However, that moment was quickly and viciously ripped away, and his smile immediately vanished.

"Time to play," growled the voice of his inner Beast. Then with no warning, Arthur's Werewolf existence grabbed hold and burst forth.

"I have been watching you deal with the cold elements for some time now, boy. I had remained silent so far as to give you a chance to adapt to this challenge and see how you faired!" the Beast growled in his head mockingly at Arthur, who was helpless to do nothing but simply listen.

"As usual, I am disgusted at your feeble, worthless surrender! Just like on the hood of that van, you have failed to put every ounce of your willpower into complete survival!" The Beast's voice fell silent for a few moments before it spoke again, almost as though it was calming itself before continuing.

"However, I have noticed that you lasted longer than I expected. But now that you gave up, it's time for ME to tag in!" it finally finished with a howling snap. The Beast DID have the ability to take control like he had done before to save Arthur's life, but he did so only then because Arthur had no other option. In his Werewolf form, the inner Beast knew that survival would take a stronghold of the boy's attention, so Arthur gave it no other choice.

The burning rage of the Beast's sheer might took hold of Arthur's near-dead frozen body. His eyes locked onto the lights of the sky. Arthur's body lurched and stiffened like he was being gripped tightly by an invisible giant. His hands began clawing deeply into the snow as his human cries became demon growls with every breath. His torso expanded without pause alongside hairs spreading out from his skin like a crashing wave throughout his body, covering him in a deep, red coat within seconds. His skull began to now reshape. It slowly grooved and morphed to give him a wolf snout forming in front of his face as his jaw lengthened with rows of sharp teeth growing out. His hands grew larger, with stronger nails becoming knife-length claws accompanied by the same for his feet. His arms and legs then expanded massively in length and width, the muscles swelling like inflating balloons. The rush of blood was active in his body, with its heat reviving his former numb self. Arthur felt the heartbeat of his body once again, and it was alive with fire. His body then ceased its forming. It was not fully complete but closer than in his fight with Cratos. He was slightly broader, and his coat was thicker and more vibrant. His clothes were now shredded tatters around him in the snow, with barely a scrap left hanging off him. His eyes finally snapped in a blink from his natural blue to a commanding yellow. Arthur threw his body upwards with arms spread wide, and he then howled into the night sky. His bellow carried through the world around him, breaking past the flow of the winds like a blade's visceral slash. Arthur raised one leg and put his foot on the ground. His shoulders were heaving as he breathed. A mist that appeared thick enough to resemble smoke began piling out from his jaw like a dragon's breath.

Arthur lifted his body, stood tall on his now strong legs, and gazed around him without hesitation. He was growling deeply within his throat. His tone was deep and harrowing to the ears. Arthur looked down and observed his hands briefly. He gazed at their surface for a moment, then turned them around and looked at his palms. His fur was red, but it wasn't thick like Cratos's black coat. He clenched his hands into fists tightly. The feel of his long nails jabbing into his flesh was oddly pleasing. He observed his body, from his vision, he was nearly like a goliath compared to his size as a human. Arthur smirked with special pride at one aspect. He was in complete control. Every other time he wasn't operating with his entire mind. Especially in the gaze of the moon, there was usually a savage Beast part of him influencing his decisions. Right now, he felt like himself. The memory of himself freezing in the snow was forgotten in his present mind. He was more than warm despite the night cold. He was boiling. Pure energy was racing through like blood, surging profusely like liquid lightning. With another mighty howl into the winds of the wastelands, he ducked his body down slightly onto all fours. Arthur then shot off running into the night, a free and powerful Werewolf feeling as though nothing could stop him.

Time became a mythical illusion for Arthur as he ran free. A limitless euphoria enthralled him; his every sense was rocketed to its maximum, with the feeling of adrenalin nearly replacing his blood entirely. From death to life, Arthur ran with every ounce of strength his legs and arms could muster. He was thrashing his legs forward continuously at top speed against the night itself. His movements were loud and powerful. The snow crashed and exploded away from his powerful leg and arms, stomping into the ground. It looked as though he was more launching himself forward than running. The blizzard continued its rage as though it was accepting the challenge of Arthur's arrogance to not die within its cold hands. The cold was more than willing to throw the worst of its storm in his hairy direction. The ferocity of its freezing blasts was an onslaught of intense cold against any warm-blooded being that was alive. Arthur Thorn was no normal warm-blooded creature, though. As the wind slapped hard against his wolf-molded face, he simply threw his head up into the skies and howled with delight. Arthur relished the elements abusing his being as his pace through the snow didn't slow by an inch.

Arthur was looking out into the snowy wasteland as he ran. He took in everything he saw as he embraced the first feeling of being completely self-aware and in control of his enhanced form. During his rush mode, Arthur felt a nearly insane lust fueling his arms and legs, which had become merely tools for his desires. He wanted to run now more than anything. The snow had almost taken his life, and now Arthur wanted to push his Werewolf abilities to their maximum. The only time he had used any of his wolf abilities was against the tiger and in small parts on the plane. Now he could see exactly his limits and surpass them all using the training he received through Cratos Mane.

Arthur couldn't tell how long he had been running in his form. It could have been an hour or several of them as far as his mind cared. However, his breath was finally starting to become heavier as he ran. His continuous dash started to catch up with his body eventually. He tensed his arms and legs to check their situation, but they seemed to be still functioning with no pain or signs of ache. Slowing his pace slightly, Arthur began to look around for something, anything. After a few more minutes of running, Arthur's eyes finally locked onto what looked like an exposed fraction of the wall from a nearby cliff in the distance. Without noticing, Arthur seemed to have located a gap in the earth that only ran deeper the further he went forward.

Approaching the beginning of this gap, he didn't stop running and headed straight into the opening. The snow walls to his left and right were raised high above his head as he descended further. His eyes were still locked on an apparent dead-end in this small snowy canyon ahead of him. Running along, he wondered how this piece of land was formed. It seemed out of place from the nearly plain straight land of snow he was running across before. There were large miles and giant snowy dunes, but for the most part, it was leveled. He speculated as he came close to the dead end.

"A fissure, maybe? Do those create canyons? Maybe it was from an earthquake. Do you get earthquakes in snowy places? I wonder where we are in the world exactly. Cratos would probably get annoyed if I asked," Arthur pondered in his head. The words of his inner mind were clear and concise. He found a wolf-like snort going out of his nose as he thought of that, then he chuckled slightly. He was feeling his wolf senses affecting his immediate reaction more than he was keeping an eye on.

The dead-end of the cliff was right against his face now. Arthur stood up on his two legs, straightening his back fully as he did. The clicking snaps of his back gave him a satisfying grin as he looked dead up the wall. The dead-end ran incredibly high up. He struggled to see the peak with the snow covering it. The snowy edge looked like it was blending in with the sky above. Luckily for Arthur, the inside was enclosed and cramped, so there was little snow or cold wind to reach him. This space gave Arthur a slight reprieve from the worst of the weather. Arthur then took a moment to pause at this time of peace, and his face twisted angrily for existing only now than before when he needed it. Gritting his teeth, Arthur looked hard at the cracked yet completely solid wall in front of him. He placed his claw on its surface. Despite it being out of the storm's wrath, it was ice cold and probably frozen solid.

"This will do!" Arthur thought as a sickening vicious grin slithered up the left side of his face. Before, it was utterly silent, but now the inner Beast spoke up, responding with Arthur's grin.

"A good time to test ourselves. Hmmm?" It whispered suggestively, trying to encourage Arthur onward. The inner Beast wasn't met with Arthurs' usual spite or hatred, but rather his smirk spread into a full grin, and Arthur happily nodded in agreement. He remembered when he punched the bullet-proof glass on the van. In his standard form, he had shattered his hand on the glass. Then he remembered when he struck the reinforced pilot's door on the plane, and it worked out well in a transformed state. Arthur clenched his giant left-clawed wolf hand tightly into a fist. His nails were digging into the palm of his hand painfully. The entire limb began to bulge densely and tremble from the effort. He pulled it back behind him like an archer stringing his arrow, then with a roar that stampeded into the heavens, Arthur launched his entire arm forward. With the strike, he twisted his whole body sideways as he did it. With this punch, he was pushing every piece of force and power he had straight through his fist as it exploded into the solid icy wall.

If Arthur had ever wondered whether earthquakes also hit snowy lands before, he certainly knew now. As his claw struck deep into the flesh of the solid rock, Arthur felt the vibrations from the force caress the soles of his feet. The ripples spread through the ground surrounding him like a million tendrils of energy. The wall around his fists cracked around the wall at both his sides spreading out like lines of broken glass. Its damage began stretching high up the cliff like a racing bolt of lightning. Arthur felt his fist embedded deep into the earth, and he then gazed at the damage he had caused. His arm was buzzing after the attack, and it nearly felt numb. He was concerned at how fragile the wall might be now. It felt around his hand as though he had just turned the wall into a mound of sand from his strike. Breathing heavily, Arthur slowly retracted his hand from the wall and observed it dutifully just in case the wall came apart on top of him. Rock and ground were falling around his fist partially as he pulled his hand out, but the wall itself held strong above him. Arthur saw how deep his fist went into the wall and how much damage he caused surrounding the area he struck.

"Overdid it a bit, it seems," the inner Beast noted, not with criticism but just with casual observation.

"Shame," Arthur grunted back at the Beast in his head.

"I was just warming up," he continued to think with smug satisfaction as Arthur wriggled the fingers of his left claw before allowing it to drop by his side. His knuckles were bloody and bare, but Arthur felt no pain. The impact from the punch was still buzzing through his body like an electric hum, numbing him. Arthur then looked around the wall admiring his work. He peered inside the hole where his fist once was and again smirked. Arthur began imagining what effect that punch would have had on a Vampire's body if he had struck it with the same force. As Arthur was about to consider throwing a second punch just to test whether he could completely break the wall apart, causing it to collapse on top of him, a dark, gritty voice spoke a few feet behind him.

"Very cute," He said mockingly, causing Arthur to whirl his body around and behold his unexpected guest.

He was very tall and of medium build. His skin was as pale as the snow around him with the familiar blood-red eyes. He wore a black shirt with a rugged dark brown leather jacket on top of it. Two leather straps were going from his shoulders to his sides, then strapped around his waist were overly large holsters with even larger-looking handguns placed inside them. He also had thick black trousers with black boots to match and brown leather gloves on his hands. The Vampires' face was littered with scars. His most prominent scar was a diagonal line that ran from his left eyebrow, down his neck, and into his clothing. On top of his head was a large rimmed, deep brown fedora hat with a row of teeth strapped all around its sides which gave Arthur a strange instinctual feeling they were all Werewolf teeth. Arthur focused his eyes on the man's holsters strapped to his sides and saw they were two shiny revolver guns. Each of them was the size of nearly the man's head it looked. The man gazed hard at Arthur with an interested glance, and he then smirked.

"I must say it's always fun watching dogs like you just throw your arms around like flailing children," he commented dryly. Arthur scowled at the man's face murderously. Arthur took a hesitant step back, readying himself for an attack. The man's left eyebrow rose, bemused.

"Calm your tail, boy. If I wanted you dead, I would have planted a shell between your eyes faster than you could sniff the powder residue."

Arthur eyed him carefully. He was unsure of this stranger's agenda if he weren't there to kill him immediately. Arthur knew this man was a Vampire, yet he seemed different from other Vampires he had met so far. He had been the only one to talk to him calmly and not just immediately hiss and thrash at him wildly. All other Vampires he had met were stylishly clothed and clear-faced. They resembled wealthy dandies that let others do their dirty work. Not this man. He looked different just through his presence. He was more robust and harder; Arthur could tell purely from his instincts. Arthur didn't make a move. He was cornered and couldn't escape where he was. His only hope was for the second the Vampire went for his gun; Arthur would try and leap forward to strike. The man observed Arthur for a bit longer, and he chuckled.

"I've been tailing you for a while, you know," he said casually, catching Arthur's attention.

"You've upset a lot of fat wallets, and those silk eaters don't forget a headache any time soon," he continued. The Vampires' left hand began to grasp the handle of his revolver. Arthur snarled in response. That was the only warning he could give. The Vampire only tutted patronizingly at Arthur.

"That's the problem with you big dogs," he voiced coolly. Then before Arthur could widen his eyes with shock, the man had his right arm extended with his other revolver firmly gripped in his hand and his finger on the trigger.

"You just don't seem to keep your eye on the ball." Arthur gulped uneasily as the end of the gun was pointed straight at him. He didn't even see the Vampires' right arm twitch. It was with a speed that was faster than he had seen Cratos able to move. His left hand was still resting on his left gun as his right hung in the air pointing straight towards Arthur. The man hummed as he saw Arthur not move.

"I could save my kind a lot of trouble if I just plant you right here and now," he mused aloud. Arthur's breath was becoming rapid as his mind went blank. He was trying to think of a plan. The man's thumb cocked the hammer, closing his left eye and staring down the sight.

There was absolute silence in Arthur's head as he could not think of a solution to this problem. Any second, the Vampire could pull the trigger, and he would be dead. He remembered being shot on the plane, but the gun there was smaller, a much smaller weapon, and the hand cannon before him now looked like one shot would take a chunk out of his entire being. This man knew where he was shooting, and Arthur knew he wouldn't miss. Arthur stared hard at the Vampire. His gaze was unblinking with the Vampires' careful yet focused gaze back towards him. The Vampire stared back at Arthur with his open eye as he waited to see how Arthur would react. But Arthur could think of nothing else but to stay still. It wasn't like in the snow, and he wasn't resigning himself to death, but he felt this was a situation where he needed to think more than fight. After a few more seconds passed, the man smiled. He opened his left eye and pulled his gun back into the air.

"But if I do such a thing before I'm told to, then I don't get paid," he finally said, tilting his head to the left slightly. Then with a flick of his wrist, he spun his revolver around his hand several times as he finished by slamming the gun back into its holster perfectly. Arthur just looked at the man with absolute shock.

"Paid!?" Arthur thought to himself in disbelief. The Vampire noticed Arthur's confused frown on his face and shook his head, disappointed.

"You're not worth my bullets. Not yet anyway, boy. You need to train hard to become something I would actually enjoy killing. Of course, it won't matter how hard you train anyway, because the next time you see me. You'll already have a hole in your head," he finished before turning his back on Arthur, then putting his hands on his pockets and casually began walking away with simple footsteps.

A part of Arthur wanted to seize this chance and leap forward to tackle the Vampire while his back was turned and tear him to pieces. He could not figure out the reason he let Arthur live. But it wasn't just the fact that it seemed cowardly and dishonorable to attack the Vampire from behind. Arthur had a feeling this guy would hear Arthur blink if he wanted to, and if Arthur ran forward to attack, the Vampire would whirl around with his guns already in his hands and fire every bullet he had into Arthur's skull. So, Arthur simply just stood there and watched the Vampire disappear as he walked upward back into the snow lands to go wherever he was before ambushing Arthur. After a few seconds, Arthur saw the cold winds of the storms cover the Vampire's body, and he was gone from sight, leaving Arthur alone to process his near-death experience with that Vampire.

All the life and energy that was born when he had transformed had now vanished from his being as Arthur simply walked onward back through the snow. He had no idea where he was going, but Arthur had the tiniest inkling that it was the direction he had been running from in the first place. But with the storm still thrashing, only a genius would be able to tell precisely. He was even more confused than when he first came across the Vampire in the alleyway that night as a human. It had only been there a few seconds, but that Vampire had somehow scared Arthur more than he ever thought possible.

"Why didn't he kill me?" Arthur continued to think to himself as he slowly put one step in front of the other. The chaos of the snow was pulverizing against his wolf body, but in his puzzling mental state, it seemed like a mere insect's itch as he carried on. The Vampire had mentioned not getting paid if he had killed Arthur.

"But aren't all Vampires rich!?" he thought further as he walked on forward, unable to think of a single answer to any question he posed to himself.

Cratos had undoubtedly told him that was the case when he first explained their enemy. Cratos had made it seem like they were all the same snobbish society that looked down upon all other life forms. That all Vampires ruled the world through politics and economics. Having all the money the world knew it had. So then, Arthur couldn't fathom why that one Vampire cared about receiving money. He also wondered why he wore vital clothing and carried guns as well as bore scars. All these questions were unsolvable puzzles that buzzed around his head unanswered. If the Vampire were waiting for someone to put a simple price on his head, Arthur wondered if he would even be able to fight against the Vampire or if he would just one day suddenly feel a hole appearing in the middle of his forehead before falling dead.

Arthur then wondered if he should tell Cratos about the encounter. Part of him wanted to smack his head for even considering not telling him, but his gut instinct was to keep it to himself. Sensing his conflict, the inner Beast spoke up again.

"Keep it to yourself for now. It's not as if the man can do anything about it anyway," he said, acting as though on behalf of the other side of Arthur's mind for him.

"But Cratos might know who that man was and give me some answers. Not knowing anything, that is the scariest thought right now," he answered back internally, followed by a dismissive snort from the Beast.

"That's not true, and you know it," the Beast said sharply, not allowing Arthur to try and fool his own mind.

"Knowing a damn thing about that Vampire won't do anything. That guy was something different. If I were you, I would wait and see if the chance to find out then comes to you. If that doesn't happen, then perhaps wait until you meet that crazy woman again." Arthur was confused for a moment, then he realized who the Beast was referring to, and he replied hesitantly.

"You mean Siren?" Arthur asked back, only for a sigh to follow.

"Yes. Obviously. That woman seems to know more than anyone else, especially Cratos. You're already hiding one thing from him. Another secret won't hurt." Arthur was puzzled at those words as he continued trudging back through the snow. The previous feeling of power he had been enjoying was now wiped from his body. Now he simply wanted to go back to Cratos and leave this night behind him. The Beast, though blunt and crass, made some sense to him. Arthur wouldn't feel any better, probably finding out about the Vampire right away. Not to mention telling Cratos about the encounter would just needlessly worry his teacher for no reason. Whoever that Vampire was, he would be long gone by now, so Cratos couldn't precisely track him down from here. As he finally came to a decision, Arthur suddenly felt his legs go entirely still in the snow. They stopped walking and felt completely numb like they had before he transformed. A nauseous drifting feeling immediately followed the numbness. He remembered this sensation. He went through the same thing before when he first entered the underground safe house. Before Arthur could say anything else, his body slumped forward, and he fell unconscious in the snow. The last thing his ears heard as he was gone was the thrashing of the storm as it began to cover his being with snow.

CHAPTER TWENTY-SEVEN

Just like the last time, when he had passed out before, Arthur awoke in what looked like a holding cell with plain grey concrete walls all around him. He had extra thick blankets covering his body which were tucked tightly around his body. They felt hot upon his flesh. Arthur sat up and looked around after wriggling himself free of the blankets; then, he smiled oddly. He wondered what time Cratos had found him; then, he asked himself how long his wolf form had lasted after he passed out. Later, Cratos would explain that he somehow came across his students face down, asleep in the snow. Anyone else wouldn't have lasted long like that, so Arthur believed that he must have been closer to the morning than he had thought. This fact meant Arthur had survived the night as Cratos wanted. He stretched his arms and back and yawned loudly. His muscles ached a little, but they weren't missing from frostbite, which was something he was very thankful to feel. The metal door ahead of him clicked several times and swung then open. Cratos walked in, holding a metal tray with a bowl of soup and bread for him on top of it with a massive grin slapped across his face.

"Morning, snowman!" he greeted cheerfully.

Arthur wolfed down the soup and bread greedily like it was his last meal. He dipped his bread into the soup, which was a delicious chicken flavor, and then he plunged it straight into his mouth. Cratos smiled as he watched Arthur eat his food and take sips from his large bowl of soup when he wasn't chewing bread. For so long, Arthur had been struck with the same bland meals served to him, which were more checking boxes of nutrition at the time than actual meals. Until right now, Arthur savored every delicious piece of the bread. He worshipped every tiny droplet of the soup on his tongue. It was perfect, and Arthur was starving. Now and then, he would take a few large gulps of water from the glass with the meal.

"Sorry if the water is room temperature. We're out of ice," Cratos said. Arthur stopped eating and looked at his teacher. They stared at each other for a few seconds before they both burst out laughing at the same time. Arthur returned to his meal, chuckling as Cratos spoke.

"You weren't in too bad a state when I found you. Somehow your body was still warm. Though I didn't want to take any chances, hence the extra blankets. You were a few miles from here which meant after you transformed, you must have had quite the fun run."

Arthur nearly choked on his bread as he didn't answer. He remembered when he walked through the snow and spoke to his inner Beast, and they both agreed that there would be no immediate advantage in mentioning the gun-bearing Vampire that confronted him in that crevice until he next spoke with Siren. So, swallowing what was in his mouth, he chuckled nervously and nodded.

"Once I was in the form, I remember going wild. I ran endlessly. Once I had calmed down a bit, I tried to run back, then I passed out randomly!" Cratos nodded as Arthur resumed his meal, quietly thankful that Cratos overlooked his lie.

"That will happen here and there. When you transform, the harder you push yourself, the worse the aftereffects will be when you revert to your human form. It is especially potent during the stages. Think of it to be sort of like a Werewolf hangover," Cratos added simply. The phrase made Arthur smile at the idea of a Werewolf with an icepack on his forehead.

"But that will grow easier to deal with as you train and progress. As you begin mastering your form at will and controlling yourself more completely," Cratos continued idly. Arthur said nothing and simply nodded as he continued eating. Unlike the other times, Arthur remembered everything about transforming into his form last night. He hadn't become a fully transformed Werewolf just yet, given he had lacked some fur on his body at the time though he knew he had been the biggest he had been. Yet Arthur was impressed with himself that he had been in complete control in the wolf form. He knew he had gotten a little carried away with the energy and rush of the transformation when he first started running, but he felt it was no different than a small child going mad on a sugar rush after eating a bunch of sweets. Arthur once again chuckled at the absurd comparison of him just being a hyper Werewolf.

"Still, though," Cratos said as he stood up from Arthur's blankets.

"That was your final test for now anyway. Once you finish your breakfast, pack whatever you need or want, and we'll be off." Arthur swallowed and looked up at his teacher.

"Where are we going?" he asked curiously. He didn't think they could go anywhere since they needed to wait for help to come for them. Cratos pulled a face at Arthur as though he had just spoken another language.

"Where? Where we've been heading too since we left Siren's," he declared, rolling his eyes. Now it was Arthur's turn to frown with confusion.

"How are we going to get there? We're in the middle of nowhere," he pointed out as Cratos chuckled condescendingly.

"There is no such thing for a Werewolf, Arthur. Everywhere in the world is connected for us at one place or another." Arthur thought for a second,

"So, we are going to hike for miles through the snow? We need to wait for the help we radioed for, right?" he asked somewhat desperately, not wishing to hike through all of that snow anymore. Cratos shook his head. Arthurs' face fell; he was not overjoyed at the prospect of traveling outside again without at least being in his wolf form.

"We can't risk the exposure, especially if the Vampires are still after us. That plane exploding had likely raised a few red alarms, you know." Arthur's face went ashen at the mention of the plane as unpleasant memories began circling on the outskirts of his mind. Then his sadness vanished as he remembered something from the Vampire last night.

"You've upset a lot of fat wallets, and those silk eaters don't forget a headache any time soon." The Vampire had mentioned that Arthur had annoyed the Vampire leaders. On the plane, the pilot had said how they had a satellite tracking their movements. Cratos was right. The Vampires were actively looking for them as that Vampire from last night was only waiting for the order to strike. A flurry of different thoughts rushed through Arthurs' mind like shot bullets in every direction. Arthur then seriously considered a life of living underground as a vole forever. Cratos noticed his students' worry and waved his hand.

"Don't take it personally. There's a Vampire most wanted list five miles long with Werewolves' names on it. They want us all dead. It is just now and then that someone sticks out more than others and becomes a target. Soon some other guy or girl will piss them off, and we'll sink away from their interest until we spit in their champagne once again." Arthur couldn't help but laugh at that remark and nod at his teacher.

"OK then. So how are we going to get to Wolf kingdom?" he asked. His teacher's grin had widened into a sinister gleam upon his student.

"That is where things become interesting!" he exclaimed and clapped his hands together eagerly.

Later on, Arthur had made a mental note to throttle Cratos in his sleep, making sure to whisper the words, "Learn by doing," to him before the life disappeared from his eyes. Arthur recalled those damnable words Cratos had told him as he unveiled the two hidden vehicles after hearing Arthur claim he didn't know how to drive one. The pair of Werewolves were zooming across the snowy wasteland at what felt like thousands of miles per hour. Arthur was barely able to keep his hands gripped on the handles of his vehicle as they charged onward. Arthur's face was a dismayed frightened horror, whereas only a few meters to his right, he saw Cratos laughing and whooping and now and then purposely aiming for the more giant snow hills so he could ramp off them. A hill or ledge would often catch Arthur by surprise, causing his heart to skip several beats as he slammed back onto the ground, nearly falling from his snowmobile. Arthur was shaking as though he was glued to a ticking nuclear reactor.

"Learn by doing!" his teacher shouted cheerfully towards him through the rush. Now Cratos was shooting forward with the kind of speed that would give even race car drivers a nauseous stomach. Cratos was still whooping and laughing as the pair traveled on. Their destination was some sort of radioed transport to take them to the kingdom. Arthur was told they had to meet the traveler because of some security issue with the safehouse if Vampire finds it. Arthur couldn't help but immensely notice how unsubtle their approach was. Even though Cratos didn't know about the gun-wielding Vampire that he had met, it was still not too long ago that they had been purposely targeted by the Vampires on a plane to be murdered. Now here they were zooming across snow lands and sticking out like cheetahs running through a children's ball pit. Arthur felt the only thing missing was a 'kill me' sign on his back for them. Cratos did mention that Vampire's interest in Werewolf targets quickly changed, but he couldn't help but think his teacher was a little too arrogant about their safety right now. But Arthur knew it wasn't like he could just call out to Cratos to keep him calm. Though given the speed they were going at, Arthur knew it would be a fruitless effort. So, he just gritted his teeth and rode on, hoping they would reach their destination soon before he crashed into a tree and Cratos would need to scrap him off the bark.

After an hour had passed in their travels, the excitement gradually had worn off Cratos, and now he was driving normally next to Arthur as the pair rolled on through the snow. Arthur was merely focused on the path ahead. Although the pace they traveled with was brisk, Arthur was keeping his eyes peeled for any sign of the people they were meeting or some sort of organized transport vehicle. The Vampire gunman was still in Arthur's head as they drove. Arthur felt like he did when he first met that woman vampire in the alley, and he then went to school the next day. Since joining Cratos and how his teacher spoke about Vampires, he had mentally decided on an idea of what they were all like. Arthur now realized that it was childish and lazy to do so, but he couldn't help making a stereotype for the Vampires when every example of them he had seen so far was the same. But now, he had met a Vampire that acted in the complete opposite way. But rather than simply adding to his knowledge of their race, it only made Arthur's mind more paranoid about how many others there might be like him. Arthur knew he and Cratos were not dropping off the Vampires radar any time soon, and the uneasy feeling of danger was becoming more than just a scared worry in Arthur's stomach. He felt like something terrible was coming for them both.

"About time you started listening to your instincts," muttered the Beast inside Arthur's head with a sneering growl as though it was scolding him. Arthur rolled his eyes and focused on the path ahead, not bothering to answer back.

"That Vampire was more formidable than your letting yourself believe," the Beast continued, picking at Arthur's nerves.

"He was just a Vampire with some guns. Different certainly but nothing fantastical," Arthur feebly replied to the Beast in his head. However, Arthur knew its response before it even spoke.

"You know that if he were as dangerous as your eyes told you, then you could never rest easy again." Arthur increased the speed of his snowmobile in his anger. He clenched his teeth and tightened the grip on the handles.

"Shut up!" Arthur snapped back out loud into the air. However, his shout was smothered entirely by the roaring of his vehicle's engine.

"You're not safe, boy. Your body is trying to warn you as I am. Listen to ONE of us, dammit!" the Beast snapped back. Arthur was about to shout back and lose his temper, but instead, he looked onward into the white void distance. He calmly exhaled and smiled as he steadied himself.

"There will always be something out to get me," Arthur finally whispered as his eyes squinted ahead of him.

"I have joined a war. I have made enemies. I will never be safe again." Arthur tensed his arms as he increased his speed further. In the corner of his eye, he saw Cratos look his way, concerned that Arthur might be going too fast to control.

"But it doesn't matter. Like always, I will take what is coming. I will walk into any trap and come out alive. I am not ignoring the storm ahead, you stupid mongrel! I am just taking in the calm before it." The Beast went quiet after that and did not speak again. Arthur smiled and reduced his speed as he calmed down and carried on in line with Cratos as before

Arthur could still not comprehend why the Beast speaks to him despite everything else that has happened to him recently. No matter how helpful the damnable animal appeared, Arthur refused to forget that creature's only goal was to gain complete control of his body for itself. It had been quite some time since his last encounter with the Beast for control of his body. That time was behind the waterfall where he first defeated the Beast. Arthur knew it wouldn't be long now until that day came again. The moon was strong last night and close to being whole, which meant the night of the complete moon was ahead, and he would again have to fight for his life. The more Arthur thought about it; he realized that he wasn't scared. He felt the opposite. Arthur remembered meeting Delfer in the Werewolf bar, teaming up with the other Werewolves to save Cratos, surviving the plane crash with him, and finally training in the underground fortress followed by their pair way to get to the Wolf kingdom. His resolve about his new life had only grown stronger with each victory. No matter what it threw at Arthur, next time, he knew deep down he would be ready to face it with all the strength and courage that had been born in him since he first started his journey with Cratos.

The pair rode on into the distance until something came into Arthur's sight. It was small at first. Appearing as a dismal black dot in the distance several miles away as they drove, it seemed to be human-shaped as they grew close. It was now about midday, and the figure wasn't moving as they came closer. The clouds had cleared slightly, and the light of day was abrupt all around them both. Yet the cold in the air was still as chilling to the bone as ever. The figure remained completely still like a statue. Arthur couldn't tell if it was even a man or woman. He looked to his side and saw Cratos. His stomach turned as cold as the snow when Arthur saw his mentor's facial expression. It was ridden with pure dread as he gazed at the figure ahead. Arthur snapped his head back and focused his eyes, doing his best to get a better look with his enhanced sight. Whoever it was, they didn't match the clothing of the gun-wielding Vampire from last night.

Arthur wanted to shout across to Cratos to ask what they needed to do, but before he could utter a single sound, Cratos did something unbelievable. Without hesitation, his teacher lifted his body forward, putting his feet onto the seat of his snowmobile, and he then stood up straight as the vehicle somehow rode onward without his control. Without even turning his way, Cratos reached inside his coat and pulled out what looked like a small knife. Arthur couldn't recall when his teacher carried a weapon of any sort, and he was even more surprised that if this person were an enemy, he would fight them with it. Saying nothing, Cratos folded his arms inward towards his chest and whipped them outward, rapidly launching the knife. Only the blade did not go in the direction Arthur expected. The metal blade launched through the air like a shot bullet and struck the chain coil part of Arthur's vehicle, severing it completely. Arthur completely totaled the snowmobile as it smashed against the ground and flipped to its side, crashing.

Arthur didn't have time to watch his teacher resume his seat and drive on at top speed towards whoever the person was. He was too preoccupied making sure the now crashing snowmobile wouldn't thrash his bones into pieces and land on his broken carcass. Remaining calm as best he could, Arthur steadied his body and kept it as still as he could let it fall onto his side without his panicked body moving it. Arthur then moved his leg out of the way as it scraped along the ground, slowing in speed and eventually coming to a grinding halt. Arthur waited a few seconds after it stopped to release his vice grip on the handles. He let go and fell into the cold snow. While none of his bones felt broken, his body was in shock from the crash. His head was pounding, and he felt disorientated. Arthur rolled on his stomach and waited for his head to clear for a moment. He closed his eyes and tried to steady his breathing, remembering his training and letting his instincts kick in. A few seconds later, he opened his eyes and focused ahead. Cratos was already yards away from him and not slowing down. Arthur knew catching up on foot would be near impossible. It didn't matter how dangerous the person ahead probably was; Arthur never thought Cratos would do something that dangerous without reason. They were meant to be a team and work together, so for him to have done that to Arthur, it must have been because Cratos assumed Arthur's immediate death. Even from where he fell, Arthur still could not make out the person. Whoever they were, they were still just blurry figures standing still in the distance. Picking himself up, Arthur clenched his fists and tensed his arms. No matter the danger, he refused to stand on the sidelines while his friend was fighting on his own. Arthur began running forward through the snow as fast as possible. He wouldn't make it at the start of what was coming, but he was damn sure he would make it there before it ended.

Cratos eyed his target carefully. He was speeding onward, able to concentrate fully now that Arthur was out of harm's way. He drove on at full speed as the figure in the distance quickly came into view. She was a tall woman with long, luxury-styled blood-colored red hair that trailed down all around her own body, nearing her elbows. She wore a long black duster coat that trailed down to her ankles with the collar up blocking the lower half of her face. Clutched in her left hand was a long drawn solid gold katana sword and in her right was what seemed like a giant steel cleaver with a handle that was as long as her forearm. Its blade was also three times the size of a normal cleaver with a curved end.

Cratos didn't need to know her name to know what she was. He held his breath as he drew closer to her. His pupils were fixated on the slightest movement she would make. Cratos knew it was no coincidence she was here. It wouldn't be the first time he had gone up against them, but it wasn't a trivial confrontation. This opponent would be dangerous even for him. As he came closer, Cratos lowered the speed of his snowmobile as she was in full sight of him now. Her eyes were equally fixated on him. They were piercing red with bottomless depth behind them. The blood lust was embedded deep within its crimson depths. Finally, Cratos came to a complete stop and jumped from his vehicle just in case she attacked. She watched him with an unchanged expression as he steadied himself straight up and looked at her. Cratos now stood several feet away with his hands by his sides. He flexed his fingers and tensed his arms a few times, preparing. Suddenly the cold of the winds around him paled in comparison to the chills running through his stomach when Cratos stared at the Vampire. Cratos removed his long black trench coat and threw it to the side. Lowering his body slightly and positioning his arms, he narrowed his eyes and deeply growled.

"After you," he muttered, and without saying a word in response, the Vampire attacked.

"That cleaver must weigh a damn ton!" Cratos screamed angrily in his head as he narrowly escaped a decapitating blow from the Vampire's heavy weapon with a quick reactive duck. The woman immediately followed her attack by thrusting her other arm forward with her katana pointed straight out to impale Cratos. With no time for a second dodge, Cratos forced his Werewolf Claws to snap out of his hand like a striking tiger and slap the golden blade aside with a monstrous snarl, curling his other hand into a fist and punching straight at her face. Without even blinking, the woman jumped backward through the air landing a few feet away. Cratos eyed her thoughtfully. He could not figure out how she was whirling around her cleaver as though it was a dinner knife. Her katana he could understand, but her figure was that of any other vampire, slim and thin. Leaving not a second longer for Cratos to think further, the woman once again darted forward with her cleaver held out behind her as she thrust her katana in front of her on its side, immediately slashing it in every possible direction at Cratos. His other hand instantly snapped into its Werewolf claw. Both his hands were now fully transformed into their wolf-like dark flesh as he threw his claws around, meeting every slash with a ringing bang that drilled through his sensitive eardrums.

The female Vampire was relentless in her onslaught. Cratos couldn't even hear her breathing out or grunting with each attack. She was as silent as the grave as she attacked with only the sound of the blades ringing through the air. Despite her impressive speed, though, Cratos was faster. Waiting for his opportunity, she slashed her sword downward, allowing Cratos to then snap his hands together like a Venus flytrap halting the blade in the air shut. Before Cratos could follow with even a blink, she then thrust up her cleaver to slice Cratos in half from the waist. Cratos gritted his teeth in anger as he was forced to slap her golden katana to the side again and leap into the air to dodge. Cratos was glowering over her for a moment as her cleaver slashed through the air he was formerly occupying. The woman didn't react with anger at his dodge. Her head simply snapped upward, looking at him as he hung in the air for half a second. She then snapped her other arm up and sent her golden katana flying straight at him like a fired arrow to lance him out of the air. With nothing to bounce off or dodge, Cratos was a hanging target as the blade threw itself forward. Reacting as best he could, Cratos transformed his entire right arm to its wolf form in a powerful flash and expanse of his muscles and threw the front of his forearm like a shield in the blade's way. Its gold sharpness sliced clean and deep through his arm, stopping only dead as the point was a centimeter from his throat.

Cratos landed on the floor and jumped back away from her to gain distance. A massive space was between them, now giving him a moment to collect his bearings. She only looked on at him as she rested her cleaver by her side and waited for him to move. Cratos looked at her with his eyes snapping to his right arm, which now had the blade of a golden sword embedded viciously through his flesh with blood seeping through the rim of both the entry and exit hole of the strike. On the blade itself, his blood ran down the metal and off the end of the tip. His transformed arm was black, with its thick dark fur unintentionally twitching with the gold blade sticking out of it. Cratos winced as he gripped the blade's handle, and without hesitation, he pulled the sword out of his arm, leaving the gaping hole through his limb open to flood out with his blood. Cratos then tested his right arm a few times. He tensed it and clenched his hand into a fist. The pain stung immensely, but he could ignore the pain and push past it for the fight for now. He allowed his arm to bleed freely and focused ahead. His other hand was holding the handle of the vampire's blade as he stared at her intensely, curious if she would ask for her weapon back. Instead, she simply remained silent and awaited his next move.

Cratos glared at the woman, hesitating. He did not expect this encounter to happen.

"What do you want!" he roared almost helplessly. The woman remained utterly silent. Her eyes were simply blinking with their redness. She was a still bottomless pool of mercilessness.

"Humph! Fine then, have it your way," he snarled. Cratos lifted her blade in front of him. He clutched its handle with both hands gripping it tightly. She remained completely still without moving as Cratos steadied himself to attack. She was not even lifting her cleaver for defense in front of her and still let it hang by her side. Cratos narrowed his eyes. He was trained enough to know this must be some sort of trap. She may be able to swing her second weapon incredibly fast but nowhere near quick enough to stop Cratos from decapitating her first. Cratos shook his head. He didn't have time to waste. He knew the tumble he made Arthur take might not have left him unconscious, and knowing the strong-headed boy, he would come after him quickly. The thought of Arthur going up against this woman worried Cratos immensely. She was made to kill the best Werewolves in existence, and the boy was still only a cub. Cratos lowered his body from his knees and began running forward, roaring as he did. The woman was completely still even now. Cratos's entire body suddenly slowed into a statue-like paralysis. He dropped to the floor like a bag of rocks. The blade slipped quickly from his hands as only his eyes were the only thing left of him that could now move. Cratos tried to move his body as best he could, but nothing budged. He tried even to summon himself into his Werewolf form, but not even a single hair sprouted. Cratos's eyes widened with shock and awe. She had cut him off from his Werewolf form.

"Poison!" he screamed at himself inside his head despairingly.

"Her blade is covered with poison, you fool. You should have known that! She didn't need to stab me. Just one cut would have done it, and throwing that cleaver around only made it easier!" The woman walked forward in the snow, taking her time as she did before, calmly standing next to Cratos, looking down on him. He was lying on his back, unable to move from full-body paralysis. Cratos was only able to stare up at her. The panic was apparent in his eyes. He saw her frown slightly, as though she was disappointed. She was unsure if Cratos was about to pull some trick out of his sleeve as she had just done to him. She bent over, picked up her gold sword by the handle, inspected it for a moment, and then refaced Cratos. A full minute passed as her eyes didn't leave Cratos's pupils. His attempts to struggle past the effects of the poison were fruitless. This venom wasn't an ordinary poison. It was specifically made to fight against the natural defenses of a Werewolf. It was the sort of thing Cratos knew Siren would have a merry dance about if she could see it in action. Odds were, if Cratos got a chance to tell her about it, she would demand five pints of his blood to try and study the damn thing. Were he able to move his lips, he would have chuckled at such a thought. However, the still-present threat of the woman loomed as she realized Cratos was finished. Shrugging her shoulders, she placed her golden blade back into its sheath that was strapped behind her back sideways. She then lifted her abnormally large cleaver high above her head. Cratos would have closed his eyes for his impending death, but he didn't dare. He was a Werewolf, defiant until the end, no matter what. He would stare her in the eyes and let this Vampire see that the warrior's life she claimed showed no fear in the end. Holding his breath, Cratos held her gaze. His eyes were steady, solid, and ablaze with steel-melting hatred. Cratos was waiting for his end to come. Her arm then slung downward without even a flinch from her face. The edge of the blade was aimed straight for the middle of Cratos Mane's neck.

The woman's blade halted in place less than an inch from Cratos's throat. It was perfectly suspended in an almost frozen stillness as the woman's head now faced away from Cratos. Her eyes were now fixated on the redheaded boy who approached them both with ferocious sprinting speed. Her face still did not change as Arthur came. His chest was heaving in and out with fatigue from running as fast as he could nonstop. When Arthur saw this woman ready to kill his teacher, he increased his speed to near demigod levels out of sheer desperation. Now here he was, standing merely a few feet away from his incapacitated teacher and the strange assailant that attacked him. Arthur saw she had a slim build with pure white skin and demon-like red eyes. She strangely reminded Arthur of the Vampire with the guns from the previous night. This woman was no ordinary Vampire, and if she could take down Cratos and nearly kill him, Arthur figured she must have been a special kind of deadly opponent.

The Vampire pulled her cleaver away from Cratos's neck and faced Arthur with her cleaver gripped tightly in her hand. She redrew her golden katana with her other hand and let both her arms hang by her sides as she watched Arthur silently. He was still tired from running and looked at her with almost maddening fury. He knew what Cratos would want for him. It's the reason he sent Arthur crashing in the first place. His teacher saw how dangerous she was and hoped to spare him, and now that he was staring at her face to face. He needed to think carefully, or Arthur knew he would be killed before he could throw a single punch. Arthur raised his hands and positioned his body sideways, turning his head and facing her firmly. He clenched his hands into fists and tensed his arms, flexing his biceps. He frowned as she remained ultimately still, waiting for Arthur to move. Arthur looked at her weapons for quick study.

"The gold sword will move faster than the giant blade in her other hand. I need to keep my eyes on the smaller one. She will try to catch me off guard with the giant one, I'm sure. I need to disarm her somehow," he thought to himself. Despite his limited experience with such weapons, he was still trying to think of a battle strategy. He frowned in his confusion. Arthur felt that he would struggle to swing that giant blade around, even if he held it with both hands, yet he recalled seeing the Vampire waving it around at Cratos with one arm like it weighed nothing.

"You MUST listen to me no matter what," purred the voice of the Beast from inside his head. Arthur, for once, heard the voice out without a snarky response.

"This one is different, boy. She is vicious. She will rip you apart before you can blink unless you pay attention and let me help you fight." Arthurs' breathing grew heavy as he considered it. He knew the Beast was right, but he also knew there would be a catch.

"Fine, but no tricks," Arthur answered back, followed by the Beast's condescending chuckle to follow.

"Tricks? We're past that boy. It'll take a miracle to get out of this with our head attached." Arthurs' teeth clenched and he scowled.

"Oh well, that's inspiring!" Arthur snorted back, rolling his eyes. The Beast's voice grew deadly serious.

"Enough nonsense, boy. Let's do this!" the Beast barked. Arthur inhaled deeply and ran forward to try his hand against the mysterious Vampire assassin.

CHAPTER TWENTY-EIGHT

"DUCK!" screamed the Beast inside Arthur's head, causing him to snap his body down in a lightning-like response instantly. Several hairs from the top of his head were cut free as the Vampire's golden katana blade slashed across him. Arthur was then immediately met with the second cleaving strike of her off-hand cleaver weapon slamming downward upon his crouching body.

"CLAP!" the Beast screamed next, making Arthur's hands quickly snap shut upon the impending death slash. Arthur perfectly and precisely clapped his hands to wrench a grip against the sides of the weapon, halting it in place. Every muscle in both his arms flared as they were instantly pushed to their limit with that clap.

"Now kick at her before she brings that katana back into you," the Beast commanded. Arthur obeyed the order and slammed his right foot forward in front of him and kicked up, connecting sharply against her stomach. It felt as though he had just kicked against a metal wall from the end of his toes. Regardless her body's resistance showed she was still knocked back slightly by several steps, but the Vampire didn't lose her balance. She took less than a second to regain herself from the kick as Arthur stood upright, looking at her.

"She was underestimating us before. Now she will up the ante. Stay sharp," the Beast grunted angrily at Arthur with serious determination.

"DODGE!" the Beast roared inside his head, nearly to the point of making Arthur wince as he jumped backward through the air pulling himself out of the line of the woman's blade swing. Arthur landed several feet away, but his eyes didn't move from her body for an instant. Even though the Beast said she would attack harder, she seemed happy to keep throwing subtle attacks than going in for the kill. Arthur couldn't tell if she was toying with him or if this was just the way she fought.

"Do me a favor," Arthur growled in his head.

"Give me some strategies other than screaming 'DUCK' or 'DODGE' inside my head, please!" he growled at the Beast

"You're still alive at least," the Beast retorted viciously. Arthur could hear in its voice that the Beast was very uncertain itself right now. Arthur couldn't tell if the Beast was being serious or messing with him.

"I can't dodge and duck away from this woman forever. I need to plan of attack, dammit!" Arthur retorted desperately. The Beast grunted.

"Against the creature that took down your mentor. Good luck there!" it snapped back sarcastically.

"I hate you so much right now," Arthur grumbled. The Beast said nothing in response and went quiet. Arthur didn't have time to tell the creature to stop sulking because the woman finally decided to step toward him. Arthur's eyes snapped on her form, observing her. He remembered his combat training with Cratos. He moved his body sideways to create less of a target for her to attack. He raised both his arms in front of him and lowered his knees slightly. He carefully calmed his heart rate by controlling her breaths. He knew if he panicked, he would die. He steadied his hands to be as still as a surgeon and awaited his chance to strike. He knew he had to precisely fight the way Cratos taught him.

"Perhaps that was his problem," murmured the Beast subtly. Arthur frowned at the comment; he didn't know what the Beast was saying.

"What the hell do you mean?!" Arthur pleaded, keeping his eyes on the approaching Vampire.

"I mean that Cratos fought her his way, and now he's lying on the floor, slumped down, ready to be killed. You've almost been cut in half so far. You can't just fight like him. It would be best if you had your personal touch added as well," Arthur thought on that. There was some sense to it. But he had no idea what his personal touch was. The Beast went silent as the Vampire held her sword arm up in front of her. She was pointing the tip of the sword towards Arthur. She then slowly positioned her cleaver behind her as she was only a few feet away from Arthur. She stopped completely dead a few feet from Arthur as he stared still at her, desperately trying to think of a way to fight back without relying on his training from Cratos. An idea then came to him. It wasn't good, and he felt it would probably backfire, but he knew he had to do something different or like the Beast pointed out, he would end up like Cratos. Without twitching a single muscle, the woman suddenly darted forward through the snow towards him with her katana arm stretched out like a piercing lance. Arthur tapped into the one thing that has saved his life more times than he could count on so far, his instinct.

Arthur moved without fear or doubt, restraining his actions. While he appreciated the value of the training Cratos gave him, something about fighting with all guns blazing felt more appealing to him. It seemed more natural. So as things stood, Arthur embraced the more animal side of his mind to help him survive and hopefully win this fight with some form of miracle.

The Vampire was no longer underestimating Arthur as she was swinging and thrusting her weapons forward with the intent to kill. The difference now was Arthur no longer needed the irritating sound of his inner Beast's scream for him to duck and dodge anymore. Arthur fully trusted his body and allowed his instincts to dictate his every move. He was avoiding the sharp edges of her fatal metal swings as though they were repelled away from him magnetically with his reflexes. Arthur's body looked like he was nearly dancing around her attacks as his body twisted and turned around her cleaver as it swung downward then across to his side without stopping. The Vampire didn't even allow a few seconds for Arthur to breathe with her endless barrage. But it still made no difference to his dodging pace. Arthur moved away from the cleavers' crashing strikes without sweating while her golden katana stabbed forward at him for his hands to slap the metal aside on its face without leaving a single scratch on his palms. Arthur's mind was clear of distractions. He was only focusing on what was before him at hand. His eyes firmly fixated on the movements of the Vampire's limbs. He was nearly seeing her attacks before her shoulders would twinge. This mindset was what Cratos had been forging Arthur into becoming. These teachings lay in his subconscious and had now merged with his natural inner resolve, creating a ferocious fighter with the cunning of a snake and the ferocity of a gorilla. Arthur repelled the Vampire's attempts to regain the upper hand in the fight and decided that defense could not be his only survival strategy. To truly win, he knew he must attack.

"Incredible," Cratos muttered with quiet awe in his head as he watched Arthur not only hold his own against the Vampire but also counter and fight back against the creature as well.

"This kid has been one exception after another. I wouldn't believe it if I weren't seeing it right now," he continued to say in his mind. His body was still motionless and paralyzed due to the poison on the Vampires sword.

Cratos had no way to warn Arthur about the poison because he couldn't even muster sound. The toxin had completely cut off communication with the rest of his body, and now he was simply a brain and eyes. The snow he was lying flat on wasn't too much of a bother, given his fur was protecting him from the cold. Still, Cratos could not believe how well Arthur was fighting. It wasn't too long ago that he was flattening the boy himself on a training floor, and now he was fighting head-on with an opponent that was ready to behead him. Cratos couldn't think of how or why this was happening. Cratos knew that even if Arthur was using all his training to his advantage, it still didn't explain his prowess.

"His flexibility…" he thought as he saw Arthur's body twist around her cleaver and across her katana.

"His reflex's…" he carried on, watching Arthur slap away the Vampire's katana strike like it was a troublesome fly.

"He's almost fighting like a Shadow…" He thought. The pieces were slowly coming together in his mind and provided him with some possible answers.

"But with the body of a Crimson," he finished stopping short in his head as he let the puzzle come together.

"But even with such a combination. Arthur doesn't know who he is fighting, and one wrong move would be his end. Arthur…please be careful!," he pleaded in his mind as Cratos could only remain watching the fight. His student and friend were staring down certain death, and he was utterly helpless.

The Vampire woman was the one backing up from Arthur's attacks now. His eyes were transfixed pieces of stone blaring upon her as his limbs moved automatically. Her weapons were being slapped aside or ducked and dodged with ease as his fists and kicks zeroed in with near-perfect force. The Vampire jumped to the side and rolled through the snow before instantly pulling herself back onto her feet and snapping her body towards Arthur. She took a few steps back and held her katana out in front with her cleaver at her side. Arthur moved toward her and observed. The Vampire nodded at Arthur. That was the first form of communication she's displayed so far.

Arthur did not return the nod. He didn't care if it was rude, she had hurt his friend, and he intended to repay that. Arthur darted forward; his feet nearly looked like a blur as he dashed forward. The Vampire woman shot her arm completely straight. The limb was barely moving forward at all, yet she released her hand, and her golden katana shot forward through the air with insane speed. Arthur barely saw the movement. The only thing to come into his vision was the hurled sword heading straight for him. Taken by surprise, Arthur brought his hand out to try and swat it aside as he had before. Unfortunately, the blade was going too fast this time and the blade shot through the palm of his hand like it was going through warm butter. The sword slid through his flesh down to the hilt, slapping against his palm. Arthur snapped his head sideways so the point wouldn't strike his face as well. The pain was searing agony, but Arthur refused to stop running despite it.

Arthur roared scornfully in a blind fit. He gripped the blade's handle with his other hand and pulled the sword free of his hand, leaving a gaping bleeding hole in the middle of his left hand. The blade's golden steel was decorated extravagantly in his blood. The pain of his heavily bleeding hand was now fueling his mind with hellish wrath. The woman turned her body and held her cleaver with both her hands as Arthur charged forward with her katana in his hand. Her eyes widened heavily as the scent of Arthurs' blood was making her embrace the oncoming attack with almost wild lust. Arthur gritted his teeth, nearly cracking them in the process. He clenched his bleeding hand with the bleeding hole and then released it. Arthur put his hand on the blade handle and squeezed it with both hands tightly. Arthur charged forward, holding the sword high above his head. As he came close next to the Vampire woman, he summoned all the strength in his body and swung down with a god's might upon her, fully intending to cut her down in two straight down the middle of her body. His eyes went blank white as a mighty roar exploded from the depths of his mouth. The Vampire woman met his challenge and twisted her body in a way that looked unnatural for a spine to endure with her cleaver swinging upward, meeting the golden katana. The two metals then met between the raging pair of fighters.

The force of the clash made Arthur feel like he had just been electrocuted, as vibrations sang up both his arms in devastating ripples. The ringing noise crashed through his eardrums viciously as the pair now stood still. The edges of their weapons were nearly embedded in each other. Arthur was breathing heavily. She hadn't budged an inch in their stance. He used every piece of his strength against her. That strike could have severed an entire tree at its base, yet she hadn't even flinched. It was as though she was made of solid diamond, and she was welded to the ground itself. The power of her strike was dancing through the depths of Arthurs' very bones, making them shudder and shake with shock. Arthur couldn't move. He wanted to step back and move his arms so he could strike again, but he was somehow frozen solid in place. His hand was bleeding out still. The blood that flowed onto his hand fell to the ground by his feet. Its pain was strangely starting to disappear. Its sticky substance continued to flow, yet the pain had nearly vanished from his mind. He couldn't figure it out. He then tried to speak, but even his jaw didn't move. His mind began to panic.

The Vampire woman moved away and let her cleaver hang from her side. She stood up straight and looked at Arthur, who stood firmly in place. She walked forward, and with her thumb and index finger, she pinched on the blood-soaked edge of her katana. She pulled it up with seemingly no effort, causing the handle to move from Arthur's grip and free it slowly. She then threw it in the air with a spin and caught it with her hand. With the blade taken, Arthur's arms slumped by his sides like dead meat.

"What the hell is going on?!" he screamed internally. Arthur was face down on the ground now, and he couldn't even flex his nostrils. His body now followed his arm's example and fell into the snow, still and motionless.

"Beast! BEAST!" Arthur shouted in his head, trying to summon his inner Beast to see if it knew why he couldn't move. A few seconds went by before the Beast finally responded.

"Don't waste your breath; I have no idea myself. This creature has tricks we weren't prepared for; it seems," it murmured in response; its tone was dim and defeated. The Beast had given up.

"NO!" Arthur roared at it. The woman Vampire kicked Arthur sharply, turning his body, so he was lying on his back. Arthur couldn't move his head, but his eyes rolled and saw that her blade's tip was now pointing straight at Arthur's throat. Her eyes were cold and expressionless. She looked upon Arthur with complete indifference. He was helpless, and she could take his life at any movement. Arthur stared her dead in the eyes with his own not blinking.

"If this, is it…I won't look away," Arthur said internally to himself. His mind was riddled with fear, but the soul of a Werewolf was still alive within him as he remained in the body of the wolf still.

"I will face death head-on!" The Vampire woman gave him a final nod as she raised the blade above her head and swung it down.

Unlike Cratos, Arthur had no person to come to his rescue. No person charged in and stopped her from killing him during this attack. He was alone with only his teacher out here lying across from him in the snow.

However, the Vampire did not claim his life right then. For some reason that Arthur didn't know, the female Vampire's arm froze solid, with the edge of her golden katana right against the skin on his throat. Only a microscope could have picked up the air between the metal of her weapon and his skin's surface. Arthur looked at her steadily as he felt his heart beating like a panicked rabbit crossing a bridge over molten lava. The Vampire stood still for a few seconds before Arthur heard her sigh underneath the collar of her coat. The Vampire looked at Arthur dead in his eyes for a few seconds more before narrowing her eyes spitefully at him. She then pulled the sword away from his neck then she looked over at Cratos for a few seconds. Finally, she turned away from the pair of them and began walking off. Arthur couldn't follow her precisely as she disappeared from his sight. Arthur heard her footsteps in the snow as she went away until he heard her no longer. He was alive, but he still couldn't move, but Arthur was at least glad that the pair of them had survived this attack.

A few hours passed, and Arthur was still motionless in the snow. The cold was probably affecting his body, but he couldn't feel the chill at all. A tiny bit of feeling began to return to him slowly as time passed onward. His bleeding hand stung, but the wound had closed over and stopped bleeding because of his Werewolf healing. It still ached like hell, but at least Arthur had the peace of mind that he wouldn't bleed to death in the snow. Not long after his feeling returned more and more strongly, and the cold chill of the snow was more apparent. Arthur knew if he couldn't get up soon, then he was sure he would eventually die like this. From the left of him, Arthur then heard Cratos begin to move. His eyes switched to where his teacher was as he was slowly rising to his feet, holding his head, and shaking himself upright, shocking his body free from the effects of his paralysis. His teacher paused for a moment as his wolf features and body disappeared and returned him to his human state. Cratos rubbed his arms and legs and slowly walked towards Arthur, kneeling by his side. His mentor said nothing and instantly inspected Arthur's hand. He lifted it and closely examined it. Cratos then placed the hand back down and looked his student over to ensure no other wounds.

"We were lucky," he grunted bitterly, the edge in his voice not filled with any sort of relief but instead disapproving worry. Cratos looked around him, seeing no more sign of anyone. The pair were left alone.

"We should have died," he muttered again under his breath. Sighing, Cratos put his hands under Arthur's body and lifted him. Despite Arthur's enormous body in his wolf form, his mentor lifted him with ease and carried him towards his snowmobile. Cratos sat on the vehicle and rested Arthur upright against him as carefully as he could. Cratos then started up the machine and headed off through the snow as they had before.

"She was not a normal Vampire, Arthur," his teacher voiced with a deep and fearful tone as they sped on forward through the snow at a casual speed. Cratos was no longer having fun driving it. His voice quickly turned angry.

"She was a part of a more powerful group of Vampires. A group of hardened fighters of a VASTLY different breed." Arthur could only listen and still couldn't move, but he didn't disagree in the slightest.

"She belongs to a special elite group of Vampires that are responsible for the most Werewolf deaths ever recorded. They have even killed an Alpha Werewolf in their existence in history as well" Cratos went quiet for a little bit as he thought hard. Arthur heard a strange rhythm in his teacher's tone. It seemed like Cratos knew about this group of Vampires more than other Werewolves might.

"They don't appear often. Only when they are summoned for a 'special' target or when they are interested in their own targets," Cratos continued, speaking with a monotone that was impossible to read at this point.

"They have lost only a couple of their group in the centuries of their existence. Nine times out of ten, a Werewolf they fight doesn't walk away alive..." he stopped for a few moments before the snowmobile sped up. Cratos clenched his fists in confused anger.

"Yet just now, two had walked away when their lives were right for their taking... that DOESN'T happen, Arthur." Arthur couldn't respond. He doubted he had anything to say, even if he could speak. That woman fought with such insane strength and expertise that she certainly lived up to the description Cratos was saying.

"They are known as the 'Hunters', and their name is something that is never spoken lightly with our kind. If Vampire leaders have summoned the Hunters after us." Cratos once again stopped talking for a long time now. Arthur was sure he could feel his teacher's body shake slightly.

"They have summoned them, it seems. That means there is no safer place in the entire world right now than the home of the Werewolves. Cyrus will need to hear what has happened." Arthur now felt nervous. After just surviving death, it seems he is only going further down the path of danger. As the pair continued the course, Cratos went utterly silent from thereon.

Arthur then had a feeling that it wouldn't be the last time he met that woman.

After some time, Arthur felt his body slowly return to him. Whatever had happened was slowly starting to wear off, and he was beginning to be able to move his body again. Though all he could do was grip onto Cratos to keep himself steady as they drove on. Cratos was ghostly quiet. His complex expression was stern and unchanging as he focused on what was ahead. The encounter with the Hunter Vampire had troubled him deeply. When they were attacked on the plane, he was upset, but this worried him in a way Arthur had never seen before. Since becoming a Werewolf, that woman had now been the most powerful opponent Arthur had faced. She was leagues deadlier than the tiger. Now she and who knows what other Vampires were also planning to come and try and kill him and Cratos. As they drove on going to the Wolf Kingdom, Arthur made a small vow to himself.

"I will train harder than anyone else," Arthur said to himself firmly.

"No matter what, I must become stronger. If more Hunters are coming, then I will need to be ready no matter what. I must become stronger to protect those I have come to know. Cratos. Delfer. I cannot be on the sidelines anymore. I need to be a player my comrades can count on. The Vampires think they have fought against the worst of the Werewolves; then they will think otherwise when they face me after my training!" Arthur steadied his breathing and mentally prepared his mind, focusing it firmly. The world had many more dangers prepared for him. Arthur was only alive now because of what Cratos had taught him, but to fight against the Vampires, he knew he would have to transcend what he was entirely. Suddenly his mind clicked to something his old teacher Mr. Wreckson had once told him after class was over and they were chatting while he finished his work. He had asked Arthur about his future and what he wanted to be. At the time, Arthur had acted sullen and said he didn't know. His teacher then simply said to him.

"Arthur, In order to make a difference, you first have to do something different" The saying didn't make sense to him until now. Arthur couldn't just go along with the usual routine with the Werewolves. He had to go a step further and become something the Vampires hadn't faced yet. That was his mission from here on.

"Look out, bloodsuckers. I am coming for you, all of you!"

In her long black coat, the female Vampire approached the man casually as she gently laid her weapons, a golden katana, and a giant cleaver, after stretching her arms side to side, on the snowy ground. Standing directly behind the man, she sighed angrily.

"I would have preferred to kill them both there and then. Save ourselves any future bother." Her voice was deep and severe, rough and dense in her scolding tone. The man chuckled and then spoke with his deep, gritty voice.

"Yes, but where is the fun in that," he replied, resting his hands on his sides a few inches from his guns. The female Vampire rolled her eyes.

"They were pathetic. We won't get any fun out of them." The man shook his head at her in response.

"I doubt it. That Crimson had you breaking a sweat for a moment there." The woman clenched her fists and scowled with a prideful sneer.

"Don't be foolish; I just underestimated the fool for a moment, and he took advantage with lightning in a bottle burst of his power. Some rookie pup shouldn't have been a problem, and as you saw it turn out, he wasn't." The man chuckled again and nodded.

"A shame, really. I would have liked to see how the boy would have fared if your poison hadn't kicked in." She shrugged, then crossed her arms, looking at him.

"I wouldn't mind seeing how he fares against you without your guns," she replied spitefully. The man chuckled again and stroked the butts of his revolvers with his hands.

"A fair point. Still though. It's as you said. He is just a pup, and from what I saw, he did damn well for a pup. Imagine how fun he will be after he completes his training." The woman shook her head again.

"He won't. The fang polishers will call for his head long before that. From what I heard, they have gone through millions covering up that plane attack." The man turned around and faced her. A smirk stretched up his scared face with the tip of his hat covering the top half of his face.

"Then do you fancy breaking into the dog's kennel?" he voiced smugly, his red eye wide and fixed on her. She looked away and sighed.

"No, but would you tell THEM, no?" she asked cryptically. The Vampire laughed now.

"I've been telling those toothless simpletons NO for the past eight centuries. But if they want his head so bad, then fine. I'll serve it to them on a silver platter." The woman chuckled.

"There's some irony," she quipped in as the pair shared a laugh.

"Besides, we haven't had a dog this spry in a long time. If he becomes more capable, I bet we'll have a lot of fun with this one," he said again with a menacing glee in his tone.

"Then why not let me kill the pup's teacher? He wasn't much," she asked spitefully. The vampire then stared at her hard. All his humor was lost from his grin, and a serious glare appeared in his eyes.

"You know why. You know who has demanded THAT mutts head. You really want to go against HER?" The female vampire shook her head, and the pair looked outward again in the direction Cratos had driven off now.

"What now then?" she asked. The man's smirk returned as he drew his gun with his right hand, holding it up close to his head in less than a second.

"We'll report back to the others. Let them all know we have a new contender in our ring," he chuckled for a moment before turning his back and walking away from the woman.

"Let's hope he's up to the challenge next time," she replied before turning away herself after him.

THE END